A FARM GIRL'S GUIDE TO RULING AS A BLOODTHIRSTY TYRANT

A FARM GIRL'S GUIDE TO RULING AS A BLOODTHIRSTY TYRANT

SCANDALS OF THE GIFTED

BOOK 2

KATY NYQUIST

Cover design by Francell Garrote

ISBN: 978-1-0394-8249-4

Published in 2025 by Podium Publishing
www.podiumentertainment.com

For Kelly Barina, my oldest critique partner.
In many ways I learned how to write from you. Thank you for being my friend for so many years.
Once you told me this was your favorite of my books but I hope to top myself in the future.

A FARM GIRL'S GUIDE TO RULING AS A BLOODTHIRSTY TYRANT

CHAPTER ONE

Less than a day after I met Countess Donya, I had fallen in love with her so deeply that I risked my life trying to save her from execution. This was despite being fully aware she was heterosexual and thus would never return my feelings. That probably made me sound like a chump. But there was something about Donya that instantly inspired in me an admiration far deeper than a mere crush. The world would be a better place with her in it.

Also, her future execution was sort of my fault.

Shortly before the disaster, I'd stood at the gates of Arahasnor, the capital city with the same name as our country, handing my papers to a bored guard.

The young, pockmark-faced man gave them a cursory glance before handing them back to me. "Enjoy your stay in the Holy City, Miss Bora," he said in the tone of someone who'd repeated those words a million times. Then he stopped and looked harder. "Do I know you from somewhere? You look familiar."

I did look like the famous Holy Maiden Ysabel. Though I had no pressing reason to keep my connection to my big sister secret, I didn't want to deal with the fuss. "I just have one of those faces. I've never been to this city before." That last part was true, at least.

Light snowflakes dropped down on us, with the white sky overhead portending a future storm. High granite walls shielded the city from my view. Tent poles and holes in the dirt, refuse of a refugee camp, lingered around the walls, despite the blight refugees either having returned to the newly restored and green Conollia or moved inside the city. The garden around the walls had been mostly covered by snow, except for a row of determined plants, namely snowdrops and witch hazel.

Since there was no line behind me, I asked, "Could you give me directions to Saint Kald's School for the Gifted?" That was my first mistake. In creating this minor delay, I sealed my fate, though I had no way of knowing at the time.

A flash of interest appeared in the guard's eyes. "Are you a new gifted?"

"Yes. A very late bloomer." Most gifts appeared in children, but I'd only developed mine at age twenty-four. Or, more likely, I just never noticed it before. Either way, the law required me to report to the school for a brief training course. That's what brought me to this city. Officially, this was to ensure I had my powers under control. Unofficially, it gave the kingdom a chance to recruit the strongest for the World Games. No chance of that for me, given what my gift was.

"What can you do?" the guard asked.

I placed my mittened hands over my cheeks to fend off the nipping cold. Even with the late afternoon sun overhead, it was still freezing. "When I'm dropped from a great height, I bounce."

He blinked. "I don't think I've heard of that one before."

"It's not common." There was also a good chance that most of the similarly gifted never noticed their ability as long as they never fell from a high location.

"Does that mean objects bounce off your skin? Could you block arrows or swords?"

"I only wish. That would be far more useful." I was clumsy and prone to bumping into things. "No, if I tripped and fell right now, I'd still get hurt. For some reason, it only works when I'm free-falling through the air. I haven't experimented with how great a fall is necessary, for obvious reasons."

He chuckled. "Completely understandable. It's a pity. I was going to ask you to demonstrate for me if you could. We'd have tried to recruit you into the guard if you could block weapons. Oh well. Saint Kald's School for the Gifted is located next to the palace, so if you follow—"

Horse hooves thundered down the road, cutting off the guard's directions. When I glanced over my shoulder, a small army of guards marched toward us, surrounding a bright red carriage. They flew the black-and-white striped flag of Sherda, a neighboring country.

The guard stood up straighter. "Pardon me, Miss Bora. I need to alert my superiors at once."

"Do you think our new queen has arrived?" I asked.

"Almost certainly." A look of shared excitement and anxiety passed between us.

As the guard stepped aside, I entered through the bronze gate. The town square spread out before me. Roads extended from a fountain with a statue of Holy Healer Noretho. The surface had frozen, and no water currently poured from the cup in the dead boy's hands. Already, people were lining the road or running forward to stand on the fountain basin for a better look at the approaching procession. Feet pounded, and shouting filled the air. I decided to take advantage of my early arrival to claim a good spot directly in front of the road, next to the fountain. That was my second mistake.

Naturally, everyone was curious. The kingdom of Arahasnor had been under a cloud of uncertainty ever since the murder of the king, the queen, and a large swath of nobility by former Head Cardinal Jiang, a necromancer who had been hell-bent on destroying the city and taking power. Our only heir was a six-year-old princess, the king's much younger sister, who'd been exiled for mysterious reasons when she was only a baby. Unofficially, everyone knew that the old childless queen had been removing a threat to her power. After the murders of the royal couple, it had taken a long time to negotiate the princess's return from Sherda. Various rumors had been flying around the country: our queen-to-be was a kind and generous girl, she was a miniature tyrant who whipped her maids, she was slow in the head. In truth, no one knew anything about the child who would control our futures as soon as she came of age.

Chattering people packed tightly against me, and the dusty winter air made it hard to breathe as our exhales melded together in white puffs. Every last cobblestone of the town square had someone standing on it. I nearly got shoved straight into the road. I grabbed the statue's arm to steady myself.

Foot guards came through the gate in two neat lines, with knights on horseback coming next. They wore white uniforms with black hats and gloves. Each sword scabbard was made of ebony lacquer. Gemstones jangled on the harnesses of the horses. The body odor of the crowd did not quite overpower the earthy scent of so many horses close together.

A crimson carriage rolled behind the knights, crunching over the light snow. It passed so close that I glimpsed a child through the window. Chestnut curls framed a pale face with a pointed nose. She must be the princess, for who else would ride in the carriage? But she had too many stress lines on her face for someone so young. Her brown eyes stared at me with a dead look I'd last seen in the blight refugees passing through my village. My heart pinched.

An exclamation came from inside the carriage, then the sound of a blow. The door popped open, and the princess tumbled out of the carriage.

My body moved faster than my brain. I leapt forward and caught the girl. We both crashed into the dirt sideways. With such a short fall, my gift was useless. I'd rolled slightly to tuck her head into my chest to protect her. My joints moaned in pain. The force of our fall was sure to leave a bruise on my shoulder and my left side.

I gazed up at the sun, stunned and slightly blinded. The princess's whimpering brought me back to my senses. I stood up and set her on her feet. "Are you all right, kid—um—Your Highness?"

The cheering and applauding crowd drowned out my question. The princess gazed up at me with wide, frightened eyes. I'd been nervous she would take offense at a commoner touching her, even to save her from a nasty fall. But she looked more scared of me than I was of her. Then, to my surprise, she threw her arms around me and hugged me.

Gingerly, I patted her back. I probably shouldn't touch royalty, but I couldn't push the poor kid away. (*Was* she the princess? I'd started to suspect she might be a body double because of her timidity.)

The carriage stopped a little ahead of us, then a man stepped out. He had short wavy hair so blond as to almost be white, bright green eyes, and the slightly pointed ears of a half-elf. Now I was quite convinced I had to be seeing things after hitting my head, because that man looked exactly like my ex-boyfriend, Falael.

A green velvet coat filled out his skinny arms. He wore so many golden chains around his neck that he clattered like dry bones. A pomander dangled from the longest chain, the perfumed ball smelling of ambergris and civet. He picked up the girl by the scruff of her neck. "Antonia, what are you doing, trying to run off? You should be more careful." Despite his words, his tone showed no concern. He tossed Antonia—yes, that was the princess's name—back into the carriage as if she'd been a package he didn't care much about denting.

"Stop! She could be injured!" I cried. The carriage door slammed shut. "It wasn't her fault. It sounded to me like someone pushed her."

"Bora!" His eyes widened. "Fancy meeting you here. It's been so long." He extended his arms. "Come, give me a kiss."

By the light of the Sun God, this *was* my ex-boyfriend.

He had a lot of nerve greeting me warmly, given that we'd broken up after he'd cheated on me with my former best friend. You'd think that would be the worst thing he could do to me, but nope, he'd also stolen my savings. I'd desired to never see him again, and it only depressed me that he'd clearly done well for himself since we'd last met since he'd joined the escort of the princess. Rings gleamed on his fingers, his collar was made of snow-white fur, and he wore one of those extremely expensive blue triangular hats with an ostrich feather sticking out. Meanwhile, I had started to sweat and was bundled up in my dirty traveling clothes. Nothing worse than running into an ex when you look like shit.

To my horror, I realized he was attempting to kiss me on the lips, not the cheek. I pushed his forehead back with my palm before he could touch me. "Falael, let's not play games. I don't like you. We didn't part on good terms. Get back in your carriage and comfort the princess."

The crowd around us murmured. Although they gave more space to someone who looked like a nobleman, I could feel curious stares beating into me. Just like Falael to always make a scene. Once upon a time, I'd believed his claims to be a victim of the constant drama going on around him. I'd been young and stupid back then, not realizing that *he* was the drama.

Falael pouted. "I understand. I broke your heart." He pulled my hand off his forehead and attempted to take off my mitten to kiss it.

I yanked my hand back, but he held on to my wrist. Who the hell had a broken heart? In retrospect, dumping me had been the best thing Falael had ever done for me. But I knew it would be pointless to tell him so. Falael lived in his own world, where he'd never done anything wrong in his entire life. I'd wasted enough of my time on him.

This walking ball of oil and perfume couldn't be reasoned with. I only smiled and said, "Indeed, I pined so terribly for you that I developed a skin disease. Rare and highly contagious."

Upper lip curling, Falael stared at me. He must have suspected I was bluffing, but rather than risk it, he finally released my hand.

A woman, perhaps a decade or two older than me, stepped out of the carriage. Long platinum-blonde hair fell over a shiny round face with two small blue eyes. Even without taking into account her pointy lace hat and heels, she towered over everyone else. Her puffy jet-black dress had been embroidered with thousands of black diamonds. Voluptuous curves nearly fell out of the silver-armored bodice. She was fat, and I could say that without judgment because I was, too. I'd spent years struggling with that word before deciding to embrace it. But I could still only aspire to carry myself with half of her style and magnificence. She wore several necklaces and multiple rings on each finger. Unlike Falael, she could pull off that much bling due to the confidence in her ramrod-straight posture. The single red ruby on her bodice gave away her identity: Duchess Hedri of Sherda, widely known as the Blood Duchess.

Officially, Hedri was called the Blood Duchess because of her ruby, a national treasure said to have once been part of a dragon's hoard. Unofficially, people whispered that she murdered maids and bathed in their blood. The baths were an old wives' tale, the dead servants sadly a fact.

People whispered and started backing away from me. Duchess Hedri fixed her beady gaze on my face. "Who is this woman, Falael?" She spat out *woman* in a tone most people reserved for words like cockroach.

Falael beamed that oblivious smile a much younger me had found charming. "This is Bora, an old lover of mine."

She glared at him. "You're cheating on me yet again?" Her bosom heaved like a ship in a storm. A crimson color filled her face.

I rapidly shook my head. "Whoa, no, no cheating going on here. Not even so much as a flirtation."

Falael tossed back his hair. "Can I help it if I'm irresistible?"

"I'm extremely resistant," I growled. "He cheated on you, too? You have my sympathies. He went after my best friend—my only friend at the time, sadly." I attempted a weak smile. My knees shook. I didn't like the hard twist in the Blood Duchess's mouth. "We should support each other. Sisterhood of women, am I right?"

Without looking at me, Duchess Hedri said, "Kill her." To Falael, she said, "Let that be a lesson to you."

My head felt light. She couldn't possibly mean it. The Blood Duchess was notorious for killing anyone who displeased her, but this wasn't her country. She couldn't just stroll into Arahasnor and start murdering citizens.

A single tear trickled down Falael's cheek. He clasped his hands together. "No! Darling, you know whatever my body might do, my heart always belongs to you. Please don't be angry at me." He hastened after the duchess as she headed for the carriage, clutching at her dress.

His melodramatic tone almost convinced me this was all an unfunny joke. Unfortunately, I knew Falael well enough to absolutely believe that he would try to kiss me in front of his extremely jealous and powerful lover, then make my imminent demise all about him.

I had to get out of there. I barreled toward the retreating crowd, hoping to lose myself among the people.

I'd barely taken two steps before my body froze. The coachman stared me down, his eyes glowing. He must have a paralyzing stare gift.

Falael clutched the duchess's arm. "She threw herself at me and tried to kiss me! Please believe me, darling."

Although I tried to object, only a strangled moan emerged from my frozen lips.

Duchess Hedri's stern look softened. "Of course I believe you, my love." She bent down and kissed him. The two of them seemed to be trying to rip each other's tonsils out with their tongues. Loud smacking sounds filled the air.

The guards around the carriage averted their faces. At least they weren't murdering me. Maybe I'd been forgotten?

The duchess broke free of the embrace. "I need to kill any other woman who dared touch you, past or future. But I'll buy you a new ring to make up for it, my handsome stallion."

"I want a diamond ring this time," Falael said, climbing into the carriage.

Just let me break free of this fucking paralyzation for one second! I'll kill them both, then die satisfied!

A Sherdan guard approached me, raising his sword. His face was as impassive as a butcher about to slaughter a pig. The dim sunlight gleamed off the blade hanging over my head.

I couldn't even move my tongue or close my eyes. Was this truly how I was going to die? The unfairness burned. Did I deserve to pay with my life just because I'd had poor taste in lovers when I'd been a teenager? Didn't almost everyone date a scumbag or two when young?

As the sword fell, a blurred red figure burst forth from the crowd. With a flick of her wrist, she sent the guard's sword flying. It struck the cobblestones with a clatter, startling the horses.

Countess Donya stood in front of me with her blade raised. She wore a red coat with a slit down the side and pants underneath, exactly like in her activism posters. The tight fit emphasized her muscular beauty. Her dark brown hair tumbled from beneath her red hat in a tangle like a wild woman. "Don't take one more step forward," she growled at the guards.

That was the precise moment I fell for her.

Duchess Hedri whirled around, her mouth a thin line. "Who are you to defy me?"

Donya panted, pushing back her hair. "I'm Countess Donya, the future queen's new regent." She inclined her head at the girl in the carriage. "A pleasure to meet you, Your Highness."

The young face pressed against the window paled and dropped out of sight. She had tears in her eyes, the poor thing. These people were twisted for making a child watch my near demise.

Duchess Hedri smirked. "Not any longer. As the princess's adoptive mother, I will serve as her regent."

"You're not even from Arahasnor. You have no authority here." Donya frowned. "I was unaware of this adoption. I suppose you'd be welcome to stay—that is to say, it would be acceptable for you to stay—we couldn't *stop* you from staying in this country, but only so long as you refrain from attacking our citizens."

The Blood Duchess snapped her fingers. "Falael?"

He leaned out of the carriage and gave her a scroll.

Duchess Hedri handed it to Donya. "King Uctor of Arahasnor agreed to allow the Kingdom of Sherda to select the regent for Princess Antonia, in event of his death without an heir. We won this favor in the last World Games. Your regency and your kingdom now belong to me."

If I hadn't been frozen, I would have cursed. I'd known our late King Uctor was a moron—honestly, the entire kingdom knew; even royal propaganda couldn't cover it up—but this was an entirely new level of stupid. Anything could be won or lost in the World Games, where monarchs wagered land and wealth as a proxy for war. Under-the-table dealings and private wagers were common. But to let your *entire damn kingdom get stolen out from under you* might be a completely new one, and to make matters worse, he'd arranged for this to happen after his death so it wouldn't be his problem. If a Sherdan noble became regent, we might as well be a province of Sherda.

Also, I was still going to die. This was small in the geopolitical scheme of things, but it sucked for me.

Countess Donya read the scroll with shaking fingers and an increasingly grim expression. Then she read it again, as if unable to believe it. "This appears to be genuine, Lady Regent." Her pug nose twitched. Though she was trying to hide her shock, her voice faltered. "I hope you'll at least allow me to guide you as a new ruler of an unfamiliar land. As my first bit of advice, you should immediately release this woman." She inclined her head at me. "Her name is Bora, the beloved younger sister of Holy Maiden Ysabel."

How did she know that? On second thought, who cared? I attempted to grunt in confirmation.

For the first time, Duchess Hedri's face lost its confidence. She probably didn't fear Ysabel, but rather my sister's husband, Dark Lord Kaine. Although he'd had his dark lord stigma erased in the last World Games, he still featured in the worst nightmares of every kingdom around the world.

"It would be a shame to have your new kingdom burned to ashes so soon after obtaining it," Donya said, a soft, unmistakable threat.

I didn't know if Ysabel would burn kingdoms for me. We'd been separated as young children, and ever since then, there had been a distance between us. She'd always been kind to me in the frequent letters she wrote but rarely talked about anything deep and personal. I'd found out about her engagement from the public town crier. But I hoped the duchess believed Donya.

Duchess Hedri's eyes flickered over me, really looking at me, as she hadn't bothered to when ordering my execution. "I've never heard of the Holy Maiden having a family. I won't let you bluff me for the sake of some powerless peasant. I'll put her in the dungeons until I can investigate. If you're right, she'll be the perfect hostage to keep Conollia in check. If you're wrong, then I'll drain her blood while she still lives." She bared her teeth. "She's not pretty enough for my blood bath, but I'll make an exception."

The blood bath was true after all. My apologies to the little old ladies in my village.

As the guards stepped forward, Donya moved to cut them off. Both parties hesitated—the common guards didn't want to be the first to attack a noblewoman, and Donya didn't want to start a fight she couldn't win.

The crowd murmured. "You're going to kill *our* Ysabel's sister?" a Conollian woman near the front demanded. Her accented voice wasn't the loudest, but the words cut through the air like a knife.

"She looks just like Holy Maiden Ysabel, except fatter," an elderly man called.

The dig about my looks was unnecessary, but thank you, random citizen.

"You'll bring the wrath of the Sun God down on this city!" a young woman shrieked.

"More like the damn Blood Duchess will bring down the wrath of Dark Lord Kaine," the older woman next to her muttered. "We only just finished repairing our walls. I worked so hard replanting the flowers."

"Holy Maiden Ysabel saved my life," another man shouted. Many more chimed in with the same sentiment. My sister had served as a healer in this city for so long, probably almost everyone had a friend or relative whose life she'd saved.

Someone picked up a stone and threw it at a guard. The sound when it struck his helmet cracked in the winter air like thunder. The murmurs of the crowd turned into growls.

The Blood Duchess surveyed the people around her with a cold, assessing look. The lines around her mouth were hard, but her eyes darted around nervously. A scroll granting her legal authority wouldn't save her from being torn to bits by an angry mob, and she knew it. The great thing about being a peasant? We weren't important enough to swear life-oaths. No magic forced us to play by the rules of the Conclave of Kings. We could rip to pieces any noble we could get our dirt-stained hands on.

"I have more important business to take care of," Duchess Hedri said. Pretending not to run away, she got into her carriage. The guards followed her lead. As soon as the coachman stopped looking at me, I could move again. I exhaled sharply.

Donya sagged down, gripping the fountain with one hand. "Sweet Sun God, save us all," she whispered.

I bent over to offer her a hand up. "Thank you for saving my life, my lady."

Looking up, she tried and failed to smile. "I finally get to meet the real Bora," she said cryptically, accepting my hand.

"How did you recognize me?"

"Your older sister wrote to me and said you'd be coming. You look just like her! She asked me to keep an eye on you while you're in the city. Unfortunately, I think that means getting you out of here as fast as possible. I wouldn't put it past Duchess Hedri to send assassins after you. She has a reputation for holding grudges for decades."

"I could turn around and leave right now," I suggested, more than willing.

"You wouldn't be safe on the road alone, and you'll be faster on a horse. Allow me to arrange an escort." Donya stood up. "Ysabel is a dear friend of mine. I swear I'll do everything in my power to protect you."

I nodded, fully aware I could use all the help I could get. "Thank you, my lady."

Five female guards in armor ran forward, pushing through the crowd. "Donya! You should have waited for us—what happened?"

"The fall of the kingdom of Arahasnor just happened," Donya said grimly.

Someone laughed nervously. Both Donya and I knew it was no joke.

CHAPTER TWO

Without a single detour, Donya took me straight to the royal stables. She gave her guards some instructions, no doubt to deal with the duchess's unexpected takeover, then sent them away.

As we approached the brick building, I said, "Surely you have more important business than looking after me. Besides, I need to register at the gifted school before I can leave the city."

"I'll offer your excuses to the school." Donya pushed the door open. "The Blood Duchess has a reputation for never letting anyone who crosses her live. She's done even more unpleasant things to Falael's lovers than turning them into blood baths. I could never face Ysabel if I let anything happen to you."

More unpleasant things? What did that mean? I didn't want to think about it, yet numerous ideas flashed through my mind. "Lovers—plural? How many times has he cheated on her, and why does she keep taking him back?"

"Too many to count, and I have no idea. Word from Sherda says that the Blood Duchess has slaughtered her way through dozens of women since taking Falael as her lover. The lives of servants are cheap in Sherda. I used to be surprised that Falael could find women willing to have him—but after what I saw today, I suspect he probably flirts with them in front of his duchess, then blames them for seducing him." Donya made a face. "He must be doing it on purpose at this point. Like some kind of twisted game. I wonder why a woman as powerful as the duchess puts up with him. He must be amazing in bed."

"Definitely not, mediocre at best," I said absent-mindedly, then flushed. "Um, personally my money would be on her enjoying the game, too. She liked watching me squirm." Sadly, based on my knowledge of Falael, I could absolutely see him getting an ego boost from countless women dying for him. Or rather, because of him. He knowingly tried to cause my death? What, did he think I'd ask him for my stolen money back? The long-cold embers of hatred in my heart reignited. I'd tried to forget about Falael and accept that I couldn't change the past. But the bad memories came flooding back as I followed Donya into the stable.

Brick pillars separated a series of horse stalls. I wrinkled my nose at the stench of straw and waste. A dark brown horse poked his snout out of the closest stall and snorted at me.

"Stablemaster Vestan?" Donya called.

"My lady! Are you with . . . Holy Maiden Ysabel? Dark Lord Kaine must be invading the city again." A handsome blond man with bright blue eyes ran toward us, flapping his arms wildly.

"I'm not—" I started to say.

He tripped and crashed into Donya. She managed to catch him despite half falling down herself. "Whoa, there!" A blush tinted her pale cheeks.

Then and there, I realized that Donya was probably straight. That awkward, flustered look as she helped Vestan regain his feet was a dead giveaway. It was certainly possible to like both men and women—I did—but when I compared Donya's current reaction to how little attention she'd given her five hot female guards in leggings, I had a strong suspicion I was out of luck. I couldn't help letting out a small, wistful sigh. Even before I'd met Donya in person, I'd deeply admired her women's rights activism and reputation as a swordswoman. I'd already had a bit of a celebrity crush on her. But even though she was only a few years older than me, she treated me like a child. I'd started with the handicap of being her dear friend's kid sister, so my expectations had been low from the beginning.

Not quite meeting his eyes, Donya said, "Vestan, this is Bora, Ysabel's younger sister. There's no invasion . . . at least, not one by a dark lord. We've got some trouble with Sherda, though."

I smiled. "An easy mistake to make. My sister and I look alike."

I'd come to look more like Ysabel the older I'd grown. We both had the same small nose, ears, and mouth. Our family had large upturned eyes, though mine were brown to her hazel. With a Conollian father and an Arahasnorian mother, we siblings had a range of skin colors, and I'd ended up a slightly lighter shade of brown. We were both short, though I'd expanded more sideways. My mother called me her plump little country mouse, which she claimed she meant as a compliment even though it didn't feel like one.

There was a mirror in each horse's stall. I avoided looking at my reflection in the closest one. I'd put so much work into getting comfortable in my body—I hadn't deliberately vomited up my food in over a year—but I still didn't like mirrors.

"Pardon me, Lady Bora," Vestan said, bowing his head at me.

"There's no need to bow. I'm not nobility." I attempted a wobbly curtsy at him before remembering he wasn't either.

Donya spoke over us. "We need your fastest horse."

I cleared my throat. "I've never ridden before."

Donya winced. "Your easiest-to-ride horse."

"At once, my lady." He turned toward the equipment hanging on the wall.

"Are you scared of horses?" Donya asked me. "Perhaps I could find a mule—wait, are you scared of mules, too?"

"I'm not scared of horses, my lady. I've just never had a chance to ride one before, that's all." I smiled in a strained way. "Too poor."

"But Ysabel gave all her siblings—" Donya visibly stopped herself. "We'll find you an older horse used to riders," she said awkwardly.

I was grateful to her for not asking any probing questions. As Donya clearly knew, my wealthy older sister had arranged for me to receive a large sum of money upon reaching the age of majority.

Thanks to my ex, I'd lost all of mine less than a year later.

Of course, I'd never told my sister the depressing and embarrassing story. Ysabel's healing gift cost her a day of her life every time she used it. Every aracoin Ysabel sent us had been purchased with her incipient death. I could only live with the guilt of receiving the first sum because I'd never asked her to send it. How could I shamelessly ask her for more?

Calum and I, the two siblings old enough to remember Ysabel, had struggled the most with our sister's inevitable death and the silent accusation lurking behind her distance. Eventually, Calum had traveled to the Holy City to find a way to save Ysabel. He must have succeeded, because she could now take a day of someone else's life to heal them instead, but he'd also somehow died. No one had ever given me an honest answer about how. Ysabel's letter, in stilted terms, said he'd died saving her. Officially he was listed as another victim in the recent necromantic rampage. I'd pestered Ysabel for months for the precise details about how Calum had died. Although I knew she must be traumatized, I had the right to know. She'd evaded my questions with the skill of a politician until I gave up.

Would Donya tell Ysabel that I'd somehow lost all my money? Would my sister think me a drunk or gambler like our father? If she ever asked, I decided that I'd demand to know what had happened to Calum in return. Let the silence between us finally end.

The sound of a wooden door breaking ripped me away from my thoughts.

The light pouring through the hole blinded my eyes, but I could dimly make out the black-and-white uniforms of the Sherdan military.

Donya reacted first. She shoved me toward the back of the stable. With her eyes on the guards, she said, "Vestan, get Bora out."

"Yes, my lady." Vestan grabbed my arm. Still stunned, I followed him. He dragged me out of sight between the last horse stall and the back wall, which had a triangular window.

Behind us, a guard said, "Countess Donya, you're under arrest for the charges of embezzlement, attempted assassination, and high treason."

Vestan shoved a crate in front of the window and half lifted me onto it. I unlatched the window with shaking hands, and he grabbed my legs to help me climb out.

A creak of metal came from the stable, but no clash of swords. It sounded like men in armor moving. Then the clang of manacles. In a rush of footsteps, the guards took Donya away.

* * *

I'd concluded that this whole mess was kind of my fault based on three factors.

Number one: the Sherdan guards had moved ridiculously fast to arrest Donya, so fast they weren't even pretending the charges were real. The Sherdan delegation only arrived at the palace minutes ago—how would they have had time to figure out if Donya was embezzling anything? Why would she have been plotting to assassinate the new queen when she hadn't known the queen would turn out to be a foreign puppet until that very day? People on the streets were grumbling and angry. A crier got tomatoed for reporting the arrest, even though it was hardly that poor boy's fault. The entire city had been locked down, both by Sherdan guards and the Arahasnor army, which had quickly fallen under the duchess's control. They weren't letting the news escape because they knew our nobility wouldn't let this stand unchallenged. They must have been planning this from the beginning, so it couldn't entirely be my fault.

On the other hand, the confrontation I'd caused between Donya and the Blood Duchess certainly couldn't have helped matters. I might have caused the duchess to move faster.

Number two: Because of me, Duchess Hedri knew that Queen Ysabel might have a stake in this matter. My sister's friendship with Donya was less well-known—if anything, they had a reputation for being political enemies. But because she'd been tipped off to possible foreign interference, Duchess Hedri had placed guards on every Bookmaker in the city. Not the gambling kind—the gifted who could create enchanted books that transmitted words to linked books around the world. As a result, Ysabel wouldn't find out about the execution until it was too late.

Finally, number three: If Donya hadn't been covering my retreat, she might have been able to escape out the window herself.

That last one alone made her arrest feel like it was entirely my fault. I'd decided to exorcise this guilt by saving Donya.

If only I could get out of the city, then I could find a Bookmaker and send a message to my sister. If anyone had the political power to rescue Donya, it would surely be Ysabel.

I didn't have the skills to sneak past the heavy watch around the gate. Instead, I bribed a guard to let me onto the wall. I pretended to be one of the young women who slipped up here on a regular basis to visit their lovers. As I walked along the wall, no one challenged me. The guards must have an agreement to cover for each other's love affairs. The top of the wall was much less heavily guarded because the only way out was a rather fatal fall.

Except for me, with my gift to bounce.

I reached an empty bit of wall near the corner tower with no guards in sight. I grabbed the wall with one hand to lift myself up, struggling to get my leg over. My wool skirt itched against my stockings. Down below, I could see snow, bushes, and tiny trees. The height made me feel faint. Steeling myself, I put one foot over the edge.

"Wait! Miss!" An elderly guard with a long white beard and mustache ran out of the tower.

I tried to leap over, but I wasn't fast enough. The guard grabbed me and wrestled me down the wall. "Please, stop! No matter what you're going through, suicide isn't the answer. Come inside with me. I'll make you a nice cup of tea and call a priest to talk to you."

Suicide must be what it would look like to anyone who didn't know about my ability. I saw no advantage to myself in admitting that I'd actually been trying to escape the lockdown—that would only get me sent to jail instead of getting sent to the priests.

Instead, I kicked, elbowed, and bit the guard's hand. His winter glove prevented me from doing any damage. He continued to smile. "I'm Sergeant Laurent. What's your name?"

I grunted around the taste of leather.

A young, extremely muscular guard ran down the wall toward us and shouted, "Whoever dumped you, he's not worth dying for! You're a lovely and attractive woman. I don't even have a girlfriend. Please date me instead!"

What in the name of the Sun God was he talking about? Oh, right, this was the guard I'd bribed earlier to get access to the wall. I'd told him that I was meeting a lover.

"That's not tactful," Sergeant Laurent said. "This poor young lady has just suffered heartbreak, and you're already hitting on her?"

"Excuse me?" The young man scowled. "It was a compliment."

"You're making her hardship all about yourself. Can't you help someone without wanting something in return?"

"Why are you always criticizing everything I do? You act like you're my father!"

Sergeant Laurent frowned. "I'm imparting the wisdom of my experience to you."

"I never asked for your wisdom, you self-righteous old coot!"

I took advantage of their argument to headbutt Sergeant Laurent and break free. I lunged for the wall.

The younger guard tackled my legs. "Stop! You should definitely consider dating me as an alternative to suicide."

Sergeant Laurent grabbed my arms. "Lovers come and go, take it from someone who's lived much longer than you. Ignore this young fool. Enjoy being single for a while and find yourself."

I was thoroughly pinned. I didn't have a chance unless I could make at least one of them let go. Inspiration struck. I batted my eyelashes at the sergeant. "Actually, I prefer older men like you."

"Huh?" Surprise made him loosen his grip.

"You criticized me when you flirted with her, too?" the young guard shrilled, pointing accusingly, which also required him to let go.

Freed, I ran past them, straight for the wall. Desperation gave me new strength. Ignoring the shouts behind me, I grabbed the top of the wall and yanked myself up.

No matter how many times I flung myself from a great height, I could never quite make myself believe I'd land safely. Survival instinct did its best to take over my body and freeze my legs. The very first time it had happened, I'd leapt to grab my little brother Benoni after some bullies shoved him out a window. I'd been trying to yank him back, not fall myself. When I'd wrapped my body around him, it had been a desperate attempt to cushion him. Instead of splattering on the ground, we'd bounced all the way to the town hall. I hadn't entirely believed what had happened, and it had taken me months to work up the nerve to try again, even with a pile of pillows below. Twenty times, I'd stared at the drop, then turned and left, before I finally psyched myself up.

On this occasion, I didn't have the time to chicken out. I flipped myself clean over the wall. Wind and small flakes of snow pelted my cheeks as I plummeted face first. The ground came rushing up very fast. That didn't stop my mind from going into overdrive.

What if my gift only let me fall safely from smallish heights, and I was about to be squashed against the ground below? Why did I only think of that after jumping? Wouldn't it be ironic if I died falling from the walls my own sister had built and bragged so much about in her letters?

My head smooshed into a freezing cold snowbank, and I bounced. High. A passing bird squawked and fled.

Huh. My gift seemed to lend me more buoyancy the farther the height I fell from. My weight decreased and my entire body became rubbery. It was a strangely ironic power for someone who was fat and not ashamed of it. (Mostly not ashamed, and I'd worked very hard to reach that place.)

I soared through the sky, bounced off the snow again, and landed in the forest. Hitting a tree trunk sent me flying into another tree. I screamed from shock, bouncing back and forth between the two trunks. My body felt no pain even as the bark dug into my face. But it was still a strange, unpleasant sensation to have my skin stretch like rubber. Each blow left more dirt and leaves on me.

My ability would wear off shortly, then this would start hurting. Head spinning, I grabbed a branch to stop my flight. Hitting the ground, I rolled. My body was so light I tumbled over the top of the snow without leaving a mark.

Eventually, I came to rest with my feet against an elderberry bush. Weight returned to my body, and I started to sink into a snow drift. The cold stung even though the impact didn't. I sat up. My heart pounded. I'd done it! I was out of the city.

I felt sorry about traumatizing two guards by making them watch me supposedly die. At least if they thought I was dead, they wouldn't chase after me. I was out and free. I could walk to the nearest town, find a Bookmaker, and summon Ysabel to save Donya.

With a lighter heart, I stood up and looked around. Fortunately I could see the path not far away. As I started walking into the forest, my stomach growled at me. All gifts came with a price, and mine made me ravenously hungry. It was a weak price to suit a weak ability. If I could make it to the next town, then I could eat.

I'd barely reached the road when a light flashed across my vision, and a tingling covered my body. I tried to grab a tree to support myself, but I no longer could control my own hands. My world went white.

Someone was sobbing. A child. My ears rang with her cries. I blinked. I stood in a little girl's bedroom. A tapestry of unicorns hung on the stone wall. Velvet curtains covered a poster bed. The other end of the room held a rocking horse and a shelf with three creepy-looking dolls with too-big eyes. A girl no older than six lay bent over a cabinet with red lashes on her back.

My hand held a whip.

I dropped it.

"A-are you all right?" I ran forward, reaching out a hand toward the girl, who had her back to me.

She flinched away from me, burrowing her head farther into her elbow and sobbing.

Of course she didn't want me to touch her. I'd been the one whipping her. But I would never do such a thing. What—how—? I'd been standing in a snowy forest! How did I get here?

Out the window, I glimpsed the royal stables and Saint Kald's School for the Gifted flying a flag just beyond. I was back in the city. All that hard work escaping, and I'd ended up back in the city! How could I save Donya now?

A tear formed in the corner of my eye. I raised a finger to wipe it away. My hand looked *white*.

I'd never had skin so pale. Nor did I recognize the long fingers decorated with many rings. I ran to the window, desperate for even a weak reflection in the glass.

Duchess Hedri's face stared back at me.

CHAPTER THREE

Princess Antonia knew how to make herself very small. It was a skill for survival she'd learned ever since coming to live with the Blood Duchess. She slouched down in her chair and let her curls fall over her face as Duchess Hedri argued with Head Cardinal Augustin.

"You haven't even provided any evidence of Countess Donya's supposed treachery," the cardinal cried.

"Are you doubting my word?" Duchess Hedri asked in a deadly tone that would have caused anyone back in Sherda to instantly drop to their knees.

Head Cardinal Augustin did not. He pointed a wrinkled finger, his long, majestic beard shaking. "Yes, I am! Embezzlement leaves a paper trail! Staging a rebellion involves moving troops! Either provide evidence or retract your slander."

Duchess Hedri smacked the royal scepter against her hand. "I'm the royal regent. My word is all the evidence I need."

With a cracking sound, Augustin straightened his stooped back as high as it would go. "You hold authority over Arahasnor the country, but the Holy City represents religious sects from around the world. We're an independent power. Any trials held within the city must be under our court system—not that you've bothered with a trial for Donya. Execution has been forbidden in this city for any crime. It's against the principles of three of our sects. You have the authority to hold Countess Donya—for now—but not to stage this ridiculous public beheading."

"Very well. The law is on your side," Duchess Hedri said. Just as the cardinal's face started to relax, she continued, "Now how will you enforce it?"

Silence filled the room. Finally, Augustin said, "Holy Maiden Ysabel won't stand by if you execute her friend."

"Countess Donya and Holy Maiden Ysabel are notorious rivals." The Blood Duchess waved her hand. "The Holy Maiden would probably send me a thank-you present."

"That's in the past. They worked together to rescue this city from the necromancer. Holy Maiden Ysabel supported Donya's election as regent—"

"Regardless, the Holy Maiden won't be able to do anything as long as I'm holding her sister hostage."

"Do you have the young woman in question in the dungeons?" the cardinal asked, looking more worried.

"Of course I do," Duchess Hedri said, flipping back her hair. Antonia knew that meant she was lying. The duchess held up a book. "I've already informed Conollia that the Holy Maiden's sister is currently under my protection, using a book seized from the countess's home that links directly to one held by Queen Ysabel. I'm certain she understands what that means, given the very graphic threats she replied with. What can a mere healer do to stop me?"

Cardinal Augustin put his hands on his hips. "Holy Maiden Ysabel will call down the wrath of the Sun God!"

"Ooo, the wrath of God." The duchess snorted sarcastically.

Enunciating each word, Augustin said, "The wrath of the Sun God goes by the name Alzira."

For the first time, the duchess flinched. Her face lost color and her hat flopped over her forehead. Antonia nearly giggled at the sight but covered her mouth in time. She'd heard of Alzira, Humanity's Strongest Monster, but knew little besides her title. How wonderful that someone existed who could scare the duchess.

Cardinal Augustin's voice became stronger. "By threatening Ysabel's family, you've released her from the restrictions against one monarch attacking another. That's a double-edged sword you're holding. Hostages can only be used once. If the young lady dies, even accidentally, while in your custody, then you'll be doomed. Let's be honest, from one leader to another. You've been moving hard and fast because your grip on power is precarious, and you know it. If you lose this gamble, your own home country will disown you. The people of Arahasnor won't accept a foreign takeover. Step down while you can still escape with your life."

The Blood Duchess straightened her hat and stared him down. "You have no idea what's headed your way. The jackals are circling your weak, rulerless country. You'll have no choice but to accept me once you see what your alternatives are."

The Head Cardinal looked her over as if trying to tell if she was bluffing. Antonia could have told him she wasn't. She'd overheard the discussion in the madcap carriage ride—about how the duchess was determined to reach Arahasnor first before the other three competing parties arrived to take over.

Finally, Head Cardinal Augustin said, "Your power derives from Her Highness." He inclined his head at Antonia. "A child doesn't pick her own regent . . . but she has the right to issue royal pardons. Your Highness, will you pardon Countess Donya and Miss Bora and request their release?"

Antonia cowered in her chair, terrified to suddenly have two important sets of eyes drilling into her.

"She refuses," the Blood Duchess said.

"Please, Your Highness. Countess Donya is a good woman and my friend. She doesn't deserve this." Augustin bent closer and lowered his voice. "Just one whisper from you could save her life."

Antonia hid her face in her arm. She couldn't defy the Blood Duchess. It wasn't fair to ask such a thing of her. She clamped her lips shut.

The duchess had murdered many people in front of her. There had never been anything she could do. She'd always told herself that. It was one thing to watch someone die, but another to be told she was responsible for it. Hoarsely, she whispered, "Please . . . don't execute anyone."

Head Cardinal Augustin straightened. "Thank you, Your Highness. What a wise move before your reign has even begun. I'll immediately—"

The Blood Duchess clapped her hands, and two guards entered the room. They each grabbed one of the Head Cardinal's arms. He looked between them. "What . . . you can't . . . I'm not under the authority of the kingdom of Arahasnor! I represent the Church of the Sun God around the world! There will be outcry when the other sects hear of this."

Duchess Hedri sneered. "You won't be able to tell anyone anything from inside the dungeons. I assure you, Arahasnor is about to have bigger problems than what happens to one measly cardinal. Especially one from a common background who was only elected because a necromancer massacred everyone actually important."

The Head Cardinal was dragged from the room, cursing and attempting to hit one guard with his cane.

Antonia whimpered. She'd known she shouldn't have said anything. She'd known it. Now she would pay.

"Come with me, Antonia," the duchess ordered. Antonia didn't resist as her guardian grabbed her wrist and dragged her painfully back to her bedroom. It would only be worse if she resisted.

"First you jump out of a carriage, then you talk back in front of company. You're an embarrassment."

Antonia hadn't jumped; she'd been shoved by Falael and the door had been loose. But it would do no good to make excuses. At least she could take the cold comfort that she'd always been destined for punishment whether she'd spoken up or not.

As soon as the bedroom door closed, Duchess Hedri ordered Antonia to take off her dress.

With shaking hands, Antonia undid the buttons. She bent over the cabinet without being asked. She didn't want to watch as the duchess inevitably went to the chest next to the rocking horse and pulled out a birch whip.

At the first strike, Antonia closed her eyes and tried to make her mind go away. She counted the grains on the cabinet. Anything to help her not think.

Another lash. Then another. She screamed with each strike. Tears overflowed from her eyes. It was harder to drift away than usual. Maybe because for a moment, it had seemed like an adult would listen to her. She should have known better. The Head Cardinal had been kind, but he couldn't stop the duchess. No one could.

The whip landed again, this time on top of her bloody cuts. Antonia screamed. She wished the duchess would become a kind person, like the woman who'd saved her from falling from the carriage. She wished it with an intensity beyond anything she'd ever wanted before.

Light exploded from Duchess Hedri's body. It was so blinding that Antonia buried her head into the cabinet and put her arms over her eyes, but the light still snuck through. An intense exhaustion filled her whole body. It was all she could do to stay conscious.

The light stopped. No one hit her again. Antonia dared open her eyes.

"Kid," I whispered. My voice sounded unfamiliar to me—deeper and richer. "Kid. You're hurt. We've got to stop the bleeding!"

I ripped a curtain off the poster bed to use as a bandage. She flinched away.

"Here." I held out the cloth. "Use this to stop the bleeding."

The brown-haired girl turned around to reveal the same freckled features and pointy nose of the girl who'd fallen out of the royal carriage earlier this afternoon. This was the *princess*? The Blood Duchess beat even the heir to the throne? Not that I doubted her capacity for cruelty, but I did wonder how she'd gotten away with mistreating someone of higher rank. I supposed in Sherda the princess had no one to stand up for her, and her royal brother had never cared about her.

Princess Antonia took the cloth from me and wrapped it over her bare shoulders. She gazed up at me with wide, anxious eyes. "Did it work?" she asked in a small voice.

I stared at her. "Sorry?"

"I wished for you to become nice, and now you're nice." A very small smile crossed her lips. Then she yawned.

I paled. "Kid—Your Highness—did you see a flash of light after you made your wish? And now you feel tired?"

She nodded. After her head fell over, she seemed to have trouble lifting it. She slumped sideways against the cabinet.

As I grabbed her, my heart raced. Carefully, I placed her down on the bed on her stomach to avoid aggravating her injuries. A body-swapping gift! No one had heard of one of those in centuries, but it had to be, because clearly I'd ended up in a different body. Given Princess Antonia's young age, her power had probably only just appeared. How had the princess picked me of all people? We'd only just met at the incident at the carriage earlier that day.

More importantly, I had to get someone to tend to those injuries. I ran into the hallway and screamed, "Doctor!"

The door nearly hit a maid in the face, so she must have been about to open it. Stumbling, she curtsied. "Your Grace." Her voice held a raspy note. A red curl poked out of her white cap. She had full cheeks and a distinctive jawline. Even with her head lowered, I could not fail to notice her beauty.

"I'm sorry," I said.

The maid nearly fell over. She looked around as if trying to tell who had spoken, because clearly it couldn't be me. "Did you say you're . . . jolly? Delighted to hear you are in such a good mood, Your Grace."

Whoa, did it ever feel odd to have people treat me with such deference that they didn't even believe their own ears when I said sorry. I fought off an urge to apologize again. For what reason, I wasn't sure. Existing? Accidentally glancing at her breasts so fast I hoped she hadn't noticed? I attempted to sound commanding, but my voice squeaked. "I need you to fetch a doctor. The princess has been injured." Or more likely, using her power had knocked her out. With such a strong power, I wasn't surprised it was one use only.

"Yes, Your Grace." She lowered her eyes, but not before I saw a flash of fury. If she'd heard the princess screaming, then she would have instantly assumed I'd beaten the poor girl unconscious. I must look like the worst scum in the world. How could I deny it had been me when I was currently occupying the body of the one responsible? "I have already summoned a doctor." She gestured down the hallway.

A short, thin man with a long face poked his head around the corner. He seemed to be trying to hide behind the high collar of his black coat. Sweat dripped down his crooked nose. He took a slow step forward.

I waved my hands. "Hurry!" I almost asked what he was waiting for, but it seemed obvious—he was terrified of the duchess. The maid had probably faked an interruption in hopes of sneaking the doctor in. At least someone in this palace gave half a damn about the princess.

The doctor rushed past me into the room. He gasped upon seeing the princess's condition, then opened up his medical bag. The maid dropped to her knees beside the bed and took Antonia's hand, murmuring something soft. The girl did not stir. I hoped this had more to do with her exhaustion than her injuries.

I stepped into the room. "Uh . . . can I do anything to help . . . ?"

Fury burned so bright in the maid's eyes that she could not hide it. My cheeks heating, I stepped backward. "Or . . . not . . ."

The maid bowed her head, and her tone became subservient. "Your Grace, I came to fetch you. You need to hurry in order to make it to the execution in time."

"Execution . . . Donya's execution? *Right now?*"

Hesitantly, the maid nodded.

I'd been too late to bring help to save Donya! Damn the insane Blood Duchess! Wait a minute. *I* was the Blood Duchess. "Stop the execution!" I screamed.

"Your Grace?" She raised her eyebrows slightly.

I turned for the door. My borrowed, too-long legs got tangled up in my heavy black dress, and I nearly fell. How did the duchess walk around in a dress covered in gemstones? *This thing must weigh as much as my whole body!* I gripped the wall, panting. "Someone get me a carriage! Ugh, and someone help me down the stairs. Dammit! I'm going to stop the execution!"

The maid and the doctor exchanged confused glances. Slowly, the maid asked, "Your Grace, have you perhaps been drinking? Or did you try any new relics with possible side effects?"

I seized on the excuse. "Yes, I must have been drunk when I ordered the countess's execution. Get me a carriage!"

The doctor cowered when I shouted. The maid leapt to her feet and offered me her arm. I noticed that she flinched when I touched her. Even though I knew this must be because of the duchess's cruelty and not my weight, I still felt disgusting. A soft, poisonous voice, one I hadn't heard in a very long time, returned to my mind: *You're revolting, a giant elephant, inconveniencing everyone.*

Donya needed me. This was no time for my issues. I gritted my teeth and moved faster. The maid got me down the stairs and spoke to a guard, who then brought around a carriage. As I collapsed into the seat, she ran up the stairs, no doubt returning to the princess's side.

This whole situation was a nightmare. Would I be killed the instant the guards around the carriage realized I was a fake? What had happened to *my* body? Was the duchess inside of it? What might she do with my face? Would it even be possible to switch back?

I pulled my knees up to my chest. Except they weren't "my" knees and feeling the jiggling and the lighter, downy hair reminded me. Every single movement of my new chest felt strange. I did not know how to flex my fingers with so many rings on them. The entire world did not quite feel real. If only this was all a dream. A tear trickled down my cheek. No, no, the Blood Duchess wouldn't cry. I had to keep up this act for at least a few minutes longer. Donya needed me. That gave me the strength to pull myself together.

I must have terrified the driver by shrieking at him to go faster. When the carriage pulled into the town square, I yanked the door open.

Once again, my legs got tangled up in my overburdened dress. I fell, landing several feet away on my hands and knees.

Looking up, I stared straight at the hastily erected scaffold in the middle of the square. Sherdan guards formed a blockade, not letting anyone close. With no time for a guillotine, they'd erected a wooden block. A guard stood next to it holding an axe. Another guard forced Donya's head down.

"Noooooooooooooooooooooo!" I screamed. I ran like I'd never run before, instantly losing my breath. This body could barely move without getting winded! My knees felt like they might pop out of their sockets. Cold air stung my cheeks.

With aching legs, I leapt up the stairs. The guards took one look at my disheveled state, blonde hair falling in frozen clumps, and fled the execution stand.

I grabbed Donya and yanked her into a hug. "Are you okay? What did they do to you? Ah! You have a bruise on your cheek! Those monsters!"

Despite the rope around her arms, Donya tried to get away from me. She growled. "I don't know what you're playing at, but I refuse to be fooled. I won't beg for my life!"

I let go. "The execution is canceled." Unfortunately, I could hardly admit I wasn't the real duchess in front of her guards, but I would explain to Donya later. "Just a little joke on my part. Ha-ha."

Donya gave me the stare that I deserved.

I struggled to my feet—ow, my knees—and clapped my hands. "Let's get my new best friend back to the palace and cleaned up. Joke time is over! I hope you all appreciated some of our traditional Sherdan humor."

The guards stared at me in astonishment. So many eyes on me suddenly made me realize the Blood Duchess favored very low-cut dresses—much lower than I felt comfortable with. I clamped a hand over my (her?) chest. Then I let go because I feared I was acting out of character. Then my hands returned because it was cold, dammit. I was freezing my tits off, literally.

From behind the barricade, the citizenry stared with undisguised hostility. Metal weapons glinted from among the crowd. A teenage boy held up a match and a doll wearing a black dress with blonde straw hair. "Burn the Blood Duchess!" he cried, setting fire to the skirt.

With a growl, a guard started toward the child, drawing his sword.

"No!" I shouted. "Don't worry, I can take what I dish out. Execution jokes. I love them. That's a wonderful effigy of me. Someone give that child a gold coin." I smiled so broadly, my face hurt.

The guard eyed me with bemusement. "If you say so, Your Grace."

The coachman actually reached into a purse and tossed a coin into the crowd. That distracted them long enough for me to drag Donya into the carriage.

CHAPTER FOUR

To call the carriage ride back awkward would be putting it mildly. I couldn't tell Donya the truth because the guards might overhear, and the carriage driver definitely would.

Donya sat in the seat across from me, staring warily. A bruise covered her left cheek. She'd looked so tall before, and now she was smaller than me. Coldly, she said, "I suppose you're taking me somewhere less public to execute me."

"No, absolutely not! I'd never—I mean, I've realized that your help would be invaluable to me in running this country." I tried my best to sound convincing. Yanking at my bodice, I tried to make it cover a little more of my chest.

Donya gazed at me with the face of someone afraid to feel hope. Then she glanced out the window. I had a bad feeling she was counting the number of guards. What should I do if she tried to run off? I didn't want to imprison her, but I desperately needed her. If only she would stay long enough for us to be alone, then I would tell her everything. "My la—um, D-Donya, I apologize for my earlier actions. Please, just hear me out. Once we're alone, I'll explain everything." I winked frantically.

Donya's eyebrows rose. "I suppose you realized that you need me as a hostage to use against Ysabel, since Bora escaped. At least that means she must have gotten out of the city."

"Oh, Bora is fine—" Except I wasn't fine. I'd accidentally committed treason, and my real body was off who-knew-where doing who-knew-what. My breath hitched. My chin wobbled. (All that fat. I was fine with fat. Fat wasn't a bad word. I felt sick. I was not fine. I wanted to *cut off the wobbly bit with a knife*.) I gagged. A sob heaved my body. I bit my lip hard to prevent another tear from slipping out.

Donya looked at me with bafflement and disgust. I could not stand to see that contemptuous look in her eyes. If we couldn't get back to the palace soon, I would break down.

Rubbing my eyes, I stuck my head up front and screamed at the driver, "Faster!"

Whatever he saw on my face absolutely terrified him. He nodded and urged the horses on.

I quickly learned that by barking orders at people, I could get stuff done. All I had to do was order the footman to find a private room, and one manifested. I'd made certain to clear the room of all staff, even ordering the guards away from the door so we wouldn't be overheard. Donya sat in the palace parlor holding a mug of hot tea. The bruising had steadily turned more purple.

I approached holding a cold cloth. "This is for your face. The doctor added herbs . . ."

She slapped my hand away. "Don't touch me."

I'd been through far too much today. Nearly being executed, throwing myself off the city wall, having my body stolen. I burst into tears.

Donya gaped with wide eyes.

"My lady, I don't know what to do," I sobbed. "I'm so scared! I'm not the duchess! I'm Bora!"

"Sherdan humor?" Donya asked weakly.

"It really is me! Princess Antonia has a body-swapping gift. I became the duchess, and she's me. I don't know how to make you believe me." I rubbed at the tears pouring down my cheeks.

Donya gazed at me only with calculation, no sympathy. "You seem to have fallen ill, Your Grace. I'll summon a doctor at the palace."

"I see that look! You want to have me committed to a mental institution." I sniffled. "Please, I needed you to save me from such a fate. Like how you saved me from Falael when we first met." Crap, that didn't work, the Blood Duchess had been there, too. "Then you introduced me to your stablemaster, Vestan?" His name was probably common knowledge. Unfortunately, I had not known Donya long enough for us to have shared any personal identifying secrets, though I lived in hopes of us reaching such a place later.

"The doctor will help you, Your Grace." Donya wasn't a good actor. Despite her attempt to sound soothing, menace slipped in. The doctor would help me be deemed unfit to ever be seen in public again.

"Um . . . I've collected all twenty of your activism posters, including the extremely rare first one, and only one, where you wore a dress."

Donya recoiled. "A stalker?"

"Please, no, just a fan." My sister would be a better source for finding a shared secret. "Ysabel talked about you in her letters. She admired you a lot." But most of what my sister had said about Donya's accomplishments had been public knowledge. I thought harder, finally digging up details from one of my sister's more vulnerable letters. "Before you two became friends, when you called her 'a heartless snake incapable of love,' she asked me if I thought it might be true. Only the two of you knew about that, right?"

Donya froze, assessing me closely. Her eyes softened. "Ysabel admired me even before we became friends? I hurt her feelings when I said that? I had no idea. Oh dear." Donya set down her teacup. "You're really Bora?" Hesitantly, she reached up to pat my back.

I collapsed into her shoulder. "I don't know what to do! Please help me!"

"By the Sun God, it's strange seeing that expression on the Blood Duchess's face." Donya put her arms around me and guided me to the sofa. "Tell me everything."

I poured out the whole story to Donya, from my escape out of the city to what the princess had done. "I don't understand why *I* got swapped when I wasn't anywhere near the princess," I finished in an admittedly whiny tone.

"Princess Antonia wished for the Blood Duchess to be a kind person." Donya tapped her chin. "That's why she swapped with you."

I rubbed my eyes. "I'm flattered, but the city must be full of kind people."

"Who else cushioned a girl falling out of a carriage with her own body?" Donya shrugged. "You also jumped off a wall to save my life. That type of self-sacrifice is rare. You remind me a lot of Ysabel." She patted my head as if I were a little kid.

I'd already known my crush was hopeless, but it still stung. I'd been placed in the best friend's kid-sister box. There would be no escaping that box.

But also, I was stuck in some weirdo's body, so what did it matter? I sniffled. Donya handed me a tissue. Blowing my nose, I said, "I'm glad I could save you, my lady."

"Please, call me Donya."

"But I'd like to go back to my own body now. Can you help me ask the princess to swap us back?"

Donya raised her hand. "Don't be so hasty. This is a prime opportunity."

"No, no, no. I'm not staying like this!" I punctuated each no with a sharp shake of my head. "If I'm caught impersonating nobility, I'll be executed! And I'm *not* a good actor, Donya." I grabbed her collar for emphasis. "When I was a kid, I was assigned to be a tree in the church performance of Holy Maiden Ava's life, and I accidentally knocked the entire stage set over on top of everyone. I knew then and there that I was never destined for a life on the stage!"

Donya patted my hand. "I know I'm asking a lot from you. But your kingdom needs you. This is our big chance to take back control."

"How about this? I'll order all the guards to leave the city, then voluntarily walk into a dungeon cell. After locking the door, you swap us back. Easy as mugging a dead man." My country accent came out stronger as my voice rose.

"Unfortunately, the kingdom needs the Blood Duchess." Donya pinched her forehead. "The late and unmourned King Uctor was childless, and he didn't care about his younger half sister or his legacy. He figured that if he could sell his kingdom once, he could sell it three more times."

"You mean besides selling the regency to Sherda . . ."

Donya counted off on her fingers. "King Uctor also promised the princess's regency—and effective control of our country—to two other kingdoms. And he promised the Sashan Guild of Slavers a thousand of our citizens in slavery in exchange for a large sum of money."

"But . . ." I gaped. "Slavery wasn't legal in Arahasnor, even before it got outlawed globally in the last World Games. He can't do that."

"I imagine Uctor thought that wouldn't be his problem since it was agreed that the guild would collect upon his death. They can't force us to hand our people over, but they can ask for their money back. The kingdom doesn't have any money. We're completely broke." Donya's shoulders sagged.

"Oh dear," I said. That didn't seem sufficient. "Oh shit."

"The Blood Duchess knew about the other rivals. She came here with a plan. She adopted the princess legally, meaning she has the first right to the regency. Sherda gave her a large sum to pay off the slavers. If the former slavers' guild gets a foothold in our kingdom, they'll bring misery and disaster. You don't know how badly we need that money, Bora."

"I know that I can be executed for impersonating a duchess!" I drew a thumb across my throat. This new information only made my position even worse. The kingdom was on the edge of collapse, everyone hated me, and three rival powers wanted my stolen throne. Nope, nope, nope. I was *not* taking responsibility for this mess. I was going back to my peaceful life with my little brother in the countryside and never setting foot outside my village again. In comparison, even my mother bossing me around and tossing passive-aggressive insults suddenly felt like a nonexistent problem, and it had gotten easier to avoid my father since the divorce. I would greet Dad's harassing creditors like old friends because at least they didn't have armies to back them up.

"I'll protect you, I swear. I'll figure something out." She did not sound confident enough to inspire any confidence in me. "If everything goes wrong, you can always flee to Conollia, and Ysabel will protect you."

"Why do I have to get exiled? I want to live in Arahasnor! It's my home!"

"Your home won't survive much longer if you don't help it," Donya said with hideous bluntness.

I looked at my hands. I didn't want to let Donya down. But if I tried to do something so far outside my capabilities, I'd only let her down later, when the stakes were much higher. "I . . . I . . ."

"I'm very sorry, but you don't have a choice at the moment," Donya said. "It's unlikely the princess will be able to swap you back right away. A powerful gift generally takes a lot out of the user."

"How long?" I asked, panic making my voice more strident.

"I don't know. Body-swapping gifts are only legend. I thought I overheard the footman telling you that the princess is still asleep."

I nodded. I'd asked as soon as we got back.

"We'll have to at least wait for her to wake up. And it will take her time after that to build up her strength. Who knows how long? Furthermore, there's almost always a distance limit on gifts. The duchess in your body is currently outside the city. If she comes back, then it will be possible to swap you two. But if she decides to leave the kingdom, you'll probably be out of luck."

I whimpered. "Why would she do that?" Surely the duchess must want to swap back even more than me.

"From her perspective, an enemy just stole her body. It would be foolish for her to head into the territory controlled by that enemy. She'll probably seek out allies in her home country."

I moaned.

"I'll send out guards right away to look for the duchess in your body, if you give me the authority."

"Yes—you can have all the authority you want. I'll order everyone to obey you as me. Just get my body back!"

Donya's face turned uneasy. "No one will believe that unless we come up with a decent excuse. I suppose I can pretend you threatened me into working for you. Even so, you'll need to make some appearances."

"Find my body . . . please . . ."

"I'll make it top priority," Donya said. "We can't have the duchess telling anyone else about the swap. If people believe her, you'll be arrested."

I hadn't even been thinking about that. I moaned even longer and more pitifully.

Donya exhaled. "I definitely don't want you to think I'm threatening you, so please don't take it that way, but it would be a very bad idea for you to leave the protection of the palace. The Blood Duchess has many enemies. Many, many enemies. In fact, there's an entire assassin organization founded by her victims for the sole purpose of killing her. Twelve assassins with personal grudges against her trained for years to take revenge. The organization is funded by countless other people who've lost loved ones to her murderous rampages. My spies inform me that they've taken the duchess leaving her country as an opportunity. The Twelve Avengers are on the move."

That was a scary-sounding name. I stared at my hands. "So I have no choice but to pretend to be the duchess."

"I'm afraid so." Donya looked sincerely sorry.

"You'll help me?" I whispered, trying not to cry again.

Donya gripped my hand. "I'll look after you like my own little sister. I promise."

Yep. I was in the best friend's kid-sister box.

Donya took charge immediately, and I was more than happy to tell the palace steward to take orders from her. We both agreed that I should speak as little as possible. Donya sent her most trusted guards looking for the real Duchess Hedri with strict orders to capture her unharmed. She also told everyone that "Miss Bora" had fallen under a spell of madness and might babble nonsense about being someone else. Then she took me to the duchess's bedroom and arranged for dinner to be sent there.

The bedroom was ridiculously big. I could fit an entire cottage in there. In addition to an enormous bed, there was a desk, a makeup vanity, and a breakfast table. The walk-in closet alone was larger than my bedroom back home. Everything looked golden yellow, from the walls to the pale silk carpet to the decorations on the baseboard. The ceiling had some poofy cloth square hanging directly over the bed. I had no idea what that was for but it sure did look fancy, with a chandelier hanging from the middle and diamonds decorating the square. The bed had a quilted headboard and a dozen different pillows. What did rich people need so many pillows for? A sweet floral scent filled the room. At first, I thought it came from the pockets of flowers on the walls, but on closer look the petals were made of cloth. It must come from the scent packets hanging in the corners.

My head hurt. This super-tall lacy hat had been fastened to my hair with entirely too many pins. As I pulled them out, I tried not to look at the full-length mirror next to the dresser. But my eyes kept getting drawn back there.

The woman staring back at me had the majestic height and waist-length blonde hair I'd longed for when I'd been the only dark-skinned girl in my small country village. She was heavier than me, and I had emotions I didn't want to feel about that. This new body was hitting all my old insecurities.

There had been a time when I'd dyed my hair, tried (and failed) to force it straight, and stuck a finger down my throat after meals to throw them up. My body and I had gone to war, and we'd both lost. One day, I'd gotten tired of hating myself so much and decided to stop listening to the mean voices both inside my head and out of it. It hadn't been nearly that easy. I'd spent years getting comfortable with my body. These days, I could look at myself in the mirror without flinching. If I didn't smile at the sight of myself, then at least I didn't cry at it either. But now I had a new reflection, and it was throwing me off-balance.

I threw the hat down on the floor. Then I took the mirror off the wall and carried it into the closet. Tomorrow, I'd order someone to take it away. A duchess could do that, right?

Among other orders, Donya had instructed the staff to bring me dinner. A tempting smell drifted off the spread of food on the oak table: roast chicken, green beans, pigeon eggs, fig pudding, and a tiny array of cakes on a golden stand. My stomach rumbled. I sat down and dug in.

The first bite of chicken tasted crispy and perfect. Damn, rich people ate well. I should savor these delicacies. But instead, I just kept eating faster.

My hands went wild, reaching for the food in front of me. It felt as if I were watching this scene from a distance, a giant woman gorging herself. I'd become a passenger riding along in this foreign body. I barely paid attention to the taste as I shoveled food into my mouth. My stomach became bloated. (It wasn't my stomach, so why should I care?) Heartburn rose up my throat. I could taste nothing but a burning sensation. There was no pleasure from this food, but I couldn't stop. It didn't matter that I no longer felt hunger. Hedri's body had control, not me.

When I returned to awareness, I'd eaten every last bit of food down to the crumbs that had fallen off the cakes. Oh no. That had been enough dessert to feed an entire dinner party! I'd eaten it all by myself!

My stomach rolled. Shame overwhelmed me. A disgusting coat of crumbs went from my lips all the way to my chin. As I brushed them off, it felt even more strange and revolting because the face didn't feel like my own. I hated that stupid double chin. I hated this body. I hated myself. I deserved to hate myself. Why had I done that? Why hadn't I stopped?

I'd lost control, and it scared me. In the space of just a day, my body had been stolen, and I'd been thrust into the middle of a national crisis. I didn't know what to do except go along with Donya's instructions. I was terrified of stepping wrong and causing people to die—including myself. My own head was definitely on the chopping block. Already I had no control over what happened to me, and to top it off, I'd lost control of my own actions, too. I felt so *stupid* and *worthless*. I gasped. More tears fell down my face. And that *damn ugly* chin wouldn't stop wobbling!

My nausea felt like a lance piercing straight into my side. I felt like I might throw up. But wouldn't it be better if I could throw up? Then all that revolting, fattening food wouldn't be inside my body any longer. I could erase this mistake.

I ran to the bathroom and stuck a finger down my throat.

The rings on my new hand cut the roof of my mouth, sending an iron taste dripping down. The pain felt like a deserved punishment. At the same time, it jolted me back to awareness. Ashamed, I withdrew my hand. I'd made a vow to stop doing that—the binge eating and the throwing up afterward.

This was the duchess's body. Who cared if it gained weight? I wasn't going to take up permanent residence in here. I couldn't possibly be stuck like this. Just the thought made me feel ill.

My senses restored, I changed into a nightgown and headed to bed. (It didn't count, what I'd just done. It had been someone else's body. I had gotten better. I wasn't weak. Over and over again, I told myself that.)

As soon as I lay down, my stomach acids decided to throw a parade. I groaned and rolled to my side, trying and failing to get comfortable.

A sudden blast of cold air struck my face. The window hung open. When had that happened? Ugh, I didn't need to feel even worse right now. I swung my legs over the bed, preparing to stand and close it.

"Not one step forward." A sword touched my throat. A raspy voice whispered, "Duchess Hedri, you killed my parents. Prepare to die."

CHAPTER FIVE

The assassins were here already! Donya had promised me I'd be safe in the palace. What was I supposed to do? I had the combat capabilities of a mouse. My gift wouldn't come in handy with no heights in sight. Should I come clean about being a fake?

I wet my lips. "Please pardon me, but I didn't—"

"If you cry for help, I slit your throat," the gender-indeterminate voice growled.

I immediately stopped talking. I could swear I'd heard that voice somewhere before.

Keeping the sword pointed at me, the assassin stepped around to stand in front of me. The moonlight illuminated her bright red curly hair. From her pointed chin to her sharp eyebrows, she was stunningly lovely. Red lipstick blazed against her moon-kissed skin. She was even taller than my current body. Her spider-thin limbs and trim frame were covered by skintight black clothing. A dark cape flowed behind her. It looked cool. Dammit, I was attracted, jealous, and also about to die!

Now I knew where I'd heard her voice. This was the Blood Duchess's personal maid, the one who'd taken the princess to the doctor. Why did the duchess have to incite murderous hatred in everyone she encountered? I whispered, "If you'd like a raise, we can talk, uh—"

"You've forgotten my name again." She scowled. "You know me as Araceli, but my real name is Ari, heir to the duchy of South Sherda."

"Nice to meet you—um, which name do you prefer?" I was a bit puzzled because Ari was more commonly a male name, but it didn't seem politic to bring that up with a sword still pointed at my throat.

The sword wavered. "Araceli, I guess?" She looked confused, then her face hardened, and the blade pressed close to my skin again.

I tried to breathe more shallowly so I wouldn't cut myself. "Wait, isn't the Blood Duchess the ruler of South Sherda? Are you two related?" Araceli couldn't possibly be the duchess's daughter—they looked too close in age. (Araceli looked about the same age as me, and I was only in my mid-twenties. Come to think of it, didn't Hedri look oddly young for a duchess? Or was I justifying my own lack of accomplishments at my age?)

"Your arrogance has reached the point where you refer to yourself in third person." Araceli sighed. "I knew you wouldn't remember my real name either. You never remember your victims. As a result, I've prepared a short presentation for you about our history together." She flared out her cloak dramatically. The sword, fortunately, lowered. I had no time to feel relieved. Red mist exploded from her garment.

It was probably poisonous. I had but seconds left to live. Slain by a ridiculously hot assassin who'd been targeting someone else! Oh, cruel world!

Instead, the mist paralyzed me in place. I couldn't even blink. I could only sweat, certain my end would be coming soon.

From her cloak, Araceli pulled out three tiny puppets and put them on her fingers. Two on her right hand, and one on her left. "This is you." She waved a puppet with blonde straw hair and a very angry face drawn in red paint. "These are my parents." The other two puppets had clearly been made more carefully, with detailed clothing and tiny buttons. The mother wore a silk blue dress, the father a doublet. They had gemstones for eyes. "You were the landgrave ruling over part of our territory after the mysterious deaths of your parents—who you definitely killed, everyone knows that. But you had greater ambitions, so you cozied up to the prince, collected blackmail around the royal court, and then—" Lowering her hands, she peered at me. "Are you even listening? Or should I just skip straight to your brutal death?"

I'd gotten back just enough motion to bat my eyes frantically. I managed a low grunt.

Araceli fished around in her pocket and retrieved a very tiny stack of papers, which she stuck to the fake duchess. "Then after you had bribed or threatened enough nobles into your control, you used your puppets to falsify evidence against my family, claiming that my parents had committed treason and spied for a neighboring kingdom—this one, ironically. You also arranged for a fake assassination attempt against the crown prince so that you could pretend to rescue him."

Whoa, I—I mean the Blood Duchess—was very evil. This could be some useful information to use against her if I survived. I got enough motion back to nod my head to show I was listening.

Araceli threw the duchess puppet to the floor, papers and all, and stomped on it, viciously enough to snap off the wig. I shuddered, thinking she surely longed to snap my neck in a similar fashion. Next, she withdrew a tiny puppet of a little boy wearing a waistcoat with short red hair and a puppet of a golden-furred dog. "This is me, and this is Mr. Wuffles."

I grunted a bit louder. Voice coming back, phew. Now, if only my legs would follow suit, then I could run. My older sister once told me that villains like to monologue, and if I were ever about to be murdered, then I should keep the killer talking. (My sister also liked to monologue, so what did that say about her?)

Araceli made her voice artificially high-pitched as she manipulated her mother's puppet. "My little Ari, I need you to be brave. Take Mr. Wuffles and run. Remember that we love you and you should definitely avenge our murders." In her usual voice, she said, "They didn't tell me that last part, but it was implied. Normally if someone kills your parents, you'd kill them back. Especially the scions of fallen noble families. Anyone who's ever seen a puppet show knows that."

I nodded before I realized I was agreeing to my death.

Araceli's voice became deeper. "The entire ducal household is under arrest for high treason." She pulled out a model guard who attacked the parent puppets, ripping them off her fingers and throwing them to the floor. I gasped. The dog leapt on the guards and then—boom, thrown to the floor, too.

"NOOOOOOOOO!" I screamed, my voice finally coming back. "Not the dog, too. Please let the dog live!"

Araceli glared. "Your vile minions didn't even spare Mr. Wuffles, but he'll be avenged."

Tears streamed down my cheeks. "That's just too sad. You lost your parents at such a young age. That damn Blood Duchess didn't even let your family dog live? She's a vile, putrid, pathetic example of everything wrong with the nobility. You should definitely kill her."

"That was the idea," Araceli said, drawing her sword and placing it back at my throat.

"I'm sorry you went through all that. Do you need a hug? I can give you a hug." I extended my arms. Ooo, I had arm movement back. I could feel my legs returning, too. They tingled all over, but I could twitch my feet again.

"An apology won't get you off the hook at this point, Blood Duchess!"

"No, I'm not the—"

Araceli spoke over me. "I've been plotting this revenge all my life. I trained in the art of the blade. I studied poisons and magic. I gathered allies among your other victims."

I clapped. "You've done so well. Your deceased parents must be proud of you."

"Stop mocking me!"

"I'm not mocking—" Upon seeing the murderous look on Araceli's face and the blade inching closer, I shut up and let her continue her monologue.

"I created a false identity and lowered myself to work for the woman who killed my family. It took me a whole year serving as your maid to swap out all your rings for fakes—wait. Where are your rings?" She stared at my bare hands.

I looked down. "I took them off to sleep."

"You *took them off to sleep*? But you never take them off! Not to sleep and not to bathe!" Araceli's hand wavered, that sword point jiggling dangerously. "I can't believe I spent years replacing your magical protective relics and the *very night* I decide to kill you, you render my hard work pointless by taking them all off!"

"Who wears rings in bed?" The duchess, apparently. No wonder the pale lines stood out so starkly on my borrowed fingers. "You sound like you've put an awful lot of work into this. Did you ever think about maybe just poisoning one of the meals you bring every day?"

"You're protected against poison. Or at least you were before I stole your Ring of Immunity. After going through all this trouble, I want to look you in the eyes when you die."

I nodded. "Yes, I can see why that would be more satisfying. But why the window? Why not just walk through the door?"

"Your door lock is another relic that explodes when anyone enters without your permission. There's one on the window, too, but I barely managed to disable that one."

"I was supposed to lock the door?"

Araceli stared at me. Then she went over to the door and opened it. It wasn't locked.

I rubbed my bedhead sheepishly. "Sorry, my bad. I'm from the countryside. No one locks their house doors, much less their bedroom doors."

"I can't believe you ruined my years of planning." Araceli advanced on me, her expression even more murderous. "The night I finally decide to assassinate you, you stop bothering to protect yourself? Am I a joke to you? Do you have an army of guards in the other room waiting to arrest me?"

I scrambled backward. "Uh, no, no guards. You see . . . the thing is . . . I'm not the Blood Duchess."

Araceli stared harder. I'd figured she wouldn't believe me. Maybe I should have screamed as soon as the sword moved away from my throat. I had a lot of sympathy for Araceli's suffering, but I refused to die for someone else's crimes.

After a moment, Araceli said, "I was starting to suspect as much." Before I could breathe a sigh of relief, she lunged forward and pinned me to the bed with one hand, the sword resting against my neck. "Where's the real Duchess Hedri, you body double?"

"I'm not a body double!" I squeaked. "I'm just an ordinary citizen of Arahasnor. The princess accidentally swapped my body with the duchess's."

"What?"

"Please don't kill me! Oh, and please don't tell anyone. Donya is counting on me to pretend to be the duchess long enough to save Arahasnor. She'll be very disappointed that I exposed myself in less than a day."

"Do you mean to tell me that the very night before the revenge I've been planning my entire life, a chance magical accident took my enemy from my grasp?" Araceli's lips pulled back in a snarl. She looked crazed.

"That's tough," I said meekly. "Not my fault, so if you'd please sheathe your weapon . . ."

Araceli's eyes narrowed. She lowered the sword slightly. "I have to admit, you're far too useless to be an employee of the Blood Duchess. She doesn't keep incompetence around for long, with the sole exception of that lover of hers. And while I could see the duchess pulling a fake act to save her life—she's quite the cunning survivor—I don't think she could ever successfully pretend to be . . . *this*."

It felt like I'd just been insulted, but I let it slide because I didn't want to die. "Thanks so much. Now if you'll kindly leave my bedroom, then we'll speak no more of this. Good luck finding the real duchess. But please don't kill my body! I want it back."

"Not so fast. I haven't schemed for so long to walk away empty-handed." While Araceli kept holding the sword a bit away from my skin, her other hand dug into her pocket and pulled out a ring. "This relic binds people to keep their promises, similar to a life-oath. I was going to use it to force the duchess to confess to framing my parents for treason. If you want to live, then you'll strike a bargain with me. Touch the diamond on this ring and vow that you're not the real duchess, you don't work for her and never will, and that you'll help me find and slay her to avenge my family."

It was on the tip of my tongue to agree to anything so she wouldn't kill me. But my big brother Calum always used to tell me that I let people push me around too much. That had certainly been happening to me lately, and I was tired of it. I ran my tongue over my lips and summoned my courage. "I have conditions, too. Promise you won't harm my real body even if you find the duchess in it. Also, promise to tell the other eleven assassins in your organization that I'm not the real Blood Duchess."

Araceli glared at me. "You don't get to impose conditions."

"I think I do. How are you going to find the real Duchess Hedri without me? You don't have the faintest idea what my original body looks like. If you kill me, your only lead is gone."

Araceli bit her lip. "The Twelve Avengers don't work together since we parted ways fearing a traitor . . . I don't even know all of their identities . . . They'd never listen to me."

I cried, "You took too long to agree to my deal! I have one more condition! I demand that you stay by my side and protect me against your fellow assassins."

"Fine," Araceli growled. "But if you want me to risk my skin protecting you, then I'm putting a time limit on it." She slammed my finger down on the diamond. "For one month, I'll lend you my sword and protect you from any and all external threats. During that time, you'll find the real duchess and bring her to me to kill. I promise I won't harm her until you swap back with her. But if you fail, then when a month ends, you'll voluntarily place your life into my hands. I bet I could lure the Blood Duchess out of hiding by threatening to kill you."

I considered it. Magical life-oaths killed anyone who broke one. That last condition had raised the stakes for me. But on the other hand . . . after the princess woke up, she should be able to swap our bodies again. Worst-case scenario, I could swap back and then run away and leave the duchess to deal with the consequences of my life-oath. It was her body who would be swearing it, after all. I decided to pad the time a little to be on the safe side. "Make it three months, and you have a deal."

"Two months."

"Uhhh . . . two months and a week."

His nonchalance unnerved me. "Show your smarmy face in my room again, and I'll have you horsewhipped." Now that sounded properly ducal! I was starting to get the hang of being nobility.

Falael smirked. "My dear Hedri, we both know you'll call me back after you start longing for me again. No one else could ever love someone as fat as you."

My breath caught. It felt like I'd been punched in my solar plexus. Falael had said things like that to me countless times. I wouldn't place the sole blame on him for why I'd started throwing up my food, but he'd been a large factor. My head spun. Stomach acid clawed up my throat. Even after so long, he still held the power to hurt me? I hated it. I hated *him*.

As Falael walked toward the door, I called after him, "I mean it! I'm done with you!"

"Like you've never said that before," he called over his shoulder as he left.

Argh! My long-desired dumping had been completely ruined! He had refused to be dumped!

If I remained persistent long enough, maybe he'd get the picture. But I didn't want to be stuck re-dumping my asshole ex until Antonia swapped my body back. I'd only wanted the satisfaction of one time before I booted him out of my life forever. Now what was I going to do?

Falael became a youthful mistake even harder to justify when I looked at what he'd become. In retrospect, he'd always been arrogant, but when I'd been a teenager, that had seemed like confidence. My siblings were the only half-Conollians, and Falael was the only half-elf in our village, so it had felt like we had a shared connection based on both being outsiders. Later, I'd realized the true source of our connection was that I had the most money of all the young ladies in the village, and Falael had wanted to separate me from it.

I'd grown up so poor I rarely had enough to eat. When I'd been eight, Ysabel developed her extremely rare healing gift, and our father illegally sold her to an organized crime boss. He'd quickly wasted all the money. My parents fought constantly, but after that they'd both started hitting each other. My mother had spent days in bed, delegating all the housework and childcare to me and my older brother, Calum.

After Ysabel became the Holy Maiden, she started sending money home, enough for us to go from nothing to practically country nobility. We received a new house and private tutors. The money came with strings—Ysabel owned the house and her tutors served as spies to make certain our parents didn't abuse us. A smart decision that I completely understood. She'd been wise to keep the money from directly landing in our father's hands, where it would soon be gone. Instead, she'd arranged trusts for each of her siblings, more than enough for each of us to purchase a business or establish ourselves in any way we desired.

I'd moved out as soon as I was able to access my trust. I'd let both Falael and my best friend move in with me rent-free. I'd been convinced by Falael to invest all of my money into his supposed lumber business. I only found out the business never existed after he and my former friend ran off to Sherda together. That same friend later wrote to me saying he'd dumped her for a wealthier woman. She thought that made us friends again, but I disagreed. Since then, Falael had social climbed all the way up to a duchess. At least teenage me had been scammed by someone very good at it.

When I was forced to move back in with my parents, I'd lied to Ysabel, saying that I needed to look after our sick mother. It was easy to deceive her when we only ever communicated by letters. Ysabel never went home. She had some sense of duty toward providing for her younger siblings, but I doubted she had any fond memories of the family who'd sold her into illegal slavery. Who could blame her?

Although my first instinct was to rely on Donya for help again, I couldn't tell her the truth about what had happened between me and Falael. I'd drop dead of mortification if the story ever made its way to my big sister. It wouldn't be fair to ask Donya to keep it a secret when she was closer to Ysabel than me.

Surely I could handle one loser on my own. If even someone like Falael made me feel helpless, how was I ever going to make it as the Blood Duchess?

While I was thinking, I went back to sleep. I'd spent too much time around people lately. People even kept interrupting me in bed! It was deeply draining.

I woke up to shouting and people rushing down the hallway. An unfamiliar voice cried, "Princess Antonia has awoken! Summon the royal doctor!"

Running to the door, I flung it open still wearing my pale pink shift. "That's great news. How is she—?"

A footman and a maid stared at me in my underthings. Then they dropped to the floor and hid their faces in their hands. "Please don't kill us!" they wailed in unison.

"Um, no, that was my mistake." Oh no, it probably wasn't in character for the duchess to apologize. "Um. Muhahahaha! You have fulfilled my exhibitionist fantasies. You have done well, now get back to finding a doctor." I slammed the door before they had time to look up and see my face flushed scarlet. Whoa, that had been awful acting. I collapsed on the bed, panting. My hair fell over my face. Seeing the pale strands instead of black made me flinch. I felt out of sorts, too tall, all wrong.

I wanted to check up on the princess, but I needed to get dressed first. Not only did I need to make certain she was all right, but my goal of getting my body back had just acquired a deadline. I really, really hoped this was reversible.

A knock sounded on my door. "I'm here to help you get dressed for the princess's coronation," Aracelli called.

"Help me?" I stared blankly.

"Most nobles have someone to assist them."

I yanked up my covers again. "I'm fine, thank you!"

"It's not as though I want to," Araceli said in a bored voice.

I got up and opened the walk-in closet, ignoring the mirror with a sheet draped over it. As much as I despised the duchess, I had to admit she had a lot of pretty dresses. Even if she was a tad overenthusiastic about plastering all of them with metal and jewels. I stared at the rows upon rows of dresses. What would be appropriate for a coronation? I had no idea. I only knew I'd be humiliated if I picked wrong. "Um, what did the duchess plan to wear to the coronation?"

"She'd been considering a couple options. May I come in and show you?"

"Yes, please." I supposed Araceli had seen me in my nightgown last night, and on a regular basis as the duchess's maid, but I still wrapped a sheet around myself.

Araceli bustled into the room. She gestured at a rack hanging in the back. "Duchess Hedri had set aside these dresses as possibilities for the coronation."

A whole rack? The gems gleamed to the point where they dazzled my eyes. I gaped until Araceli took pity on me. "What color do you like?"

"Red is my favorite color," I said.

"A good pick for your complexion, too—or rather your new complexion." Araceli selected a bright red dress covered in small rubies. "What do you think?"

"Gosh, it's pretty." I stepped forward and took the dress. "Err, can you turn around?"

With a roll of her eyes, Araceli obeyed.

Lacing covered the back, and it took me ages to loosen it before I was able to pull the dress on. But I couldn't figure out how to retie it. I couldn't even reach. Eventually, I whispered, "Help."

"Turn around and lift up your hair," she said in a polite but firm way.

Mortified, I obeyed. I'd have liked to cover myself up, but there was too much exposed skin everywhere. I felt awkward as her hands moved over my back, lacing me up. She'd tried to kill me last night, which was part of my discomfort. Also, she was very pretty and smelled nice, like lavender.

"Shouldn't we give the princess time to recover before trotting her out in front of a crowd?" I asked.

Her voice softened. "I spoke to her, she's doing well. Countess Donya believes we're at risk of more challengers to the throne if we don't move fast."

"Well, I can't argue with Donya." I gasped as she tightened up the laces.

"I told Countess Donya that I'd uncovered your secret and about my promise to protect you, but not the part where I might end up killing you." Turning me around, Araceli adjusted the bows on my front.

"Uh-huh. We don't want to stress her out." I nodded.

"I thought you might tell her later, but I barely even talked my way out of a dungeon cell before reaching that part. If you tell her, make sure you explain that you took a life-oath to help me. Not just a regular oath, one that will kill you if you break it."

"Oh, you think I should tell her the truth?"

"Why are you asking me?" Araceli glared. "I'm not your friend. We're barely allies."

"I'm sorry." I looked down and shuffled my feet.

Araceli exhaled loudly. "I'm sorry for snapping. Now sit down so I can do your hair."

"Thank you so much!" I beamed.

Araceli stared at me. "*You're* supposed to pretend to be the Blood Duchess?"

". . . Yes?"

She pinched her forehead. "This is hopeless. No one is going to believe that you're Duchess Hedri. They'll take one look at you and scream shape-shifter. If I hadn't sworn a life-oath to you, I'd be outta here. Since I did, I'll offer some advice. You don't thank servants. You say, 'Hurry it up, and if one hair falls out of my hat today, then I'll have you whipped.'"

"I can't say that! What if I hurt someone's feelings?"

Araceli considered this. "Think of the person you hate the most."

That was easy. I thought of Falael. My brows scrunched up.

"Like that," Araceli said. "Keep that expression on your face all day, and try not to talk."

As she instructed me, her hands flew in rapid motions. She created a looped braid from my hair, then placed a red pointed hat on top. A ruby gleamed from the center. The soft silk veil fell over my face. It looked lovely. I even smiled at my reflection for the first time since the swap. But I shouldn't say so, right? It wouldn't be like the duchess to give out compliments. But it was only the two of us here, and I wouldn't want her to think she hadn't done a good job. "You're so talented. Thank you."

Araceli shook her head. "We're doomed."

Donya entered the room carrying a tray of pastries.

"I'm full," I said quickly. It was true—after how much I'd eaten last night, it would be a while before I got hungry again.

"I thought you might eat breakfast with Princess Antonia." Donya waved at the doorway. A little girl clung to the frame, wide-eyed. She definitely looked like she could use more meals.

I smiled at the princess. "Please, come in."

She didn't move.

Donya leaned over and whispered, "I told her about the body swap, but I'm not sure she believed me."

Araceli met the princess's eyes. "It's true. This isn't the real Duchess Hedri."

Princess Antonia darted into the room and grabbed Araceli's skirt. She peered out from behind the cloth at me.

I knelt down. "Nice to meet you. My real name is Bora."

Araceli patted the princess's head. "She won't hurt you. I'm quite certain of it at this point." A note of unhappiness lurked in her voice. She wanted me to be the real duchess, or at least be better at pretending.

The princess's tense shoulders relaxed. She clearly trusted Araceli. They must have known each other from long before their trip to my kingdom. Stepping forward, the princess curtsied flawlessly. "Good morning, Mother."

"You don't have to call me that. And definitely don't curtsey to me. I'm not anyone important." I waved at the pastries. "Would you like some?"

"I . . . can?" She leapt for the table before I could give an answer. I wouldn't have thought pastries a rare treat for a princess, but she crammed an entire apple tart into her mouth as if she feared it would be taken away.

"Slow down, you'll choke," I said. Lowering my voice, I leaned toward Donya. "Does Her Highness know how to swap me back? Um, I know we can't right now, but Araceli needs to kill the duchess later." And I needed to not be killed by Araceli.

Princess Antonia overheard me. "Sorry, I tried with a frog and a mouse, but I couldn't do it. Look at the bright side, you can stay with me forever and ever. I'll let you have all my pastries if Mean Mother never comes back." She shoved the plate in my direction.

"Thank you, Your Highness—" I faltered as Donya gave me a pointed look. "I mean, Antonia." It would be hard to get used to calling the princess by her first name. It was even harder to get used to looking her in the eye, but I did my best. "I promise that we won't leave you with the duchess after my body gets swapped back. We're going to find a way to take her down, and Araceli is going to, uh, make sure she doesn't hurt you again." I sat down and took a strawberry tart. I couldn't turn down food offered as a gesture of friendship, so I took a small bite. "These are delicious. Thank you for sharing." Strawberry had been Calum's favorite. The memories hit me suddenly and unexpectedly, making me blink back tears. I looked down before anyone noticed.

Donya sat at the table across from me. "Princess Antonia has a powerful gift, so it must have a heavy price. Her exhaustion could be part of her price but not all of it." Or she could have been knocked out by the beating, but neither of us wanted to say that in front of the princess. "Without knowing her price, it will be difficult to figure out the conditions that she needs to replicate her magic. Most people know their price instinctively after the first time they use their magic, but the princess *is* very young."

"Not a clue," Antonia insisted around a mouthful of pastry.

"I've been researching if there has ever been another case of a similar gift, but that will take time. We'll figure this out. I give you my word," Donya said.

I certainly hoped so. I looked down at my new tummy and fat thighs and lost my appetite. Pushing away my half-eaten pastry, I asked, "Did you contact Ysabel?" At a time like this, it would be lovely to receive advice from my politically savvy Holy Maiden sister.

"About that . . . the duchess took my book linked to Ysabel's, and I can't find it." Donya winced at the look on my face. "I don't trust regular mail with this news. If someone intercepted a letter, they'd have evidence enough for the Conclave of Kings to order your execution."

The reminder of the stakes made me feel ill. "Do we need to have the coronation today? I don't feel ready. Antonia is still recovering."

"Yes, we have to. It will be a rush job, not as properly fancy as it should be, but we need to have you formerly decreed as regent before the other kingdoms show up demanding the position. You don't need to do anything for the ceremony, Bora. Just sit at the front of the church where I direct you. When I call your name—the duchess's name—come up and repeat the oath."

"Not a life-oath?" I asked, sneaking a glance at Araceli. She was wiping a crumb off the princess's face. Antonia smiled at her in return.

Donya snorted. "The world would be a different place if royalty swore real life-oaths to protect and serve their kingdoms. No, these are just words."

"Can Araceli accompany me?" I asked. "She's serving as my bodyguard after trying to assassinate me last night."

"After what?" Donya shrieked. Whirling on Araceli, she growled, "You didn't tell me that part!"

Huh, maybe I shouldn't have said that. At least not in front of the child? But this ordeal was headache inducing, and I preferred to keep my number of lies to the minimum. "Relax," I said. "We've settled that. She even swore a life-oath to protect me."

Princess Antonia whispered to Araceli. "You finally tried to kill her? Don't do that again. She's nice now. I made sure of it! I helped!"

Araceli curtsied to Donya. "I'm Araceli, also called Ari, the rightful heir to the duchy of South Sherda."

Donya stared. "You're the long-lost heir that the duchess has been trying to murder for years? You didn't tell me that part either! Wait, you're a man?"

"You're a man?" I repeated. I'd assumed her puppet wore male clothing because she'd been a tomboy. Araceli seemed so elegant and feminine and devastatingly attractive. Though she'd look great in a waistcoat too.

Araceli tossed back her hair. "I'm trying to figure that out at the moment."

My first reaction was, *Wait, you can do that? Dammit, no one in my village asked me before they pigeonholed me as the unmarriageable fat girl looking after her parents! I'm jealous!* I'd always thought of an identity as something that got forced on you rather than something you could pick out for yourself . . . Things really were different for the nobility. My second thought, however, was the realization that nobility didn't generally get to pick their gender. There had been a big scandal when Donya went around wearing trousers. Where did Araceli get the confidence to decide her own identity? Even when confused, my first instinct in any given situation was politeness. "I wish you the best of luck figuring it out. Do you want me to call you he or she?"

"Either is fine, but you'd better stick with 'she' for now or you might slip up in public."

"Good point. Thank you."

Araceli hissed to Donya, "She keeps saying thank you every five minutes. I don't think this masquerade will last long."

Donya rubbed her forehead. "Her part at the ceremony won't involve any talking, other than repeating the oath. Now, I'm going to arrange a small lunch meeting with a few close allies before the ceremony."

"Do I have to?" I whispered, perilously close to a whine. This sounded like a great chance to expose myself.

Twirling a lock of hair, Araceli looked me over. Her frown deepened. "It might be better if we tell everyone that she's sick."

Donya exhaled and steepled her fingers together. "Remember how Arahasnor is broke? We're even worse off than your average broke kingdom. The government has only been running since the king's death because I've been personally funding it. Not with money from my county; that would be unfair to my people. I won a large sum betting on the World Games."

Gambling didn't seem like Donya; I would guess there was a story there. "It doesn't seem right for one person to pay for the government."

"It would be more unfair if the cook who made us breakfast doesn't get paid," she said. "But it was a lump sum, and I'm out. One noblewoman funding the whole government is simply impossible. The rest of the nobility should help, but their tax rates are a joke. We need allies."

"Everyone will surely pull together to stop our kingdom from being taken over by foreign invaders." I laughed. "Just kidding, even *I'm* not that naïve."

Donya cracked a small smile. "It might be possible if I could convince the most important nobles that we have a real chance of survival. I've explained that you're on our side now, but some people want proof, which is understandable. If I could only find the Head Cardinal . . ."

"Mean Mother threw him in the dungeon," Antonia said. "She made everyone promise not to tell."

"Ah! Head Cardinal Augustin! I have to let him out!" Donya ran out the door. There went my last chance to delicately bow out of this lunch meeting.

CHAPTER SEVEN

Donya had directed me to a walnut chair at the head of the table and instructed me to remain seated and speak as little as possible.

A dozen people filed into the room. Each one bowed or curtsied before my chair and introduced themselves. I was never going to remember all of them. I smiled and nodded. Then I remembered to frown instead and nod.

An elderly man in white robes only slightly inclined his head at me. I assumed he must be important enough to give me the greeting of an equal. Or maybe he just hated me, judging from how he glared.

"Your turn," he said coldly.

I realized I was supposed to incline my head in return. "Oh, I'm sorry!" As I did, he coughed. "Are you feeling unwell?" I asked.

He glared even harder. "The dungeon proved cold for my lungs."

The dungeon . . . wait . . . this must be Head Cardinal Augustin! "I'm so sorry!" I cried.

In the corner, Donya buried her face in her hands. It just slipped out. I didn't even mean to apologize for throwing him in there since I hadn't done that—it was only a sorry-something-bad-happened-to-you. The cardinal raised his eyebrow very slightly, then turned and walked to his seat.

By the time everyone was seated, my throat felt dry and sweat dripped down my forehead. I picked up the small golden cup in front of me and drank from it. The beverage was so small, I downed it in one gulp. Hopefully, this wouldn't be all the water we'd get with lunch.

Everyone stared. Donya pinched her forehead.

"Isn't that the water for washing our hands?" a noblewoman in a blue dress whispered. She sounded like she was genuinely doubting herself, but as soon as I saw the white towel lying next to the cup, I knew she'd been right. I wanted to sink into the polished wooden floor.

Donya jumped in before I had a chance to respond. "I know that looks a lot like the Arahasnor washing cup, but it's actually a Sherdan toast cup. Just look at the little line of diamonds around the top of the cup—that's the giveaway. Everyone, let's drink a toast to the health of our new lady regent." She picked up her cup and drained it. Under Donya's aggressive glare, everyone else drank as well.

I wanted to cry. Thank goodness Donya had saved my heinie. How many other such mistakes would I make?

Several maids brought in the real water in crystal glasses. Next came glasses of red wine. Then a celery soup with a hot bun.

This time, I was determined to wait for someone else to eat so I could watch what they did. No one made a move toward the soup. Instead, everyone gazed at me with hungry eyes.

Donya clapped her hands. "It's the honor of the duchess regent, the highest-ranked person, to begin the meal."

Sweet Sun God. I had to go first. And everyone was staring at me.

I reached for a piece of bread to dip into my soup. Donya shook her head frantically.

Right, nobility probably didn't do that. I reached for the spoon.

Donya shook her head even harder. She touched a different spoon at the top of the plate.

It mattered which utensil I used? Why did we even need more than one spoon? I picked up the spoon from the top, dipped it in the soup, and took a sip.

The slurp sounded worryingly loud in the silent room. Hopefully no one noticed, because immediately they all went for their own meals. I ate slowly, scared of doing something wrong or spilling on my expensive clothes. Everyone around me drank their soup so elegantly and took small bites of bread.

The man on my right turned to me. "What do you think of the plans to add additional guards to the city walls?"

"A great idea," I said. After all, I'd been able to sneak out pretty easily, which didn't bode well for our security. "We should pay the guards more, too." Then hopefully they'd be less susceptible to bribes.

From the other end of the table, a woman cried, "You already want to raise taxes to pay off our debt! Now you want to spend even more on guards? There's barely any purpose for them since we made peace with Conollia. We should be laying off half of them."

"Oh," I said, shrinking down in my seat. "Maybe not, then."

Questions flew at me fast and furious. "Will you negotiate with Sherda to lower their tariffs on our turnips?"

"What's your response to the Head Cardinal's demand to limit the number of chickens in the same coop under the prevention of cruelty to animals law?"

"Should we dismantle the stadium from the last World Games or use it for entertainment?"

"How do you plan to pay off the debt from hosting the World Games?"

"Is it true that we're in debt to the Dragon Emperor? You know how terrifying dragons can be about debts . . ."

"What is your reply to the latest protest march by the Construction Guild demanding their unpaid wages?"

"Do you think redleaf should be legal?"

I blurted out, "*Red leaves* are illegal? Whatever do you do in autumn? Arrest all the trees?"

Everyone was staring again. I hated that.

Donya laughed loudly. "What a funny joke! Such a clever way to avoid the controversial subject of drug legality, which surely should be saved for a more formal occasion than lunch."

I sank down farther in my seat. I'd barely even understood their questions. Unfortunately, I understood the part where a dragon might eat me. I wanted to go home.

The next course was beef brisket. The giggling of two maids drew my attention. I looked over in time to see one of them spit into a plate.

I jerked my eyes away as if I'd been the one to do something wrong. The maid placed the spittle-tainted food in front of me.

A delicious smell rose off the beef, but I didn't take a bite. I suddenly regretted consuming that soup. Given how much everyone in this city hated me, it wouldn't surprise me if it had been poisoned. At the least, I bet someone had spit in it, too. I felt sick.

Donya frantically gestured at the fork I should use. She didn't understand the real reason I wasn't eating. I tried to smile at her, even though I felt terrible. I knew it wasn't me who everyone hated . . . but it still felt awful. I pushed around the food on my plate, trying to make it look like I'd taken a bite. At least that was enough to convince everyone else to eat.

The young lady sitting next to Donya asked, "Has Sherda been discussing the team lineup for the next World Games?" From her smile, she was attempting to do as Donya requested and switch from politics to small talk. Unfortunately, this was still a blank to me. I didn't know the name of a single Sherdan Gifted Knight.

"Nice attempt to trick me into revealing vital political secrets." I tapped my nose. "I'm not going to squeal like a swine mouth."

"A what mouth?" She peered at me from behind her fan. "Are those Sherdan words?"

"Yes?" I snuck a glance at Donya.

"Who wants to talk about religion?" Donya asked in desperation.

The subsequent bloodbath fortunately distracted everyone from me.

"That could have gone better," Donya said as we walked back to my room. "Head Cardinal Augustin thinks I have you under mind control. But he wasn't upset about it—he thought it was a great idea. He promised me sanctuary if I got caught."

"I'm sorry," I said.

"No, no! I'm the one who should be apologizing to you." Donya sighed. "Ysabel always . . . um, I should have realized that you would require more preparation before appearing in public."

No doubt she'd been about to say that my older sister always had impeccable noble manners. But Ysabel had been taken in by the Church at a young age. We'd had very different upbringings.

"It's not your fault," I mumbled. "I should have told you that I couldn't do it." I just hadn't wanted to disappoint Donya by whining too strongly.

"You can't avoid attending the coronation this afternoon. I'll try to run interference to keep anyone from talking to you. It's just, I'll be so busy with other things during the ceremony . . . If only I had time to find someone to accompany you."

"I wanted Araceli to come and protect me from the rest of the Twelve Avengers, remember?"

"And she already knows about the masquerade! Perfect!" Donya smiled. "She'll need a disguise or everyone will wonder why you brought your personal maid as an escort. I'll go talk to her."

Donya left me alone in my bedroom. I sat on my bed and tried not to cry. My dress felt itchy and the gemstones were poking my legs even through all the petticoats. How did the duchess wear this awful thing all day? I felt scared to move for fear a boob might pop out.

When someone knocked on the door, I sprang to my feet. "Give me a moment," I called. My voice sounded embarrassingly close to tears.

Instead of Araceli, a young male voice called, "This is a delivery for Her Grace. From Falael."

By the time I rubbed my eyes and opened the door, I found a bouquet of roses lying on the ground. I groaned. Would I have to put up with my ex for my entire stay in this unwanted body?

Rounding the corner, Araceli looked at the bouquet. "The page left them on the floor and ran? I don't blame him. Last time the duchess was fighting with Falael, she threw his gifts and sometimes heavier items at the poor people who had to deliver them."

"I'll feed Falael these roses, thorns and all," I hissed. At Araceli's look of surprise, I explained, "He's my ex. Me in my original body, I mean. He stole a bunch of money from me, then set me up to die by flirting with me in front of his jealous, bloodthirsty lover." I didn't know why I told her. Perhaps I wanted to get it off my chest to someone. "I can't stand having him around me constantly. I will scream, I swear it."

"Do you want help getting rid of him?" Araceli asked. "I've had to live with him for a year, and I can't stand him. He tried to have me executed for accidentally mispronouncing his 'noble elven name,' which sounds like a food. I'm only alive because he didn't recognize me later. He never remembers servants' faces."

"That sounds like him. I'm sorry, and I could use help, thanks. What did you have in mind?"

"I'll pretend to be your lover at the coronation to make him give up."

"That's not a bad idea. But I wonder if he would truly let go so easily? It might just make him more persistent. He's the type who wants whatever he can't have." I toed the flowers.

"I see you're familiar with that perverse personality of his." Araceli grinned. "We'd need to deeply humiliate him. You should bring more than one lover. Say the word, and I'll find the most handsome male prostitute in the city."

Bringing a prostitute to the new queen's coronation? Objectively, this sounded like a terrible idea. But my temper had been hanging by a thread for the past day.

Everyone kept telling me I wasn't enough like the Blood Duchess. Well, I bet I knew what the Blood Duchess would do.

I met Araceli's eyes. "If we're doing this . . . let's go all out."

A smile tugged at her lips. "I excel at that, Your Grace."

I sat across the table from my prospective employee with my arms folded. Araceli stood guarding the door. The prostitute leaned back in the chair with his hands behind his head.

Steepling my fingers, I attempted to look stern. "I hope I've been clear about the terms of the job. You must be willing to immediately flee the country of Arahasnor." I couldn't let some innocent soul get mixed up in this in case the Blood Duchess took back her body from me later.

The young man nodded. "That's why I volunteered. I already have tickets for a carriage out of town this evening. I'm here to earn some travel funds."

"You aren't involved in anything criminal, are you? Uh, I mean besides your actual profession . . ." I looked him over for any signs of connections with organized crime. Muscles bulged from every part of his body. A tattoo of a dragon curved down his neck. His left cheek had another tattoo with a character I didn't recognize, but it looked like the language of Faan, where he probably came from. His jet-black hair had been cropped short. He had deep-set monolid eyes, long eyelashes, and a smile a tad too brightly red to be natural. I usually had a thing for the pretty-boy type—he had too many muscles for my taste. But purely objectively, he was a very handsome man. He'd need to be, in order to succeed in his line of work.

He rubbed the back of his neck. "It's not like that. I haven't done anything wrong. I simply ran into some trouble with two clients. Naturally, most see me anonymously. How was I supposed to know two of them were mother and daughter?"

I winced. "Rough luck. So hideously awkward that I can see why none of you would ever want to see each other again . . . but why do you need to flee to another country?"

"The woman had a husband, who also found out, and now they're getting divorced. Their son sent me a threatening letter saying that he's the lover of a powerful and homicidal noblewoman, and he's going to have me murdered for homewrecking his family, so I—"

"Hold up." I raised my hand. "Is this son's name Falael?"

"Whoa, was that a lucky guess or are you a Seer?"

"Do you mean to tell me that sitting before me is the man who fucked both Falael's mom *and* his sister?"

He winced. "Do you know the guy? Please tell me he isn't a friend of yours."

I giggled. It turned into a laugh. I clasped my hands together, turned my gaze up to the ceiling, and prayed. "Sun God, I know I've never been a particularly attentive follower. After recent events in my life, I started to feel lost and alone, like no one was up there looking after me. But now, my faith has been restored! Everything happens for a reason!"

"Uhh . . ." My guest stared at me as if he feared I'd lost my mind. He glanced at Araceli. "Is she okay?"

"I increasingly doubt it," Araceli said.

I reached across the table and grabbed his hand. "What's your name?"

"Lao." He sounded uncertain.

"My dear, wonderful, miracle-from-god Lao, remember how I told you that I needed you to pretend to be my lover so I could ditch an ex who wouldn't accept we were over? My ex is *Falael.*"

Lao's eyes lit up. "You mean you're going to pay me to humiliate the guy who tried to murder me? I'll give you a discount!"

My grin felt like it would split open my face. "No, I'll give *you* a raise."

While Lao ran off to fetch his outfit, Araceli rummaged through my closet. "We need the perfect weapon for your grand revenge."

"But we already picked a dress . . ." And I didn't want to even think about undoing all that lace.

"Not sexy enough. How about this one? The duchess got banned from her last church for wearing it, but since the Head Cardinal is now on our side, he can't throw you out." She held up a red silk dress with a scandalously low bodice. Holes between the laces would bare part of my stomach. Small rubies had been interwoven into the fabric. A slit ran down the side to reveal my leg from the thigh down. It would also expose a fair bit of my back.

I flinched. It was a lovely dress, and I knew it didn't suit me at all.

Araceli beamed. "This is the perfect make-your-ex-regret-being-dumped-by-you dress. I'll find the matching ruby necklace and—" She stopped. "What's wrong? Does it show a little too much skin? I don't want to make you uncomfortable."

"It's the type of dress the Blood Duchess wears," I mumbled. I ought to get used to it. Switching to a permanently modest dress style would make me look suspicious. If I couldn't act the part, I could at least dress it.

But the notion of wearing that lovely, scandalous outfit filled me with a strange mixture of longing and humiliation. I could picture what people back at the village would say: *That fattie thinks she's pretty. How embarrassing.* My own mother would have gently told me that such clothing didn't suit me. It would suit my beautiful Holy Maiden older sister, but not me.

Araceli set down the dress and met my eyes. "But?"

"I don't have the confidence to wear that," I blurted out. Immediately, I regretted my candor. I looked down to hide my blush.

Araceli bit her lip. "If it makes you uncomfortable, then we'll go back to the old dress for today. Tomorrow we could come up with an excuse for why you changed styles to something that covers more, such as the duchess injuring her shoulder. I could slap on some fake bandages. But if you like the dress and it's about what other people think—why do you care? Let them think what they want. Wear what you like."

I'd never been able to do that. I'd never been comfortable in my own body. But this was the Blood Duchess's body. That thought felt oddly freeing. "Do you think it would look good on me?" The question came out weak and pathetic. Desperate for approval.

"You'd be stunning." Araceli sauntered over and held the dress up to my body. She turned me to face the mirror, then smiled. "Mmm, yes, this will show off all the right assets. You have a great rack."

I looked away. "They're just lumps of fat."

Araceli snorted. "Everyone's breasts are lumps of fat. That's what makes them so wonderfully soft. Skinny people's breasts are also made of fat and tend to be smaller for that reason. Nothing wrong either way. Some like them small, some like them big, and I like them big. You happen to possess some particularly fine ones. Embrace your assets."

My face felt hot. "I'll try on the dress and see if I like it. Could you let me do it alone?" I asked in a small voice.

"Of course. This dress isn't too complicated. You should be able to fasten it yourself." Araceli took out a golden necklace with a sizeable ruby surrounded by white diamonds. "Wear this. It will draw everyone's eyes to the right places."

She winked at me, and I flushed scarlet.

* * *

Before Araceli left, she helped me undo the lacing on my first dress. The second one was less complicated, on account of having a lot less fabric. After putting it on, I didn't dare look in the mirror. If I did, I'd change my mind. While waiting for Araceli and Lao to get ready for our grand show, I had entirely too much time to doubt myself. What had I been thinking? I'd make a fool of myself! Everyone would laugh at me! I clutched at the front of my dress and tried to yank it up to cover a bit more. Alas, that only bared more of my navel.

"We're ready." Speaking in a deeper voice this time, Araceli threw open the door.

I squeaked and hid behind a dresser. I wasn't ready! I hadn't mentally braced myself!

Lao sauntered into the room first. He wore tight black pants and black boots. His white shirt had been left open, revealing the tiger tattoo curled around his belly button and an impressive set of pectoral muscles. His longish hair had a windswept look. He'd added a touch of blue makeup around his eyes. Overall, he looked like a man who could have strutted off the cover of a romance novel. Devastatingly handsome but definitely not appropriate for a noble ceremony. I hissed, "Araceli, maybe this is a little too far—"

"Call me Ari. For today, switch to thinking of me as a man."

I laid eyes on the transformed Ari and lost all ability to speak.

He wore a gleaming black vest—and nothing underneath it. His bare, lightly muscled arms ended in black gloves. The scaley pants left very little to the imagination. Red locks puffed out around his head like a crown. A splash of purple gave his eyes a sharpness like those of a hawk. He'd acquired a cane with a silver orb that he twirled between his dexterous fingers.

"Gah," I said.

"Yes, that was precisely the effect I was going for." Ari glanced sideways at his reflection. "Hmm, I think I like how I look as a man, too. Now I'm even more confused."

"You'll find yourself someday," Lao said with a sympathetic look. "You're young! You have plenty of time."

"Your clothes," I said weakly. "They look great on you. I truly mean it." Ari was exactly my type. It was all my brain could do to function.

"Thank you." Ari gestured at me. "Come out and let me see if I picked the right dress for you."

Forcing my hands to stop covering myself up, I stepped out from behind the dresser. I looked anywhere but at Ari.

"Oh my." Ari whistled. "You look every bit as stunning as I expected. Please, wear that. It looks so much better on you than it did on the real duchess."

"But we have the same body," I protested. "And she had more dignity. More confidence."

Ari snorted. "She had overconfidence. And she wore too much jewelry. She didn't have your pleasant aura. With your sweet smile, you'll be conquering hearts."

Lao winked at me. "Hot damn. If you change your mind about wanting to keep this strictly a show, then let me know."

I blushed as red as my dress and told myself that he couldn't mean it. He must flatter his clients all the time. Besides, this wasn't even my body. My current body was even heavier than my original one, which made me think confused thoughts about the heated gazes from these two.

"The terms of the deal were clear," Ari growled, stepping in front of me.

"I do threesomes for extra," Lao said hopefully.

I hadn't realized it was possible to turn even redder. "M-maybe I should get a coat."

Ari immediately whirled around. "You are forbidden to cover up that masterpiece of a dress."

"But . . . it's cold . . ."

"The duchess's carriage has a heating relic."

I looked at the floor. "I'm not sure I can do this."

Ari's gaze softened. He tilted up my chin and looked me in the eye. "Right now, you're not Bora. You can be whoever you want."

Ari was right.

Right now, I was the notorious Blood Duchess. I could do what I would never have dared if I'd been in my own body. Who cared if people looked down on me? The duchess would take the blame for everything I did. It gave me exuberance and a newfound freedom. "Thank you," I whispered.

Ari smiled. "You're not supposed to thank me, Your Grace," he said, but his tone was teasing.

"Are we doing this?" Lao asked.

I straightened my shoulders. "We're doing this."

CHAPTER EIGHT

I strode into the chapel with Ari on one arm and Lao hanging off my other.

The crowd parted before me, gasping and muttering as they realized that yes, the Blood Duchess appeared to have shown up at the coronation escorted by two prostitutes and dressed like one herself.

Shocked whispers followed us down the aisle. But who cared? If I'd understood one thing over the past day, it was that my reputation as duchess had already hit rock bottom. I had nothing left to lose. At the very least, I wanted to make Falael taste a fraction of my own pain from all those years ago when he ran off with my former best friend.

Since this was a royal church, each pew had cushions with armrests between them. A dozen pillars ran down the walls, supporting the domed golden ceiling. The seats toward the front became wider and were decorated with gemstones. The front row held a series of thrones, placed on a lower level so they didn't block the view of those behind them.

The Head Cardinal already stood at a golden podium. The giant stained-glass window behind him showed Holy Maiden Ava ascending to heaven. The archway above the stage was decorated with detailed paintings of past saints' deeds. Three golden chandeliers lit the room. A dizzying amount of gold gleamed from the statues and decorations around the church. The room smelled like smoke from the candles, and a large number of people in heavy clothing pressed close together. The princess and Donya were already on the stage, but I refused to look in that direction. Donya was going to be furious, but that was a problem for future Bora. Princess Antonia waved at me before the Head Cardinal jerked her away and covered her eyes.

The front row had one seat still empty. Falael sat to the right of what must be my seat. He looked up with a smile. "You're here! I brought you a present—" The smile faded as he saw the two men next to me.

"*We're* here." With a malicious smile on my lips, I leaned my head against Lao's shoulder and tugged Ari's arm closer.

"I believe you're sitting in my seat." Ari fixed Falael with a glare so intense he leapt up without a thought. I wasn't even the one being glared at, and I was sweating.

"Allow me, Your Grace," Lao said, helping me step up to the throne in my wobbly high heels. He glanced at Falael with a bored expression. "Oh, you're still here? Aren't you too old for this line of work? I see a gray hair."

Falael turned bright red. I was going to give Lao yet another raise.

"There are only two seats. I guess I'll have to sit here." With a wicked grin, Ari planted himself on my lap.

The crowd gasped audibly. Everyone was staring at me. I felt my cheeks heat. Ari was entirely too close, pine cologne drifting off his neck. I feared that I must be sweating so hard everyone could smell it. Thinking about it made it worse. From the podium, the Head Cardinal glared at me exactly like the priest from my village. That look had featured in my childhood nightmares. Maybe this was a step too far.

Ari gave my arm a small squeeze. It brought me back to myself. I couldn't back down now, not in front of Falael.

"Why, thank you," I cooed, putting my arms around Ari. Crap, was I touching his chest? I might be, but I'd gone too far to back down.

"Don't leave me out!" Lao spoke in a coquettish voice unlike the one he'd used during our interview. He draped himself over the arm of my throne. "You look tense, Your Grace." Nimbly, he massaged my shoulders. "It must be the stress of looking at that ugly thing." He cast the shaking Falael a look of pure disdain. "I don't know why you kept him around this long . . . pity? What's his name again? Falafel, like the street food? Oh, now I remember him! His family has been a constant supply of clients for me." He winked.

At that precise moment, Falael recognized Lao as the prostitute who'd slept his way through all his immediate female relatives—and now finished by stealing his lover. Falael's expression was beautiful. His eyes widened, his mouth tensed, then his entire face turned purple. I would have liked to remove that moment from time and keep it in a scrapbook.

I was going to make Lao *rich.* I'd let him take his pick of the duchess's jewelry. It wasn't like it was mine anyway.

With a strangled gasp, Falael fled the chapel.

Lao unfolded a blue fan and started fanning me. "Ugh, someone needs to chase the stench of him away."

Head Cardinal Augustin silenced the whispers and gossip with the sheer force of his presence. His voice cut through the air like a blade. "We're here today for an important moment in history." Then he launched into a long lecture that got off topic several times to discuss his real passion: laws to protect farm livestock from animal cruelty. Princess Antonia's eyes were clearly drifting shut.

I spent the entire sermon trying very hard to keep my expression stern. Both Lao and Ari were pressed close to me, an interesting sensation, especially for someone who hadn't gotten any recently. It was Ari I felt hyper-aware of . . . maybe because he'd be the one I'd have to face after this? Or maybe because he had that irresistible grin and flashing dimples I'd noticed from the moment I'd laid eyes on him? Every time he brushed me, it gave me goose bumps.

Outside the church, Falael wailed so loudly that he shook the chandeliers: "I've been greatly wronged! My love has been trampled upon! My pure heart!"

Cardinal Augustin glared harder, but even his deadly gaze couldn't penetrate walls. He spoke more loudly, finally wrapping up with an admonishment about royal duty for the princess. When he looked at her, she straightened and opened her eyes wide. That had been shorter than most sermons. In all fairness, we hadn't given the Head Cardinal much time to prepare his speech.

Donya draped Antonia with the purple Robe of Royalty, which looked like a blanket on her short frame. Then she helped the princess climb into the stone Coronation Throne. It was a solemn moment, and everyone in the room went quiet. Unfortunately, that made Falael's wailing sound even louder. I would have felt guilty toward the princess for ruining her big moment, except she was giggling. I suspected she hadn't liked Falael much, just like most people with the misfortune of knowing him.

Next, the Head Cardinal anointed the princess using a silver chalice of holy water. A choir in the back started singing, finally drowning out Falael's crying. Cardinal Augustin presented Antonia with the coronation regalia: an orb, scepter, sword, shield, and too much jewelry for one person to wear. Then Donya took them away before they crushed the princess with their weight. Finally, he handed her a written oath. By then, luckily the crying had stopped so she could be heard. She read it out loud, then signed her name at the bottom.

When called upon, I read the oath of regent. No one asked me to stand up, which was probably for the best because my leg had gone to sleep.

Turning to the crowd, Cardinal Augustin bellowed, "The Sun God blesses the new queen!"

The crowd screamed the traditional response: "May the queen remain true to her oaths, and we will remain true to ours!" I missed my chance to shout, but I mouthed along.

Finally, a crown was placed on Princess Antonia's head, and she became Queen Antonia. The spiked golden crown was clearly too large for her, so it had been heavily padded with an entire new layer of fur. The tips were razor sharp—legend had it a few past kings had used this crown as a weapon. Antonia looked pale and tired. I tried to smile at her, but the Head Cardinal continued to cover her eyes whenever she glanced in my direction, which was probably for the best.

At this point, everyone was supposed to come up to the stage, swear allegiance, and kiss Antonia's hand. Typically there would be a royal parade and a huge ball afterward, but I'd heard it had been canceled for lack of time and money. The new monarch usually gave a speech, but fortunately no one expected that from six-year-old Antonia.

I tried to stand, but by then both my legs had pins and needles. Ari supported me as I wobbled. As the new royal regent, I had to go first. I kneeled down. Cardinal Augustin firmly had his hands over Antonia's eyes. Squirming, she complained, "I've seen the duchess and her horrible boy toy do all sorts of gross stuff in front of me."

"That word is not appropriate for you to speak, Your Majesty," the Head Cardinal said sternly.

"What word? Toy?" Antonia pouted. "Toy isn't a bad word!"

Cardinal Augustin had very expressive eyes, and they told me to get my vow over with quickly and then get out of here. I obeyed. A long line of nobles waited to give their own vows. After I stepped off the stage, Ari and Lao fell in step beside me.

Outside the chapel, Falael knelt in front of the door. "So cruel! You can't treat me like this!" he wailed, grabbing my feet. "How could you claim that you loved me, then humiliate me in public?"

I remembered a thousand times Falael had claimed he loved me. He loved me, and that's why he had to control what I ate and lecture me about my country accent, to make me *better*. He loved me, so I needed to trust him and not ask him any questions about where the money was going. He loved me, so how could I question why he draped himself all over my best friend? Shouldn't I be happy that they were getting along? Didn't I trust him?

I had no regrets for the next part of my plan.

At a wave of my hand, a trio of guards stepped forward. "Falael, you're under arrest for fraud," the sergeant said. His fake business had stolen not only from me but also quite a few others in my village. The warrant had been active for many years.

Falael's eyes went to me. "But . . . you promised you'd remove that old arrest warrant when we came here!"

"I'd only do that for a current lover, not an ex." I swept off to my carriage, an escort hanging off each arm, ignoring the pleas behind me.

* * *

After giving Lao his pay and bonus, I was in quite a good mood. "That was a great idea," I told Ari.

"You pulled it off stunningly. The look on his face!" Ari beamed. "Would you like me to help you unbutton your dress? It's a bit trickier to get off than on."

I froze. Objectively, I knew that Ari and Araceli were the same person. But Ari seemed so masculine and Araceli so feminine. I couldn't imagine letting a man help me change, even if only partway. "I . . . uh . . ."

Ari didn't push it. "I'll send another maid."

He opened the door to reveal a stern-faced Donya.

I took a step backward. "I'm sorry!" I lowered my head, then snuck a glance at her expression.

Donya massaged her forehead. "It's fine. A small scandal isn't important in the scheme of things. Honestly, I was afraid you'd show up and apologize to everyone. Instead, you did something the Blood Duchess would do. It was an enormous scandal, but I can't deny she'd do exactly that if she wanted to break up with her current lover."

I twiddled my thumbs. "I had a very important reason. I promise." My voice got weaker with each word, because I couldn't possibly tell Donya the reason, not when my words might make their way back to my sister.

Donya turned to Ari. "I know I asked you to make her seem like the real duchess, and you definitely succeeded. Nice show of initiative. Just don't get any funny ideas."

"Funny ideas?" I asked in a high-pitched voice.

"I assume that you were only acting. If that ever changes, you'll talk to me first." Donya fixed Ari with a glare, gesturing at her eyes, then back at him. "Or . . . uh . . . there will be consequences. Big consequences, that is to say, um, entirely appropriate consequences for the situation."

By the Sun God, Donya was trying to give Ari the protective-big-sister talk. She wasn't great at it, but since I had a younger sibling myself, I recognized the signs. Ugh, this was yet more proof that Donya didn't even see me as a woman at all.

Donya turned back to me. "I hate to ask anything more of you after the busy, stressful day you've had, but the delegation from the Sashan Guild of Slavers is arriving tomorrow to collect on our debt. We crowned Queen Antonia just in time."

I groaned.

Donya bit her lip. "I'll take care of everything. I'll arrange it so you don't need to talk."

She looked so worried, how could I add to her stress? "I'll be fine. I promise."

As soon as Donya left, Ari asked me, "Are you and Donya close?" His tone was deliberately neutral.

"We've only known each other for a few days."

"But you're basically doing all of this for her." His voice held a resigned note.

I flinched. "Why would you say that? Is it that obvious?"

Ari made a sound in the back of his throat as if this explained a lot. Before I had time to deny any further, he left, calling over his shoulder, "I'll send another maid to assist you. And thanks for letting me help you get revenge on your ex. It was fun."

After dinner, I'd been banished to my room with orders to read an etiquette book. Only after I curled up in the armchair with my legs tucked under myself did I remember that I'd promised to write to my family while I was in the city. In my defense, I'd been going through a lot lately. I sprang up. My unfamiliarly long legs tangled together. I hit the carpet with my chin. Oof. I could only be grateful the floor was so padded.

As I rubbed my bruise, I soothed myself thinking that it probably hadn't been long enough for anyone to get worried. I'd promised to write a letter as soon as I found the school. If I delayed much longer, though, they would worry. Or at least, my mother would worry. Just about everything worried her and sent her to bed for days on end. On the other hand, my dad had forgotten my sister's name by the time she became famous. My little brother Benoni mattered the most to me, and I knew he'd worry the most sincerely. He'd been deeply wounded by Calum's death. Our oldest brother had been more like a parent than our actual parents to both of us. We'd lost two siblings in infancy, too, but there was no denying that Calum's abrupt, mysterious murder had hit the hardest.

Benoni was a serious, quiet kid. Teachers tended to mistake that quietness for obedience, but he'd always been willful. I would not put it past him to head into the city to find me if I didn't write to him. Benoni was too young to help, and my parents . . . they would be the opposite of help. Fantasizing about them being useful made me laugh a little. My mother's top priority would be the low cut of my dress, and my father would try to loot the palace for anything he could sell.

I briefly wondered if I needed to warn my family about the duchess in my body, but she didn't even know they existed, much less where they lived. She would not find them. If I wrote the truth in a letter, there was a risk of it being intercepted. For that matter, there was a risk of my father selling me out to the highest bidder. Even if I only told Benoni, I couldn't risk our parents reading his mail. I decided it would be better to lie and pretend everything was fine.

I sat down at the writing desk in the duchess's room and quickly scrawled out a very short letter claiming the school had kept me busy. I also used expensive postage as an excuse for why I might not be able to write again anytime soon. I'd try to send a few more letters, but I didn't want anyone counting on it.

It was hard to write with larger hands than usual. My handwriting came out messy. Hopefully that would be attributed to excitement.

The Blood Duchess had a fancy seal. It took me a few tries to use it, and it came out looking like a lump, but that was better because how would I explain a noble seal on my family letter? I tried to smooth out the wax a bit.

Now, how should I mail the letter? I could wait and give it to Donya tomorrow, but I was overdue to write.

I'd already changed into a comfortable dressing gown, but it was more modest than what the duchess usually wore, so I stepped outside my door. Were nobles supposed to have people waiting around for their orders? I didn't see anyone. If only I could find one person, I could order them to summon Donya or Ari.

At first I thought I'd walk until I found someone, but this palace was so big, I quickly feared I couldn't even find my way back to the bedroom. A lot of rooms were boarded off, probably because Donya lacked the money to maintain them. I might have made a mistake.

When I heard a sound outside, I ran to a window. A man below was shoveling snow. I wrenched the window partly open. "Excuse me! Could you please—?" Oh no, I'd used please. Maybe I should start over and sound more ducal?

He looked up, screamed, and fell on his face.

Apparently I didn't even need to try to terrorize people. I bit my tongue to stop myself from apologizing. "I'm looking for Countess Donya or my maid, Araceli."

Stumbling to his feet, he ran.

I sat down, leaned against the wall, and tried not to sob.

Fortunately, Ari found me a few moments later. "I knew you'd gotten lost." He held hands with Antonia, who waved at me.

"I swear, this place is more twisty than a hangman's rope," I grumbled.

In a loud whisper, Antonia said, "Don't feel bad, Araceli doesn't know the way around yet, either. We had to ask for directions twice."

"Is it Ari or Araceli today?" I squinted, realizing the outfit wasn't as telling as usual. From the trousers I'd assumed male, but that was a female blouse with floral embroidery.

"I'm not sure today. Maybe in between? He or she is fine. Ari is a more gender-neutral name, I suppose."

"Ari, then," Antonia said firmly.

"If you're not sure, you can always call me 'they' or 'Ari.' How can I be offended when I'm not always sure myself?" Ari winked at me.

I stood up. "I'll call you my lifesaver for rescuing me before I died of dehydration in this maze. I wasn't sure if the poor man would actually find you. The duchess must have done something dreadful to him. I should make it up to everyone the duchess has hurt. What if I asked all past victims to come forward?"

"You haven't been around Arahasnor long enough to terrorize people yet," Ari said. "This is pure reputation. I don't recommend an open call for people to receive compensation. You'd get too many scammers, and you wouldn't even know who was telling the truth."

"Mean Mother hurt too many people," Antonia said.

"That's also true." Ari turned back to me. "It's not your crimes to take responsibility for, so try not to let it get to you."

My shoulders sagged. They were right. Donya would want to throttle me for suggesting something so out of character and money-wasting. I didn't intend to be in this body long enough to take responsibility for all the crimes, yet it didn't quite sit right with me. Every time someone flinched away from me, I felt awful. I'd honestly rather they spit in my food.

Antonia patted my arm. "*I* feel much happier with you here."

For her sake, I smiled. "Thanks." To Ari, I said, "I wrote a letter to my family, to keep them from worrying. How do duchesses send letters?"

"Too many people want to spy on the Blood Duchess's mail. I'll send it for you. I've got ways of sending secret messages. It's kind of you to not want to worry your parents."

"I'm grateful." I gave Ari my letter, not correcting the misunderstanding. I couldn't complain about my difficult parents in front of two orphans.

Ari tucked the letter away. "We were going to the library to research body swapping. Would you like to come along?"

"Yes!" I cried.

Antonia shifted her feet. "See, I'm trying to fix you. Although if you did want to stay, I'd make sure you ate cake every day."

I would have been flattered except I knew this came from a place of low standards. "If we catch the Blood Duchess, we can throw her in prison."

Antonia pursed her lips. "You make a tempting argument, but I want her to die."

Whoa, the look in the little queen's eyes was dead serious. I gulped. "I leave the murder to Ari."

"Red is your color, but you're too adorable to be covered in blood." Ari winced. "Sorry, that was habit. I used to flirt with the Blood Duchess sometimes as a way to appease her. It kept her . . . manageable. I'll try not to do it in front of Countess Donya."

Oh, of course Ari only flirted out of habit. It was selfish of me to feel disappointed just because I'd enjoyed feeling wanted. "Donya's not scary at all." I shrugged. "Don't let that silly threat of hers bother you."

Antonia grabbed Ari's hand. "Yeah! No one can threaten us now that I'm queen."

There was a long list of people threatening Arahasnor, but I didn't burst the kid's bubble.

The three of us somehow found the library. Probably because it was the biggest room on this floor. Although I'd complained about the palace being overly large, I immediately adored this haven to readers. The shelves stretched up twice my height, with equally tall windows in between. The second story had comfortable nooks for reading. A giant globe stood in the middle of the room: twice my height, with the unexplored parts of the world whited out. Its silver stand had a brilliant diamond on top. A mural of Umeko, patron saint of librarians, spread across the ceiling. The place was so uncannily silent, it felt like a shrine, especially with the sunset casting colors through the glass.

Standing still, I inhaled the scent of so many books. "Where do we even begin?"

"I asked the librarian to set aside any books about body swapping earlier, claiming the princess had read a fairy tale about them and wanted to learn more."

Competent people were also my type. Damn, I was surrounded by people too good for me.

First we all sat on the floor and divided the books between fiction and nonfiction. Unfortunately, only one book sat on the nonfiction side. Antonia looked through some picture books while Ari read over my shoulder.

The story was a myth about a saint who swapped a rich man and a poor man for a day to impart moral lessons. "Are we sure this isn't fiction, too?" I asked.

"Saint Adil's existence is well-documented. Although, he lived two thousand years ago, so it's difficult to tell fact from fiction in his legends." Ari sighed. "There doesn't seem to be any information about his price."

Antonia pinched her arms. "I don't feel any power. I'm sorry."

"Don't hurt yourself." I gently tugged her arms away. "It's fine." It wasn't fine, but what else could I say?

"There's one bit of good news." Ari pointed at a picture of a funeral in the book. "It seems that if one of the swapped people dies, the other can still live on in the new body."

The widest grin spread across Antonia's face. "We can hack and stab old Mother to bits and still keep new Mother."

I coughed. "Uh, the story isn't a complete guarantee. Also I still want my body back. Please don't hack me to bits."

"It's useful to know." Ari closed the book. I started to pile them up. "Don't bother, you're too important now to clean up after yourself. It would look suspicious."

Frowning, Antonia pinched her arms again. It was starting to worry me. I clapped my hands. "Let's not talk about Duchess Hedri any longer. We should all go to bed. Thanks for helping me find some new information."

"I wish it had been more helpful," Ari said.

We headed to Antonia's bedroom first. When the door opened, I saw the chest of whips and flinched. Antonia followed my gaze and flinched, too.

"That's still in your bedroom?" No wonder Antonia was jumpy. This wouldn't do at all. "We should throw it out."

"Can I burn it?" Antonia asked hopefully.

There were a lot of practical reasons to say no, all of them overruled by a pair of big, adorable eyes. "That sounds like fun. If we're not keeping you up past your bedtime . . ."

Ari smiled. "I won't tell the tutors if you don't."

We lugged the chest down to the kitchen, thinking the room would be empty this late. But when we stepped through the door, a dishwasher screamed. "The Blood Duchess has an iron maiden!"

"What's an iron maiden?" I called after her retreating form.

"A torture device." Ari set down the chest with a grunt. "As if Duchess Hedri would ever waste so much blood, especially belonging to a young woman."

I hoped that was a dark joke. "Where's the furnace?"

The furnace wasn't large enough for the entire box. But it was an enchanted relic strong enough to incinerate even the metal bits. Antonia fed the whips in one at a time. The glee on her face did not look entirely sane. But I would swear she held her head higher with each whip destroyed.

When I reached for a whip handle to help the process move faster, both Ari and Antonia flinched.

"Sorry." I dropped the whip. "I'm sure you want to do it yourself." It was an excuse to cover up the trauma I'd seen. I felt like an idiot. I should have known better than to touch a whip by the handle in front of them.

At least I hadn't ruined the evening. Antonia skipped her way back to her room when we were done.

After we put Antonia to bed, Ari kindly walked me back to my room, since I certainly couldn't have found it on my own. "Thanks," I told her, pausing in the doorway.

"I should be thanking you. Your idea helped Antonia. She's very important to me. I didn't plan to get attached to anyone when I infiltrated the duchess's household for revenge, but I couldn't help it." Ari reached out and pushed a lock of hair behind my ear, as if offering proof that it wasn't scary to touch me. "You're not the Blood Duchess. You don't need to apologize for her crimes."

"I'm sorry."

We looked at each other and laughed.

CHAPTER NINE

The next morning, Donya and I faced down the representative of the Sashan Guild of Slavers across a polished granite table.

He looked so ordinary. I couldn't quite get past that. I'd heard horror stories about the Guild of Slavers. In fact, after Ysabel had been sold by our father, when we had no idea what had happened to her, I'd deliberately sought out every horror story from the pamphlets distributed by abolitionist activists in our country. Like picking at a partly healed scab, I hadn't been able to stop myself. The contents had given me nightmares.

This young man had light brown hair, a heart-shaped face, and green eyes. He smiled at me with a kind expression. He didn't look like someone who'd ever beaten another person. He looked like he would have trouble lifting any sort of weapon with his frail arms.

Donya gestured. "This is Arrand, the spokesman for the Sashan Guild of Slavers."

Even his name sounded ordinary. It only made me all the more tense, waiting for the other dragon claw to drop.

Arrand coughed. "We've changed our name to the Guild of Indentured Servitude after the outcome of the last World Games." He seemed completely relaxed, while Donya looked wan and strained. He smiled at me. "My congratulations on your regency, Your Grace. I'm pleased that your plan went so well. Now I've come to collect on our agreement."

He spoke as if he knew the Blood Duchess personally. I'd never before had to deceive someone who'd known her well, except for

Falael, who barely counted due to his political powerlessness. Sweat dripped down the back of my neck. I tried to sound distant and aloof. "There was never any doubt of my success."

Her lips white and pursed, Donya said, "No agreement that the duchess made with you would ever hold up in Arahasnor's courts without the permission of our queen."

"Of course," Arrand said mildly. "I'm confident we can come to an arrangement that will pay the late king's debt and perhaps even benefit your kingdom as well." I didn't trust his gentle voice or equally gentle smile.

The door was flung open so hard it must have left a dent in the wall. A messenger page rushed in. His chubby cheeks were bright red and a lock of sweaty blond hair stuck to his nose. "Riot . . . at the back of the palace . . ." he gasped.

Donya shot to her feet. "I'm sorry, I have to handle this. Perhaps we can meet another time?"

"Her Grace and I can continue the discussion without you. Surely the royal regent doesn't need a babysitter?" Arrand raised an eyebrow.

The tip of Donya's nose turned crimson. "I . . . that's a rude thing to say!"

Arrand chuckled. "My apologies. If the kingdom is in a great enough crisis to require the duchess's attention, then of course we can reschedule. Is it a crisis of that magnitude or just a few peasants causing a stir?"

"It's merely a minor incident." Donya wasn't a particularly good liar.

"I'm delighted to hear it." Arrand beamed and took a sip from his teacup. "The duchess and I will excuse you to handle this no doubt minor matter."

I locked eyes with Donya over his head. My gaze was frantic, hers concerned. She mouthed, "Just make small talk. Don't promise him anything. Don't let him trick you into agreeing to anything that sounds even remotely like a promise."

What could I do but nod?

Casting one last worried look over her shoulder, Donya left. As soon as the door closed, I could hear her running down the hallway.

I gazed at Arrand, who calmly sipped his tea. "What do you think about the weather?" I asked weakly. "Will we get another snowstorm or is the season over? Personally, I'd welcome a sign of spring."

Arrand set down his teacup. "Ah, yes, spring, when countless farmers in Sasha will need workers to replace the slaves freed by Dark Lord Kaine. Did he need all of them, I ask you? He didn't just take the Conollians, who he claimed had been acquired via legally questionable raids. He stripped us of slaves we'd had for generations!"

"Um," I said. Actually, I wanted to tell him how little sympathy a half-Conollian like me had for the plight of slavers, but that would make no sense coming from the Blood Duchess. I clamped my lips shut to prevent anything from escaping.

"I can't tell you how delighted we are that Arahasnor's debt provides us with a new source of workers. King Uctor promised us one thousand slaves."

"Slavery has been rendered illegal around the globe by the last World Games. I couldn't let you take our citizens if I wanted to," I snapped. Surely that didn't count as agreeing to anything—it was more the opposite—but I still feared Donya wouldn't approve of me slipping out of character or starting a fight. "Um, leaving that aside, when do you think hats will go out of fashion? They're nice enough, but I'm ready for more creative hairstyles."

Arrand spoke over me. "Fortunately, my guild is nimble and prepared to change with the future. I present the new alternative to slavery: indentured servitude!" He beamed at me.

I shouldn't ask. I had to ask. "Indentured servitude?"

"It's a contract where the indentured servant agrees to work without pay for a fixed number of years in exchange for food, clothing, and shelter. Contracts can still be bought and sold, so the time limit is the only real difference. We're advertising it to our clients as the new and improved slavery, where you still don't have to pay your workers, but you also don't even have to look after them once they get old. You can simply cast them out on the streets with nothing if they get sick."

A pit formed in the center of my stomach. "This is legal?"

"We've investigated the new laws quite carefully and already have test cases in progress. I can assure you, no one will be dropping dead from broken life-oaths. How fast do you believe you can select the debtors? Within the week would be preferable."

I felt control of this situation slipping through my fingers. "We're *not* giving you a thousand of our citizens no matter what you're calling it now."

"Since the contracts expire in twenty years, we'd need four thousand servants. Although, of course, sometimes contracts get lost or altered, and the workers end up being forced to stay until they become too old to work." Arrand winked at me. "Perhaps if you agree to deflect any inquiries concerning missing contracts over the next two decades, we can make it three thousand?"

"I'm not agreeing to that," I said, desperate to emphasize that I was agreeing to *nothing*.

"No need for a pretense now that we're alone. I already have the contract that we arranged back before you claimed your regency." He removed a paper from his pocket.

I didn't agree to this atrocity, Donya, I swear! I can't be held responsible for what the original Blood Duchess did! Sweat dripped down my nose and dampened my armpits. What should I do? Deny everything? Pretend I knew what he was talking about? Babble some more about the weather?

"As per our agreement, the Guild of Indentured Servitude has sent you Gifted Knights to help you quell the current riots."

I stared at him. "You planned those." I had no evidence, but I knew it the way I could smell a rainstorm or tell when the crops back home were about to sprout.

"Don't you mean *we* planned the riots?" Arrand chuckled. "We both knew what would happen when you allowed me to buy up every bit of debt in this city. Your kingdom didn't have legal slavery even before the last Games, so receiving papers of indentured servitude would come as a shock to the average citizen. Of course they'd direct their rage at the palace, since the late king is the one who failed to pay those who worked on the stadium and necessitated them buying food on credit."

Now I understood what Donya's political allies had been talking about during the meeting yesterday. They'd said something about King Uctor going into debt to build the World Games stadium. But I hadn't been politically savvy enough to follow that to its logical conclusion: that there must be workers going hungry and going into debt because they'd never received their pay. I felt ill.

"There's no need to look concerned." Arrand's smile became even more hateful, if that was possible. "We took this into account, remember? The guild has hired mercenaries to supplement your own guards. Between the two of us, we have more than ample forces to control the city. If we massacre the first group of protesters, it will discourage a repeat." It horrified me, how casually he spoke of it. "I'll summon my forces." He stood up.

"No," I said.

Arrand frowned. "No?"

I'd promised Donya to do nothing. But I couldn't let this happen. "No. The agreement is off!"

"Why the cold feet now? Did you find another buyer? No, our idea hasn't spread far enough yet. We've both already sworn, and I won't agree to remove the spell binding you to our oath. Surely this isn't an attack of conscience?" Arrand snorted. "The average citizen is better off in servitude. We feed them and clothe them. They sold themselves for money that allowed their families to survive. Without a buyer, they'd starve. We're providing a valuable role allowing the lower classes to be useful instead of burdens on society. They should be grateful to us."

My world went white.

Because I'd been a young child the day my sister Ysabel had been sold, my memories had become faded and confused. I remembered her screaming as they'd dragged her into the cart. I remembered Calum asking our father when Ysabel was coming back and the look on his face when he learned that she wasn't. And I remembered rocking my newest baby brother to sleep that night because my mother had been crying too hard to do it herself.

The weight of that one day had infected our entire family like rot in the roots of a tree. My mother had blamed my youngest brother because Ysabel's gift had been revealed when she'd healed him. And probably because Mom was too much of a coward to blame my father. She'd barely even looked at or touched her youngest child. Benoni had only been three years old when he'd asked me if he was going to hell because he made his sister disappear.

For years, my other siblings and I had lived in terror, afraid our father would do the same to us when the money ran out. We'd been unable to stand up against his verbal, and sometimes physical, abuse. All of us except Calum, who would pick fights with our father as if he wanted to get beaten. Calum had blamed himself more than anyone else could.

When Ysabel had resurfaced as the Church's Holy Maiden, suddenly both my parents had acted like everything was all better. But it wasn't all better. The sister who returned to me wore a mask in public and had panic attacks in private. Ysabel's healing ability cost a day of her life every time she used it, and the Church was draining her dry. She didn't even fight it. She acted like she didn't care. I always wondered what the men who'd purchased her had done to her, to make her not even care if she lived or died.

I'd tried to talk to her about it, but it only made her angry. She didn't open up to anyone, even—especially—her family. I didn't know what to say to Ysabel. We were sisters, but after so many years apart, we were also strangers. In a sense, a bit of our sisterhood had been stolen. We might never be as close as we would have been if we'd spent our entire childhoods together. My youngest brother didn't even know Ysabel at all. A part of my family had been taken away that we could never get back.

Then Calum had gone to the city to save Ysabel and come back in an urn.

Yet this smug, smiling man said that I should be grateful to him for providing my abusive father with the opportunity to sell my sister.

I snapped.

"Guards!" I shouted. Two Sherdan guards in black-and-white uniforms entered the room and saluted. I pointed with one of my brightly painted nails. "Arrest this man!"

In all honesty, even after I spoke the words, part of me didn't think they'd actually do it. But without hesitation, the guards seized Arrand's arms and dragged him down the hallway.

His face went crimson. "You can't—this is an outrage!"

But I could. I remembered the day the Blood Duchess had casually ordered me murdered because Falael had kissed my hand. Now I was the one holding that power. It was terrifying and maybe a little exhilarating.

Arrand cried, "My Gifted Knights will—"

"We'll take you hostage to stop them from attacking." I was coming up with my plan as I went along. I didn't even know what my next step would be. I only knew that I couldn't let him start a massacre.

"We had a deal! You swore a life-oath!" Arrand stared at me as if expecting me to fall over dead on the spot.

Yet as the knights continued to force him down the hallway, nothing happened. I hadn't known if life-oaths taken by the real duchess would affect me or not, and I hadn't known about this life-oath at all.

No invisible chains tightened around my heart. Apparently life-oaths affected the person who'd sworn them, not their body. Wait, did this mean I wouldn't be able to ditch my life-oath to Araceli by fleeing back to my own body? That could be a problem. Um, this didn't mean my real body had dropped dead, did it? Probably not since the duchess hadn't broken the oath, but I was treading on completely unfamiliar territory.

"The Conclave of Kings will hear about this!" Arrand shouted before being dragged around a corner.

That could be an even bigger problem. The Conclave of Kings prevented any members of their organization from attacking another member through strict life-oaths. They'd want to know why I hadn't fallen over dead after arresting a representative of the Guild of Indentured Servitude. Then they'd be required to take action against me.

What had I done?

Araceli ran down the hallway, a sword and scabbard clashing with her maid's uniform. "There you are! Donya sent me to take you out of the palace." Her mouth flattened into a grim line. "The rioters are about to break in."

CHAPTER TEN

The Conclave of Kings would never get a chance to kill me if an angry citizen with a rock bashed my head in first. Rather than something witty and philosophical about this irony, "Murmph?" emerged from my mouth.

Araceli seized my arm. "Follow me. I'll take you to a carriage."

"What . . . how . . . wait!" I jerked my arm free. "How could rioters get past the guards so quickly?"

"Countess Donya refused to employ the guard against them," Araceli said. "I respect her for that choice. It's not ideal to let a riot break down the palace gate, of course, but people who have been tricked into indentured servitude are angry for a good reason. Ever since the duchess arrived, this city has been on the edge of a revolution. One wrong move could turn this situation into a bloodbath. The rioters have exclusively focused their anger on the Blood Duchess, since they correctly blame her for selling their debt to the slavers. If you're not here, they might dissipate."

As the person currently stuck in the Blood Duchess's body, this failed to comfort me. "Wait. The real duchess had a plan with the former slavers' guild. They brought Gifted Knights here to quell the populace. I took the representative hostage to stop them, but someone has to tell his Gifted Knights or they might attack anyway."

"Good move on your part." Araceli stopped trying to grab me. "I'll find the captain of the guard."

"You think I did the right thing?" I asked, desperate for reassurance.

"There will be ramifications for this, but I don't think you had much choice if he was about to start a massacre."

That wasn't the reassurance I'd hoped for, but it was better than nothing.

Araceli frowned at the look on my face. She grabbed my shoulders. "Bora, I promised to protect you, and I will."

A palace guard ran down the corridor, shouting, "The royal stables' staff have revolted! They're refusing to provide a carriage for the duchess."

Araceli winced and bit her lip. "That's going to make it harder, but I'll still find a way for you to escape. Somehow. Huh, protecting people is a lot harder than assassinating them. I could kill you half a dozen ways, but getting you past a mob will be a lot harder."

"People are angry because King Uctor owed them unpaid back wages, right? Why don't we pay them back? There are so many fancy things here." I gestured at the portrait on the wall and the golden candlesticks next to it.

"Even if you sell everything in the palace, it won't pay off the entire royal debt. The late King Uctor had a spending problem well before the World Games."

Even so, I wanted to help the people I could. "If I don't at least sell off what I can, then won't the debt be even larger?"

She hesitated. "You've got a point. Frankly, I'm out of ideas."

The guard listening to us in confusion finally interrupted. "That's a portrait painted by the late and great Jdalj. You can't just give away our cultural heritage! It will end up pawned for a cheap price and sold off to a foreign country where we'll never get it back."

Ugh, I didn't have time to sort out cultural heritage from expensive junk. "How about the duchess's jewelry?" I suggested. None of that actually belonged to me, and it didn't belong to Arahasnor either. If there was any heritage in there, it wouldn't be ours.

"You start gathering the jewelry while I head off the slavers' Gifted Knights. Don't do anything before I arrive." Araceli then spoke to the guard, giving orders.

* * *

Back in the duchess's bedroom, I headed straight to the jewelry box. Something hard slammed against the window, making the glass pane rattle. I jumped, nearly dropping the box. Another impact followed moments later. It sounded like a rock. This time, the glass cracked with a groan. Though I knew it was risky, I pulled back the curtain to peek.

A crowd of angry citizens stood below. Their voices rose in an incoherent shout. A group of men clustered at the front held a makeshift battering ram made of logs tied together. They thrust it at the palace gate. The iron groaned in response.

Donya stood on a balcony, trying to speak over the crowd. She was completely alone, without a guard to protect her. "I won't let the slavers take any of you! I promise!" she screamed into the wind.

"You can't promise that, my lady," someone shouted. "Just step aside. It's the duchess we want."

Araceli had told me to wait for her, but I couldn't wait. This crowd looked on the verge of exploding.

I threw open my window. "*I* can promise you that I'm going to throw the slavers out of the city. Under my leadership, the royal treasury will completely pay off its debt. Here's a down payment!"

I dumped the duchess's jewelry box out the window. As I'd hoped, the stampede for the jewelry distracted the entire crowd, including those holding the battering ram.

Donya's eyes jerked over to me. "Get back inside!" she cried, her voice faint over the chaos.

"I have everything under control," I said.

An old man near the front of the mob pointed at me. "Don't be fooled! She's trying to distract us. She'll never keep her promise. Get her!"

Ha, it wasn't like they could do anything to me while I was several stories above them.

Someone below hurled a rope. It glowed golden, likely due to someone using their gift. The rope fastened around my wrist and yanked me over.

I had seconds to regret all my life choices as I fell.

I landed directly on one of the spikes of the fence surrounding the palace. My gift made my skin bend so the metal didn't pierce me. Then I bounced.

What a wonderful moment to confirm my gift still worked even though I wasn't in my own body. The buoyancy made me a bit lightheaded. I wasn't out of danger yet. The mob screamed incoherently. As I landed on an adjacent spike, it slid off my rubbery skin, and I tried to grab it. No matter what, I must land on the side of the fence away from the mob.

My sweaty hands slipped. Flipping around in the air, my bottom landed on another spike and bounced again. This time I managed to kick the fence.

I fell backward. After landing on the snow below, I bounced three times before I lay still on my back. My life flashed before my eyes. It was mostly boring, except for after I became the duchess.

Snow soaked through my dress as I stared up at the mob, fortunately on the other side of the fence. Unfortunately, several people held bows and arrows and could easily shoot me from between the bars. Though winded, I got to my feet, prepared to run.

"It's a miracle!" the old man cried. "The Sun God saved the Blood Duchess! She must have truly changed her ways."

Donya may not have been skilled at deception, but she successfully seized the perfect cue. "It's true! The duchess has repented for her bloody past. All the royal family's debt will be repaid. We will also be paying interest in order to compensate for any hardship you incurred due to our late repayment."

An "Oooooh" ran through the crowd.

For a moment, I thought myself safe.

Then a young child threw a fist-sized rock at me. It sailed through the fence bars and smacked me in the forehead, catching me completely unprepared.

I felt blood dripping down my face and swayed, woozy from the pain. But I feared falling over and passing out. If I did, then the illusion of a miracle would be broken. My vision blurred and doubled.

An odd silence fell over the crowd. A cold breeze ran through the air, slashing at the cut on my face. The moment teetered on the edge of violence.

Then Araceli ran out the palace door. "More debt repayment! Get in line!" Guards followed her holding candlesticks and vases and other knickknacks snagged from around the palace. "We need to record the names of each person and the value of what they receive."

Oh yeah, I probably should have thought of that. We definitely didn't have enough money to pay everyone twice if people decided to lie. People might also lie about their names, but that sounded like a problem for Araceli to handle. My problem at the moment was remaining vertical.

Whether from the promise of money or the threat of the guards, people started to line up in an orderly fashion. Quite a few of them slunk off into the shadows, including the one who'd thrown a rock at me. I would consider those the smart people. The real Blood Duchess would have been collecting names for a far more sinister reason.

Araceli pulled me to my feet. "You're either crazy or a fool," she said, but I would swear there was a note of approval lurking behind her words.

"I can be both," I said, then passed out against her shoulder.

I woke up lying on my back in bed.

Looking at my pale hand, I briefly wondered who had painted my nails and why my skin color had changed. Ugh, did my joints feel unusually sore? Why was my head heavy from excess hair? Who'd hit me on the forehead?

Reality came rushing back to me. I must have survived the mob, because I was back in my bedroom. The duchess's bedroom. Same difference. I felt nauseous. I'd nearly died, and it was all the fault of this stupid body. It hadn't worked properly or been fast enough when I'd needed it the most. Ripples of fat sagged off my bones. I glanced at my tummy, felt sick, and looked away. It wasn't my body. I didn't like it. I didn't *want* to be the Blood Duchess. I had a mad desire to rip off my skin and throw this whole body away.

I moved, probably to do something nonsensical, but a stabbing pain in my head stopped me.

I raised a hand to touch my aching temples. Someone had bandaged my head injury. I'd also been changed into a lacy nightgown. Even if it had been necessary, it was still unnerving to have been changed in my sleep. Looking down at my thick, pale, naked thighs, I felt an even stronger sense of disconnect. Did it even matter who touched this body? It wasn't mine. But it was still unpleasant. I felt a grumbling in my stomach and an ache in my back from where I'd slept wrong. If only I could leave and get back to my own comfortable skin.

"May we come in?" Araceli called.

"Yes," I replied in a hoarse voice. I could use someone to stop me from being alone with my thoughts.

Araceli entered, wearing a maid's uniform. She tugged the young Queen Antonia behind her. "Antonia—Her Majesty—heard about your injuries and wanted to see you."

"Just call me by name when we're alone. It feels weird otherwise." Antonia pointed at my bandage. "Did people do that to you because they thought you were the real duchess?"

"Err . . ." I glanced at Araceli for help. I didn't want to lie, but I didn't want a child to blame herself either.

Gently but firmly, Araceli said, "They did. That's why we're researching to help Bora return to her correct body."

Antonia gnawed at her lip and peered up at me from under her lashes. "You must be angry at me. I understand. I wouldn't want to turn into the duchess, either. She's mean and a lot of people don't like her."

I winced. "This situation isn't ideal, but I don't blame you. It was an accident. And if you hadn't swapped us, the duchess would have killed Donya before I could stop her."

"I don't want the real duchess back." Antonia looked at her golden slippers. "But I don't want you to get hurt either. And I don't want to be hurt myself."

"I promise I won't leave you with that horrible woman," I said. "We'll get rid of her and let Donya be your regent instead."

Araceli nodded. "That's right. If Arahasnor doesn't allow executions, then there's always poison. A friend of mine has poison that can melt someone's innards. We can make sure she suffers for all the pain she caused us."

I frowned. Was that an acceptable thing to say in front of a child? But Antonia looked thrilled. She bounced up and down. "Finally she'll die instead of other people! It's a promise!"

I worried about this kid.

Just when my last set of visitors had left and I'd started to drift off, someone new knocked on my door.

"Huh?" I called in a sleepy voice.

"It's Donya. How are you feeling? Should I come back later?"

"Ahhhhhh!" I sat up and started straightening my hair. I must look a fright, with my forehead bandaged and one of my nails chipped in my fall.

Why did it matter? This wasn't my body. But I still didn't want Donya to see me like this. I gave up taming my hair for fear I'd disturb my bloody bandages.

"Are you all right?" she called. "I thought I heard a cry of pain. Should I summon the doctor again?"

"No, no, I'm fine, I was just . . ." I didn't have an excuse. "Come in!"

As Donya entered my bedroom, I yanked my sheets up to my neck to cover as much of my body as possible and huddled in my burrow of pillows like a small furry animal.

Donya took a seat by my bed. "We need to talk about the fallout of arresting a diplomatic representative."

I chuckled nervously. "How much trouble am I in?"

"I don't blame you, Bora. Not one bit. What Arrand tried to do . . ." Donya's mouth flattened into a thin line. "I'm furious, too. There was no other way to stop him. He had permission from the real duchess to bring his Gifted Knights into the city and use them against civilians. Taking him hostage was a reckless move—but it worked. We successfully forced everyone connected to the guild to leave the city by threatening Arrand's life."

"Oh." I gnawed on my lip. It surprised me that anyone cared about him, but I figured he paid their wages. "What about the debt?"

Donya rubbed her forehead. "We can't pay that debt. We simply can't. I've run the numbers thousands of times . . . and we don't have the money. Not if we sold this entire palace. I suppose just flat out refusing to pay them was unethical, but not as unethical as handing over our innocent civilians to cover the late king's reckless spending."

"They're going to complain to the Conclave of Kings."

"I'm sure they will. But complaints take time. Dark Lord Kaine built up an army while the Conclave was still trying to figure out what to do about him. Ideally, I hope we can swap you back before the Conclave acts."

I sat up straighter, my headache lessening slightly. "That would be perfect! Let's make this whole mess the real duchess's problem! Have you found her yet?"

Donya winced. "No, I haven't. I assumed that she would head back to Sherda . . . but either I guessed wrong or she slipped past our guards. We're still looking, I swear."

"Oh." I sagged back down. Although I told myself that I couldn't swap back even if we found her, it didn't assuage my worries. For all I knew, my body could already be dead. I was stuck in this palace and couldn't even help with the search.

"I'm reaching out to all my contacts, seeking someone with a gift for searching for people across long distances. In the worst-case scenario, I suspect the duchess will come back to us at some point. She must want her body back."

"I hope so," I muttered, picking at the flab on my arm. I didn't want to be stuck in this unfamiliar meat shell. My real body had my freckles and curly hair like my brother Calum. I wanted that connection to him back. "Uh . . . if she comes back, won't she have a revenge plan?"

"We'll have to handle that as it happens. We have a more urgent situation." Donya folded her arms. "I came here to talk to you about the debt situation. You promised to pay off all the king's debt to the citizens who prepared for the World Games, but we don't have that money, either." Her tone held a note of reluctance, as if she didn't like what she was about to say.

"I'm sorry," I muttered.

"I told you, I'm not blaming you. It was the only way to defuse the mob at the time. I have an idea, but I need your help."

"I'll do anything."

"Don't agree so quickly." Donya frowned. "This could be risky and difficult. Here's the problem: Our treasury is empty. After the damage to the city due to the undead rampage and the unpaid wages after the World Games, the people can't afford increased taxes. Selling your jewelry will only put a dent in the debt. We need the nobility to cough up the money."

"Raise their taxes," I said.

"That's not so easy. Nobility don't pay taxes, technically—they pay tribute. Though I've heard the terms used interchangeably by people. The amount is settled as a result of the National Games. Just like in the World Games, the monarch and the nobility each swear life-oaths to abide by the outcome of the competition. It can't be changed until the next National Games. But you're in an unusual position."

"I'm a peasant pretending to be a duchess. I have no life-oaths."

"Exactly! You can break the agreement between the crown and the nobility and demand a higher tribute. Because King Uctor fared so poorly in the Games, tribute has been low for a long time, and I know they have the money. Even though you're not oathbound to anyone, the nobles are still bound to you, so they won't be able to refuse. They can and will complain, but they'll have to hand over the money. We're in a unique position with you due to the body theft. You're the only monarch who could become a total tyrant, because you're not the real duchess."

Slowly, I said, "Even if they're suspicious, they can't act against me without proof that I'm not the real duchess. They'll complain to the Conclave of Kings, but that takes time, like you said."

"Exactly!" Donya nodded. "We can take their money and use it to pay off the government's debts to our citizens. Furthermore, because you're not under the influence of any life-oaths, you can also threaten the representatives of the other two countries who are planning to show up and try to take over our kingdom. I couldn't attack a diplomatic representative the way you did today." Donya touched her chest. "My life-oath would have killed me. The real duchess couldn't, either. But *you* can."

Because I was a peasant. I'd never been important enough to swear a life-oath before I got swapped with Duchess Hedri. The delicate system binding together the power structure of this world simply didn't apply to me.

"Then we'll swap you back, and leave the Blood Duchess and Sherda to take all the blame with the Conclave of Kings. Sherda will probably renounce the duchess if she's seen as going too far. We'll kill the duchess before she can reveal anything." Donya's tone was uneasy when speaking of murder, but she didn't shy away from the words. "We can let the Blood Duchess be the villainess while we do what must be done to save the kingdom."

My fingers clenched around the blankets. "I'll do it."

Donya shifted. "Bora, I want to be sure you understand what I'm asking when I say that we're going to make you into the villainess. You'll threaten powerful people. You'll have to commit high treason. Ideally, everyone will blame the duchess. In the second-best scenario, we'll pin this on an unnamed imposter. But if anyone ever finds out that it's you in there, then you'd be accountable for all those crimes. We're talking crimes on an international scale. The Conclave would never stop hunting you."

I understood perfectly. We didn't actually have the duchess captured or any way to guarantee I could be swapped back. The plan was to leave the duchess holding all the blame in the end. But if anyone found out the truth first, then *I'd* be executed for these crimes.

But I'd been the one who put Donya in this position with my reckless decision to arrest Arrand and my promise to the mob to pay off the crown's debt. I had no right to refuse to do what needed to be done to dig us out of this mess.

"I know." I met Donya's eyes. "I'll do it. I'll become your villainess."

CHAPTER ELEVEN

My hands trembled under their pearl-covered gloves. I couldn't do this. Confront the most powerful nobles in the kingdom and demand their money? I wouldn't even be able to speak! I'd throw up all over them!

If only Donya had let me take notes. She'd given me an entire speech to present before the gathered nobles. I appreciated that. But she'd said it would be too obvious someone was puppeteering me if I read off a sheet of paper. The Blood Duchess had always made her speeches short, spontaneous, and filled with threats. Apparently even if pretty much everyone of power suspected the duchess was under mind control, we still couldn't be obvious about it. When Donya had caught me trying to write on my hand, she'd made me put on gloves.

My stomach twisted. I stared down at my luxurious golden dress, puffed out with a hoop and embroidered with real gold. This wasn't me. These luxuries didn't belong to me. Even this body wasn't rightfully mine. I was going to get caught.

"Are you okay?" Ari asked. He'd shown up at my door dressed in a guard's uniform with his hair fastened under a cap, so I assumed today was a "he" day, but I figured I should probably ask to be sure.

"I'm just happy to have you along. Donya wasn't included in the invitation because she has already agreed to the new tax rates. I nearly begged her to come anyway, but she has so much else to do. Besides, we can't make it too obvious she's telling me what to do. I'm grateful to have someone else at my side who knows the truth." I tried to smile. "You're Ari right now, is that correct?"

"Yes, I felt like that today. You don't mind?" Ari tugged on his cap. "I'm scared that someone will recognize me and ask questions that might trouble you."

I snorted. "Nobles don't look at the servants' faces on the best of days. Today? When I'm trying to raise their taxes? You'll be the least of their concerns."

Ari laughed and patted my shoulder. "You're right."

Even his small laugh restored a bit of my confidence.

Taking a deep breath, I tried to channel my older sister's spirit. Ysabel had a knack for walking into any setting and making herself heard. Despite coming from the same origins as me, she'd managed to fit in with the royal court. Ysabel would hold her head high, stride into that room, and talk them out of all their gold. People would open their purses to her and somehow like her even more afterward.

Yes, that was the spirit! Be a graceful swan, like Ysabel!

I lifted my chin, stepped through the door, and immediately banged my head on the chandelier.

Ow! Why did my new body have to be so tall?

Ari grabbed my hat before it could hit the floor and stuck it back on. Everyone stared at me. Despite my best efforts, my cheeks flushed. That had not been what Ysabel would have done. My perfect big sister had natural grace and balance. If only she was here, not me.

Behind me, Ari cleared his throat. "Presenting Duchess Hedri, the royal regent."

Oops, I had been supposed to wait for him to introduce me before I went in. I had screwed up again. My blush deepened. My arms swinging awkwardly, I power-walked to the throne. The chorus in my head chanted, *Let's get this over with, let's get this over with.*

A row of Sherdan guards lined the carpet leading to the throne. I passed opulent marble pillars, paintings, and busts of deceased monarchs. The sheer amount of gold hurt my eyes. Several dozen noblemen and ladies sat on tall oak chairs with golden sun decorations on top. The weight of their eyes bore into my back. A bead of sweat slipped down my nose as I pushed aside a red curtain hanging around the throne. Then I sat down.

Light blazed down on me from a glowing relic shaped like a sun. It made this heavy dress even hotter. At least the last monarch had installed two layers of cushions on the throne. The whalebone of my corset dug into my bottom. A curl had slipped out of my braided hairstyle, probably when my hat fell off.

Keenly aware of every eye in the room on me, I tucked the curl back in.

Ari marched forward and stood at my right with his hand over his chest. "Our noble regent has an announcement to make."

My mind went completely blank. I couldn't remember a single word of my prepared speech. The bright lights from the chandeliers overhead spun.

Without missing a beat, Ari continued talking. "In light of the recent riot, Her Grace has made repaying the crown's debt to our past employees a top priority."

That had been the first line of my speech, and the prompt jogged my memory. I took a deep breath. "In order to host the World Games, the residents of this city worked overtime to construct a stadium and housing for dignitaries. Countless employees waited on the guests and supported the games. The Church generously agreed to pay for half the costs and has already fulfilled their end of the bargain. However, the royal treasury stands depleted, and we've been unable to pay the hardworking citizens who labored tirelessly to make the World Games a success."

All the nobles stared at me. I couldn't read their expressions easily behind their face powder and fans. But no one was smiling.

"This nonpayment has caused serious hardship among the citizens of Arahasnor. Many have gone into debt purchasing food for their families, only to be exploited when the Sashan Guild of Slavers"—I think I was supposed to use their new name, but I forgot it—"purchased the debt on a massive scale. Although I have taken swift action to prevent them from enslaving our citizens, our economy remains in a state of crisis. Several merchant companies are on the verge of shutting down because they weren't paid for the royal purchases of food and building supplies during the Games. If we let them collapse, it will result in massive unemployment. The portion of the royal debt owed to Arahasnor private citizens is . . ." I subtly lifted up the top of my glove to check the number written on my skin. "One million aracoins."

I could buy a third of the property in the city with a million aracoins. Holy shit, that was merely the debt that we owed on the World Games? Did that mean the total royal debt was even higher? Sweet Sun God, we were all so doomed.

The beating sun relic made perspiration drip down my forehead. "The nobility of Arahasnor benefitted greatly from hosting the World Games." I think I accidentally skipped part of my speech about the poor citizens who couldn't afford basic necessities and a family who froze to death from lack of firewood, but too late now. I had no choice but to keep forging ahead. "Countess Lealonie, you've made a fortune off the trade deals you negotiated with dignitaries." Here, I'd been instructed to stare at a woman in a yellow dress, but I was so stressed out that my vision had gone blurry. I kept going. "Duke Pierre, you sold crops to feed our guests at a premium, but this drove up food prices for everyone else in your dukedom. All the nobles in the northern region sold lumber for construction. You all asked to be paid in advance and at double the market rate. What good luck for you pigeon pluckers—commoners can't even refuse a royal building order, much less negotiate prices." I hadn't been instructed to say that last part. The sarcasm and country slang had slipped out. "If you don't know, a pigeon plucker is Sherdan for a brilliant businessman, by the way." Of the con artist variety.

My head hurt, and the overheating from my clothing was making me cranky. My next words came out clipped and sharp. "When Arahasnor agreed to host the World Games, we were told it would bring a flood of coins into our kingdom. Well, it did—except all the coins ended up in the pockets of the people in this room. The average citizen was forced to provide labor on credit, then the crown refused to pay them later. It's been a long, hard winter. Just earlier this week, a family of six was found frozen to death in their house. The father had worked constructing the World Games Stadium while the mother served food and drinks during the Games, but neither received pay, so they couldn't afford firewood." Good, I found a way to work that back in. "The crown requests a temporary tax hike to specifically apply to profits received from the World Games in order to pay our citizens the money they rightfully earned."

Perfect! I managed to remember the entire speech! Proud of myself, I beamed at the crowd. No one smiled back.

A woman wearing a hat with a dove nestled on top snapped open her fan and peered at me from behind it. She raised her hand.

Donya had instructed me on how to recognize the most important nobles in the kingdom, but most of that information had deserted my memory. "Yes. You. Please speak," I said.

"Is this a voluntary request for donations?" she asked.

Tough question. Donya had told me that I needed to convey the sentiment that it was voluntary, but they still had to do it. Not an easy line to straddle.

"Everyone in this room has the status of a noble, and the benefits that come with it. Traditionally, the nobility is supposed to pay for their daily privilege by defending the kingdom upon need. In practice, the nobility holds all the power, so it has always been easy to tax the citizenry as they—ahem, as *we*—please and give nothing in return. If you look into your heart and consider your duty to your kingdom, then I believe you'll find that you owe this to your people and your country."

The eyes staring through the fan looked entirely unimpressed. "Tax rates are decided during the National Games. You can't change them until the next year."

"Unless those present vote in agreement." I smiled the strained smile of someone who knew full well I was asking people to vote to raise their own taxes. "Please do consider that the current tax rates for nobility are the lowest in a decade." Unreasonably low. According to Donya, the king had lost massive political support after the failed trade embargo against Conollia, and he'd been trying to bribe his vassals with low tribute rates.

A man in a poofy wig cleared his throat. "Is it a problem if the guild removes some debtors from the city? Those who can't pay for their own food are only a burden on our kingdom."

My hands clenched on my armrests. I felt that same anger rising again. I'd grown up often hungry. I knew there wasn't the tiniest chance this man had ever missed a meal. "People are going hungry because we owe them money. They're good, hardworking citizens. They don't deserve to be turned into slaves under a thinly veiled premise." It wasn't okay for anyone to go hungry or be enslaved, but I thought it more likely the assembled nobles would care about theoretical taxpayers.

My appeal didn't work. Disapproving murmurs ran through the crowd. "King Uctor promised them money, not us," the nobleman said.

"But you all benefitted from the World Games." My voice came out more plaintive than I liked. I straightened and tried to adopt the harsh tone of the Blood Duchess. "The man who made the decision to buy on credit has regrettably returned to the Sun God. But the king's debt binds the entire country of Arahasnor. All of you had the option to refuse when the king asked you to sell him materials for the stadium—commoners couldn't turn down a royal request. The royal treasury is empty, so in order to pay our citizens what they are owed, we must all contribute. Countess Donya contributed all of her personal money and World Games winnings to keep the government running this long." She hadn't told me to throw in that part, but I felt salty. "I'm asking you to reach into your hearts and find compassion."

A worrying lack of compassion stared back at me from the increasingly hostile faces.

"I simply don't see how any of this is *my* problem." A lady in a yellow dress stood up and headed for the door. The rest rose to follow suit.

"Wait! Please!" I shouldn't have begged. I was screwing this all up. Tears stung the corners of my eyes.

Ari stood at attention and bellowed, "Arrest anyone who tries to leave!"

The guards shot into motion, blocking off the door and crowding around the nobles. A shocked hiss ran through the crowd. A woman pretended to faint, then got up off the floor after she realized no one was paying attention. I cast Ari a grateful look. He winked at me.

I clapped my hands. "Everyone, please sit down." I didn't want to arrest anyone, but I couldn't just let them all leave, either. That would mean failing Donya and all of Arahasnor.

"You can't do this," someone in the middle of the crowd said in disbelief. "A noble who attacks another noble dies from violating their life-oaths."

Everyone stared at me, alive and showing no sign of strain. I tried to smile confidently, but it came out as a grimace.

"It's a bluff." With those confident words, the crowd moved for the door again.

"Stop," Ari growled. The guards raised their pikes to bar the door.

"The Conclave of Kings will hear about this!" The noblewoman in the yellow dress marched toward me.

I flinched. I knew this was a mistake, because her smile widened with triumph.

She lowered her voice. "If the Conclave of Kings learned of how you've beaten your ward, then your regency could be called into question."

Anger wiped away my anxiety. She'd known that the real duchess had been beating Antonia. How many people in this room had known and done nothing to protect that poor child until their own interests were being threatened?

I steeled my resolve. Raising my voice, I cried, "Arrest them all! Some time in the dungeons will let them think about how they'd like to vote."

The woman's face paled as a guard grabbed her arm. I stared her down with all the fury in my heart.

The nobles didn't fight. None of them were armed, and they largely seemed confused and disbelieving about the situation. As they were dragged out of the room, they all kept shouting about life-oaths and the Conclave of Kings.

Once Ari and I were alone in the throne room, I sagged back into my seat. By that point, I'd soaked my expensive dress with sweat. "Do you think I went too far?"

"You went exactly far enough," Ari said. "Don't worry, we'll just let them cool their heels in the dungeons for a few hours. We're not going to actually hurt anyone. But we needed to do this in order to prove that life-oaths don't kill you. That puts the nobility in quite a tight position—their life-oaths still stop them from raising troops against you, but you can do whatever you please to them in return. You have all the power here. They'll cough up the money you need to stave off Arahasnor's destruction."

My hairstyle had fallen apart. I pushed sweaty strands off my forehead. "Someone who controls an army but isn't bound by life-oaths . . . doesn't that make me a dark lord?" The title had always been gender neutral, probably because the dark lady was what adherents to the Sun God called the adversary. Who got declared a dark lord revolved around politics rather than any exact definition. The Conclave of Kings had been known to quibble over whether the leader of a large bandit group counted. But the primary purpose of the entire system was to prevent war from breaking out. Anyone who led a country had to swear life-oaths not to wage war, or be declared a dark lord and have every country in the Conclave unite to destroy them.

"That's correct, but I wouldn't worry too much about the Conclave of Kings," Ari said. "They spent two years sending Dark Lord Kaine warning letters while he was building up his army. By the time they get around to doing something about you, you'll be back in your real body, and I'll have killed the duchess. No one will ever know what happened. They'll be left confused as to how Duchess Hedri broke her life-oaths."

"We need a cover story." Body swapping was a mythological power, but other types of magic could be used to change appearances, create illusions, or control people. "If we don't have an explanation for breaking the life-oaths, it will become a bit too obvious that I'm an imposter."

"Then you might lose control of the Sherdan guards." Ari frowned. "The nobility will hesitate to attack you because they'll die if they're wrong, but the guards didn't swear life-oaths."

I'd been thinking about this since my conversation with Donya, and I'd come up with an idea. "My sister told me the treasonous former Head Cardinal Jiang had a relic that could break life-oaths. A cane he carried everywhere. She said the Conclave of Kings ordered it burned after his death because it was deemed too dangerous to exist, but she secretly kept it." I smiled at the memory, because that kind of trick was exactly what Ysabel would do. As someone who'd been bound all her life to become a human sacrifice, of course she'd see the value in keeping around something that could break life-oaths. Also, she'd always been a sneaky weasel. "My sister made half a dozen fake replicas and gave one to Donya."

Ari beamed, catching on to my plan. "Good idea."

"Jiang took his cane everywhere. Any noble in Arahasnor would recognize it. The cane's power became notorious after he used it to kill the former king and queen."

"Even better." Ari rubbed his hands together.

I started to feel hopeful about this whole messy situation. "Should I go pick up the cane, then head to the dungeons to negotiate?"

"No, let the nobles seethe and worry a bit longer." Ari chuckled. "There's no rush. You should sit back and savor victory. You deserve a break."

"That might be the nicest thing anyone has said to me lately," I said, gazing into his eyes.

Of course, at that precise moment, a messenger boy burst into the room. His collar was disheveled, and his armpits had soaked his red uniform with sweat. Terrified eyes locked with mine. "Dark Lord Kaine has breached the city!"

CHAPTER TWELVE

A dozen Arahasnor guards burst into the room on the page's heels. They shouted over each other as they bumped into the furniture. Dammit, I needed to start learning to lock doors. Absolutely nothing good ever happened to me when someone came busting in. Next time I got promised a break, I would barricade the damn door.

I stood up and cupped my hands to my mouth. "Silence!"

The voices rose to a crescendo.

Ari banged his sword hilt against the wall. "Silence! Let the ranking officer step forward and explain the situation."

For some reason, it worked when he did it. Maybe I needed to get my own sword.

An Arahasnor guard walked up to the throne and saluted. He must be the captain, judging from the plumes in his helmet. "Your Grace, just minutes ago, an explosion occurred at the South Wall. Three intruders entered through the hole. The guards on duty only glimpsed them from a distance, but they heard a woman in a white dress shouting loudly at the other two, and they recognized the voice of Holy Maiden Ysabel. The woman accompanying the Holy Healer could only be her bodyguard, Alzira. The man wore a distinctive black helmet marking him as Dark Lord—I mean, King Kaine."

I was baffled that my sister had reached the Holy City so quickly. Since she'd apparently only shown up with a group of three, they must have been using a magical method of transportation that could only carry a small group. Not that she needed a larger one—either Kaine or Alzira alone could equal an army.

"Which direction did they go?" Ari asked.

The captain looked at Ari as if he'd lost his mind. "Do you think we followed them? He's moon-damned *Dark Lord Kaine*!"

"You could have at least tried to tail them from a distance." Ari raised an eyebrow, distinctly unimpressed.

The captain muttered something about not getting paid enough. In a louder voice, he said, "It would have done no good to track them. They vanished into some sort of swirling dark portal. Then minutes later, the portal appeared in the guest bedroom in the palace where Countess Donya has been staying. King Kaine dragged her through the portal, then vanished."

"Oh, that's all right, then." I exhaled in relief. "Donya and Ysabel are good friends. I'm sure Kaine came to rescue her because of the duchess's—because of *my* little execution joke. Donya will explain that was all a big misunderstanding and now we're on the same side." Or rather, Donya would explain to my sister and her team about the body swap. It would be a huge relief to have Ysabel and her two walking armies on my side.

"Not necessarily." The captain looked uneasy. "Part of the bedroom wall exploded when King Kaine activated his portal through it. Some debris struck Countess Donya on the forehead. She fell unconscious, then Kaine and Alzira dragged her through the portal."

"Oh dear. Did she look badly hurt?"

"The guards on duty couldn't tell. They barely arrived in time to see her taken away."

I still believed Donya was in no danger, because my sister's healing ability could erase anything short of death. Surely Donya would shortly be on her feet and explain this entire misunderstanding.

I clapped my hands for attention. "Set patrols to watch for any sign of Ysabel or her escorts. If you find them, tell me and I'll go talk to her—"

The captain coughed. "Actually, I came here to deliver my resignation. I'm not fighting Kaine whether he's a king or a dark lord. The man is the living incarnation of terror and destruction. I'm not paid nearly enough. I wouldn't fight him if you offered to make me the next king."

The Arahasnor guards behind the captain all raised their hands. "I'd like to resign too," one said. A chorus of agreement came from the rest.

I felt a headache coming on.

As a dark lord, naturally Kaine had quite a terrible reputation. I'd almost forgotten just how frightened people were of him. Being half-Conollian, I'd had a lot of sympathy for his cause from the very beginning. Conollia had been abused by neighboring countries and raided for slaves before Kaine had taken charge. I didn't think he was a bad person. I'd only met him once, at my sister's wedding. Kaine had swept me off my feet in an effusive hug, then told me that we were family now and he'd always help me if I ever needed it.

Then my father had tried to crash the wedding despite being distinctly uninvited, and Kaine had made a serious attempt to murder him before Ysabel stopped him. Despite being kind to me personally, he was a very dangerous man. His ability let him steal the gifts of others. Although he'd calmed down on the destruction and theft since going legitimate and marrying my sister, he possessed as many powers as a walking army.

I sighed. "I hope you'll reconsider. I truly do believe that this is a misunderstanding. It will blow over shortly. I'd never order any of you to fight King Kaine. However, if you want to resign, then I can't force you to stay."

"I'll consider returning to my job if this city is still standing by the end of the day," the captain said with worrying frankness.

From the wall, a Sherdan guard cleared his throat. "You're letting them resign? You're not going to execute them? You won't torture their entire families to death?"

"Of course not!" I recoiled.

For some reason, Ari started making funny faces and mouthing something I couldn't understand.

"In that case, I'd like to resign, too." The Sherdan guard unbuckled his sword.

This started a clamor of every single Sherdan in the room falling all over themselves to quit. Suddenly, I understood what Ari had been trying to communicate. We couldn't afford to lose our entire force like this!

I tried to talk, to bargain and offer additional pay, but the chattering of the room was too great. No one was even listening to me.

"May I speak?" The mild-sounding request cut through the chaos like a beacon of order. So piercing was the voice that most of the crowd fell silent.

The elderly guard who'd spoken was Sergeant Laurent—the exact same man who'd tried to stop me from throwing myself off the city wall just days ago. His brow wrinkled and he put his hands behind his back. "I completely understand how everyone feels. However, if we allow word of Kaine's invasion to spread at the same time the guard quits, then this city will be overtaken with chaos. I would like to suggest that we take the duchess up on her generous offer not to fight Kaine and instead spread word that Countess Donya will negotiate with him. This should restore peace to the city."

I took advantage of the room's silence to add, "I'll pay everyone double today as hazard pay." Oh dear, I'd need to shake even more money out of the nobles in my dungeons.

The Arahasnor captain eyed me nervously. "And we won't have to fight Kaine?"

"If you see him, immediately surrender. Please. We don't want a war with Conollia." I tried to smile reassuringly. "This is truly all a misunderstanding."

A Sherdan guard said, "Many of us volunteered for this mission because you promised citizenship for us and our families in Arahasnor. You said there would be free land since the border had recovered from the blight. But we've yet to receive the papers or be allowed to invite our families to join us here."

Why did I have a feeling the Blood Duchess had never intended to keep that promise? "What an oversight on my part! I'll have those papers to you by the end of today."

The Sherdan nodded. "Then we're also willing, as long as we aren't expected to fight a dark lord. Former dark lord. He's equally deadly either way."

As the guards started to file out of the room to spread word across the city, I called out to Sergeant Laurent, "I'd like to give you a promotion."

He flinched. The tips of his ears went red. "No need, Your Grace." He fled the room, blending in with the crowd.

I had a feeling he didn't believe me about the promotion. He probably thought I might threaten him for refusing to fight Kaine. The Blood Duchess's reputation was absolute trash. I sighed and whispered to Ari, "I was serious about wanting to give him a promotion. His name is Sergeant Laurent. We've met in a different body." I also wanted to find a way to tell him that the woman he'd tried to save was still alive. Maybe it wasn't that important in the grand scheme of things, but I didn't like to think of him feeling guilty about my nonexistent death.

"Sure, although first I'm worried about Queen Antonia. What if she was targeted for kidnapping, too?" Ari said.

If Ysabel had any reason to think the young queen might also be in danger from her guardian or if she simply wanted a hostage, she just might. "Let's go check on her together."

We were both too nervous to talk, instead focusing on moving as fast as possible. Ari led me down the hallway to Antonia's bedroom. I knocked. "May I come in?"

Silence answered me. Then Antonia whispered, "C-come in." Her voice sounded choked, as if she'd been crying.

Immediately, I pushed open the door. "What's wrong?"

This room had bad memories from when I'd first had my body forcibly swapped. The furniture looked luxurious and ancient, from the claw-footed dresser to the bed with heavy magenta velvet curtains. But it didn't particularly look like a bedroom for a child. The dolls on the shelf were too neat and fancy to have ever been played with. The desk was too large for a little girl. I needed to get this kid some proper toys.

Obscured behind the curtain, Antonia sniffled.

I ran into the room. "Are you hurt?"

The curtain was flung backward. A boy sat on the bed with a knife pointed at Antonia's throat.

I screeched to a halt. On second look, he wasn't a child, but rather a halfling with a thick black beard and icy blue eyes. He wore leather armor, and a smirk twisted his wide mouth. "Take one more step forward, and your daughter dies."

A tear trickled down Antonia's cheek.

I raised my hands in surrender. "Please don't hurt her!"

"Take off all your rings, Blood Duchess . . ." The halfling frowned. "You don't have any rings."

"They're awfully heavy," I said. Plus, Ari already stole all the ones with magical properties.

"You won't trick me," he growled. Antonia whimpered as he jostled the knife at her throat. "Show me where you're hiding your rings."

"I don't have any! I'm sorry! Please stop, you're hurting her!"

Behind me, Ari snarled, "Durnip, what in the name of the Dark Lady are you doing?"

"Ari?" The halfling blinked. "You're here, too? What are you waiting for? Hurry up and stab the Blood Duchess."

"You fool, let Antonia go!" Ari pinched his forehead.

"But she's my hostage!" Durnip protested.

"Doesn't this situation seem strange to you? The Blood Duchess would have already stabbed straight through poor Antonia's body to get at you. She only adopted the girl so she could have a claim as royal regent for Arahasnor. I'm ashamed to be part of the Twelve Avengers with the likes of you. Why would you possibly imagine the Blood Duchess would be a good enough person to care about the child she took in for political reasons? There was no point in pretending to threaten her!"

"Who's pretending?" Durnip twisted Antonia's hair, making her yelp. "After the Blood Duchess is helpless, I'm going to kill her daughter in front of her to make her pay for what she did to *my* family."

The temperature in the room dropped. Ari's eyes narrowed. The rest of his face barely twitched, but there was danger in his expression that hadn't been there before. Very slightly, he shifted his neck.

Rings on a chain hanging under his shirt glowed before a red light shot forth from one of them and filled the entire room with a blinding blaze.

I cried out, my hands going over my eyes. When I could see again, Durnip's knife had eroded to nothing.

I knew what I had to do. I ran forward to pull Antonia away from him.

"Wait!" Ari cried, but I was already moving, and I wasn't sure if I could reverse my momentum.

Shoulder slamming into the bedpost, I picked Antonia up. She trembled slightly in my arms. "I've got you," I said.

Smoke spewed from Durnip's mouth. It eroded the bed curtain and shot toward my face.

Ari moved between us. He held up one of the rings around his neck, and it formed a golden shield.

My heart hammered as I stared at the tattered cloth falling in threads to the floor. That had almost been my face. I ought to have had a bigger reaction, but I felt numb.

Ari clubbed Durnip over the head with the butt of his sword. "He's got an acid-breath gift. I tried to warn you."

"Sorry," I croaked. "You saved my life. Thank you."

"Don't worry about it. You did well." Ari looked up and directed a blazingly brilliant smile at me.

Antonia stirred in my arms. "I was so scared!" She leapt away from me and flung herself at Ari, sobbing.

Ari rubbed her back. "I'll hug you later all you want, but first I need to take this man away before he has a chance to hurt anyone again."

Antonia let go and wiped her tears. "I'm okay. I can be brave."

I suspected this wasn't the first time she'd needed to be brave in a dangerous situation, and it made me sick. "What are we going to do with him?"

Ari prodded the unconscious assassin with a boot. "Tricky. I was going to try to persuade him to help me find the real duchess, but I'm not sure I want to work with someone who would threaten a child. He's not easy to imprison with his gift. I suggest a stone—"

Before Ari could finish, black mist rose up from the ground and fastened around Durnip's unconscious form. The air reeked of dead leaves and decay. A low voice whispered, "Traitor." A shadowy tendril leapt out at Ari. He jumped backward, but it drew a line of blood down his cheek. One of the rings fell off his chain, a smoky quartz, and vanished into the darkness.

Durnip sank into the shadows and vanished before I could do more than gape.

Antonia shrieked and fell backward.

Words failed me. I pointed. "What?"

Ari applied pressure to the cut on his face. "Shit. The Living Shadow. The twelfth assassin, and the deadliest. I know nothing about them. They always work alone. I'm surprised they even rescued Durnip. And it was also odd that they targeted me first instead of you . . ."

"It sounds like you've been labeled as an enemy," I said. "I'm sorry."

"What are you apologizing for?" Ari shrugged. "Don't look so worried. No matter how tough the Living Shadow is supposed to be, the real duchess still lives. If it hadn't been for you, then *I* would have killed her first, not number twelve."

Antonia clutched tighter to his leg. "I'm sorry. I ruined all your plans."

"Nah, don't worry about it." Ari patted her head. "I can handle any shadow."

I didn't feel nearly as confident, but I wanted to reassure the child. "Of course! Ari is the strongest assassin, don't you know?"

Antonia's tears started again. "I did what he told me. Was that bad? Am I bad?"

"No, no, it's okay. It's better to cooperate in situations like that." I waved my hands.

Ari's face turned stern. "No, it's not okay. It's understandable, and I forgive you. That doesn't mean it's always okay to put yourself first. Someday, you're going to be capable of doing more than you were in that moment. You'll have the power to protect other people as well as yourself. If you feel bad, then remember this feeling and be braver next time."

That seemed awfully harsh to me. Antonia gulped and stopped her tears. She nodded.

It took us a little while to coax Antonia enough to make her let go of Ari's leg. Then we took her downstairs to visit the royal doctor's office. Although she had no outer injuries besides a pinprick to her neck, I was still worried enough to insist on it. We left her there while Ari went to arrange a permanent guard duty around her. After what had just happened, we couldn't leave the young queen alone again.

As we walked back from the doctor's office, I said, "Antonia already felt guilty enough. There was no reason for you to make her feel worse."

Ari shook his head. "I respect you for your easy ability to forgive your near death. But Antonia is not an ordinary little girl. She's a queen. There will come a day when putting herself over other people will turn her into a tyrant as bad as the late King Uctor. There may come a time when she is called to die for this kingdom in return for all the power and privilege she currently holds. If she's not willing to do that, then I will do everything in my power to support her abdication. But this kingdom cannot survive another bad monarch. Even a mediocre one might break us. An ordinary person with ordinary levels of selfishness, given the absolute power of a queen, becomes a monster. Monarchs can only go one of two ways: They must be selfless or tyrants."

The words rang true. Yet my heart could not accept them. "She's a very small girl to bear such a burden."

"My parents raised me to believe in noblesse oblige. By the time I was Antonia's age, I already understood there were circumstances under which they might sacrifice my life for the duchy. Since Antonia never knew her parents, I'm doing my best to impart the lessons she needs to learn." Ari shrugged. "Power is a burden, but it beats being powerless. Every child in this city who is starving because of the late king's selfishness would trade places with Antonia. Hell, they'd have traded places even when she was getting beaten, because plenty of them get beatings without the crown."

I knew Ari was right, because I'd once been a starving child on a barren farm. "Even so, I'd hope for a better life for children than starvation and being asked to carry adult responsibilities."

If only the world could be better. I didn't have the power to upend the entire system of monarchy, not even in my current unique position, but I'd like to move the world in a better direction. If I could get a few minutes from the crises to breathe.

Ari patted my shoulder. "We're already making progress toward helping this city. Then, the country." His gaze grew pensive. "It's been a long time since I thought about anything except revenge. Next time we have a break from assassination attempts, let's sit down and come up with a better plan. I still have lessons on leadership rattling around in my brain."

Since he'd reminded me of my danger, I asked, "Can I have one of those rings?"

Ari clutched at the necklace under his shirt. "No, I stole these fair and square."

"But they originally belonged to the duchess." Admittedly, I didn't have any legal or moral right to the Blood Duchess's possessions, despite me currently using them. My shoulders sagged. "I'm afraid of being attacked by another of the Twelve Avengers. The Living Shadow seems able to pop up anywhere."

"Their power has conditions. Admittedly, I'm not sure what they are . . . which means it's difficult to say when you're safe." He tilted his head, considering. "Most of these rings take skill to use. If you accidentally triggered the ring I used earlier with a stray thought, then you might summon up a barrier through your arm and chop it off."

"Oh." I winced. "Never mind."

"I didn't say no. I was considering what might be safe to give you." Ari removed the chain from around his neck and pulled off a ruby ring. "This one lets you detect danger. From now on, I'll stay close enough to you that you can always shout when you need help. If you keep an eye on the ring, you'll be able to summon me whenever you need me."

I slid the ring onto my finger. "Thank you so much."

"That ring was one of my favorites." Ari winked. "You're lucky you're cute."

I flushed. "You think I'm cute? But this is the duchess's body . . ."

Ari laughed. "That part certainly is strange for me. I meant your mannerisms are cute."

This only made my blush deepen. Was I reading too much into that laugh? I could be. I was awful at reading people.

To disguise my nervousness, I examined the ring on my finger. "How does it detect danger?"

"When a threat to you is nearby, it—"

The ruby exploded with crimson light.

"Glows?" I asked weakly.

A hand grabbed the back of my neck and yanked me through a portal. I barely glimpsed Ari's shocked face before the darkness closed in.

I landed on my back on a stone floor. Dazedly, I stared up at herbs hanging from the rafters. Between the barrels on the walls and the cool air, this seemed to be a windowless basement. No one would hear me scream down here.

My sister Ysabel's scowling face loomed over me. She was flanked by Alzira and Kaine, both fixing me with equally murderous glares. Ysabel wore a white silk dress and silver high heels. Even with the heels, she was short and thin as a wraith. Despite her sticklike wrists, she'd put on weight recently, entirely located on her stomach—wait a moment. That was a baby bump.

I gasped. "Hey, I'm going to be an aunt! I'm so excited!"

Ysabel planted the heel of her boot directly on my neck and ground down. "You have ten seconds to tell me where to find my little sister, or I'll kill you."

CHAPTER THIRTEEN

I gasped and choked, unable to breathe. The pointed heel drove directly into the most vulnerable part of my neck, bringing burning pain. My vision narrowed into a black tunnel with a single ray of light. I had the horrifying realization that despite the comedic nature of this situation, I could seriously die like this, murdered by my own sister. The pain of my buckling throat threatened to swallow my mind. I could barely speak. "P-please . . ."

Ysabel very slightly lessened the pressure. Hatred twisting her face, she hissed, "Five seconds."

"It's me! Bora!"

Ysabel stared at me. I'd prepared myself for disbelief, but I only got total incomprehension.

I spoke rapidly while I had the chance. "If you'll only ask Donya—"

"Don't address Donya by her first name as if you're friends!" Ysabel stomped on my throat again.

I gurgled. Red spots danced before my eyes. As my neck jerked, I glimpsed Donya lying on top of a blanket on the floor with a bandage around her head.

The instant the foot raised and air returned to me, I screamed, "What did you do to her?"

Kaine and Alzira immediately pointed at each other and said at the same time, "He did it!" and "She did it!"

"You blew up the wall with one of your thousand interminable gifts," Alzira growled.

Kaine pouted. "You got in my way when I was trying to pull Donya to safety. I saw you elbow her in the forehead."

"I did not!" Alzira reached for her sword hilt. "How dare you blame me for your errors, you unworthy dog."

"You want to go at it again?" Kaine rolled on the balls of his feet, his palms starting to glow.

"You're both responsible," Ysabel said.

Immediately, the two of them stopped and hung their heads. "Sorry, Ysabel," they mumbled.

"Why are you two picking a fight instead of healing Donya?" I shouted.

"How dare you cast aspirations on the Holy Maiden's generosity!" Alzira cried. "Ysabel promised Donya to never use a day of her own life to heal her, and she wouldn't take a day of Donya's life without permission unless the injury was lethal. She said Donya would wake up shortly. Are you questioning Her Holiness's healing knowledge?"

"Oh, that makes sense." That was just like my older sister, to be unwilling to take even a day of someone else's life without asking first. Too many people had done that to her already. It was only recently that she'd obtained the ability to use someone else's lifespan instead of her own to heal. "Yzzy, you're such a good person, even if you did step on me. Still, you didn't recognize me, and I know you must be worried, so consider it forgiven."

For the first time, I noticed my sister's disheveled condition. The bags under her eyes left her face hollowed out. She clearly hadn't combed her hair, which for Ysabel was quite unthinkable. Dirt stained her dress and, to be honest, she didn't smell like she'd had a bath lately, either.

Tears filled my eyes. "You must have rushed here to save me. Thank you. But you shouldn't be overstraining yourself if you're pregnant. Please sit down and rest."

Ysabel fixed me with a glare that could melt steel. "Now why are you acting like *we're* friends, you bitch?"

"Eeeek! I'm sorry!"

Ysabel's tone filled with malice. "Tell me where my little sister is, or I'll torture you for the information."

"Ooo! Let me!" Kaine waved his hand to volunteer. "I'll rip off her fingernails."

Alzira sneered. "Why waste time on such games? Let's skip straight to breaking her fingers."

"Do you want her to pass out from pain?" Kaine snorted. "Clearly you should let me handle this."

"I can torture people for Her Holiness every bit as well as you!" Alzira went for her sword again. "I'll do it slowly so that she feels every bit of Donya's pain."

Weren't you the one who injured Donya to begin with? "Err . . . ah . . ." I'd been trying to interject, but they were talking too loudly, and my throat hurt too much to shout.

Ysabel placed a hand on her forehead. "I'm too delicate to watch someone being tortured . . . so I'll leave, and you can figure it out between the two of you."

To my horror, my sister turned and started to walk away.

Desperation forced a scream from my aching throat. "Wait! Yzzy! I'm your sister, Bora!" My brain groped around for a memory from our childhood to convince her. I spoke rapidly: "On my fifth birthday, Uncle Urew gave me a porcelain baby doll. You were jealous, so you stole it after I refused to swap toys. After Mom gave my doll back, you buried it in the backyard, but you told everyone that I'd lost the doll." This was the perfect story to convince Ysabel, because back then she'd lied that I'd lost the doll and everyone had believed her. She'd only whispered the malicious truth late at night to me, so only the two of us knew how she'd disposed of my birthday present.

Ysabel stopped. She looked over her shoulder. Her eyes narrowed. "I'm impressed at the level of research you put into this absurd deception. Alas, your source failed you. Bora stole *my* doll, so I buried it out of spite so neither of us could have it." She turned and resumed walking away.

My fury overwhelmed my fear. I leapt to my feet. "Ysabel, you *fucking* liar, that was my doll!"

Ysabel flipped back her hair. "I would never steal a doll from my precious little sister."

She dared say that *to my face*? "Oh yes, you would! You used to 'borrow' my stuff all the time! Even though you always got better toys than me because you were older. I was perpetually wearing your hand-me-downs. And the *one* time Uncle Urew got me the better present, of course you had to have it." Kaine and Alzira gaped at me, but I didn't even care, my face flushed and panting, too focused on my sister as she spoke over me.

"That's why you stole my doll, because you were jealous of me."

"I was too scared of you to steal anything belonging to you. You used to be a huge bully, Yzzy. You would pinch me and pull my hair until Calum dragged you off me."

Ysabel sniffed. "I'll have you know that I was a very protective older sister."

"Protective, yes, I'll give you that. You were always the no-one-messes-with-my-little-sister-but-me type." When I was young, whenever other children had tried to tease me or insult my weight, Ysabel had chased them off with such scathing insults that they didn't dare come near me again. "I never realized how much you'd been protecting me until after you . . . you left." Because then, with my protector gone, the bullies had come after me in earnest. "Even if you didn't let other people mess with me, you *did* mess with me yourself, Yzzy."

"Um, I—" Alzira started to speak, only to close her mouth at the look on my sister's face. Kaine had already beaten a retreat to the doorway.

Eyes smoldering, Ysabel hissed, "Don't pretend to be the innocent one. You used to tattle on me to Mom for every last little thing."

"I told Mom when you got into trouble for your own good."

My sister snorted. "Still being sanctimonious after all these years? You didn't care if I said my prayers every night. You just wanted to get me in trouble. After I buried the doll, you went around messing up my chores and then told Mom that I'd slacked off. And she believed you!"

"Pshaw, you had that coming."

"Now you're admitting that it wasn't 'for my own good,' you little monster?"

I crossed my arms. "Are you admitting that you stole my doll?"

"It was my doll first!" Ysabel shouted.

"No, it wasn't!"

"Do you want to ask Uncle Urew?"

My eyes screwed up. "Fine, next time we see him, let's ask him. Then you'll see."

"No, then *you'll* see." Ysabel scowled. She turned to Kaine and Alzira, watching with slack-jawed expressions. "Sorry, it looks like she's my real sister after all. No torture allowed."

With a frown, Kaine edged back into the room. "Light of my heart, I've only met your sister once, but she definitely didn't look much like the Blood Duchess. Are you, uh, certain? I know you have your little problem with faces. Can I speak to you alone for a moment?"

Given that my sister was born unable to see people's faces, and often failed to recognize her own family, his conclusion made sense. Also, his hand was touching his hammer. I inched away.

Ysabel pinched the bridge of her nose. "Kaine, even *I* can tell this isn't my sister's body. It's way too tall. But that's definitely Bora inside of it. I don't know how this happened." She turned to me. "Do you have a disguise gift like Calum? You told me that you could bounce." Her tone held a slight note of accusation.

"It's not a gift. Or rather, not *my* gift." I shrugged. "It's a long story." My voice broke a little, and I massaged my throat.

Ysabel's shoulders sagged. "I'm very sorry. I could heal you, but I'm not sure the damage is worth a day of your life. And I don't have any left of mine. I'm sorry."

"Hey, what does that mean?" My voice rose with concern.

"The only reason Ysabel can live is because of a regeneration ability. She has none of her own days left to give." Despite the calmness of Kaine's explanation, his gaze burned. Every muscle in his body tensed. I had the prickly sensation of facing down a wolf ready to lunge.

Then we were absolutely *not* going to let my sister heal me—or anyone—with her own life. I met his gaze with an equally fierce one of my own. He looked surprised.

"This silly little injury isn't worth the price. I'm feeling better already." I exaggerated a bit to make her feel better. Honestly, I felt glad my sister wasn't spending her life so recklessly any longer. If Kaine had been behind this change, then I approved of him. "I'm thirstier than a cow in heat, though."

"Here." Kaine spun his hand twice, first making a cup appear, then filling it with water.

What a useful ability. I chugged the water. "Thank you. Huh, I feel way better."

"I added rejuvenating properties to the water." He watched me closely, then nodded. Turning to my sister, he said, "I don't know Bora well enough to tell if it's her, but she's no duchess. Nobility doesn't know anything about cows."

"I *do* know my own sister." Ysabel's shoulders sagged. "Or at least, I ought to. I really am very sorry." She hung her head.

"Aw, Yzzy, you couldn't have known. You were only threatening the duchess because you wanted to save me. It means a lot to me that you'd come all the way out here to rescue me. Although you shouldn't torture people." I rubbed my neck. It didn't even feel bruised.

Ysabel put her nose up in the air. "I'm not a torturer. I was going to stop them before they actually broke a finger—I figured the threat would be enough to make a spoiled duchess talk."

"I wasn't bluffing," Kaine said.

"I know you weren't—that's what made you so convincing." Ysabel laughed.

I wondered if I believed her. Ysabel was always good at putting on a façade of being an innocent little angel, but she generally did whatever she felt she had to in order to protect her own. No matter. I didn't blame her for trying to save me. I'd let her put on a good face in front of her little sister. "I told you, I'm not angry. Except why didn't you tell me that you're pregnant? I'm a bit angry about that."

Ysabel frowned. “I *did* tell you. Then you passed along the information to our mother, who started nagging me to reconcile with her because she wanted to be a grandmother, so I stopped telling you things I didn’t want Mom to know.”

“I never got that letter! I had no idea!” I paled. “Mom must have been going through my mail. Please, Yzzy, you’ve got to believe me. I’m not a child any longer—I don’t tattle. I know you have valid reasons to be upset with both our parents.”

Ysabel smiled, a mixture of relief and joy. She pulled me into a hug. “I believe you.”

It felt nice to get a hug from someone after everything I’d been through over the last couple of days. Even though my sister smelled sweaty and slightly dirty, I still melted into her embrace. I sniffled. The tears snuck up on me, because after so much stress, someone was finally comforting me.

“There, there.” Ysabel patted my shoulder. “It’s okay. You can cry.”

Even after spending so long apart, it amazed me how easily I drew comfort from her. We’d fallen back into the old pattern of how she used to comfort me after another kid insulted me. I hid my face in her shoulder, a little embarrassed to show my tears with two other people present. “It’s just been . . . it’s been so hard . . . ever since I accidentally got stuck in the duchess’s body.”

Ysabel made a sympathetic noise in the back of her throat. “What a dreadful thing to happen to you. Where’s your real body?”

“I . . . I don’t even know.” I sniffled again. “The Blood Duchess ran off in it. For all I know, she’s already gotten me killed.” I started crying in earnest.

Ysabel hugged me tighter. “We’ll find a way to get your body back. Then I’ll take you on a lovely relaxing vacation back to Conollia. You might consider moving there. I don’t know why you’d want to live with Mom when she goes through your mail. Did she guilt you into looking after her?”

I chuckled nervously, still unwilling to admit to my sister how Falael had scammed me out of her money (purchased dearly with her own lifespan). “Enough about me! I’m fine.” I took her by the shoulders, stepping slightly away. "Let's talk about you. I'm so excited about my new niece or nephew. Do you have baby names picked out?"

Ysabel frowned. "No, we're still going to talk about *you*. How you ended up body-swapped is way more urgent."

"Oh, right." I bit my lip, trying to figure out where to even begin. "You know about the Blood Duchess declaring herself regent, right?"

Wrinkles formed on Ysabel's forehead. "The last I heard, Duchess Hedri sent me a letter demanding I acknowledge her as Arahasnor's ruler or she'd kill my sister. I assume you didn't take yourself hostage."

Kaine nodded. "Yeah, because I swore to chop off the head of whoever threatened my sister-in-law. Let me know if that was you so I can take it back."

Alzira crossed her arms. "I, too, swore to murder whoever threatened Her Holiness's sister, and I do not treat my word as lightly as this fool." She gestured toward Kaine. "Even if you sent the threat, you still have to die."

"It wasn't me!" I shouted. "The Blood Duchess tried to arrest me. Donya helped me escape. I fled the city. I planned to ask you for help, Yzzy. There was a flash of light, and I turned into the Blood Duchess. Everyone has been trying to kill me ever since!"

Ysabel put her arms around me and glared at Kaine and Alzira. "Both of you, take two steps back and face the wall. You're scaring my little sister."

Hanging their heads, they obeyed.

Ysabel rocked me, stroking my hair. "Did you see anyone around who might have swapped you?"

"We know who swapped me. Princess—I mean, Queen—Antonia did it by accident. She wanted someone kind to replace the Blood Duchess, who was beating her."

"No wonder she ended up with you, then." Ysabel tucked back a lock of my hair. "Does the queen know how to swap you back?"

"She doesn't. We still haven't figured out the price of her gift, so we don't know how to trigger it. She did get tired and faint after using her power. She was out for a while."

"For such a strong ability, it must have a higher price than mere exhaustion." Ysabel raised her voice. "Kaine, have you ever heard of a body-swapping gift?"

His voice muffled from facing away, he replied, "That's not one of mine. Sure does sound useful, though. I don't know what price it has."

Ysabel turned back to me. "We'll figure it out. In the worst-case scenario, I know ways to alter physical appearances."

"Actually, I need to stay in this body for now." I swallowed. "It turns out the late king sold out our country to more than one group. The Guild of Slavers showed up next."

My sister's face transformed, her eyes turning glacial and her fingers whitening as she squeezed her hands into fists. She looked ready to rip out someone's throat with her clenched teeth. I knew her well enough to see the hint of fear as well as anger lurking in her eyes.

I knew exactly what she was thinking. "We won't let that happen, Yzzy." I put a hand on her arm. "Donya came up with a plan. I'm going to act the part of a villainess to save Arahasnor." In short order, I filled Ysabel in on everything that had happened.

When I was done, Ysabel touched her forehead as if dizzy. "Wait, you made the assassin who tried to kill you into your bodyguard?"

"It was only a small misunderstanding. Araceli is a wonderful person."

"And you took over a country . . ." Ysabel swayed.

"I didn't have any choice. I wanted to run away, but I couldn't let the slavers take over." I peered at my sister's face through half-open eyes. "Are you angry?"

"Oh, I'm angry, but not at *you*." Ysabel paced the basement, waving her fists. "I can't believe that as soon as I take my eyes off Arahasnor, this happens. People think they don't have to be afraid of me just because I moved to Conollia? They're in for an unpleasant surprise!"

From the floor, Donya groaned, low and long.

Both Kaine and Alzira leapt away from the wall to tend to her. Alzira gasped. "Your Holiness! She's stirring."

Donya sat up and rubbed the bandage on her head. "What happened to me?"

Immediately, Kaine and Alzira pointed at each other and chorused, "It wasn't *my* fault."

Ysabel raised her voice. "Donya, how could you drag my sister into this mess by letting her pretend to be the Blood Duchess? I asked you to look after her! Not use her!"

"I'm sorry." Donya hung her head.

"She didn't drag me into anything," I said. "Don't shout at her; she's injured. We didn't have any good options. I couldn't have left the city because the duchess is being targeted by the Twelve Avengers. I had no choice but to pretend."

"They're the Eleven Avengers, now," Kaine said. "One of them accepted a contract on my life a few months ago. Honestly, not even the most skilled assassin I've killed."

"Thank you for coming to save us, Ysabel," Donya said.

Ysabel winced. "It was a rather more violent rescue than I intended. And I was too late. If not for the body-swapping incident, you'd have already been executed by the Blood Duchess." Her shoulders sagged. "I'm sorry. Bora is right—I have no right to criticize you for doing your best in a bad situation."

"I'm impressed you got here so fast," Donya said.

Kaine raised his hand. "I can teleport short distances. I obtained the ability by figuring out how to merge three of my minor abilities."

"He's gotten even more indestructible," Alzira muttered in a dissatisfied voice.

"The ability still has some kinks to work out," Ysabel said with one eyebrow raised.

It was then that I realized how cold it was in the cellar. I couldn't figure out why the temperature had dropped several degrees. My sister glared at her husband. He looked at his feet.

Ysabel put her hands on her hips. "You claimed you could get us through the city walls without needing to blow them up."

Kaine mumbled, "I did, dear."

"And what's currently at the South Gate?"

"A hole in the city wall, dear. I'm sorry, dear."

"Not to mention the smoking ruins of the gardens I carefully constructed around the gates!"

"I'll buy you new flowers and help you plant them, dear. I'm sorry, dear. I love you, dear."

"Why do you insist on destroying my carefully constructed city walls every time you come here?" Ysabel threw up her hands. "I get it, plenty of local fools keep provoking you. I wouldn't blame you one bit if you ravaged the city at this point. Burn down the palace and slaughter the inhabitants if you must, but my walls were innocent. The walls did nothing wrong."

My drama queen sister must be joking. Still, I found this whole conversation bizarre. Anyone seeing the fear in Kaine's eyes would have questioned who was the dark lord and who was the holy maiden. What was so important about some granite walls? But Donya muttered under her breath, "He damaged the walls again? He's in so much trouble."

I coughed. "I hate to interrupt this riveting conversation, but Ar—people will be worried about me. Since you sort of kidnapped me."

Donya shot to her feet. "How long has it been? What time is it? Oh no! The Dwarven Caves sent word that their delegation will arrive by evening! We have barely any time left to prepare."

"Why would the dwarves come here?" I asked. Dwarves were notoriously insular and rarely traveled outside of the World Games.

"They're the second group King Uctor sold the kingdom to."

"Oooo." I nodded. "That sounds bad."

"The Dwarven Caves, huh?" Ysabel steepled her fingers. "Now I wish I'd brought Ua'la'sur along. They're terrified of her. Kaine's teleportation could carry three people at most—but no matter. She already gave me certain inside information about the dwarven leadership. It will be my pleasure to help you out with this one."

As my sister threw back her head and laughed evilly, I realized she'd definitely have been a better dark lord than her husband.

CHAPTER FOURTEEN

As soon as we marched up the stairs, Araceli stormed down the hallway. She wore the same black assassin outfit as the time she'd tried to kill me. All the running had left her face flushed and her hair disheveled. Rings covered all of her fingers. A glowing light from a golden band pointed at us. "Found you!" she cried. "If you're one of the Twelve Avengers, too, this isn't the real Blood Duchess—"

"It's all right." I stepped between them with my hands raised, hoping to stave off a fight. "Meet my sister, Ysabel. She came here to rescue me."

Araceli lowered her hand. "She knows who you are now?"

"Yes." I smiled to show the danger had passed.

"Ysabel, as in the Holy Maiden?" Araceli flushed. She dropped into a curtsey. "It's an honor, Your Holiness."

"A pleasure to meet you," Ysabel said, inclining her head, "unless you're here to assassinate my husband after trying to kill my sister?"

"No, my target is Duchess Hedri—the *real* duchess. I'm Araceli, Your Holiness."

"A potential suitor for Bora," Donya whispered to Ysabel. "I already gave her the Big Sister Intimidation Talk."

"Nice. I knew I could count on you." Ysabel gave Donya a fist bump.

I turned crimson, a color painfully evident on my current pale skin. If I'd overheard that, Araceli might have, too. Talk about mortifying! Why did my older sister live to embarrass me, even dragging innocent bystanders into it? "It's not like that! Araceli just pretended to flirt with me to help me deal with a problem—" I still didn't want to explain about Falael to my sister. "It wasn't a big deal. There's nothing between us."

"That's right." Araceli seemed to wither. "I should get changed. Most of the palace knows me as a maid, not an assassin, and I plan to keep it that way. This clothing has magical protections, or I wouldn't have worn it."

"It looks great on you," I said. "Uh, I'm very grateful you came to save me." The attempted mass resignation of the guard had made it painfully obvious I couldn't count on many people in a crisis. "Seriously, thank you."

She shrugged, seeming uncomfortable with the praise. "It's nothing. As you said." She turned and walked away.

I might have said something else, but then Ysabel swept past me. "To the royal planning room," she ordered. "We have a great deal to discuss before the dwarven delegation arrives."

The planning room was full of world maps, spread across the stone table and plastered on the walls. Though it was a fairly large room, the filing cabinets and racks of maps made it seem cramped. There were no windows, only a gas lamp overhead. The space reeked of gas and parchment. A world globe sat next to the golden throne at the head of the table. Waves moved slightly across the painted water. If I looked closer, I could also see the real-time movement of storms. Naturally, my sister sat on the throne. No one would have dared challenge her for it. Once we were all seated, Ysabel took charge like an expert. "My dear friend Ua'la'sur used to be queen of the dwarves, and she dished out all the dirt to me."

My sister knew the Queen of Nightmares? I whistled under my breath. I couldn't say I was surprised, not with the company she usually kept.

Ysabel continued, "There was a big scandal recently when the secretary of the treasury cleaned out a good bit of the government's money and ran away to a foreign country. It caused serious unrest. The prime minister tried to cover it up, but word still got out. Ua'la'sur even had people reaching out to her asking if she was interested in starting a rebellion to return to power. She wasn't."

Smart woman, I thought. Being a ruler isn't as much fun as it looks from the outside.

"This is bad news," Donya muttered.

"Why?" I asked. This all sounded like useful blackmail material.

Ysabel said, "As Donya has guessed, this move to take over Arahasnor is the prime minister's ploy to hold on to power. He's probably planning to pretend that buying our country is where all the money went—even though he got the rights to the regency dirt cheap in the Games."

Donya said, "If it's a matter of politics and pride, then the dwarven delegation won't back down easily. Even worse, they may be spoiling for a fight. Nothing like foreign conflict to help a leader raise his popularity at home. They'll be looking for trouble with us."

Kaine leaned back in his chair. "Some leaders are the worst. Who would drag their people into a war just for pride? My honey bunny taught me that's what assassination is for—when someone pisses you off but there's an army between you and them."

Ysabel gave Kaine a sweet look. "They can't wage war on us—they're oathbound like all nations not to fight any other signatory to the Conclave of Kings. They're probably aiming for a long, twisty court case. Unfortunately, we can't afford to take a long time. Our strategy will be to get rid of all foreign threats quickly, then swap Bora and the Blood Duchess back."

I nodded vigorously, badly wanting to be back in my own body.

Ysabel's lips peeled back into a feral grin. "For that reason, we need to convince the dwarven delegation that we're far more trouble than they're willing to bite off. We need to show them a real villainess."

I didn't like how everyone looked at me as she said that.

"To start, we'll have Bora take me hostage," Ysabel said.

I raised my hand. "Why am I doing that?"

"So we can pretend that Kaine is being threatened into protecting you," Ysabel said. "We need an excuse to use my hubby's firepower without involving Conollia in the political machinations."

I nodded. "That makes sense." I remembered how absolutely everyone in the city had been terrified of Kaine's arrival. No one wanted to fight the former dark lord.

Kaine shrugged. "I could just destroy the dwarves without the need for this song and dance."

Ysabel raised an eyebrow at him. "Didn't you just say that good leaders shouldn't drag their people into conflict?"

"Oh, it won't be necessary to call in the Conollian army. I can take them by myself. If they're causing trouble for my sister-in-law, then this is personal."

"You're a king. Everything you do involves Conollia."

"Not if I threaten them to never come near my country," Kaine insisted.

Ysabel sighed. "If we bring home a war with the Dwarven Caves, then Durrian will be very upset with both of us."

"Oh." Kaine's brow wrinkled. "We can't have that."

"Just picture his tired, stressed-out, *sad* face."

Kaine shuddered. "We'll do it your way, dear."

"Thank you." Ysabel turned back to me. "After we put on a show and threaten the dwarves a bit, then we'll switch to bribery. I know the location of their missing secretary of the treasury. I'll let you offer that up as a trade, so they can give up the rights to our kingdom but still save face."

I tapped my chin. "The carrot-and-stick approach. Clever." It felt good to have Ysabel around again. If only Calum was still here too . . .

Cradling her head in her hands, Donya mumbled, "It's way better than anything I came up with. We might as well try." She sounded absolutely exhausted. I was glad Ysabel had shown up to help her. If only I could have been more use before this. I was in way over my head, and I knew it.

Ysabel patted Donya on the shoulder. "Chin up! This is going to be fun."

Both Donya and I gave her the glare that she deserved.

When I'd agreed to act the part of the villainess, I hadn't fully thought through what it would entail.

As Araceli tied up the laces on the back of my dress, I groaned. "I don't think I can do this."

"You did great last time." Araceli patted my shoulder.

"Last time I was riding high on adrenaline and anger." I gnawed on my lip. This had all seemed so much easier in the planning room. Now I had to go out there and threaten people way more important than me. My hands shook.

Araceli stepped around to face me and meet my eyes. "Would it help if I stay somewhere nearby so I can rescue you if you start to falter?"

"Yes, please," I whispered.

"Then I will. I'll help you get through this. Turn around so I can do your hair." Araceli spun me to face the mirror.

A stranger stared back at me. Today's dress was red as blood with a ruffled skirt, rubies dotting the bodice and the long, flowing sleeves. A cloth rose jutted at the hip. The dress was strapless with puffs of lace around my shoulders and a massive ruby brooch centered between my breasts. It bared an embarrassing amount of cleavage. My ears felt heavy from the long teardrop garnet earrings I wore. The combination of a crown and a heavy golden necklace made me feel like my head was being pulled downward. The rings on my fingers were all fakes, but I had no choice but to wear them as the duchess's famous style no matter how much they hurt my knuckles. The duchess's long blonde hair frizzed in all directions before Araceli grabbed clumps and started to tame it into a braided bun.

I shifted. I was sweating again. Ugh, I always felt hot in this body. As I moved, my stomach jiggled. I flinched as I watched the waves in the mirror. It brought back an old, dark impulse. Keeping busy had staved off the thoughts. Now they returned.

At one point, I'd hated mirrors. I'd covered every last one in my house. It had taken me a long time to reach a tentative truce with my body. This body? It wasn't me, so I had no self-love for it. I'd never even liked Duchess Hedri before I'd been forced into such great intimacy with her, which made it even harder. The cold blue eyes staring at me in the mirror reminded me of the duchess casually ordering my death.

My back and knees hurt, all the more when I'd been stuffed into strange fancy outfits. I couldn't get used to the height. The body didn't move how I was accustomed to and kept bumping into things. It was *fat.*

Years ago, late one evening after leaning over the toilet retching, I'd noticed that my teeth had signs of decay and my hair had gotten thinner. My knuckle had a callus from sticking it down my throat so many times. I'd tortured my body trying to make it look like I wanted it to and ended up hating myself even more.

Then and there, I had decided to stop letting the word "fat" have power over me. It hadn't worked so easily, of course. I'd faked it until I made it. (Mostly made it.)

Now I'd been thrown off my equilibrium. I lurked uneasily inside this strange, heavy body. It felt unfair that I'd somehow gained weight without doing anything except being body-swapped. Irrational, I knew. That was hardly the most unfair thing about this situation. I'd been trying to stop caring about weight at all. But it bothered me the most. I felt torn between desperately trying to shed the extra pounds with another round of gorging myself on food and throwing up because it was a lost cause. I knew how easy it would be for me to slip back into doing both.

"I look awful," I whispered.

Araceli removed a pin between her lips to speak. "You look great."

I glanced down at my feet, away from that horrible mirror. "I didn't mean to insult your handiwork. You've done the best you could with the materials you had available."

"I'm not flattering you. Or myself. I mean it."

"Uh-huh," I mumbled, wanting to change the topic.

"Just look at you." Araceli swept a hand down my dress. "Magnificent, every inch. You've got eyes like a pair of diamonds. They perfectly suit that sharp chin. Such soft, voluminous hair. I was always jealous of the duchess's hair, to be honest. Mine is so thin. Your bosom . . . hmm, I'd probably better stop before I sound crude, but suffice it to say the dress complements it. The heels make you look even taller and more imposing. The real duchess rarely wore high heels, so I'm glad you let me put you in them, because they match the style you have going. Between the spiky metal on your dress and the crown, you look like a battle goddess ready to burn this city down if it doesn't bow before you."

"When you say imposing, you mean fat, right? All the rubies in the bodice only make me look even thicker around the middle. The skirt is huge, and I hate it!" The words poured out of me like a torrent.

"Some people like big women," Araceli said. "Not everyone, of course. Court fashion says a woman shouldn't be tall. I say bullshit. Anyone who isn't into giant, big-boned women won't be your target audience. So what? Rather than trying to make yourself smaller to suit other people, why not play up your strengths? Go ahead and show off those long legs with some heels. Adorn a gemstone on every acre of flesh. Let the ample bosom have freedom. You look magnificent."

The passion in her voice moved me. I gazed at my reflection again. This time, I also took in Araceli standing next to me, holding my shoulders. She had such sincerity in her gaze that I couldn't help but believe she meant every word. When I looked at her eyes, then back at my reflection, I could start to see what she saw. The duchess did look intimidating, confident, and dangerous.

"Uh, thank you." I tugged at a bit of lace on my sleeve, blushing again, unable to meet Araceli's eyes except in the mirror. "Soooooo, do you like big women?" Sweet Sun God, I hadn't meant to ask that, it had just slipped out.

"Of course I do. What do you think that speech was about?" Araceli winked at me. "You don't seem comfortable in this body—did you used to be skinny?"

"No, actually, I, uh . . . I wasn't comfortable in my original body, either." I looked away. "Not all of the time, at least. Sometimes. I'd gotten better about it."

"I bet you were adorable, just like you are right now." Araceli seemed about to say something, then she stopped herself. "Not that it's any of my business. I hope I didn't make you feel uncomfortable."

"No, not at all! You made me feel much better. Thank you. You did a wonderful job on the outfit—no backhanded compliment this time, just a sincere one."

"You're welcome." Araceli patted my cheek. "You're a goddess, and if she doesn't see it, that's her problem." A note of wistfulness entered her voice.

Araceli left while I was still trying to puzzle out who "she" was. I supposed the dwarven ambassador must be female?

A page poked his head in the door. "Um. I've been given a message from Countess Donya. She said the dwarven delegation has arrived. She promised to stall them as long as possible while you make it to the throne room."

I had no time for further pondering. It was showtime.

CHAPTER FIFTEEN

I sat on the golden throne, sweating and trying not to let it show. My eyes slipped over to the side door where Araceli had promised to stay in case I needed her.

The throne room was empty except for Ysabel, Alzira, and Kaine. Alzira fingered her sword hilt while Kaine leaned against the wall and dozed off.

Ysabel paced the carpet in front of me. "How do I look? Properly disheveled? I did the best I could on short notice." My older sister wore a plain white smock resembling a prisoner's clothing. Manacles, made of solid gold, chained her wrists together. I wondered how she'd gotten those on such short notice. She'd ordered a page to the correct store with confidence, like she purchased fancy chains all the time. Her curly hair fell over her shoulders in a tangled mess. Wet streaks imitating tear tracks ran down her cheeks, and she had a smudge of dirt on her face.

"You look very much like a prisoner," I said. And it was unfair how good it looked on her.

"Do you think the bare feet are too much?" Ysabel lifted a foot to examine her soles.

I hadn't the slightest idea. "I think it's fine?"

"Let's practice." Ysabel sat on the floor next to my throne and looped her chains over the royal specter so it looked like I was holding her close. "Remember your line?"

I cleared my throat. "I have taken the Holy Maiden hostage. I have no fear of the Conclave of Kings or Dark Lord Kaine!" Oh no, my voice came out too squeaky. I tried to deepen my tone. “Ahem. If you take one step forward, I’ll strangle her pretty little throat.”

“Woe,” Ysabel wailed, dabbing her eyes. “Please, don’t hurt me!”

Alzira drew her sword. “How dare you threaten Her Holiness. I will smite you!”

“Eep! I’m sorry!” I squealed, cowering down in my throne.

Ysabel drew herself up to her full height, letting the chains slip off the specter, and glared. “Alzira, did you just draw your sword on my sister?”

Alzira flinched. “I’m sorry, Your Holiness. It was a reflex. I forgot that it was all an act for a moment because you sounded so convincing. You’re an amazing actress.”

“Don’t try to flatter your way out of this one.” Ysabel tapped her foot. “If you can’t stick to the script, then leave until we’re done.”

“I need to guard you, Your Holiness!” Alzira protested.

“You can guard me from the balcony.” Ysabel inclined her head above. “Stay out of sight, and if you make one more sound, I’m banning you from the throne room entirely.”

“Yes, Your Holiness.” Alzira sighed, slinking away.

I exhaled in relief as soon as she left. Just the pressure from Alzira’s glare had nearly made me wet myself. Had Araceli called me intimidating? Clearly it was only on the outside. Alzira could have scared a real goddess, much less a fake one like me.

“Sorry about that.” Ysabel returned to kneeling by the throne. “Your next line?”

I tried to remember. “As long as I control the Holy Maiden, then Dark Lord Kaine is my servant!”

Ysabel burst into sobs. “Please, someone save me!”

“Hmm?” Kaine jolted out of his slumber at the sound of his name. His gaze fell upon Ysabel, huddled against the throne and crying.

Kaine’s eyes narrowed. Energy exploded from his body in waves, freezing the room in place. Every muscle in my body wanted to run, but I couldn’t move. His iron irises pinned me in place. Softly, yet with weight behind each word, Kaine asked, “Did you make my wife cry?”

Only a moan came from my mouth. This time I did piss myself. Just a little. I'd never been more grateful for the massive layers of fabric hiding my shame. I couldn't blink. I could barely even breathe. My chin wobbled like a dinghy in a storm.

Kaine reached for the hammer on his back. "I'm going to destroy this country now."

"Stop!" Ysabel shrieked.

Kaine blinked. "If wifey-poo cries, that means it's time for me to lay the smackdown. Don't worry, dear, I'm already inside the walls, so I can't harm them. I'll be careful to step around the flower gardens as I burn the city down."

Ysabel massaged her forehead. "I'm not truly being taken hostage, I'm pretending. Don't you remember the plan we discussed?"

Kaine shrugged. "There were words. You said I couldn't beat up the dwarven delegation, but I'm still not clear on why. We've got Jiang's old cane to deal with any pesky oaths holding me back from battle. I can kill anyone who stands in your way. If this plan makes you cry, then it's a stupid plan. I won't let you keep on suffering for everyone else's sake. I made a vow to never let you sacrifice yourself for the greater good again."

"Darling, I'm acting. I'm not crying for real." Ysabel lowered her voice. "Like those times when you cry and say no, but you don't actually want me to stop."

Dark Lady be damned. I just learned far more than I ever, ever wanted to know about my sister's sex life. Going to shove that deep down my memory hole and never think about it again.

Kaine's eyes lit up. "Ooo, I understand now. Got it, carry on."

Ysabel turned back and tossed her chains at me. "Ready to begin again?"

I whispered, "Uh, Yzzy? Could you make your husband leave? I'm too scared to say my lines with him here . . ."

Ysabel turned to Kaine. "Love, would you do me a favor? Could you go to the balcony and stop Alzira from leaping out and attacking every time I pretend to be threatened? I'd really appreciate it."

"Of course." Kaine beamed. "Anything for you, honey bunny."

"Thank you. You're the only one I can count on." Ysabel kissed Kaine before he left.

As soon as Kaine was gone, I could breathe again. Even when he hadn't been actively on the verge of murder, his very presence had filled the room with pressure. Why were all my sister's allies a bunch of psychos?

A page stood at the entranceway and bellowed, "Presenting the dwarven ambassador, Gen'le and his secretary, Ma'qas!"

The delegation was here already? But I hadn't finished practicing yet! I paled and cowered on the throne.

Ysabel collapsed to a heap at the foot of the throne, her hand over her forehead as if in a dramatic faint. Her chin trembled and her eyes even took on the dull, lifeless quality of despair.

I thought back to that play I'd been in as a child. Where I had failed at my role as tree, my older sister had been on the center stage acting her heart out in the part of Holy Maiden Ava, Bride of the Sun God. She gave me the silent treatment for a week after I accidentally knocked over the painted forest and clonked her over the head during her big moment. Come to think of it, that was around the same time my doll from Uncle Urew went missing. She definitely took revenge! So much for her proclamations of innocence!

A row of guards in Sherdan uniforms strode in first, lining the room to protect the lady regent. Then the dwarven ambassador followed, a man in a silk doublet with a thick, black beard. A dwarven woman trailed after him in a modest purple dress buttoned up high. She carried a notebook.

Ambassador Gen'le stopped before the throne and bowed his head slightly. "Duchess Hedri, the late King Uctor promised control of the future regency of Arahasnor to both my country and yours. Obviously this puts both of our nations in a difficult situation. We're prepared to negotiate who will step aside in exchange for compensation."

Completely reasonable words. Unfortunately, I had no intention of handing my country over to either foreign power. Also, Arahasnor didn't have nearly enough money to pay compensation. That's why I had no choice but to be unreasonable in return.

I threw back my head and laughed. "You think you have the authority to negotiate with me? A new country like yours that carelessly tossed aside your nobility and let commoners vote? What nonsense! Maybe your brains are as small as your bodies!"

A muscle twitched in the ambassador's cheek. "Regardless of your opinion of my nation, our claim is valid. We brought documentation." His gaze held contempt, and it made me inwardly squirm.

That insult had been both over the line and frankly none too clever either. Somehow, I kept my chin raised. I was ashamed of how I was acting. But I was *supposed* to be evil. How else could I sell this deception?

I sneered. "Do you think I care about your documentation? Pieces of paper aren't power. This is power!" I spread my arms wide, pointing at the guards. "And this is power!" I jerked on the chains holding my sister.

Ysabel immediately burst into tears. Damn, she was good at crying on command. If only I had that skill—although I wished I could *stop* crying whenever I wanted to.

Ambassador Gen'le startled, noticing Ysabel for the first time. She'd been crouching behind the throne before. "Who is this? What have you done to this poor woman?"

"I have taken the Holy Maiden hostage! I have no fear of the Conclave of Kings or Dark Lord Kaine. If you take one step forward, then I'll strangle her pretty little throat." Good, I remembered my line. My voice didn't waver—I was getting better at this. Was I supposed to do something now? Belatedly, I yanked on the chain again.

"Please, don't hurt me!" Ysabel gazed up, clasping her hands pleadingly. Her curls fell artfully over one eye. My sister had a talent for weeping beautifully. Her sobs sounded delicate instead of grating on the ears. Her shoulders heaved in a way that showed off her chest. Even her makeup remained intact.

Ambassador Gen'le shuddered. "You . . . how could you do such a horrible thing? Do you want Dark Lord Kaine to devastate the world? The Conclave barely stopped him the first time! Everyone knows he adores his wife."

"That's exactly why I've done it. As long as I control the Holy Maiden, then Dark Lord Kaine himself is my servant. I'll be unstoppable."

"Please, someone save me." Ysabel batted her eyes imploringly. Her tone was filled with heart-wrenching terror. But I knew better. When my older sister was actually scared, she tried to hide it behind a mask. She was too proud to let other people see her fear. In my sisterly eyes, I could tell she was having fun playing this role.

Ambassador Gen'le, however, looked completely taken in by my sister's act. He stepped forward, reaching out a hand as if to help her. His secretary grabbed him and pulled him back.

"Uh-uh." I wagged my finger as if at a disobedient child. "Do you want your kingdom to burn under my armies and Kaine's power?"

"You're holding the leash on a dragon," Ambassador Gen'le growled. "Kaine can't be controlled."

I agreed. After what had happened earlier, I was fairly certain if I'd been actually threatening Ysabel, then I'd already be dead. But the knowledge it was all fake lent me courage. I jerked on the chain again. "Kaine won't dare make a move as long as I have his darling wife in my possession."

Ysabel buried her face in her hands. "Please, forget about me. Even though the Blood Duchess threatened to rip off all my fingernails and use my blood for her facial massage. She said she would cut off my flesh bit by bit. Even if I die, it will be worth it to stop this madwoman. She even threatened to slaughter every woman prettier than her in the city."

I what now? Yzzy, are you framing me for more crimes? This is like our childhood all over again. Then I remembered that I was supposed to be a villainess, so Ysabel was helping me. I put a finger to my lips and laughed from my belly. "Oh-ho-ho-ho-ho! Why stop at the women? Any man prettier than me should die, too! Unless they're willing to serve in my bed, of course."

Ysabel dabbed her eyes. "When I think about what she did to that horse who bit her . . ."

Even the crime of animal abuse had been hung around my neck now? What was I supposed to have done to some poor, innocent horse? Despite the lack of details, Ambassador Gen'le looked deeply impressed and intimidated.

"She even threatened to rip the fetus from my womb early and send it back in a box to my husband!" Ysabel clutched at her stomach.

Big sister, you're going a bit too far! I didn't want to become quite that twisted. How had she even thought of something so deranged?

Ambassador Gen'le gasped and swayed on his feet. "A new dark lord has arisen! The most terrible one yet!"

Hey, I hadn't even done anything yet. At least this meant everything was going according to plan. Was it time to move on to the next stage yet?

Sure enough, Donya flung open the door and strode in. She was followed by a series of maids holding jewelry boxes. "Your Grace, please accept these offerings, and in exchange, don't hurt the Holy Maiden any longer."

Ysabel fell over sideways as if just being in my general presence sickened her.

The maids paraded forward, presenting the Royal Jewels. The sacred treasures of our kingdom for centuries—which, frankly, was the only reason they hadn't been sold off yet.

The dwarven ambassador and his secretary gaped as each treasure was presented. A pearl necklace, an emerald ring, a string of rubies, a diamond-studded circlet. The maids placed each one on my body, including a crown on top of the first crown. The flow kept coming, until I was wearing half a dozen necklaces, three rings on each finger, and bracelets nearly to my elbow.

So heavy! I could barely move!

Finally, Donya knelt down and presented an emerald set in a golden flower brooch. It glowed brightly, casting rainbows across the room.

Ambassador Gen'le inhaled deeply. He knew the legend behind this particular piece: Holy Maiden Ava was said to have blessed it such that as long as the brooch remained in Arahasnor's borders, the royal line would always continue. The perpetual light it exuded was proof of its divine power. Because it was so important, the brooch was never worn. It was kept locked up in a safe in the palace treasure room and guarded at all times. For Arahasnor to bring this out and offer it to me was a violation of our traditions and a sign of complete and utter submission.

I turned up my lip. As planned, I recited my line: "You dare offer me an *emerald*? Don't you see that I'm wearing red? This doesn't match my outfit at all!"

"This is the greatest treasure of Arahasnor," Donya said. "You ordered us to bring all treasures to you." Not the best actress—her delivery came out flat. Perhaps we could pass it off as numb terror?

Summoning all my nerve, my heart pounding in my chest, I picked up the brooch. Then I threw it at Donya's face.

As it bounced off her nose and hit the floor, I wanted to sob. So much money! More than I'd ever touched in my entire life! Enough to feed my entire village! I wanted to sink into the floor and die. Instead, I composed my lips into a smile. "Oops, sorry, my hand slipped. Maybe because your greatest treasure was a bit too lightweight? Don't you think that a proper gemstone should be double that size?"

Donya knelt down and picked up the brooch. "I'm very sorry, Your Grace." The gem looked intact. I thought. I hoped. It had better be intact, or I would be in so much theological trouble. Wait, did I see . . . a tiny chip? My heart attempted to leap out of my throat and strangle me.

Ambassador Gen'le looked as though he might faint. "The sacred treasure of Ava!"

I wanted to faint even more than he did. What if I fell over dead from sacrilege? I'd begged everyone to let me use a fake, but they all said it wouldn't glow properly. I was going to get struck by lightning from the Sun God. I'd never dare go outside again.

To falter now would ruin everything and waste all my efforts. Nothing for it but to keep pressing on with this act until the bitter end.

I yanked on my pearl necklace. "Hmm, these don't look big enough. I still don't feel satisfied. I desire more jewelry." Actually, one more necklace might cause my neck to snap. Everything felt so heavy, I'd tip over if anyone pushed me. "Don't you think I could fit four rings on each finger?" I stretched out my hand. It took a lot of effort, given how weighed down I was. The bracelets rubbed uncomfortably against each other. *Please, just let this be over already.*

"This is all the jewelry in the royal coffers," Donya said.

"Humph! Then I'll have to send Kaine to conquer another country for me." I turned to look at the two dwarves.

The ambassador took a step backward. His cheeks paled and his beard twitched.

With great effort, I stopped my head from nodding over under the weight of two crowns. "I've heard the Dwarven Caves mine the greatest treasures in the world. I know! I should conquer *your* nation next."

Ambassador Gen'le clutched his assistant's arm.

"Oh no! Please don't!" Ysabel clasped her hands together. "I'm sure they never meant to try to claim what belongs to you. They'll leave and never do it again."

The ambassador nodded furiously. "We'd never dare stand up against your might. We'll sign papers forfeiting all claim to Arahasnor, then leave at once." And likely report me to the Conclave of Kings the instant they left, but I didn't blame them for saying whatever they needed to in order to get out of this situation.

"Humph." I tapped my chin, pretending to consider. "But I still desire jewels."

"Your Grace, the dwarves predominantly mine gold and silver, not gems. Please have mercy on them," Ysabel pleaded.

"Oh, well." I leaned back on my chair. "I hardly need gold—I have too much of it already. Perhaps I can be merciful and merely demand a tribute of what gems they do possess. Get those two lowly creatures out of my sight."

Ambassador Gen'le scrambled toward the door, casting Ysabel a look of gratitude and sympathy. Donya left quickly to prepare the meeting room for the next stage.

I narrowly stopped myself from collapsing. I had to keep my chin raised just a little longer, until they left. Then Donya would get them to sign the papers forfeiting any claim on Arahasnor and offer them the location of the treacherous treasury thief as compensation (and a distraction). Hopefully that would end this particular mess—especially because we still had quite a few more messes to go.

Secretary Ma'qas lowered her head and approached the throne. She was a mousy woman with short brown hair and beady eyes. Taking off a pink pearl bracelet, she held it out to me. "A tribute for Her Grace."

I looked at her quizzically. Why would this woman offer me her jewelry when I hadn't even asked for it? Had I terrorized the dwarves so deeply? I felt awful about stealing from someone. Unfortunately, I had no way to turn this down and remain in character. I'd find an excuse to return her bracelet to her later.

I reached out my hand. "It's the least you can offer me, peasant."

Before I could touch the bracelet, the door slammed open so hard it dented the wall. Araceli strode in. She wore a maid's uniform, but she'd ripped open the front to make it more low cut and hiked up the skirt. Pouting, she posed with a hand on her hip. "You ugly bitch, how dare you try to seduce my darling with a trinket? Do you imagine you can rival me, the Blood Duchess's current favorite?"

I had no idea what was going on. I hadn't given Araceli any kind of cue about needing her help. I thought I was doing great. Plus, we'd almost been done, and the last thing I wanted was to drag this on even longer until the crowns gave me brain damage. But Araceli had thrown me a cue, so I needed to roll with it or else it would look strange.

"No one could rival your beauty, my darling." I blew Araceli a kiss. "Come over here."

Araceli boldly sauntered over and leaned her head against my shoulder. Lightly, fortunately, because just a little more weight would have sent me tumbling over. Her hair tickled my nose with a strawberry scent.

Secretary Ma'qas backed away. "I'm sorry to have offended."

"Do you think an apology is enough to make up for insulting the duchess's lover?" Araceli pursed her lips. "Darling, kill her for me."

My spine went rigid. What was Araceli talking about? This wasn't part of the plan. Obviously, I'd never kill someone, but I didn't know how to get out of this. I bought myself time to think with another fake evil laugh. "Death wouldn't make up for insulting you, my beauty. What if we torture her instead?" I gazed into Araceli's eyes as if love-struck, trying to telepathically convey, *What the hell are you doing?*

Araceli simpered. "What a wonderful idea." She reached out and caught Ma'qas's wrist, forcing her to drop the bracelet. "You have lovely fingers, slut. Do you think you'll still look as pretty after losing a few of them?"

"Enough!" Ambassador Gen'le cried. He looked terrified out of his mind, but to give him credit, he stomped forward and yanked Ma'qas away. "I must protest! This is a diplomatic mission. We have immunity."

"Do you think diplomacy means anything to me? I could have both of your heads hanging from my throne in seconds." I had no choice but to say that. After all, the entire plan hinged on the dwarven ambassador believing I was quite capable of killing him. But how was I going to back down now?

To my horror, a guard drew his sword. No! I hadn't meant it!

My mind went numb. I flashed back to that day by the fountain when the real duchess had so casually ordered my death. For a moment, I sincerely believed the guard was about to kill me instead, and my lips froze.

"Stop in the name of the Sun God!" Ysabel clasped her hands together. As she gazed up through her lashes, she looked the picture of piety. "If it means saving this innocent woman's life, then I'll offer up my head instead."

I snorted. "Don't you know that you're my precious hostage? I'll only display your pretty head after I'm done using you."

Ysabel squared her shoulders. "If you harm these innocent people, then I'll bite my own tongue and commit suicide."

Thank you, big sister, for giving me an out. I sneered. "A weakling like you could never follow through. But it would be a shame to lose your tongue—I so very much enjoy your terrified pleas. Let the ugly one go." I squeezed Araceli's waist. "My precious dove, I'll buy you a new necklace to make it up to you."

Araceli pointed at the secretary's bracelet lying on the floor. "I want that pearl bracelet. No one but me should dare touch it."

I would have agreed to anything to end this. "Anything for you."

Ambassador Gen'le grabbed Secretary Ma'qas's arm and hustled her away, pausing only to whisper a weak thanks to Ysabel.

The guards followed after them—planning to keep them from running away.

As soon as they were out of sight, Ysabel unchained herself. "I have to go talk to Donya. I'll direct her to whisper some things to the ambassador to terrify the Conclave of Kings so much that they'll dither instead of immediately gathering an attack against us. You did perfect, Bora. I'll praise you as much as you deserve as soon as I return." She ran off.

When the door closed behind my sister, I collapsed into my cushion. I yanked off both crowns, followed by as much of my jewelry as I could. The pounding in my head didn't stop.

Araceli ran forward and took off her maid's cap, throwing it over the bracelet. "You didn't touch that, did you? Please tell me you didn't touch it."

"I didn't! What the hell were you doing?" I shouted. "You went too far!"

"I had to—"

"No, you didn't! We'd already successfully threatened the dwarves. You didn't have to terrorize that poor woman." A sob caught in my throat. I'd held off until everyone else had left, but now the tears threatened to erupt. "Did you know that the first time we met, the Blood Duchess tried to kill me just because I was Falael's ex-lover? It was the scariest moment of my life. She stomped on me like I was an insect. I never, ever wanted to be the kind of person who would do something like that to someone else. I feel so ashamed and sorry toward Secretary Ma'qas!"

Araceli paled. "I didn't know that happened to you. I'm sorry."

"Do you know why I played along with your act even though it made me feel like the worst scum?" I glared. "Because I trust you! I know you must have had a good reason to do what you did. Please, explain it to me!"

"Secretary Ma'qas is one of the Twelve Avengers. She was trying to kill you."

"Oh." I slumped down on my seat. I was crying now, not because of the news but because as soon as I no longer had anger to sustain me, the tears leaked out.

Araceli put an arm around me. "You did a good job."

"I'm embarrassed to be acting like this." I sniffled. At least I hadn't broken down in front of Ysabel, who'd done such an amazing acting job and been perfectly fine afterward.

"You were strong when it counted." Araceli patted my back. "You have nothing to be ashamed of."

A sizzling sound drew my attention to the floor. I gaped as part of Araceli's maid cap eroded away, revealing the pearl bracelet underneath. "What in the name of the Sun God caused that?"

"Ma'qas specializes in poison. Most of the Twelve Avengers stayed separate to keep our identities protected so one person getting caught couldn't reveal the others. But Ma'qas and I trained together from a young age. I know her face, and I know her tactics. I had to stop you from touching the poisoned bracelet without breaking the act, so I used the first idea I could think of. It was what we did to chase off Falael, so I thought you'd be able to respond to the cue on the fly."

My voice came out as a whisper. "If I'd accepted that bracelet, I'd have died immediately." I couldn't tear my eyes away from it as it ate a hole into the floor. "You saved my life. Thank you." I sniffled. "And I yelled at you afterward. I'm sorry."

"Hey, don't worry about it," Araceli said. "I understand why you felt scared. I was making it up as I went along, too. Your sister saved us both from talking ourselves into a corner. Not that a guard could have killed Ma'qas—she'd have annihilated him. But it still would have caused a serious hitch in our plan."

"What plan would have caused you to forget your revenge, my old friend?" a new voice called. Ma'qas dropped down from the balcony, landing before the throne. The formerly mousy expression had been replaced with a predatorial gaze and a hard twist to her mouth. She had ripped off her jeweled jerkin to reveal leather armor underneath.

There was anger on her face, and despite being in the same room as her sworn enemy, she glared at Araceli instead of me. This was a very personal rage, a betrayal deep enough to lure her out into the open. "I never thought you'd turn traitor, Ari. But I'll kill you along with the duchess."

CHAPTER SIXTEEN

Gazing sadly at the assassin, I groaned. "It feels like anytime someone opens a door unexpectedly, I always get bad news. Araceli, why do we never get any good surprises?"

"Why do you never lock the doors?" Araceli countered.

Hey, I was already working my ass off pretending to be the duchess. How could I remember to lock doors, too? I whispered, "It's not my fault this time, the guards should have done that."

Araceli glared at Ma'qas. "And you! You should know better than to attempt a frontal attack on the Blood Duchess. If she were the real thing, you'd already be dead. Speaking of which, she's not—"

"I knew you'd noticed me," Ma'qas said. "You're so confident, you didn't even bother to lock the doors. There's no point in stealth, so let's see if your trap can kill me." A chain whip unfolded from her hands and lashed at me.

I yelped. Araceli shoved me sideways. I landed on my hands and knees on the carpet. The whip shattered the sun globe hanging over the throne. Bits rained down on me, and I felt grateful for my lack of exposed skin.

Araceli leapt between us, holding out her hand. A diamond on her pinky glowed, forming a shield.

Ma'qas stared. "You have her rings. The Blood Duchess gave you her rings." Her tone turned from stunned to furious. "I'd almost dared hope it was all a pretense, but you must be truly bound to her. Was that act back there real, too? Did you fall in love with the woman who murdered your parents like something from a bad play? I never took you for someone so shallow and pathetic."

"Listen to me, please," Araceli shouted. "She's not the duchess."

"Tell me more—" Ma'qas leaned in as if listening, then she lashed out with her whip.

The metal dagger at the end of the whip curved at my neck, so fast it must be a relic, too fast for me to duck. A beam of light blasted from Araceli's hand, severing the metal in two.

With no more words, Ma'qas dropped the whip and drew a longsword from her back.

I ran and crouched behind the throne. I wanted to help Araceli, but I knew I would only get in the way if I acted recklessly. Should I throw something? But I might hit Araceli. I always made my siblings chase after the ball when I threw it too far off during games of catch . . .

A beam of light extended from Araceli's ring. Gripping it like a sword, she blocked an attack. The two combatants strained as they locked weapons. They seemed to have once been friends. Would Araceli be upset if I summoned the guards and they killed Ma'qas? What should I do?

"Just give me a moment to explain," Araceli cried. "You know I'd never forgive the Blood Duchess. *This isn't Duchess Hedri!*"

Ma'qas's lack of reply was a refusal to listen. She dodged sideways, trying to stab Araceli between the ribs.

Araceli sidestepped, the blade sliding past her. "Can't you trust me just a little? I know we were always rivals, but I thought we respected each other."

"I could almost believe you mean what you say." Ma'qas eyed her opponent coolly as she came to a halt. "Mind control?"

"Please let her talk. She's nothing like the duchess."

"Are you kidding me? That stunt back there was exactly like the Blood Duchess! Who else would dare throw Ava's sacred treasure or take the Holy Maiden hostage?"

I was a little flattered that my performance had been so convincing. But now wasn't the time for such thoughts. While distracting us with talk, Ma'qas's left hand reached for a dagger strapped to her back. A green light glowed from her fingertips.

"Look out!" I screamed. Fearing my warning would be too late, I lunged forward and grabbed Ma'qas's ankle, yanking hard.

The dwarf tumbled to the ground. Kneeling over her, I said, "I'm so sorry! I didn't mean to hurt you, I just had to stop you."

Ma'qas leapt to her feet, but she didn't attack. She stared at me. "What did you just say?"

"Um, I'm sorry. I'd like to make a good impression on Araceli's friends." I smiled winningly.

Ma'qas's whip went limp. "Whoa, that's not the Blood Duchess."

Araceli nodded. "I know, the apologies convinced me, too."

"I should have figured from the unlocked door." Ma'qas shook her head. "Seeing that expression on her face is creepy."

"I'm sorry!" I cried.

"*Extremely* creepy," Ma'qas mumbled. In a louder voice, she asked, "Is this a magical disguise? Did you kill the real duchess? I'd be disappointed at missing out myself, but it would still be good news."

Man, it was a little embarrassing how everyone kept catching on to my act, but at least this time it turned out for the best.

Araceli shook her head. "A body swap. Unfortunately, the real thing is still roaming free in Bora's body. Ah, by the way, this is Bora."

Ma'qas sheathed her sword. "Why this risky masquerade?"

Araceli and I exchanged glances. Even though she was one of the Twelve Avengers, Ma'qas was also a dwarf. I didn't know how she'd react if she found out that we were planning to scam the dwarven kingdom out of the rights they'd won in the last World Games in order to protect our own nation. Nor could I think up a decent excuse.

"We're turning the Blood Duchess into a dark lord," Araceli explained. "After she becomes the target of the Conclave of Kings and hated by the entire world, we'll swap their bodies back. She'll never be able to survive."

"Hmm." Ma'qas tapped her chin. "A more vicious revenge than merely killing her. I approve."

Either she didn't have that much loyalty toward her kingdom, or it was outweighed by her hatred of the duchess. A lucky save either way.

"Of course, I'm still going to try to kill the duchess after we swap back their bodies," Araceli said. "But she's gotten out of seemingly impossible situations before."

Ma'qas nodded. "She survived my poison the last time. In fact, she didn't even notice I'd poisoned her. I didn't think it would work this time—it just seemed worth a try. Especially since she wouldn't notice if I failed, like she didn't notice my last dozen attempts. She's entirely too tough. But not even she could survive a full crusade from the Conclave of Kings."

"Don't you think it's fitting, too?" Araceli grinned. "Duchess Hedri always skirted on the edge of what she could get away with. Sherda allows nobles to murder, as long as they don't target anyone important. When she went after other nobles, she used assassins or framed them for treason. It would be satisfying to see her die, but even more satisfying to see her properly executed for her crimes."

"I've always liked how you think." Ma'qas grinned back. "Very well. My lips are sealed concerning this plan of yours. In exchange, I want you to let me help when you're ready to kill her."

I exhaled in relief. It seemed to be settled. I felt grateful for that first night when Araceli had tried to kill me, because I wouldn't have lasted long in this masquerade without her. At the same time, I didn't entirely like how Ma'qas smiled at Araceli, though I had no good reason why. It was a friendly smile, full of shared understanding from someone who clearly knew Araceli much better than I did.

"Have a Bookmaker create a pair of linked books for us," Araceli said. "I promise to write to you. In exchange, will you help us find the real duchess?"

Ma'qas raised an eyebrow. "You don't know where she is? Whoa, I am rapidly losing faith in this plan."

"If I did, she'd already be in a dungeon." Araceli shrugged. "It's not an insurmountable obstacle. We've got her body. We have the gifted who caused the swap to begin with. But I confess that knowing where to find her stolen form would take a weight off my mind. Tie off one last loose end."

"A very, very big loose end," Ma'qas growled.

Although I knew she was right, I resented the tone of voice. I'd been careening from one crisis to another since I'd ended up stuck in this body. There had been no time for anything except survival. At some point, had I stopped even thinking about getting my body back? The realization unnerved me. I'd enjoyed some aspects of having power, but surely it hadn't been enough to make me forget about my original goal. Had it? "Donya has been trying very hard to find Duchess Hedri. Surely she can't cause that much trouble while stuck in my impoverished peasant body?"

Ma'qas crossed her arms. "You might be unpleasantly surprised. The duchess clawed her way up from minor nobility once before. I'd bet she has a few contingency plans in case she falls from power—allies or money tucked away. It's strange you haven't heard from her. Strange and worrying."

"Then help us." Araceli's tone turned wheedling. "You were always better at tracking than me."

"Flattery will get you everywhere." Ma'qas shrugged. "I'm only agreeing to this because I can't have my revenge if you two fools lose track of the Blood Duchess. I'll have a pair of linked books made, and you get me a portrait of her real body." She gestured at me.

"Done," Araceli said.

"I'll find an excuse to leave the delegation and stay in town." Ma'qas turned away and vanished out the door.

Once we were alone, I said, "Nice. Fast thinking."

"It wasn't entirely a lie. I've given some thought already to how satisfying it would be to see the duchess face justice." Araceli's gaze became distant. "Even though I accepted it as unlikely a long time ago, I've always wanted to prove that she framed my parents."

"Thank you for helping find my body, too. It's been worrying me," I admitted. Even worse, I'd been helpless to do anything to speed up the pursuit.

Araceli patted my shoulder. "I know. Do you want to get some food? I'm hungry."

My stomach growled in response. "Before, I could barely eat for nervousness."

"Then you deserve a treat. Come on."

Back in my room, I sat in the armchair and Araceli perched awkwardly on a stool while we devoured strawberry muffins from a basket. "To a successful day," Araceli said, toasting me with a muffin.

"Don't boast yet," I said. "We haven't heard from the dwarven ambassador."

"We're just letting him fret. You terrified him. He'll give us whatever we want."

"Thank the Sun God that Ysabel came up with such a great plan, and she was there to cover for my poor acting." I laughed. Ever since we'd been children, Ysabel had been a natural leader, and I'd been a natural follower. Even if I hadn't been the younger one, our dynamic probably would have been the same. It felt like a relief to have her show up and take charge.

Araceli frowned. "Your acting was *amazing*. Frankly, I thought your sister overacted a bit. You're the one who convinced the ambassador that you were ready and willing to kill him. Don't sell yourself short."

"Oh, I didn't mean it in a bad way! I'm relieved that Ysabel came to help." Yet as soon as I spoke those words, they didn't feel true. Why? I definitely hadn't wanted to keep fumbling around alone. Still, I wished I'd been able to handle this entire mess without my sister's help.

Ever since I'd been a small child, I'd relied on Ysabel to protect me more than my abusive father or my self-centered mother. Ysabel had put food on the table when we'd been poor. She'd protected our entire refugee camp from the wealthy and powerful. And she'd done it by draining her life. For years, I'd been too ashamed to look her in the eye because I knew she was dying to save us. But what could I do? It wasn't just me—my little brother needed food and protection. I had never been able to tell her to stop. I'd known she wouldn't listen to me, so it would have felt disingenuous to tell her to stop, as if I was merely unburdening my own conscience by pretending to give her a way out that she couldn't take. If only I'd had power, if only I'd been able to help her, then I could have told her to stop.

"It's gotta be annoying sometimes, being the little sister of the famous Holy Maiden." Araceli wiped a crumb off her lip. "Honestly, I find your sister a bit exhausting."

I immediately defended her. "She's bringing all her energy to help us pull off this act. It can be difficult when people compare us, but that's not *her* fault."

Araceli studied me as though she could see the truth in my eyes. "You can complain if you want. I won't tell anyone. You certainly got the worse role in our little play, the villainess to her tragic heroine. A little jealousy would be normal. You can vent to me, and it will stay between the two of us."

"No, it's not like that. I don't think so, anyway." I hesitated. Was I jealous of my sister? Ysabel had always been more than me: more beautiful, more smart, more brave, more strong, more charming, and more magical. For that matter, she'd even won the unfortunate title of more tragic. She'd been doomed to die young from the moment her healing gift had manifested. I would have rather cut out my own tongue than presume to show jealousy to her face. Keeping it to myself was the absolute least I could do. Now that Kaine had found a way to save my sister from losing her life when she healed, did I have the right to feel jealous of her? Did the heavy feeling under my chest come from petty envy? Maybe a little. I'd never wished for Ysabel to be any less than the magnificent big sister I adored, but I wished I could be a bit more like her. Then she wouldn't be the only person carrying all the burdens in our family.

I blurted out, "I wish I'd been able to handle this whole mess on my own, so my pregnant sister didn't need to drag herself to a whole different country to rescue me. She should be resting at home. I'm glad to have her on my side, and I certainly think our odds of success are better with her. But I've always relied on Ysabel, and she's never once relied on me. She's done too much for our family since she was only a child herself. I wish I could be the one to protect her sometimes, too."

Araceli gazed at me, a soft look in her eyes. "That's just like you, Bora. I should have known. You're not the type of person to get jealous." She chuckled. "I love that kindness of yours."

I looked down. "Uh, I don't think my kindness is an asset at the moment, not when I'm pretending to be a villainess."

"It's the reason I'm still here," Araceli said.

"Oh." My cheeks warmed. I still thought I hadn't done a very good job as the Blood Duchess, but if I'd convinced Araceli to stay, then at least I'd contributed something to the team. "Thank you. Talking to you helped me understand my feelings a bit better."

But that didn't change anything. If I just kept on doing what Ysabel said, then everything would turn out all right. Ysabel was the smartest person I knew. Right now, it was more important to save my country than to assuage my jealousy or pride. Even though I felt a bit disappointed in myself.

Ambassador Gen'le handed me the paper forfeiting the Dwarven Caves' claim to Arahasnor. "Even if the Conclave of Kings doesn't punish you, you'll receive your karma someday."

Since he had believed my threats to torture Ysabel, I couldn't blame him. If anything, I admired his courage for being willing to say it. Even though I'd committed to playing the part of a villainess, sometimes it felt exhausting to be hated by everyone. How would a villainess react? I stuck my nose in the air and sneered. It probably looked like I was constipated.

Ambassador Gen'le opened the door to his carriage. "Come, Ma'qas. Let's leave this evil place."

Ma'qas cleared her throat. "I'm sorry. I'm staying here. You see, the Blood Duchess has fallen in love with me and demands me as her concubine."

I choked. Then I remembered that we needed an excuse to keep Ma'qas around. It was of vital personal importance to me that she track down the duchess in my body. Even if I didn't like the story she'd come up with one bit. "Uh, that's right," I said. "Muhahahahaha." My evil laugh sounded weak even to my own ears.

Ma'qas placed a hand on her forehead. "After we left the throne room, she dragged me back to her quarters. I was helpless to resist."

I what now? First my own sister falsely accused me of all nature of horrors, and now this? I felt faint.

Ambassador Gen'le puffed out his chest. "This is an outrage. No matter what devilish powers you may control, I can't allow you to take one of my own people prisoner for your dark lusts."

I had no idea what to say. How did this escalate so quickly? Even if I had to pretend to be a tyrant, a moral line must be drawn! I would not accept this false charge!

"No, I've decided to stay on my own." Ma'qas reached up and captured my hand. "I've fallen in love with the duchess!"

I choked again, then turned it into an evil cackle.

Ma'qas swooned on top of me. "I already belong to Duchess Hedri, body and soul. I'm a helpless pawn of her evil wiles. My body can't resist her. She's completely conquered me."

The dwarven ambassador stared at me with both horror and fascination, as if trying to penetrate the dark secrets of my seductive wiles.

Don't look at me like that! I don't know what the hell she's talking about, either. Subtly, I tried to push Ma'qas off me.

"Are you certain?" Ambassador Gen'le demanded.

Ma'qas sighed and snuggled closer to me. "I'm sorry, sir. I can not give up this unimaginable pleasure."

The ambassador's eyebrows crawled to his hairline. He was looking at me with even more shock and perhaps curiosity. I couldn't take it any longer. I grabbed Ma'qas's arm to lift her off me.

Ma'qas took this as an invitation to jump onto me and throw her arms around my neck. "No! Not in front of the ambassador!" She made a high-pitched cry of pleasure.

I'm the one being assaulted here! By the time I wrenched Ma'qas off me, the dwarven ambassador had climbed into the carriage and fled this scene of debauchery.

Panting, I glared at Ma'qas. "You really couldn't think of a better excuse than that?"

Ma'qas winked. "I'm just taking a little revenge on Ari."

What did Ari have to do with this?

"Do you need anything before you look for the real duchess?"

"Ari already arranged for my travel funds." Ma'qas chuckled. "I'd better leave before I get attacked with real intent to kill this time." She darted away.

I turned around to find Araceli dressed in her maid uniform again. She glared after Ma'qas with undisguised murderousness. As soon as she noticed me looking, her face softened. She coughed. "Sorry about her. She was always provoking me back when we were training together. She thinks she's funnier than she actually is."

Still confused, I said, "Eh, I guess the Blood Duchess's reputation can't get any worse at this point. It won't be my problem after I switch back." I was becoming increasingly desperate to ensure that happened. I couldn't possibly survive in the duchess's body with all the messes I'd created. Too many powerful people had reason to want me dead.

"I hate to drag you from one disaster to another, but we've already left the nobles in the dungeon for longer than we planned. I don't particularly care about their whining, but we do need to hurry up and get their money."

Oh, crap, I still had Arahasnor's most prestigious nobility locked in my dungeon. Just one of half a dozen executable crimes I'd committed lately. "Let's go." I needed a distraction from the off-kilter way Ma'qas had left me.

"Are you certain? If you're tired, it can wait."

I cracked my knuckles. "Actually, I'm in the mood to let out some aggression." With my current level of annoyance, I'd never felt more prepared to play the part of the evil Blood Duchess. "Does my grin look suitably terrifying?"

Araceli studied me. "You definitely look like someone got you up too early in the morning."

"Excellent." My smile widened. "Let's put on another show."

CHAPTER SEVENTEEN

I swung the replica of Cardinal Jiang's cane as I walked down the dungeon stairs. Ysabel met me at the bottom, this time wearing an elegant yellow dress. She winked at me. "Excellent acting today."

"You carried it, really," I mumbled.

Ysabel lifted up my chin. "Nonsense, you were fabulous. Bring more of that energy. We need to visit the representative from the Guild of Slavers before we talk to the nobles."

"They're calling it the Guild of Indentured Servitude now," I snarled. "I think we should turn it into the Guild Out of Work."

Ysabel grinned. "Yeah, that energy. I'm in a hurry to throw that bastard out of my city, but first we need to intimidate him badly enough that he'll go back to the guild and tell them not to mess with us again. Ideally forever, but I'll even settle for buying some time to rebuild the city."

"I'm getting good at intimidation." I swung the cane again. It bounced off the walls and hit my shins. "Ow."

Ysabel rolled her eyes. "Let me do the talking. I'm the innocent Holy Maiden, and you're the evil duchess threatening me. Just stand behind me looking wicked, and I'll handle the rest. You know I've got your back, baby sis."

"Of course."

Opening the cell door, Ysabel strode in. The room had stone walls. Arrand sat on a simple wooden chair next to a cot. His head immediately shot up, and his eyes went to the cane I carried. I could almost see him making the connection to my supposedly broken life-oaths. His nose twitched like a ferret's.

Ysabel's chest heaved. She wiped a tear from her eye. "I'm relieved the Blood Duchess hasn't tortured you yet."

"Holy Maiden," Arrand said very coldly. He didn't seem moved by her innocent act, and I could guess why. Ysabel had married Dark Lord Kaine, the guild's greatest enemy. This particular audience didn't have any sympathy for her.

Ysabel gripped the wall. "I was so terrified that the duchess had already carried through with her threat to rip out your hair and glue it to your ass."

Hey, Yzzy, do you have to keep framing me for increasingly creative crimes? I stood straight and tried to look like someone who had the faintest idea what my sister was talking about.

Arrand sneered. "Did you manage to seduce this hideous beast to your will like the last dark lord?" He gestured at me with a contemptuous expression.

"How could you say such cruel words?" Ysabel dabbed at her eyes. "The Blood Duchess took me hostage to force my husband to aid her crimes. If you don't give up on Arahasnor's debt, then she'll destroy the guild."

"I'm sure Dark Lord Kaine needed a lot of convincing," Arrand said sarcastically. "Did you have a threesome with your husband and the Blood Duchess, you slut?"

Anger rose within me hot and fast. No one called my sister a slut. Standing behind Ysabel, I cleared my throat. I made a gesture as if removing someone's hair and ramming it up their ass. It was a creative gesture, but Arrand got the meaning. His face paled. "How terrible that the wicked duchess took a holy maiden hostage. Very evil."

"Isn't it?" Ysabel beamed, then remembered to wipe the smile off her face. "Fortunately, I persuaded Duchess Hedri to release you, under the condition that you sign a paper forfeiting any debt owed by Arahasnor to the Guild of Indentured Servitude."

Arrand growled, "This is an outrage. A contract under duress would never be enforceable."

Ysabel arched an eyebrow. "Then it seems to me that a great many of your guild's contracts wouldn't be enforceable. We'll let the

Conclave of Kings decide. Perhaps they'll hear the case sometime in the next century. In the meantime, sign this." She waved a paper.

Arrand looked over the document. "You're not even going to offer us a single coin?"

"Arahasnor is broke." Ysabel shrugged. "I could let you punch me instead."

I wondered what Ysabel was doing, but then I remembered her request to be silent. I'd interfere if necessary—I'd never let anyone punch my pregnant sister in front of me.

Arrand growled, "Don't tempt me, you little snake."

Ysabel clasped her hands together. "I feel overcome with guilt to be assisting the vile Blood Duchess, even under duress. Yet the Sun God has illuminated my soul, teaching me that the answer to all sin is suffering. He has granted me a divine vision." She raised her eyes to the ceiling as if staring straight up into the distant sun. "Through the power of your sacred fist, I will be cleansed of sin."

Arrand looked wild-eyed. "You have no idea how badly I want to do it, you crazy bitch."

"Better yet, stab me! My blood will purify me!" Ysabel cried.

"I'd do it in a heartbeat if I had a knife!"

"Here you go." Ysabel handed Arrand a knife. Then she screamed, "Help! This man attacked me!"

Kaine burst through the door. "Ysabel!"

Alzira ran in close behind him, screaming, "Your Holiness!" Both of their eyes fell on Arrand. "How dare you, sinner!" Alzira shattered the knife to shards while it was still in his hand.

"But—" was all Arrand had time to say before Kaine and Alzira fell upon him.

Ysabel linked arms with me and strolled out of the cell, closing it behind her. Strangled cries of pain came from inside. As we headed down the chilly stone hallway, she said, "Don't worry, I told them that he had to be in good enough shape to sign the paper afterward. Now we have an excuse to deny the guild's debt. They just attacked the Holy Maiden."

I blinked. "Will that work?"

"It's the type of legal case that only the Conclave of Kings could decide, and it takes the Conclave a long time to do anything." Ysabel shrugged. "We could drag this out for years. Decades, even. Mainly I just wanted an excuse to hit the slaver a few times before we throw him out."

I could understand that. "Are we talking to the local nobles next?"

"Yes, we ought to." Ysabel frowned. "That situation will be harder to handle. Some of them know me perhaps a little too well to be fooled by my acting. Others might enjoy my suffering too much. It might be better if you intimidate them alone. Do you think you're up for it?"

I swallowed. A childish part of me didn't want to let my big sister down. "Uh . . . can you tell me what to say?"

Ysabel grinned. "I already prepared a script."

Ysabel had arranged for the guards to herd all the nobles we'd wrongfully abducted into the prison yard outside for my speech. Though it was a sunny day, the high stone walls cast long, dark shadows. Snow buried the grass. As soon as I stepped out, everyone's heads shot up. Several immediately fastened their gazes on the replica of Jiang's cane. Baleful glares hit me from all directions. I was close enough for them to attack me, if they had the nerve. I shivered, not just from the cold. This lot did not look as intimidated or remorseful as I'd hoped. I reminded myself that Kaine was lurking just inside, ready to come out if I shouted.

Standing in front of the prisoners, I cleared my throat. "Listen up, pigeon pluckers. I've come to dictate my terms."

"You can't dictate terms!" the lady in the yellow dress shouted. Countess Lealonie, if I remembered correctly. "You're a duchess of Sherda, not even from our country."

"Oh, so you remember that I'm the Blood Duchess?" I bared my teeth. "From the way you've been talking to me, I thought you had no idea."

This won me a brief silence. "Since you refused to negotiate with me the first time, you've lost your chance. You'll give me anything I ask for, or your lives and lands will be forfeit."

The silence was promising, or so I thought. At least it meant everyone was too scared to shout the insults I could see hovering on their red faces.

Eventually, Countess Lealonie said, "As if you aren't going to run my lands into the ground with your reckless spending anyway."

Something about how she said it got to me. Not even angry, just bitterly resigned. At this point, I was supposed to threaten to hang them all upside down by their heels and extract all their blood. I glanced down at the script on my hand, where I was pretty sure I'd misspelled "exsanguination."

Then I sighed, and said, "I don't need more jewels and dresses. I need the money to pay off the former king's debt. I have no qualms about kicking out the Guild of Indentured Servitude without paying them, but I need to at least pay all the workers who built the World Games stadium."

Maybe I was making a huge mistake. I probably shouldn't show any weakness in front of enemies. But I couldn't help trying.

Countess Lealonie snorted. "The last time King Uctor said we needed to accept a tribute hike for the good of the nation, it turned out he had to offer up compensation because he'd groped a foreign queen. Given that you seduced and abducted the dwarven ambassador's secretary, it looks like you're following in his footsteps."

By the Sun God, how had that rumor made it all the way to the dungeon already? Guards could be such gossips. I winced. "I'm not giving the Dwarven Caves a single aracoin. I booted them out after forcing them to renounce their claim on our kingdom. You may not like me, but right now, you need me to save your country."

Countess Lealonie crossed her arms. "Arahasnor is going to hell. That's why I need to keep every last coin in my own lands, to look after my own people."

It was selfish but in an understandable way. Probably my extravagant and reckless behavior of late hadn't inspired any trust. Heaving a huge sigh, I plopped down on the ground. The damn heels were killing me. "What would you want the crown to do with your money?"

Countess Lealonie eyed me warily. After a long moment, she said, "My county needs a new bridge. We share a border with Conollia, and the bridge was destroyed during the fighting. It's impacting our trade routes. I've got the money to fix it, but I need agreement from the Conollians, and I lack the authority to negotiate that."

"I can do that! Kaine is my—I mean, I took his wife hostage, so he'll have to listen to me. Deal." I spat on my hand, then held it out for a shake.

Countess Lealonie gave me a very funny look. Belatedly, I remembered that nobles didn't do that. But before I could wipe my hand off, the countess grabbed it and shook. "Deal."

I was immediately swamped by nobles shouting out their own requests.

By the time I gave orders to the guards to release everyone, I felt satisfied. They had probably only negotiated with me because I'd forced them. But there had also been some good ideas for improving the kingdom among their demands. It got me thinking. So far, I'd been strictly on the defensive—fighting for my survival and hopefully stopping my country from going down in flames. It would be wonderful to do something productive for a change.

"How did it go?" Ysabel asked, falling in alongside me as we walked up the stairs. "You've got a dirt stain on your dress! Did anyone throw dirt at you? Just say the word, and I'll have Alzira put a sack over their heads and beat them anonymously."

"No, no, I got tired and sat down." I hesitated, then admitted to everything I'd done. I waited for my sister to scold me.

"Sweet Ava, you did brilliantly! I'm impressed. Those are even some good ideas for improving the kingdom. Except that one landgrave who wanted the self-portrait of Jdalj hanging in the throne room, but we can let him have that ugly thing. It will give me an excuse to redecorate." She patted me on the shoulder. "When did my baby sister grow up and get so smart? I'm proud of you."

"Thank you." I tried not to blush. Her words meant more to me than she would ever know. I'd melt into a puddle before ever admitting to her how much I admired her. "Now that I have a breather before the next crisis, I think I should do more for the kingdom. I have all this power. It seems like a waste not to use it. But I'm not a politician or scholar. What would you do?"

Ysabel hesitated, twirling a curl with her finger. "We have to be practical. There's a limit to how many changes the nobility will accept in a row."

"No, we don't." I spun my sister around and grabbed her by the shoulders. "We've already threatened the nobility into submission. I'm a tyrant!"

"If one of my ideas goes wrong . . ."

"Then blame it all on the Blood Duchess. Yzzy, that's the beauty of this crazy situation! We don't have to take responsibility for anything. This is the perfect chance for a social experiment. We can try out whatever we like, and if it doesn't work, then we scapegoat the Blood Duchess."

Ysabel bit her lip. "Now that you mention it . . . I've always wanted to make medical treatments free for the poor."

"Free? How would the doctors make a living?"

"The royal treasury would pay the doctors. As a healer, I always set aside a certain portion of my time for people who can't afford to pay, but I can't help the whole city. I know doctors who can barely keep their practices going because their principles compel them to help those who can't pay. I also know doctors who will turn a patient out onto the streets if their clothes aren't nice enough. People become prey to scammers because they can't afford legitimate treatment. If medical expenses were the responsibility of the crown, then no one would have to die because they couldn't afford treatment." Ysabel became increasingly animated as she spoke. "We could work with existing charity programs run by the Church. Honestly, I'd love to make it so that no one ever had to go bankrupt from medical expenses, but our treasury is too empty and our populace struggling too much to raise taxes. We need someone else to fund this particular experiment. Fortunately, I have a lot of Church contacts."

I grinned. "That's a wonderful idea. Head Cardinal Augustin seems like a good person. I bet he'd help."

"I'd also like to devote funds to training more doctors. We don't have enough, currently. I'd written up a plan, but I could never get it past the last Council of Cardinals. The new one owes me their positions."

As we reached the duchess's office, I gestured her inside. "Sit down, and we'll plan out who we'd need to talk to first. If anyone gives you trouble, then I'll threaten them for you. I'm getting better at that."

Ysabel sat down in the chair across from my desk. "Speaking of which, I'd love to educate certain nobles who have been difficult for me to work with in the past. We could make them take classes about sexism and other forms of discrimination."

I thought of some of the difficulties I'd had in communication when even a handshake turned into a tripwire. "Throw class differences in there, too. It would be wonderful if we could all come to understand each other better."

Ysabel rubbed her palms together. "I had to sit through hours of memorizing their complicated family trees for etiquette class. Now they have to sit through this! It will be so much fun!"

My sister's motives might be less than pure, but I still thought it a good idea.

As she chattered on, I realized this was the first time we'd been alone together since our reunion. A pit formed in my stomach. I was afraid to ask her this question, but I'd never have peace until I did. Ysabel was smiling. I didn't want to ruin that. But if I didn't ask now, then I'd keep on finding excuses, until later became never.

I had to know.

"Yzzy?"

"Hmm?" She looked up.

I swallowed. "How did Calum die?"

CHAPTER EIGHTEEN

My sister's face froze. It was painful to watch every line harden. "Why are you asking me this now?"

I wet my lips. "Because this is the first time we've been alone together since you came to the city. Because being in the place where he died makes me think about him constantly. Because I've always needed to know the truth."

Ysabel's voice became distant. "I told you what happened."

"You told me that Cardinal Jiang murdered him, but not how or why. That's not enough. Please, Yzzy, he was my brother, too! I deserve to know!"

Ysabel did not speak. Her eyes were wide. It took me a moment to realize that she was very slightly shaking. Sweat crept down her neck. Her mouth opened and her throat bobbed, but no sound came out. She was having a panic attack.

I leapt to my feet and ran around the desk. Dropping to my knees before her, I grabbed her hands. "Breathe. Can you breathe with me? Inhale. Exhale."

Ysabel met my gaze. Tears leaked from her eyes. After a few stuttering breaths, she started to match my pace.

"Inhale. Exhale." I breathed deeply to demonstrate. "Good, good." I squeezed her hand. "You're doing great."

Ysabel drew in a shaky breath. She released my hand to wipe her eyes. The flush faded from her face.

Where was my handkerchief? Had I left it in my room? I found one in the desk drawer and offered it to her. "I'm sorry, Yzzy. I shouldn't have asked. You don't have to tell me anything."

"No. You have the right to ask. He was your brother, too." Ysabel stared at the crumpled handkerchief in her fist. "I owe you an explanation."

It bothered me how she said that, like a defendant before a judge. "Not if it's going to make you suffer."

Gazing off into the distance, she spoke as if she hadn't heard. "Calum joined Cardinal Jiang's guard to spy on him. He kept it secret—only Uncle Urew knew. He did it for me, in order to find a way to stop Jiang from sacrificing me."

"Wait, Jiang tried to do what now?" I blurted out before I could stop myself.

Ysabel looked up. "Oh, right, you didn't know. I didn't tell anyone. I only told Calum because I was angry at him. I should never have told him. He'd be alive if I hadn't."

"Hey, don't say that. Look into my eyes. Breathe." I took her hand again. A part of me felt hurt my sister had never trusted me with this information before, but I shoved that part deep down, because this moment wasn't about me. (And honestly, she'd probably been right to think I would be useless. But now wasn't the moment to dwell on that.)

Ysabel's hand hung loose in my grip. She barely seemed aware of me. "Cardinal Jiang planned to sacrifice me in a magical ritual to obtain immortality. I'd sworn a life-oath not to escape him."

"Why would you—?" I stopped, realizing I sounded too accusatory.

Ysabel answered me anyway. "He threatened our people. He would have killed me anyway. I just didn't want him to kill more people while he was at it." She half sobbed. "Jiang caught Calum and took him hostage to have extra leverage to use against me. If I'd given in to him, if I hadn't fought him, then Calum would still be alive."

"No!" I grabbed her face and forced her to look into my eyes. "You can't know that. Jiang probably would have killed Calum anyway."

"I could have arranged his safety by forcing Jiang to swear a life-oath—no, he could break life-oaths—but if I'd rescued Calum faster . . ." She was hyperventilating again, stuck on a past she couldn't change.

I didn't know what to say to her to make her believe me. "It's not like that, Yzzy. Calum would never want you to blame yourself."

Even as her hand shook in mine, Ysabel's voice took on that horribly distant tone again. It scared me. "I tried to have it both ways. I tried to save both of us. Maybe I wasn't as selfless as Calum. I struck a deal with Kaine to defeat Jiang in the Games, break my life-oath, and rescue Calum."

"Which is what Calum would have wanted you to do!" I said loudly. Our big brother had always protected both of us. "The so-called cardinal turned out to be a demented necromancer. You couldn't have let him win."

"I remember when Jiang launched his rebellion. He met me just inside the city. He had Calum. He smiled at me. Then he slit Calum's throat."

I gasped.

Ysabel wrenched away from me. She put her head in her hands, her fingers digging deep into her scalp. "It's my fault that our brother is dead. I failed Calum. I couldn't tell you because I was afraid you'd hate me."

"It's not your fault!" I nearly screamed it, even though I knew my words would make little difference. If our positions had been reversed, I would have blamed myself, too. What were words except empty nonsense? "I'm sorry I made you tell me." I wanted to know, but I hated the pain I'd caused her. "I hate *Jiang*. I'm so angry at what he did to you and Calum. I'm glad he's dead. I want to dig up his bones and burn whatever is left of him."

Ysabel looked up at me with teary eyes. "But it *is* my fault. Everything happened because of me. If I didn't exist, then Calum would be alive."

"If *I* didn't exist, then Calum would still be alive and you'd never have been sold into slavery and fallen into that necromancer scum's clutches."

Surprise erased the agony from Ysabel's voice. "That doesn't make sense."

"Yes, it does. After Dad sold you, he told Mom that he could afford to lose you because they had another girl old enough to work around the house. Therefore, if I hadn't been born, none of this tragedy ever would have happened."

"That's hardly your fault!"

"I could say the same to you."

"Who knows if Dad was even telling the truth?"

"Again, I could say the same about Former Head Cardinal Jiang and his improbable promise to ever let Calum go."

Ysabel shook her head. "It's not the same."

"My claim is exactly as logical as yours."

Tears overflowed from Ysabel's eyes. "There must have been a way I could have saved Calum," she whispered. "There must have been something I should have done differently. I'd only just reconciled with him, then he died. I want him back! I miss him so much!"

"Me, too." I wrapped my arms around my older sister, and we wept until our tears had run out.

After we'd both cried our way to exhaustion, I helped Ysabel stand up. Not only did she look exhausted, the pregnancy was clearly wearing on her, too. She never used to move so slowly.

When I opened the door, Kaine stood on the other side. "Can I take you back to our room? Do you need a hot drink?"

"How do you always do that?" Ysabel asked with a mixture of affection and exasperation. "How do you have a supernatural ability to know when I've been crying?"

Kaine blinked. "I've got enhanced hearing, but this time, it was too loud for me to need it. Who am I going to murder?"

Ysabel laughed. "No one, unless you can kill Jiang again."

"I could dig up his bones and burn them."

I nodded. "That's what *I* suggested."

Ysabel massaged her temples. "The drink sounds nice. I'd like to lie down for a bit. Bora, we'll talk more about our political plans later."

My sister leaned on her husband as she walked away, his arm around her shoulders. Her hair fell slightly out of her bun, over his large fingers. He murmured something to her, then she collapsed deeper into his embrace.

Alone, I considered what I wanted to do. There was no doubt plenty of work setting my deals in motion, but I didn't have the energy. Nor did I want to be alone. I knew exactly what I wanted.

I wanted to see Araceli. I felt surprised by the intensity of the desire. If we could just be in the same room or exchange a few words, it would make me feel better.

I nearly asked the closest person where to find Araceli, then thought better of it. I'd make a huge fuss and have absolutely no reason for it. How would I explain myself?

As if in a trance, I walked back to my room, opened the door, and fell face first onto my bed. I stayed like that until a maid came by to tell me that I was wanted at dinner. She wasn't Araceli. I didn't know why that disappointed me so much.

Ysabel met me at the dining room door. "We're having a family dinner tonight. Just you, me, Kaine, and your 'friend' Ari."

I squirmed internally at the emphasis she put on the word *friend*. "Why Ari?"

"I should be asking you that," Ysabel said in a mischievous way. "Kaine agreed with me. In fact, he insisted. He said it was a necessary rite of passage."

What did that mean? I had no time to ask before Ysabel whisked me inside. The round tower room was surrounded by windows on three sides, overlooking the snow-covered gardens. At first I thought the table stood on a carpet, but it was actually a tile pattern embedded in the floor. A mirror on the ceiling made the small room seem bigger and brighter. The ebony table had been covered with roasted chicken and mashed potatoes. Each cushioned chair had a golden butterfly on the back. Kaine sat next to Ari, who I knew was currently Ari from his white shirt and trousers.

Kaine stuffed a grape into his mouth. In his typical blunt fashion, he asked, "Are you a she or a he? It may affect the particular nature of the threats I level against you."

"Today, I don't feel much like either, but 'he' fits best at the moment."

Kaine's eyes widened. He leapt to his feet with his arms extended, shouting, "New friend!" as he attempted to hug Ari. Ari held him off with one hand.

Ysabel pinched her forehead. "Love of my life, we've talked about this. No hugging without asking first."

"Sorry." Kaine lowered his arms. "Can I hug you?"

"Err, I'd rather not," Ari said.

"I'm completely fine with that." Kaine sat down. "Sorry again. I got a little overexcited about meeting someone like me."

"We're alike?" Ari sat up straighter.

"It's not exactly the same, but it's close enough to make us friends," Kaine said. "I was born female, but I realized pretty early on that I identified as a boy. I know it's not so straightforward for everyone."

Ari nodded. "I thought I might be like that for a while, except the other way around. I think the longer I presented as a man, the more it bothered me that no one saw me as a woman, but then when everyone saw me as a woman, I had the same problem the other way around."

"The elves call that genderfluid." Kaine leaned forward. "I know a woman with a body-modification gift who changed my body into the form I wanted. The change is complete. It even allowed me to become a father. Should I introduce you?"

"Thank you, that's a very generous offer, but there's no need. I've never felt like I was in the wrong body. I just . . . don't think my body is who I am. Just an arbitrary box that causes other people to put stifling labels on me."

"Boy, do I ever feel that," I muttered, thinking of how everyone back in my village used to look at me with a mingling of pity and indifference. When both of them looked at me, I flushed. "I didn't mean to intrude. It's just that I know what it's like to be uncomfortable with your body. I had to deal with"—I didn't want to admit to making myself throw up—"bullying. Uh. I know that's nothing like what you've gone through. Err, since it's a lot more common to be fat. Most people don't care. Only a few jerks make a fuss about it." My tongue was all tied up, and this wasn't coming out right. "I was trying to say that I admire you both for taking charge of your own identities. Uh, I've never had any conflicting feelings about my gender. But if I did, I bet I would have bottled it up and hid it for my entire life."

Ari touched my hand. "I respectfully disagree. I think you're a lot braver than you give yourself credit for."

"Thanks." I flushed. "I confess I'm curious to learn more. This is a new concept to me."

"I've wanted to talk to you about it for a while," Ari said, meeting my gaze. Something in that look sent shivers through me. "I'll answer your questions if you answer mine."

"Sure! What causes you to change between genders?"

"The first question, and already I can't answer." Ari smiled ruefully. "I don't know. It just happens. Sometimes over a long period of time, sometimes a couple times a day. Sometimes who I'm talking to or what I'm doing affects how I feel, sometimes it doesn't. Trust me, I find it more confusing than anyone else. When I don't follow how I want to express my gender, I don't feel like my honest self."

"I think you answered me perfectly," I said.

Kaine nodded. "I get it. I used to feel like a foreigner in my body. It drove me crazy when someone called me 'she' and I'd just think 'Who's that?' Like a gut wrongness."

"Yes! Exactly!" Ari snapped his fingers and sat up straighter. "A constant, nagging itch. It can be frustrating that I have to dress up one way or another to get people to see me how I want. Sometimes I don't want to change clothes in the middle of the day. But I suppose I should be grateful that Arahasnor has so many gendered uniforms. Makes it easier."

"In elven society, some people go by 'they' or use another gender-neutral pronoun," Kaine said.

Ari shrugged. "I'd heard that, but I'm not sure it's right for me. I like it when people perceive me as the same gender I identify as at the moment. It gives me a feeling of satisfaction that I'm not sure I'd get from 'them.' Sometimes I'm fine with any pronoun, but other times it matters to me. I suppose it wouldn't be a big deal if everyone just called me 'them' all the time. Do you think I should stick with that? Would that make it easier on other people?"

Kaine shrugged. "That question makes my head hurt. Who knows what's easier for other people? Who cares? Just do what you want. If you want to be 'he' tonight, then be 'he.'"

I chimed in. "I agree. 'It wouldn't be a big deal' doesn't make it sound like you want that. You should do what you want. I admire that about you."

"I find it admirable, too." Kaine smiled. "You're living your life freely. You had no problems at all telling me as soon as we met. But I never would have told you if you hadn't said something first." He looked away. "You're a lot more honest than me."

Ysabel cleared her throat. "Love, don't be hard on yourself. You haven't had the luxury of being honest because you lived a fair bit of your life surrounded by people who wouldn't let you. In the early days, a large portion of your army wouldn't have followed you over something as stupid as what was inside your pants. Even now, a lot of your followers would find it hard to accept. When you're surrounded by hostile neighboring kingdoms, you don't have the luxury of not caring about a potential internal rebellion."

Ari nodded. "That's very true. I'm lucky in many ways. I was born noble. I was born to a pair of very understanding parents, who let me dress and act however I pleased growing up, and who had the power to stop anyone who mocked me or looked down on me. My life would have been very different if I hadn't been born lucky, and I know it. I would never look down on you for facing different choices than I did."

Kaine sniffled. "That means a lot to me." He brushed a tear from his eye. Ysabel put a hand on top of his and squeezed. He immediately flung his arms around her and hugged her.

"It goes without saying, but everything you tell me in this room, I will keep in strict confidence," Ari said.

"Right, I should have asked you to keep it secret before I opened my mouth." Kaine shrugged. "I've never much cared about the opinions of people I don't care about, but I'm too busy rebuilding Conollia to deal with even more fights. If people found out that it's possible to steal my powers by overcoming my will, they'd know I could be replaced, then—"

Ysabel clamped a hand over Kaine's mouth. "Stop talking."

"Everything in this room is a secret," he protested, muffled.

"That doesn't mean you can blurt out anything!" She put the former dark lord into a headlock.

The price of Kaine's gift related to overcoming his will? This was highly confidential information. No wonder my sister had turned red from fury. I would do everything in my power to forget about this just in case I ever met a mind reader.

Politely pretending he hadn't heard an international secret, Ari asked, "Is it my turn to ask you a question, Bora?"

I flushed under his stare. "Oh! Sure!"

"Do you prefer me as Ari or Araceli?"

I nearly said that I liked both equally. But something in Ari's wistful gaze told me that this question was very important to him. I shouldn't take it lightly or toss off a kind but insincere answer. So I took a moment to think deeply.

And the conclusion I came to was that I liked both equally. "Honestly, I can't imagine you without both sides to yourself. They're both you. I like how you switch between them. I can't possibly pick one I like more than the other, because you're always still you."

"Oh," Ari breathed. Very slowly, he reached across the table to cup my chin. It felt like we were the only two people in the room.

Except, of course, we weren't. Kaine slammed his hands down on the table, rattling the dishes. "Oops, I forgot! I was supposed to threaten you because Bora likes you. You seem like a great guy, so it's probably not necessary, but don't ever hurt her on purpose. If you hit her, you're dead. Good talk." He grinned contentedly and reached for a drumstick.

If my face got any hotter, I'd be able to fry an egg on it. "Yzzy . . ." I growled.

Ysabel chuckled. "Don't look at me. It was entirely his idea. I couldn't talk him out of it if I tried, though I admit I didn't. My baby sister deserves a few proper older-sibling threats. Ari, you should be more afraid of me than you are of Kaine. He'd only kill you. I'd make you *suffer* and *rot* before you died."

"You're embarrassing me," I groaned, hiding my face in my hands. I didn't dare look at Ari. I might die. One more word from my sister and I was about to scream so loud, my pronouns would be ban/shee.

Ari frowned. "You're wrong. Bora likes someone else, not me."

I did? I ventured to peek between my fingers. Ari's downcast eyes looked sad. Sweet Sun God. I hadn't thought he would ever . . . toward me . . . I mean, I'd wondered when he'd asked, but I had told myself not to get my hopes up.

Head in her hand, Ysabel smirked. "I won't upset my little sis by sticking my nose in further. But as one last free piece of advice: Look at her face."

Ari turned his neck. Our eyes met. He turned so red that his freckles vanished.

While we were both sputtering, Ysabel said cheerfully, "You should serve yourself before Kaine eats everything."

The rest of dinner passed in a less dramatic way. Kaine and Ari exchanged stories. I filled Ysabel in on what had been happening at home, telling her that Benoni hadn't dealt with any bullying lately and had made a few friends. I was avoiding talking directly to Ari, and I knew it. My heart couldn't stop hammering.

Ysabel raised a hand to touch her forehead. "No dessert for me tonight. Please enjoy yourselves without me."

Kaine was on his feet in a heartbeat. "You're not feeling well?"

"Just a headache," she mumbled. "My back hurts, too. No more than the usual pregnancy symptoms. I'm fine."

Kaine put an arm around her shoulders. "I'll take you back to our room. Then I'll give you a massage."

"Thank you. You're so good to me." Ysabel's eyes welled up. She raised a hand to cover her face. "Don't worry, I'm not upset. I've been crying easily ever since I became pregnant. Kaine keeps threatening everyone." She laughed through her tears.

"You should rest." I made a mental note to find some herbal headache tea for her. I had a particular blend that I liked.

Kaine lifted Ysabel up into his arms in a bridal carry.

"I can walk," she grumbled, but she didn't sound like she meant it.

"And I can carry you." He kissed the top of her head and swept her out of the room.

"My, how romantic," I said, pressing my hand to my heart.

"Would you like a massage, too?" Ari was looking at me again in that way that gave me butterflies.

I swallowed. "I don't need you to take care of me, and my back doesn't hurt."

"What if I want to anyway?"

I couldn't imagine saying no to that, even though I was terrified I'd somehow screw this up. "Y-yes?" It came out as a high-pitched squeak.

Smiling, Ari offered me his hand. My heart hammered a mile a minute the entire walk to my bedroom.

In my room, I lay down on my stomach. Ari placed his hands on my shoulders and massaged. I hadn't realized how much tension had been there until he started to release it. I sighed. Normally I wasn't fond of being touched, but I told myself that it wasn't my body anyway. That gave me enough distance to lean back and let the sensation wash over me. I could feel my insecurities melting away. By the third circle, I was leaning into the rocking of his hands.

"Is that the right amount of pressure?" Ari asked.

I sighed. "A little harder, please."

Ari followed the lines of tension down my back, circling my spine. As he bent over, far closer than a professional masseuse, I felt his body heat against my back. Tingles swirled in my belly.

Ari's breath tickled my neck. Slowly, he leaned in. With agonizing gentleness, he turned my chin and lowered his head down to the pillow, our gazes locking. Our faces were so close I could taste his breath. Then he kissed me.

CHAPTER NINETEEN

Fortunately, I didn't have time to panic. My mind went blank. I kissed him back.

Ari moaned into my mouth. His hair slipped out of his cap, falling long and lovely around his shoulders. That slightly flustered look on his face did naughty things to me.

My heart fluttered. I rolled onto my back. Ari was on me immediately, straddling my waist and pressing kisses against my neck. "You feel so good," he whispered, kissing his way down my throat.

"You have amazing hair," I replied, running my fingers through it. "You're so handsome."

He stiffened, just slightly, but I felt it. "Is that the wrong word? Do you prefer beautiful?" I asked anxiously.

"Maybe? I think . . . I don't feel like Ari right now. Not since dinner ended. I'm sorry, I should have said something." Araceli bit her lip and twisted her hair.

"You're saying something now," I said encouragingly.

"Do you still want to continue?" Araceli looked away. "It's fine if you don't. I won't be offended."

"I told you that I liked every side of you, and I meant it. I'm insanely attracted to you right now." Immediately, I worried that had been too clinical. I'd been trying to avoid another gendered term.

It won me a small smile from Araceli. "The feeling is very much mutual." She brought her hand up to cup my face.

It wasn't *my* face. But I wasn't going to think about that. Ever since Falael had trashed my self-esteem, I hadn't once been able to stop the intrusive thoughts during every intimate moment. I didn't want to mess this up. Maybe I could find power in this not being my body. The Blood Duchess was strong and confident and fearless. I could believe that someone as amazing as Araceli would want the duchess's body. As for me? I'd rather not think about if that bothered me because I would. Not. Mess. This. Up.

"Is there anything else I should know? Anywhere you don't want to be touched?"

"I'm fine with touching. When I'm like this I . . . I don't want to have sex like a man. But touching is fair game."

I hummed under my breath. "That leaves plenty of ways for us to have fun."

In a frustrated voice, Araceli said, "These clothes don't make me look like a woman." She looked down and waved at the trousers.

"Then take them off." I tugged at the top of her shirt, feeling the threads stretch. The Blood Duchess probably tore off her lovers' clothing. I yanked harder, channeling my villainess persona.

The trousers followed, sliding to the floor with a soft clang from the belt buckle. Oh, what a sight. That alabaster skin looked frail, but an assassin's muscles were anything but. Wild red hair puffed out like a tree in the heart of autumn. The desire in those dilated pupils warmed me. "I love your tattoos," I murmured, tracing the number five formed from a thorny vine.

"All of the Twelve Avengers have a tattoo in the order that we joined. It's a symbol of our resolve."

"Oh." I withdrew my hand, afraid I'd poked a delicate subject. Better for neither of us to think about how Araceli had once wanted to stab the heart I was currently borrowing.

"Here are my fun tattoos." Araceli lifted up her hair to show a beautiful butterfly with one monarch wing and one wing made of marigolds. "This one represents my promise to be true to myself." She twisted to show the crown on her other shoulder. "I got this one the day I decided to protect Antonia with my life."

"They're lovely. I'm not the kind of person who gets tattoos, but I do like yours." I swallowed. "Did the needles hurt? I'm not brave enough." My villainess confidence was slipping away. Suddenly I felt nervous about someone so attractive getting a look at me. Except it wasn't me; did that make it okay? I *wanted* that to make it okay. I did not want to wonder if Araceli would still want me in my own body. I feared to ask. At moments like this, it was better not to let my brain get in the way.

Araceli took my hand and kissed each knuckle. "You are brave and beautiful. You defeated Falael, the Guild of Slavers, the dwarves, and your own nobility. A mere needle would never scare you."

Taking a deep breath, I summoned up the manic energy I'd felt in the throne room that day I'd tossed Ava's sacred treasure. I took Araceli's hand and kissed it in return. "I'll fear nothing with you at my side."

Araceli waggled her eyebrows at me. "I showed you mine. It's only fair if you show me yours."

I ripped off my dress so fast the fabric tore. It was the most expensive clothing I'd ever destroyed, and I didn't care.

Araceli pushed me back onto the bed and straddled me. She buried her face into my breasts. "I love these," she moaned. "Damn. Holy damn. I could happily die smothered to death like this."

I giggled. "Don't die—ah . . ." A lick made my neck arch, then I couldn't speak except in gasps. For a brief moment, I flashed back to Falael telling me that my breasts sagged. Usually here was where I started to feel gross and hate to have that part of my body touched, but this time I told myself they weren't my breasts. This wasn't my body. I could just lie back and enjoy this and not think. (The lovely compliments weren't being paid to my own breasts, but I wouldn't let that bother me. For once I wouldn't be a screwup. If I could only get this intoxicating desire by being the duchess, then I'd still take it.)

Araceli glanced up at me, gaze coquettish and amused. I whimpered, knowing I was being teased. Then coherent thought was gone again as she kissed downward and licked my navel. I moaned, and my thighs involuntarily squeezed together. "You're so damn sexy."

"Flattery will get you everywhere." Araceli tugged down my underwear to kiss the place where hair met flesh. "Mmm, these are getting in the way."

"Take them off," I said, striving to sound less desperate as I lifted up my hips.

Araceli yanked them off and tossed them over her shoulder. Hazel eyes drank in my exposed skin.

I shivered under her heated gaze. "Sorry, I didn't groom myself, I didn't know that—"

"Absolutely do not apologize. You look delicious." She bit her bottom lip. "I want to taste you."

I'd be burned at the stake before I'd turn that down. "Oh, yes."

Her fingers explored with agonizing gentleness. I moaned at the first lick, my hips moving in time with her tongue.

"I could happily die crushed between these, too." Araceli kissed the inside of my thigh.

"Don't joke, *you're* the one killing me. You're going to drive me insane if you don't get inside me."

"As you wish," Araceli murmured, then slid in a finger. She kept licking me as she pushed in and out. The maddening pressure and wetness formed a pool of heat in my belly that exploded. I collapsed backward with a piercing scream.

Araceli licked her fingers, her confident grin returning. "That good?"

"Yes, it was that good." I pecked her lips. I could taste myself, but it didn't bother me, an odd feeling.

She tugged me down into the bed next to her. Then she buried her face into my breasts and fell asleep there, like a cat who'd found the perfect ray of sun.

I smiled and looked at the red locks spread across my shoulder. I wanted to do this again. And again. And again. I wanted soft moments and exciting ones both inside and outside the bedroom. I wanted to have many more meals together. I wanted to introduce Araceli to the rest of my family. I wanted to shop for clothes together and find matching outfits. I wanted to go back to my childhood home and show her the spot where Ysabel had buried my doll. I wanted so many things that my heart ached with it. What would happen in the future when I stopped being the duchess? Would Araceli no longer have a reason to stay? Would I become a peasant again while Ari took back the duchy? Would she be attracted to my real body? I didn't know if we could have a future together. But I wanted it so badly.

Like that, I nearly fell asleep. But that would have been unforgivably selfish, and I strived to be a better quality lover. Nudging Araceli, I whispered, "Your turn." I lifted her up in the air and placed her on the side of the bed.

She gasped as I manhandled her. I smirked. "You liked that."

"You surprised me," Araceli insisted, even as her hands went up to grab my shoulders.

I'd never been so pleased to be tall and strong before now. "You liked it, my flower."

She chuckled in acknowledgment. I'd found a good nickname, then. "I'd never turn down an offer from you."

Our lips connected. I ran my hand down her body and circled a nipple. She smiled into my mouth, rocking closer into me.

I let my hand go down farther. She gasped and held me tighter as I rubbed her. The sweat of our bodies filled the air. I was tired, but oh, how I wanted this. I needed to make her unravel as she'd made me. Each sultry pant told me I was on the right track. Inching my hand downward, I asked, "Should I give you a finger?"

"HEDRI, STOP!" Araceli screamed, shoving me off the bed.

It felt like a bucket of ice water had been thrown over the room. Araceli gaped at me, wide-eyed and trembling. Slowly, I raised my hands and backed away. "I'm sorry."

"You've done nothing wrong." Araceli gripped a fistful of red hair. "Shit. That wasn't because of you. I thought . . . I thought I could handle it."

I grabbed a chair on the other side of the bedroom and sat down. "We never did talk about how I'm not in my own body." In retrospect, that seemed like a huge blunder. I'd been so caught up in my own insecurities that I'd never considered how Araceli might feel about making love to the body of the woman who had plotted her parents' deaths.

Araceli gulped. "This is on me. I should have guessed that might happen, and now I've made you feel worse about yourself."

"No, no, you haven't. I'm selfish for not considering how you might feel."

Araceli pushed her hair out of her face and sighed. "As you know, I used to flirt with the Blood Duchess. It was a good way to control her. Duchess Hedri wasn't interested in women, but she liked people to be in love with her. It fed her ego. She trusted me because she thought I loved her."

"That must have been difficult."

"Honestly, I did find her body objectively attractive."

"I had some idea about that."

Araceli sagged against the wall. "That's why I thought I could do this with you, without making an ass of myself."

"You're not an ass."

"I even thought it would be nice to have the haughty duchess's body writhing under me and at my mercy."

"That's a little ass-like." The words popped out before I could stop them. What was I thinking, hitting poor Araceli at her lowest point? I froze, mortified. "I'm sorry for saying that!"

Araceli threw back her head and laughed until her air ran out. She wiped a tear from her eye. "When you have that look on your face, you're so different from the Blood Duchess, it's miraculous. When I was touching you, I completely forgot who you were."

"That's nice to hear." I swallowed. "I was a little nervous that you might only want the duchess's body, not me."

"That's not true at all. I never once thought about touching the real duchess like that. I only wanted it because of *you*." Araceli waved at me to come closer again. Slowly, tentatively, I sat down on the bed next to her. She took my hand. "We really should have talked first. I could have told you there was a chance I might freak out, so you wouldn't be caught off guard. I was trying to push my way through."

"You didn't have to do that." I felt hurt that she would think she couldn't talk to me and nervous I'd somehow caused it. "I'm sorry if I pressured you."

"You didn't!" She nearly leapt up with the force of the words. "Please don't blame yourself. I've always lived by a motto of 'seize the moment.' An assassin's life can be short. I thought we might not have another opportunity and took a chance. I honestly don't regret anything we did, only that I might have hurt your feelings."

"Hey, you don't need to worry about me. It went wrong when I tried to touch you back, right?"

Glumly, Araceli nodded. "I didn't feel scared when I was the one touching you."

I hung my head. "I really am sorry."

She squeezed my hand. "For the last time, you have nothing to apologize for. I was encouraging you. I was enjoying it, until I saw your face—the duchess's face—and suddenly I forgot who was touching me."

"We could try again, when I get my body back. If you still want to then." I glanced at her sideways.

Araceli leaned against me. "Bora, if I find you devastatingly attractive in the body of my worst enemy, I guarantee I will like you no matter what your real body looks like. It's the person you are inside that I'm attracted to."

When she put it like that, it made me feel much better. For the first time, I was able to relax against her.

"I'd still be willing to try again with you like this. Honestly, if you got a haircut, it might make a big difference."

"I could get a tattoo," I half joked. The notion was intriguing, after seeing how good tattoos looked on Araceli. My mother would freak out, but I wanted to be past the point of caring about that. Looking at Araceli's messy locks, I longed to brush back her hair but feared taking the initiative to touch her. "Seriously, you don't have to do anything that makes you uncomfortable. I'll get my real body back, then this won't be a problem."

Leaning in, Araceli touched our foreheads together. "I'm grateful that you're willing to give me another chance."

"After the way you rocked my world? I'd beg you for it," I insisted.

"That would make you look nothing like the duchess." Araceli smiled and held out her arms. "Want to cuddle?"

I was quick to take her up on that offer. We fell asleep together, intertwined.

A high-pitched voice cried, "Arrrrrrrrrrrrrrrrraceli! Where are you?"

I rolled over and tried to put my head under my pillow. But someone else was already using it. A beautiful face with waves of red hair. This must be what sailors felt like, glimpsing a mermaid rising out of the waves. I smiled.

"Arrrrrrrrrrrrrrrrrrrrrrrri!"

Groaning, I sat up. My doorknob rattled. I had no time to stop it from opening. All I could do was drag my sheet up over my naked chest.

Queen Antonia bounded into the room. "There you are!"

"Huh?" Next to me, Araceli finally stirred.

As she sat up, I hastily tugged up the sheet to make sure it covered both of us.

Antonia put her hands on her hips. "You promised to take me out for a walk this morning."

"Yes, I did," Araceli admitted. "I thought I still had time." Her gaze fell on the rays of sunlight coming through the window. "I'm sorry. I'll get dressed as quickly as I can, then come over. In the future, you need to knock before entering people's bedrooms."

"Sorry." Antonia pouted. "You weren't in your room."

"Why would you look for Araceli in my bedroom?" I asked, holding the sheet close.

"Because I'm not stupid." With a withering glare, Antonia strode out.

As soon as the door closed, I groaned and collapsed backward onto my bed. "I feel responsible for traumatizing a child."

"She's not traumatized." Araceli pecked my lips. "I watched my whole family die; that was trauma. Children are robust—and should know better than to burst into bedrooms. I'll teach her not to do that before she walks in on something more explicit." She picked up her clothes off the floor.

I cleared my throat. Unfortunately, this made Araceli turn around to look at me before I'd thought of what I wanted to say. I knew I ought to say something. I couldn't just let the bod that had rocked my world stroll off without a single word. My voice came out rather small as I admitted, "I had a great time last night. Um, in spite of how it ended."

"Me too." Araceli smiled. Her hand reached out to brush a lock of hair off my face. "And as far as I'm concerned, ending on cuddling was a great note. Next time, I'm not going to rush into anything physical without getting a handle on my thoughts. However, I'll cuddle you some more tonight if you want."

"*If?* Of course I want to!" Whoops, had I said that last part out loud? Judging from the smirk on Araceli's face, I had. I flushed. "We can talk after you get back from your walk. Maybe over a private dinner tonight." That would give me some time to compose my mind from the puddle it had melted into.

"I'd love that." Araceli gave me another smoldering smile, then regrettably started covering up that sexy body with clothes.

Later that day, I sat at my desk going over all the palace financials, looking for errors or signs of embezzlement. I lacked the skills to help with official paperwork. I knew it and acknowledged it. But I still wanted to do something more to help my sister than just stamp whatever she gave me with the royal seal. It was hard, boring work. My bedroom desk was a bit too small for me. The thin seat cushion was insignificant for sitting for a long period of time. As I rubbed my aching forehead, I reminded myself that I'd asked for this. Ysabel had been content to let me spend the day lazing and eating chocolate. But no, I wanted to be useful.

I had to admit, I'd been hoping to help more with getting my body back. That goal had just taken on a new urgency. However, we'd yet to hear from Ma'qas. Ysabel said she was speaking to her own contacts, but apparently most of them only trusted her, so I couldn't help with the search. So far my sister's information network in Arahasnor had come up worryingly blank. It was looking more likely the duchess had left the kingdom the longer we couldn't find her.

What if the Blood Duchess had gotten mugged on the road, died, and been buried in a shallow grave? I might never find out. Then what would I do?

A knock interrupted my fretting. "I knocked this time!" Antonia said unnecessarily.

"Yes, you did, thank you. Is Araceli with you? You may come in."

Antonia bounded into the room. "No, but I came to talk to you about Araceli." Her lower lip jutted out. "I'm here to threaten you about what will happen if you ever hurt my Ari." She made a tiny fist.

"Oh, really?" I swiveled in my chair to face the child.

Antonia bit her lip. "I know I'm not very scary, but I'm the only one who Araceli has got."

"No, no, I think it's very sweet of you." I tried to keep a straight face.

Antonia scuffed the carpet with her shoe. "It's not fair that your sister, her husband, and Countess Donya all threatened my Ari, but no one has threatened you yet."

"My sister, too? That dinner with Kaine wasn't bad enough?" I flushed with mortification. We would be having words later.

"Araceli said that your sister is way scarier than the dark lord, but she sounded impressed about it."

"I could have told the world that," I muttered. The Conclave of Kings had never gotten between Ysabel and the last cookie.

"Araceli didn't seem mad," Antonia reassured me. "She likes your sister. But someone's gotta threaten you too in order for it to be fair."

"I completely understand." I folded my hands. "Lay it on me."

Antonia placed her hands behind her back and cleared her throat. "Araceli has been like a parent to me. The first person who cared about the mean duchess hitting me, and she even promised to kill the duchess for me. She's still working on that one, but it's the thought that counts."

"You're doing great," I whispered.

"I know a kid doesn't scare a grown-up." Antonia looked at her feet. "But after I reach my age of majority, I'll have all my power as queen. Then I'll have people I can send to beat you up."

I sat up straighter and nodded. "Yes, good point."

"After I figure out how to control my gift, I could body-swap you with a slug. Then I could squash the slug." Antonia pulled out a notebook from behind her back. "I have drawn pictures to demonstrate." She flipped to a crude stick figure of a girl wearing a crown and stepping on a very large slug. An arrow helpfully indicated that the slug was named "Bora."

I applauded vigorously. "Wonderful drawing. You have quite a talent, I love how you drew the slime dripping off my repugnant slug body. I feel very threatened. I'll never do anything to hurt Araceli, I promise."

Antonia beamed. "Thank you! I spent ages on the slug. I redrew it twice." She closed her notebook. "I don't want you to get too scared. I like you—a lot. You're good for my Ari."

"Thank you," I said, sincerely touched.

"Araceli used to be very lonely before you swapped places with the mean duchess. She smiles a lot when you're around. You're funny."

I flushed, thinking of the many ridiculous situations I'd gotten myself into lately. "I'm basically a clown," I mumbled.

"I mean it." Antonia stomped her foot. "You make Araceli smile. That's important. Araceli used to be very angry all the time, but ever since you came, there have been smiles. Araceli would never talk about what would happen after she killed the duchess. I begged her to stay with me and become my new parent, but she said that she couldn't promise she'd be able to. She never admitted it, but . . . I was afraid she planned to die."

I swallowed. "That's tough. I'm sorry."

"Ever since you came, Araceli talks about how to protect you after you swap bodies and her plans to stay and help our kingdom. She talks as if she has a future." Antonia's eyes welled up with tears. She tugged on my sleeve. "Please don't go. Please stay with my Ari."

I wanted to promise right away, but I feared that would be irresponsible. I couldn't make promises to this kid that I might not be able to keep. I didn't even know what Araceli wanted from me. I'd already started thinking long-term, but maybe to her, we were a mere fling. I probably should have asked before last night. Now, it would break my heart if she turned out not to be serious.

I tried for a balance between honesty and diplomacy. "I like Araceli a lot. I don't plan on going anywhere, as long as she still wants me."

Antonia frowned. "You sound like you think Araceli might leave you. But Araceli is the one who thinks that you don't like her."

"Huh?"

"I asked her if you'd stay with us forever, and she said that you liked someone else."

"I do?" I looked around as if expecting this mysterious person to materialize.

"Yeah, she thinks that you like the countess." Antonia studied my face. "If you like Araceli, then you should tell her. Then she'll feel better. And I won't have to turn you into a slug and step on you." Antonia skipped out of the office.

I was dumbstruck. Did I like Donya? I used to have a crush on her. But I'd never seriously seen her as a real possibility. Before I'd met her, she'd been my celebrity crush, someone I admired for all the activism work she did, and after I'd met her, she'd been even more awesome in person, but also even more unattainable. I'd adored her more as an ideal than as a person. I'd found her attractive, but I'd never seriously imagined a life together with her. Not the way I'd been fantasizing about living and growing old together with Araceli.

These were two very different feelings. I'd had a crush on Donya, but I was in love with Araceli.

Love. I tested the weight of the word, trying to see if it fit. Perhaps it was a little early to say love, but I was definitely falling hard in that direction.

Queen Antonia was right. I had to talk to Araceli. I couldn't possibly let her think that I had used her for a brief moment of comfort while liking someone else. If there was a chance that my feelings might be mutual, then I wanted to seize it.

I leapt to my feet—then immediately developed doubts. Was I dressed well enough for this talk? I'd put on a rather formal gown from the duchess's closet. Maybe I should have gone with something a bit sexier. Had I checked my teeth since breakfast? Did my breath smell?

I needed to primp myself first. Just then, a guard threw my door open. "Your Grace! You're needed at once."

I should have locked the door. Bad things always seemed to happen when I left my door unlocked. It had started to feel like a jinx. "Unless it's a city-wide crisis, it can wait."

"Yes, Your Grace."

I started to close my bedroom door. (This time, I would lock it.) The guard stuck his hand in the way, shouting, "What are you doing, Your Grace?"

I stopped before I hurt him. "Didn't you say it could wait?"

"I meant yes, it's a city-wide crisis, Your Grace."

I groaned. "Have you told my—Holy Maiden Ysabel?"

"That's the problem, Your Grace." The guard hopped from foot to foot. "A mob of concerned citizens is storming the palace, demanding that you release the Holy Maiden from your evil claws. Their words, not mine."

CHAPTER TWENTY

Why did it constantly feel like I was careening from one enemy trying to kill me to another? I barely had time to think as I raced for the front gate. According to the guard, my sister had already headed over. If she planned to put on an act, then she would need my help. I was worried about what my sister's husband and bodyguard might do.

I found a mob of concerned citizens waving pitchforks at the front gate and shouting, "Free Holy Maiden Ysabel!"

Where was my sister? Hadn't the guard said that she'd come out first?

"Noble citizens!" Ysabel's voice pierced the air. She stood on a balcony above. "The Sun God thanks you for coming to my aid during this difficult time. However, the Sun God has a plan. I have accepted this plan, even though my role is difficult." Her shoulders heaved. She pretended to brush a tear from her eye. Then she buried her face in her hands and fake-sobbed. "You must leave, or the Blood Duchess's cruel wrath will descend upon you. But do not fear. The Sun God will protect me."

A hefty woman wielding a rolling pin stood in front of the mob and eyed my sister. "Everyone, it's okay! She's just faking it again!"

A relieved sigh went up from the crowd. A man muttered, "She clearly has the duchess under her control, just like how she controlled Dark Lord Kaine. Good for her."

"No wonder we've been getting paid for all our old labor at the Games if Her Holiness has taken charge."

"Yeah, I wondered about the signs advertising free doctors. The Blood Duchess would never do such a thing. I should have known our Ysabel would be pulling the strings."

A woman in the back cupped her hands to her mouth and shouted, "Keep it up, Holy Maiden! Congratulations on the baby!"

I couldn't help but feel indignant that my sister was getting all the credit for the ideas and plans we'd come up with together. On second thought, the alternative would be the duchess getting credit. Between those two options, my sister was better. I got no credit either way.

Ysabel's hands dropped from her face. Her tragic martyr expression was replaced by a scowl. "Hey, what do you mean about faking it *again*?"

Before my sister could do anything stupid, I took the stairs at a run.

By the time I reached the balcony, the mob had dispersed.

Ysabel paced, muttering, "I still don't see what she meant about *again*."

I guided her inside. "You're important to people in this city. I noticed as soon as I came here. On my very first day, everyone saved my life for your sake. I'm glad you've got people who care about you. Hurry up and come inside. It's freezing, and you're not even wearing a coat." I put my arms around her to warm her up.

"Don't you start, too," she grumbled. "Kaine has been driving me crazy with his fussing since I got pregnant."

"Yzzy, I'm your sister, don't try to bullshit me. You love being fussed over."

"Even I have my limits, okay?"

I didn't believe a word of it but decided to allow her to have her illusions. "Let's get something hot to drink." My smile froze as Donya came down the hallway toward us. She carried a letter and had a worried expression. "Please don't tell me it's another crisis."

Donya grimaced. "I could tell you a bit later, after you have time to get warm."

My shoulders sagged. "Please just lay it on me now. Otherwise I'll worry too much to enjoy the respite."

Donya held up the envelope to reveal the seal. "We've heard from the last person who King Uctor sold the kingdom to: the Dragon Emperor."

The Dragon Emperor of Faan came by his name honestly: He could turn into a dragon large enough to eat our palace. He ruled an empire so vast that our entire kingdom would fit into a single province. Sure, we had Kaine, the last victor in the World Games, but the Dragon Emperor wasn't even allowed to participate because he couldn't fit into the ring. A massive fire-breathing lizard would never be afraid of my cheap villainess act. Back in my village, a common saying had been "as unlikely as a dragon forgiving a debt." We were doomed.

My hands shook so badly, a bit of warm milk from my mug sloshed out, and I had to set down my drink. Kaine, Ysabel, Donya, Ari, and I were seated around the planning table. Ari had acquired a new black doublet and high boots, but even this dashing look couldn't distract me from my anxiety.

Leaning over, Ari whispered, "Casual looks good on you, too."

"This old thing?" I flushed, glancing down at my yellow wool dress. The neckline seemed awfully high, so I shifted it down a little. Huh, when had I gotten the confidence to do that?

Ari lowered his voice even more. "I adore how easy it would be to rip it off you."

Suddenly I felt hot all over. I had an overwhelming urge to confess my feelings right here, right now. Screw waiting to get him alone.

Ysabel kicked me under the table and snapped me out of my daze. Nope, now was not the moment, even if near-death adrenaline was tempting me. We might all be about to die in dragon fire. Was it so wrong for me to want one last time before my painful demise?

Donya opened the letter. Her jaw dropped.

Ysabel sipped from her own mug with a coolness I could only admire. "Don't keep us in suspense. How bad is it?"

Donya turned the letter to face us. "There's only one sentence written: *I don't want your trash kingdom.*"

Ysabel spat her milk across the room. It nearly hit me, but I ducked in time. Ari exhaled in relief.

"Is it a bluff?" I asked, afraid to believe good news. Good news never happened to me. "Maybe this is an elaborate ploy before he arranges a subtle invasion. Dragons have a bottomless capacity for greed. Everyone knows that."

A huge smile spread across Donya's face. "No, the more I think about it, the more I believe it. Arahasnor isn't near Faan. We'd be a very inconvenient province for them to manage. If the Dragon Emperor took over our kingdom, then he'd also take responsibility for our debt. From his perspective, he'd be losing money instead of gaining it. You know how dragons feel about losing gold. We're like a morsel too small to swallow."

"This is good news." Ysabel didn't look happy, though. Her knuckles had turned white on her mug. "If the Dragon Emperor wants to be a fool, then let him. Arahasnor has many great assets. I can't think of them at the moment, but—my gardens! The city has beautiful gardens and truly majestic walls."

I understood how offended my sister felt. Was our kingdom truly so awful as to make even a dragon forgive a debt to get rid of us? "We've got treasure, too," I insisted. "We have cultural heritage. I've never been a huge fan of Jdalj's art, but we have the largest collection of it in the world. What about the royal jewels? Doesn't he want to hoard the royal jewels?"

Donya cleared her throat. "Actually, I think the Dragon Emperor was after the Sacred Treasure of Ava. He's tried to purchase it several times. The dwarven ambassador spread it around far and wide that the Blood Duchess destroyed it. I suspect the Dragon Emperor lost all interest in us after hearing that."

"It was only a small chip!" I wailed. "It can be repaired . . . right?"

Ysabel raised a fist. "This is outrageous. That shitty dragon tried to take over our entire country to get *one emerald*?! Is the rest of Arahasnor worth nothing to that smug lizard? My homeland is broke, our nobility is useless, our farmland low quality, and our people will riot at the slightest excuse. But we are not complete and utter trash!"

Kaine had been dozing off with one hand on his elbow, but upon hearing this, he raised his eyes. "You know I'd conquer your homeland if you ever asked, my dear."

Ysabel sniffled. "Yes, but you'd be doing it for my sake, not because you actually want Arahasnor. It's not the same." She turned imploring eyes on me. "Surely there are good points to being the ruler of Arahasnor?"

I couldn't think of any at the moment, but I wouldn't let that get in the way of my wounded national pride. "I've nearly been lynched a few times, but that just goes to show we have a very politically involved citizenry. The Dragon Emperor is too much of a coward to rule us."

"Exactly!" Ysabel cried. "Where does he get off thinking he's better than us, with his elite bureaucracy and efficient road system? Our rambling roads where none of the addresses make sense are part of our national charm."

"You're right, it *is* insulting," Donya said slowly. "Our nation is as tough as dirt. No other country could have survived as many trade embargoes as King Uctor's poor diplomacy brought down on us. I'd like to see a foreigner decipher our insanely complicated recordkeeping and nonsensical tax system. To say nothing of balancing the politics of an independent church living within our borders that refuses to acknowledge our authority."

Ari groaned. "Donya, I count on you to be the rational one."

Ysabel said, "Our criminal element could mug the tame organized crime in Faan. If a dragon went to the bad part of town? We'd see a sudden rise in gemlike scales being sold on the black market and dragon steaks offered in street food stands."

"Don't count the countryside out," I insisted. "A dragon couldn't last on a diet of insects like we do in hard times."

Ysabel raised her fist in the air. "Tell that lizard he'd better get back here and try to conquer us, or I will skin him for a pair of boots."

"Yeah! He's big enough to make boots for everyone here!" I cried.

Donya was about to write that down before Ari shouted, "We don't want another nation trying to conquer us, remember?"

An embarrassed silence fell across the room as we all realized what madness our patriotism had nearly driven us to. Ysabel sniffled.

"You're right, I know. Even so, there was no need for the Dragon Emperor to be insulting about it. He acted like there wasn't a single object or person in all of Arahasnor worthy of hoarding! Where does he get off? He doesn't know us. He hasn't even seen my petunias." She rubbed at the tears forming around her eyes. "Aargh, I wish I could stop crying. I'm not even sad, I'm *angry*."

Kaine put an arm around her. "Do you know what would make you feel better? I'll put a hole in that stupidly long wall around Faan. I can pretend it was an accident."

The sound of breaking glass drew our eyes to the other side of the room. A clown wearing a bright purple wig, giant shoes, a red nose, and a puffy rainbow shirt burst through the window. He licked a rusty knife and cackled, "Blood Duchess, today is the day—"

Without looking over his shoulder, Kaine punched the assassin under the chin. The clown went through the wall, leaving a body-sized hole. Judging from the distant sound of crashing, he'd also flown through the royal stables and a few other buildings.

Kaine looked over his shoulder. "What *was* that lightweight thing? Was the latest Avenger a fly assassin?"

On second thought, I decided maybe Kaine could take a dragon after all. It was good to have him on our side.

From the ceiling, Alzira complained, "I was about to do that. I thought it would be polite to let him finish his speech first." Holy shit, had she been in the room this entire time?

I turned to Ari. "Was that a friend of yours? I'm sorry. We could go check if he survived the fall . . . though I have my doubts . . ."

Ari snorted. "Nah, that guy was always an asshole."

Ysabel and I went to the kitchen together to return our dirty mugs. Only afterward did I remember I had servants now. I needed a chance to talk to her anyway. I'd recently mailed another letter full of lies to Benoni and our parents, and I felt guilty contemplating even more lies in the future. I tugged her into a cushioned nook in the hallway. Light from the curved window made it the perfect reading spot. "Yzzy, a moment?"

"Apparently we have all the time in the world now that Faan *can't even be bothered to conquer us*," she grumbled.

"Can I tell Benoni the truth about how our older brother died? Next time I see him in person, of course. I can't risk a letter ever since I found out Mom goes through our mail."

To my surprise, Ysabel stiffened.

"I wouldn't without your permission," I reassured her, even though I really did want permission. Our youngest brother shouldn't be the only one out of the loop. It would be unfair. "He took Calum's death hard. I caught him talking to someone not there several times."

"Plenty of people talk to themselves. Maybe it helps him think."

"He was talking to Calum."

"Oh. I'll see about arranging for a counselor; the elves have made amazing strides in that area." Ysabel wrapped her arms around her shoulders. "Sure, you can tell him. If you think it will help."

"Is something wrong?" I asked.

Ysabel wouldn't meet my gaze. "Aren't you angry at me?"

"For threatening Ari?" I blinked. "Nah. He didn't seem to mind. Just look at how casual he was with you today. I think he took it in the spirit it was meant. The queen came by to threaten me in return this morning. It was adorable."

Ysabel looked at me as if I'd gone insane. "No, because I caused Calum's death!"

I gasped. "No, you didn't. Surely you know that, Yzzy. His death wasn't your fault."

"He died because of me. Isn't that the same?" There was no real question in her voice, only a dull resignation.

"It's not the same at all! Would you blame *me* if Calum had died saving my life?"

"That's not what happened, though." Tears formed in the corners of my sister's eyes. These were real tears. Like the mob, I knew when my sister fake-cried. This was different from her mere frustration over the emperor's letter, too. She was trying so hard to hide it, I could tell. I wanted so badly to hug her again, but she was leaning away from me. Yzzy had a tendency to shut down when deeply upset.

I groped for something to say before hitting upon an idea. I didn't like it, but I was desperate. Time to admit what I'd vowed to never tell her. I took a deep breath. "My ex-boyfriend stole all the money you gave me."

Ysabel's head shot up. "Huh?"

"He pretended he was investing it in a lumber company. He cheated on me with my best and only friend, then fled the country with her. That's why I had to move back in with our parents."

Ysabel's hand clenched into a fist. "I'm going to murder him," she said, her voice low and sincere. "What's his name? What's his last known location?"

"It's fine. I've taken care of it. I'm not a kid any longer. I can handle my own enemies."

Ysabel didn't seem to hear me. "I'll grind his body into powder and feed it to him! I'll make him suffer and beg before he dies!" She trembled with fury. The look in her eyes had turned diamond hard. She wasn't exaggerating.

"Are you mad at me?" I asked.

"You? Why would I be angry at *you*?" Ysabel stared at me in confusion. "I suppose I'm upset that you never told me. Why *didn't* you tell me? I would have given you more money. I never would have let you be forced to live with our abusive parents."

"Dad is rotten to the core, sure, but Mom isn't so bad, and after the divorce, now it's just the two of us."

"Mom makes you suffer with words, and I'm not sure that's all that much better."

I thought about the direct correlation between my mother's constant jabs and my hatred of my body. "Point taken."

"Mom always went after you the hardest. I think it's because you never insulted her back, and you always forgave her." My sister bit her lip. "I hated listening to you cry late at night. Sometimes when I was a kid, I'd make her angry on purpose so she'd go after me instead. I used to worry a lot about what would happen to you, after I . . . left home."

Left. What a nice euphemism for being sold into slavery. "You shouldn't have worried about me, Yzzy. You had it so much worse. I wish I could have stopped them from taking you away."

"Why didn't you tell me?" Ysabel repeated. "I thought that Mom had successfully emotionally blackmailed you back into her clutches. I was going out of my mind because nothing I said could persuade you to leave. I would have thrown money at you in a heartbeat if it got you out of that house."

"That's why I couldn't tell you." I swallowed a lump in my throat. I was perilously close to tears. "You bought every coin that you sent me with a day of your life. How could I explain that I'd lost something so precious because I fell for a smooth-talking pretty boy? What if you had to do more healings in order to make up for the lost money? I wouldn't have been able to live with the guilt. I already hated myself for being stupid enough to think the most handsome man in town would ever love a fat fuck like me."

All the color drained from Ysabel's face. "Death is too good for him. I'm going to make him suffer slowly."

"There's no need. After I swapped with the duchess, I had him arrested for fraud." That was the only reason I had the confidence to have this conversation with her. I could not have lived with myself if she had to save me yet again. "He was mine to handle."

"Good for you." Ysabel pulled me into a hug. It felt a bit strange to have her so much smaller than my current body. She didn't even come up to my shoulder. I had to bend down to hug her. Patting my back, she murmured, "Oh, Bora. I hate that anyone dared to make my precious baby sister feel unworthy."

"Are you angry at me for losing your money?"

"Of course not."

"Would you have hated me if I'd told you back when it happened?"

"Of course not!"

I hugged her closer. "Then why won't you believe that I don't blame you for what happened to Calum?"

"That's different," Ysabel muttered into my chest.

"Yeah, it's different—you were held prisoner by an evil necromancer for years. I stupidly gave a hot asshole all my money. I practically had it coming."

"You know that's not what I meant."

"I love you, Yzzy." I pressed my chin over the top of her head. "Please be as kind to yourself as you are to me. Please don't blame yourself any longer. Calum would be furious if you blamed yourself. He never let anyone push around his younger siblings, not even themselves."

Ysabel made a choked sound like a sob. "I'll try."

"That's all I ask." I rubbed a circle onto her back.

"It's awesome that you took down that scammer ex yourself."

"One of the top ten moments of my life."

"When did my baby sister get so amazing?" Ysabel's voice finally held a trace of a smile.

"I've been proud of myself lately," I said, and for once, I meant it.

I remembered that I still needed to find Ari/Araceli and confess my feelings. I felt a welling of confidence. Somehow, I knew I would find the right words to say. Whatever the obstacles of my current body and my insecurities, we would get through them together.

Unfortunately, at that point, I heard the sound of blaring horns.

Ysabel rubbed her eyes and looked out the window. "What's going on?"

A booming, gift-enhanced voice cried, "Presenting the representative of the Conclave of Kings!"

For once, I wasn't behind an unlocked door, and it hadn't done me any good. Trouble had found me anyway. "Haven't we filled our quota of crises today?" I moaned. "Is it too late to force this godawful kingdom on the Dragon Emperor?"

Ysabel paled. "I thought we'd have more time before the Conclave made a move. Can you stall them? I'll bring Kaine and Alzira."

The old Bora would have been too scared. The new Bora wouldn't let her sister down. "I'll intimidate them so badly, they'll be shaking in their boots."

Ysabel patted my arm. "I knew I could count on you." She left at a run.

I'd taken off a lot of my jewelry because I found it too heavy. Fortunately, I still had most of it stuffed into my purse. I would have been too nervous to leave such expensive jewels lying around. As I ran down the stairs, I crammed on rings and bracelets. I tossed a ruby necklace over my head, getting my hair caught. Stopping at a mirror, I straightened my curls. I yanked down my bodice and hiked up my skirt in order to look properly like the Blood Duchess.

With my head raised high, I stepped outside. A row of guards in silver masks lined a golden carriage. The plumes on their helmets told me that these must be Gifted Knights. But I refused to be intimidated. I had my own guards standing at the palace gate and guarding the wall. The same guards who had turned tail as soon as the mob showed up, but I told myself that the Conclave's representative didn't know that. *I'm not Bora, a simple country girl. I'm the Blood Duchess. Fierce and unconquerable. Terrifying and beautiful.*

The lead knight bellowed, "Announcing the representative of the Conclave of Kings."

I tossed back my hair and laughed wickedly. "What a fool, setting foot on *my* territory. I, the Blood Duchess, will—"

My words died in my throat. The woman who stepped out of the carriage had curly black hair, brown eyes, and a short stature supported by high heels. Those facial features had stared back at me from the mirror for my entire life.

She was *me*.

Or rather, she was the real Blood Duchess.

CHAPTER TWENTY-ONE

"Ah. Uh," I stammered. My mind had gone completely blank. All my fake confidence in myself as the Blood Duchess had vanished in the face of the real Duchess Hedri.

My body seemed like a foreign thing now it had been dressed up, perfumed, and bedecked in such large gemstones. I felt distant, as if in a dream.

In a flash, she'd stepped past the wall of guards to come so close I could have reached out a hand and touched her (my?) shoulder. She raked me with her eyes. A sneer pulled back her lips. "I see you've been enjoying yourself inside my body, thief. You made me look like a mess." Her eyes swept the courtyard, taking in the wreckage left from the last two mobs. "Clearly you weren't able to handle your situation at all."

Her poise and dignity showed flawlessly in every word and gesture. It seemed so much better than my own fake confidence. Frankly, she wore my body far better than I did. Her blue dress perfectly accented her curves. (My curves? This had the potential to get confusing real fast.) In my state of shock, every last ruffle on the dress became vivid. A huge diamond necklace drew attention to the scandalously low dress line. My hair looked shinier and more voluminous than I'd ever managed to style it myself. I'd have fallen flat on my face if I'd attempted those high heels. A bit of makeup had turned my plain face beautiful. Funny, I'd always hated my double chin, but on the duchess I hadn't even noticed.

A nasty voice in my head whispered, *She's superior to you, no matter what body. You never could have made yourself look so beautiful.*

Everything you have now is only because everyone thinks that you're the Blood Duchess. Without that, you're just a plain country mouse that no one listens to, respects, or cares about.

I knew I ought to do something. Say something. Even running away would be better than standing here waiting for her to order my arrest. But my cowardly feet refused to move. The guards were staring at us—both hers and mine. I swayed as the world around me spun.

A cloud of doom wrapped inescapably over me. Deep down, I knew it was all over.

The real Duchess Hedri raised her hand high to wave a parchment. "I am your rightful duchess. I have a scroll from the Conclave of Kings verifying my true identity. Although even without that, I'm sure the difference between me and her is quite obvious." She gestured at me, then placed a hand on her chest. "The superior quality of nobility can't be faked. Guards, arrest this imposter!"

I closed my eyes, waiting for the hammer to fall.

"Ours isn't the real Blood Duchess?" one of the Arahasnor guards asked from behind me.

Duchess Hedri sniffed. "Of course not. Could you possibly imagine me as this pathetic, cringing thing? Her name is apparently *Bora*. Ugh. How utterly common."

"Bora, the Holy Maiden's sister?" The guard grabbed my shoulder.

I was utterly convinced he was about to slap me into chains. Instead, he pushed me behind him. "Stay back! We'll protect you."

A dozen more guards leapt forward, forming a barrier in front of me.

"Did you not hear me? This woman is an imposter!" Duchess Hedri cried.

"Exactly! The only reason we didn't leap to help her sooner is because we thought she was *you*." The guard glanced over his shoulder. "I'm sorry, Miss Bora. If I'd known that you weren't that horrible Blood Duchess, then I would never have abandoned my post when the mob came. I would have protected you with my life. Also, I watched one of the maids spit in your food but didn't do anything.

Please forgive me. I'll make up for it by defending you to the last drop of my blood."

Duchess Hedri's smugness dropped off her face. "What do you think you're doing? I ordered you to arrest this peasant!"

"We don't take your orders." Sergeant Laurent stepped forward from the crowd. Coolly, he spat at the duchess's feet. "You're a foreigner. You're not welcome here. We won't let you lay one finger on one of our own."

A rumble of agreement came from the guards.

"She's a good one. She made sure we all got paid on time! We should have realized sooner that she was too nice to be the Blood Duchess."

"We'll protect our Holy Maiden's family no matter what."

"No one wants you in charge! I'd rather obey one of our own people."

"She stopped the slavers from taking over the city and drove off the dwarves."

Hey, that *was* me! I felt a warmth under my chest.

Duchess Hedri whirled on one of the Sherdan guards who had been part of her original escort. "What are you waiting for? School these insolent rebels!"

The Sherdan guards shifted. The captain shot a nervous glance at me, then mumbled, "Actually, we'd rather keep that duchess."

"What did you just say?" Hedri hissed.

The captain puffed out his chest. "She kept her promise about paying us and giving us citizenship. You didn't." With increasing confidence, he continued, "I don't see any proof that you're the real duchess. Just look at her over there, dressed up in ducal finery." He jerked his head at me, where I stood in a state of shock. "She looks like a real duchess to me. You can't prove otherwise."

Duchess Hedri went white with shock, then red.

I cleared my throat. "Sorry, did you not realize how unpopular you are?"

Duchess Hedri shrieked, "Gifted Knights! Attack—"

A blur shot through the crowd and leapt in front of me. Alzira, Humanity's Strongest Monster, stood before me with her sword pointed at the sky. "Take one step forward, sinners, and I will bring down the wrath of heaven upon you," she said menacingly.

From behind me, Ysabel said, "The wrath of heaven is an asteroid large enough to crush your skull. Don't take one more step toward my sis—uh, I mean, my kidnapper. I'm very attached to my kidnapper. I'm the sort of person who becomes brainwashed very quickly."

Remembering my sister's inability to see faces, I said, "Ysabel, she already knows who I am. That's the real duchess."

Ysabel did a double take. "Dark Lady, that's your body shape. Uh. I mean, the Sun God has bestowed upon me a vision suggesting that this complete stranger spend some time in the dungeons."

"How dare you!" The duchess no longer looked composed or dignified. Sweaty hair stuck to her face. "I'm the official representative of the Conclave of Kings. I demand a trial for this imposter."

"Interesting." Ysabel eyed the duchess coolly. "We'll think about it."

"We will?" I gasped.

At the same time, the duchess growled, "The Conclave ordered this trial. The people who rule this world. It's not optional."

Ysabel swept back into the castle, calling over her shoulder, "I suggest you find an inn for the night. This isn't your castle yet."

Sitting in my office, Ysabel handed me a cup of tea. "I find this particular herbal brew calming for my nerves. It helped me quit the redleaf."

"Thank you." I blew on the cup. Staring into the liquid depths, I tried not to panic. "Was the duchess right about us not having a choice except to go to trial?"

"We've got a choice: trial or war."

"Oh dear."

"Realistically speaking, we can't stall the Blood Duchess for long. She's the representative of the Conclave of Kings. As much as I'd like to throw her in a dungeon until we figure out how to swap you two back, that would be an act of war."

"Ah." My shoulders sagged. "Then we're in a lot of trouble." I'd only just started to get my confidence back when the guards sided with me. Now it was gone.

"Actually, this may be an opportunity." Ysabel tapped her chin. "It's very, very interesting that the Conclave of Kings sent the Blood Duchess as their representative. If they'd sent a delegation of important people from various nations, that would mean they're backing her claim. But they didn't. They sent her alone."

"My grasp on international politics is weak." I took a sip. The tea tasted bitter. "What does that mean?"

Ysabel stared off into the distance. "I'll bet Arahasnor's neighbors didn't like seeing a land-hungry nation expand next door to them. It sets a dangerous precedent, to let Sherda pull such a trick. Countries with traditional enmity to Sherda would oppose it. Of course, Sherda has allies, too. It must have been a split vote. This was a compromise option."

I looked down at the steam rising off my tea. "They're letting the duchess succeed or fail on her own?"

Ysabel smiled. "Exactly. See? You should give yourself more credit. You caught on to the politics right away. They sent the duchess here with her identity verified by their Seer and gave her authority to call for a trial. But they didn't immediately rule in her favor."

"We still have a chance." I spoke as if trying to convince myself.

"In a sense, I think the Conclave of Kings has been using the Blood Duchess the same way our side has been using you—that is to say, as a scapegoat. If she succeeds, then they'll accept her as regent. But if she fails, they'll deny all connection to her. Either way, the matter gets settled without them needing to risk anything." Ysabel bared her teeth. "I suspect a large part of their motivation is that no one wants to risk a conflict with my dear Kaine."

I drank more tea. My tongue had started to become accustomed to the flavor. "The Blood Duchess is in the right. I stole her identity and her authority. How can we possibly win the trial?"

"A trial with the fate of a nation at stake won't be fair or unbiased. Those with the authority to judge will be the cardinals and the nobility." Ysabel smirked. "The cardinals hate the duchess for arresting the Head Cardinal, and the local nobility doesn't want a foreign regent. They're already biased in our favor."

"But I'm not the real duchess. That's a fact."

"Oh, my dear naïve sister. I'm telling you that people don't need to think that you're real to vote for you. They just have to think that you're a better option than Duchess Hedri. Frankly, she set the bar somewhere in hell."

"Then do you want me to pretend I'm still the Blood Duchess?" At the thought, I shook my head. "It's impossible. They'll bring in Seers to detect if we're telling the truth."

"You can truthfully say that you didn't steal the duchess's body. The swap was accidental. Therefore, we just have to make sure the question is phrased how we want."

"I can't truthfully say that I'm the Blood Duchess!"

"Seers can be biased or bribed, just like noble juries." Ysabel gave me an assessing look. "They'll ask you questions about your past, though. Perhaps we should go with the amnesia route. It doesn't need to be a convincing story. The Conclave sending Duchess Hedri alone is practically tacit permission. They'll accept the outcome of this trial, even if it's nothing but a convenient fiction."

I slammed my teacup down. "Yzzy, I don't want to be stuck like this forever! I want to go back to my real body!"

"Oh." My sister frowned. "Of course you do. I'm sorry. I got carried away scheming. Oh dear. That poses a problem."

I didn't like the sound of that one bit. My love life depended on getting my body back. That was such a selfish consideration, I didn't dare raise it. Nor was it something I wanted to talk about with my sister. I had plenty else to say, though. "Duchess Hedri is currently in my body! If you make her into a criminal, then how will I ever go back to being myself?" Up until now, I'd been content to do whatever I needed to inside the duchess's body because I didn't plan to live there for the rest of my life. If both the duchess and my real body became criminals, then I'd have no retreat left. I felt like a box was closing in around me. My breathing grew heavy.

Ysabel hung her head. "You're right. I'm sorry."

That wasn't the answer I'd wanted from her. I'd wanted her to tell me that she had another clever solution. "What will we do?" I asked in a small voice.

Ysabel fiddled with her teacup. "I'll think of something." Her usual confidence had deserted her voice.

"What happens if we tell the truth?" I asked.

Ysabel seemed to consider this. "You didn't swap the bodies on purpose, and we could prove it. I could protect you from retaliation, using my own and my husband's political influence. But Duchess Hedri would become the rightful regent of Arahasnor. She would take over the kingdom as she'd originally planned. We've even chased off the other challengers for her."

My heart sank to my stomach. The tea inside me gurgled. I whispered, "If there's no other option to save Arahasnor . . ." I couldn't quite bring myself to say it. I couldn't be brave enough.

Ysabel reached over and grabbed my hand. "You don't have to do this. I'll come up with a new plan."

"What will happen to Queen Antonia? The duchess abused her."

Ysabel paled with horror. "Maybe she can flee to Conollia with us?"

"Can she, without starting a war?"

Ysabel's shoulders sagged. "No." She straightened. "I'll think of something. Give me more time."

But I didn't believe there was truly another option.

My sister left me alone to my tea and my cowardice, trying to decide if I had what it took to sacrifice myself for my country.

As I nursed the last dregs of my tea, I heard a knock on my window. I looked up.

Ma'qas balanced on my windowsill. With a cheerful grin, she said, "Good news and bad news. The good news is, I found the Blood Duchess."

I sighed. "Yes, I know. She marched into the city and put me on trial."

Ma'qas had the grace to look sheepish. "Ah, I see you already know the bad news. It's not my fault! She had already reached the Conclave Headquarters before you sent me after her. It was too late from the beginning. She must have headed straight there after the body swap.

It always would have been difficult to stop her. She was surrounded by too many guards for me to do anything by the time I caught up with her. But I have more good news! The Living Shadow called together the rest of the Twelve Avengers. Although, we're the Ten Avengers now—"

"I know," I said. "My brother-in-law killed two of you. One before this mess started, and the clown recently. I'm sorry."

Ma'qas shrugged. "Don't be. I never liked those guys. Besides, anyone stupid enough to fight Dark Lord Kaine deserves what he got. Sorry, *former* dark lord. He's still the scariest bastard to walk the face of the earth. I don't know how your sister can handle him."

I had some idea, but nothing I'd say out loud. "I think they're good for each other. Such a cute couple."

"The point is, turns out the Living Shadow knew all of our identities and summoned all of us for the final assassination. That thing might not be as scary as Kaine, but it is a far more subtle and efficient killer."

I had a bad feeling. "You gathered to do what, exactly?"

Ma'qas beamed. "To kill the Blood Duchess! Fear not, I explained to them that she's in your body now. They won't come after you any longer. They'll go after the real one instead."

"But they'll kill my body!" I slammed my teacup down. This time, it cracked. "I was planning to go back to that."

"Tough luck." Ma'qas shrugged. "Sorry, but we all want revenge, and we don't have any attachment to you. I suggest you learn to love the body you currently have. Ari seems to like it." With that, she climbed out the window.

I screamed after her, "That's my body! It is not yours to kill! Get back here!" I kept shouting until my throat gave out, to no effect.

Ma'qas didn't know what she was talking about, unfortunately. If I couldn't swap back, then my love life would forever have the flag of doom hanging over it. Araceli was not the only reason I wanted my real body back. But that particular consideration did weigh heavily on my mind. Even though Araceli was willing to try with the duchess's body, I didn't want to cause more trauma. Plus . . . you know . . . it was very scary to think of someone killing my body!

I still needed to talk to Araceli. It had faded from my mind in light of the many, many shocks of the day. But it would be discourteous to not say something complimentary to the lover who had rocked my world last night.

Rather than show up empty-handed, I stopped by the kitchens for a snack. Then I stole a cluster of flowers from a vase and hid them behind my back.

I'd planned to talk to Antonia first, but as it turned out, both people I needed to speak to were in the same place.

Araceli sat on the floor of Queen Antonia's room. A tiny table held four empty teacups. Two dolls filled up the table as guests.

Raising her teapot, Antonia asked, "Would you like more, Lady Araceli?"

"It's Lord Ari right now."

Antonia nodded gravely. "My apologies. You may now wear the lord's hat." She offered a tall top hat.

I cleared my throat. "I have additional refreshments." I held up a cheese pastry.

Antonia's eyes lit up. "Lady Bora! Please join us." She pushed aside a doll to make room for me.

I presented the flowers to Ari. "For you."

He smiled. A faint flush crossed his cheeks. "Thank you." He looked around, failed to find a vase, and stuck them inside the empty teapot instead.

"I don't mean to interrupt, but I have an important question to ask you." I fixed my gaze on Antonia. "Can you swap me back with the duchess?"

Antonia paled. She looked down and pinched one of her hands. "I don't know how. I'm sorry," she whispered. "I've been practicing with my magic tutor. I couldn't do anything with the insects. My tutor even volunteered to let me test my gift on her, but nothing happened. I can't feel the same emotions as when I did it the first time."

"Didn't your tutor also say that distance might be a factor? What if we got the two of them in the same room? Do you think that would help?" Ari asked.

Antonia slapped the table. "I can't!" Tears welled up in the corners of her eyes.

"Hey, don't worry about it. I didn't mean to upset you." Over Antonia's head, my eyes sought out Ari. His face was grim. I couldn't mention the urgency of the situation and the threat to my body, not in front of a child.

Antonia sniffled. "I'm sorry. Please don't hate me."

"Of course I don't hate you. I'm the one who's sorry for bringing it up."

Ari said, "It's not your fault. She's been upset ever since she found out that the real duchess is back in the castle. I just finished calming her down."

And then I had come in here and ruined it. I winced. Carefully, I sealed all my feelings about my body's possible murder into a box for later. Ever since I was a small child, I used to set aside my feelings whenever my mom got upset and needed comfort, so I was good at that. "Shall we return to the tea party?"

We played for a bit, but Antonia's heart didn't seem in it. Her hands shook, and she kept glancing at the door. Eventually, her tutor came by for a history lesson, and we got booted out.

"You've heard?" I asked once we stepped into the hallway.

"Yes." Ari bit his lip. "I'm going to protect you. If this all goes wrong, then we'll run away from Arahasnor. You, me, and Antonia. I promised her that I'd take her, too, rather than leave her with the duchess again."

"Thank you." I held out my hand and Ari accepted it. I squeezed. After a moment, I said, "I have an important question for you. Please answer honestly. Don't worry about sparing my feelings. Would you really still like me if I was in my original body?"

"Yes, absolutely," Ari said. "I like *you*. Honestly, it would have been easier for me if you'd been in your original body from the beginning, instead of looking like the woman I hated for so long. I would have liked you even sooner, if not for that. Now, I like you no matter which body you have."

I stared off into the distance. That was the answer I'd wanted to hear. I could run away with Ari and Antonia if I could get my real body back.

Except would it really be that easy? As long as Antonia was the key to the duchess's regency, she'd always be hunted. I risked causing global turmoil. There might even be a war. How many lives would be lost because of my selfishness?

It terrified me to think of staying as Duchess Hedri. Up until now, no matter what outrageous thing I'd done, I'd been able to tell myself that it was the Blood Duchess, not me. I'd never planned to take responsibility. If I went through with this, then I'd be stuck with every single insane thing I'd done for the rest of my life. My throat tightened. My heart raced. It became difficult to breathe.

"Bora?" Ari patted me on the back. "Are you all right?"

I swallowed hard. It took me two tries to speak. "What if I can't get my real body back?"

"Then I'll learn to love this one." Ari took my hands. "I meant what I told you before. I'm willing to keep trying. I rushed it too much, forcing myself before I was ready. With time, I'm sure I can accept your current body."

These were the first words to make me smile since the bad news. "I really like you. I mean it. Antonia said something that made me realize you thought that I liked Countess Donya. I used to have a crush on her, it's true. She was the cool hero who I admired. But that was only an idle, unattainable dream. I never seriously fell for her. You're the only one I can picture spending the rest of my life with."

"Bora . . ." Ari whispered. He seemed unable to speak. He took both of my hands in his.

"I'm crazy about you. I want to stay with you forever. And I want to protect you, too. That's why I've decided to accept this trial. I'll pretend to be the Blood Duchess for the rest of my life."

Ari paled. "You don't have to do that. It's too much to ask from you. We can still run away."

"I don't have to, but I'm offering it anyway." I stared straight into his eyes. "Just promise me one thing. Please never forget who I really am. Please always call me Bora. I need you to see my real self, even if I have to pretend for the rest of my life." My voice caught.

Ari pulled me into a hug. "I will. I promise. Bora, Bora, Bora," he whispered, chanting my name over and over again, like a prayer. "I'll keep you safe." His hand touched my neck with his diamond ring, seeking out skin contact. "I release you from your life-oath."

The chains briefly manifested around my heart, then dissipated. I was free. I gasped, clutching the left side of my chest.

"It doesn't seem likely that we'll meet the deadline, but I wanted to be certain anyway. I've wished for a long time that I treated you better when we first met."

"Let me do it, too." I took Ari's hand, touching the diamond ring. "I release you from your life-oath."

"Appreciated, but unnecessary." He kissed my hand. "I haven't been sticking around for the oath for a while now."

I flushed.

"One last thing." He took off another ring and slid it onto my finger. "This has a shielding power. It can create a bubble around you. Physical objects will bounce off. Nearly no magic is strong enough to enter or exit the bubble. Oh, except this ring." He pointed to another emerald one on his right middle finger. "This ring can create a blade that cracks the bubble. I'm keeping this one, since I need to be able to reach you if you fall unconscious."

I nodded. "Makes sense. Are you sure you want to give up such a valuable ring to me?"

"You might need it more than me," Ari said.

I winced, struggling to argue with that one.

"You can turn the ring on and off with a thought. You need to be touching it for it to work. Give it a try."

I pictured a bubble. A glowing golden sphere appeared around me. "Whoa." I looked at Ari. "You're inside the bubble."

"Because I was standing next to you when you activated it. You can fit two people inside. It's useful if you want to protect someone, but if you're not careful, you could also trap an enemy inside with you."

"I'll remember. Thank you." I let the bubble drop. "I feel much better now." A little better, at least. Physical attacks didn't scare me nearly as much as being stuck as the Blood Duchess for the rest of my life. I didn't want to accept the consequences for everything I'd done while running around pretending to be her. I definitely didn't want responsibility for all the crimes she'd committed before we'd even met. Also, I wanted my own body back.

But I'd made my resolve to sacrifice myself for my shitty, impoverished, dragon-rejected country and the people inside it who I cared about.

Ysabel burst into my office, her hair wild around her face. "I have a plan. If we fake the little queen's death, we should be able to take her out of the country and avoid a war. As for saving Arahasnor . . . I'm still working on that one."

I turned around. I wore the duchess's signature red dress and all her jewelry. "You don't need to worry about it. I've decided to stay as the Blood Duchess."

Ysabel took in my serious expression. Her face collapsed. "Bora . . ."

"You can't talk me out of this. I didn't make the decision because of anything you said. Don't blame yourself. I have my own reasons. I have something that I have to protect, even if it means sacrificing my body and my identity. You can't change my mind, big sister." I smiled, an expression tinged with melancholy. "Time to become the villainess I've been pretending to be."

CHAPTER TWENTY-TWO

My heels clacked on the wood as I strode into the courtroom. It had no windows, but high stone archways had been painted with bright floral patterns. The gray walls suited my bleak mood. The Saint of Justice and numerous past judges glowered at me from portraits leading up to the judges in front. Cardinal Augustin sat on a slightly raised seat, with half a dozen lower seats behind him. I recognized most of the nobles as people whom I'd recently thrown in jail. I winced, then attempted to use my fan to hide my un-duchess-like expression.

There had been a long argument about my outfit for the trial. Araceli thought that I should dress to look my best. Ysabel thought I should wear a serious, modest costume in contrast to the real Blood Duchess. Her reasoning was that everyone already knew I was a fake, so it would be better to seem like a more stable, serious ruler. Araceli insisted that it would be a sign of weakness and accused my sister of wanting to make me look like a good puppet. Ysabel said there was nothing wrong with appearing to be a puppet as long as you yanked their strings back.

In the end, I'd cast the deciding vote. I picked my favorite low-cut scarlet dress, with a tall matching hat decorated with cloth roses. The largest rose bloomed as big as my head. My sister had taken her defeat in good grace and immediately switched to teasing me about caring what Araceli thought of my looks. Then she and Araceli had gotten into another fight over who would do my hair. In the end, they worked together to create a jeweled spiral bun and apply my makeup.

I kept my chin high as I walked down the stairs. With jewelry covering nearly every bit of exposed skin, I no longer felt less dressed than Duchess Hedri, sitting in the pews in her scandalously skintight black gown. (Though I had to admit, she looked so good being me, it was making me think maybe I'd been too hard on my own looks. Maybe confidence did have a lot to do with it. Maybe I'd always been pretty, and I'd just never let myself see it.)

I finally felt strong and ready to take on this farce of a trial. The dress ruffles kept anyone from noticing my knees shaking, anyway. As the defendant, I strode to a podium. The real Duchess Hedri sat in the pews, surrounded by her Gifted Knights.

A formal trial in the Holy City was typically very, very short. The high concentration of Seers among the Church made it easy to deliver a verdict. Typically, a Seer would take testimony from related parties and easily discern who was lying and who was telling the truth. Only in rare occasions would one party exercise their right to call in a second Seer. If the two contradicted each other, then the trial went to the jury. We fully expected that to happen this time. Sweat dripped down the back of my neck. My overly heavy hat made my head nod over.

Ari stood next to me, dressed as my bodyguard. He gave me a small nudge that restored my fading confidence. Sitting next to my sister, Queen Antonia waved.

Now that I'd gotten so close to the Blood Duchess, maybe it would be easier for Antonia to use her magic on us? I mouthed, *Can you swap us?*

Antonia's small smile faded. She shook her head vigorously.

I sighed. Even though I'd mostly given up on going back to my own body, it would have been nice to have the option. Since I'd clearly upset Antonia again, I regretted asking.

I touched the protective ring that Ari had given me. I drew strength from it, not just the potential for protection but also the reminder that I had someone watching my back.

A middle-aged woman in a black court official robe stepped forward and held out her hand. "Please take my hand, then give your name."

No one who touched a Seer could lie. Seers themselves couldn't turn off their gifts. This made it impossible for them to be bribed, so testimony while touching a Seer was sacrosanct.

However, this woman was no longer a Seer. Years ago, Kaine had found her drunk and crying at a tavern late at night because her natural ability to force all her lovers to tell the truth while touching her had ruined yet another romantic relationship. Kaine had offered to take her power. At the time, he hadn't even asked for anything in return (to Ysabel's despair). My sister had been the one to point out how handy it would be to have a fake Seer in their pocket. Since she'd be revealing herself as a fake with our blatant lies during this trial, Ysabel had offered a large enough amount of money to retire comfortably for the rest of her life. She'd accepted, and we'd obtained our fake Seer.

I took the offered hand. "I'm Duchess Hedri of Southern Sherda, the Lady Regent of Arahasnor." I wanted to follow this up with some grand Blood Duchess-like declaration. Something about how I'd have everyone hung up by their heels for doubting me. Maybe throw some jewelry at the floor. But I couldn't work up the will. I was too nervous.

The Seer inclined her head at me, then turned to the podium. "She speaks the truth. Do the ladies and gentlemen assembled have any other questions?"

Head Cardinal Augustin said, "We came here to determine if she's a fake, and she's not. The trial is over." He sounded nervous. I didn't think deception came naturally to him. He was probably only going along with it because the Blood Duchess had tried to kill him and nearly taken over the kingdom.

My eyes swept the pews. I was banking on these people hating the Blood Duchess more than me, even though I'd thrown most of them in jail lately.

Countess Lealonie immediately said, "She's the real duchess. The trial is over." She winked at me. Apparently, that time I'd thrown her in jail had been forgiven. I was very glad I'd already gotten Kaine's permission to build her bridge before this happened.

An immediate chorus of agreement came from the surrounding nobles. Whoa, not the tiniest bit of hesitation? Not even one dissenter? The Blood Duchess was even more unpopular than I'd realized. Despite all my hard work terrorizing people, I clearly remained the lesser evil.

"We object to the Conclave of Kings interfering with our kingdom."

"It's not as if they showed up when certain parties attempted to steal our country out from under us."

"Our lady regent is a real pigeon plucker!"

I winced at the street slang I'd once pretended to be a compliment. Had the nobleman believed me when I'd claimed that it meant a smart person? Or was he being deliberately ironic? It didn't matter, as long as he supported my claim.

At this point, we all fully expected the real duchess to demand a second Seer. If the testimony ended up split, it would go back to the jury. This would lead to a longer trial, but after how quickly everyone had supported me, I had confidence in my victory. I didn't quite feel safe yet. But I did let my grip on the podium loosen.

Ysabel sniffed loudly. "I hope that no one will doubt the Seer that I personally vouched for. To do so would offend the Sun God . . . and hurt my feelings."

Kaine sat up where he'd been dozing in the pews. "Hmm? Did someone hurt your feelings, love?"

Alzira drew her sword. "Point my blade at who I must slaughter, Your Holiness." The entire room flinched. Energy sparked through the air. Even I might have cowered under the podium, if not for Ari touching my arm reassuringly.

Ysabel placed a restraining hand on her bodyguard's shoulder. "Please, sit down. The Sun God has not called upon your services . . . yet." Her gaze swept the room, landing on the real Blood Duchess.

"I accept the Seer's testimony," Duchess Hedri said.

Wait, what? I didn't like how she said it. She was a little too calm. My sister looked surprised, too—she couldn't have expected one little threat would do the trick. This all felt too easy. The duchess continued, "I have one more charge to lay. I accuse Duchess Hedri of treason and the murder of the former duke and duchess of South Sherda, as well as their young son. Oh, and the family dog too."

Ari's hand slipped from my arm. He'd gone slack-jawed with shock.

Dark Lady. What could the duchess be playing at? I could follow the first half of her plan. She'd already realized that no one in Arahasnor would voluntarily vote for the destruction of their own country, so they'd pretend to believe my story even if she called in a second Seer. Although she might have dated Falael, she wouldn't have lasted this long by being completely stupid. She must know that the Conclave of Kings wasn't on her side. Then she'd decided to expose her own crimes so that she could force me to confess my real identity or be executed in her place.

But I didn't understand what she planned after that. High treason was an executable offense. If I confessed to the body swap, I'd get in trouble, but then she'd become the traitor and murderer. If I didn't confess, I might die if I was convicted, but the duchess would still be powerless and stuck in my body. I supposed a fresh start in a new body would be better for her than dying, but she didn't seem like someone who enjoyed poverty. Plus, the Avengers knew the truth and would still come after her—to say nothing of my sister. Was it as simple as her being determined to drag me down with her out of spite? I had trouble believing she was suicidal. Looking at the smug twist in her lips, I felt convinced that she had another plan.

What should I do? I saw no benefit in confessing. The court was still biased in my favor. For now, I would deny everything. "I have no idea what this peasant is talking about." I'd hoped my voice would sound confident, but it came out shrill. I snuck a glance at Ari. He'd turned white and was trembling. There was pain in his eyes, but also a growing rage.

Duchess Hedri continued, "Due to the destruction of all physical evidence, I've provided an artifact that can record memories."

She held up a small mirror. "This has captured direct images of the massacre."

Like an idiot, I wondered where she'd gotten the memories. Then I realized that of course she'd cast her own memories into the mirror. Just how blatant could she be? Did she have no shame? Probably not. My own attempts to resemble her hadn't even come close to this level of shamelessness.

The duchess displayed the mirror. The images were . . . very bad. The jury looked ill; several had to turn away. Ari started to silently choke at the sight of the duchess murdering his parents. I reached out to him, but he turned and fled the courtroom. I completely understood. If someone had shown my brother dying up there, then I would have run off to throw up. I wished I could chase after him, but as the defendant, I wasn't allowed to leave while the trial was in progress. I had no choice but to watch. My fingers tightened on the podium. *Someone, anyone, go after Ari!*

As if in response to my silent prayer, Antonia leapt up and ran after Ari. I breathed a small sigh of relief.

With a smug smirk that I longed to rip off her face, the duchess turned to me. "Do you plead guilty or innocent?" I'd never known my own voice could sound so malicious and contemptible. It screeched against my ears.

Ysabel waggled her eyebrows frantically at me. I had no idea what she meant.

I cleared my throat. Remembering the lame excuse we'd joked about earlier, I said, "I have amnesia."

The sound of my sister slapping her own forehead echoed around the room. Apparently that hadn't been what she meant for me to do.

Duchess Hedri's smirk widened. "Then a Seer's testimony would be useless. What a shame. But I think my mirror has provided ample evidence of your crimes."

The assembled jury muttered amongst themselves. They were all fully aware of the truth about this situation. Whereas it had been easy to pretend not to know about the body swap, it was hard to deny this. Furthermore, how would we explain it to Sherda? An Arahasnor court didn't even have the power to dismiss charges of treason based in Sherda.

"Wait." The door flung open. Ari stood in the doorway. He was wiping his mouth, and his eyes were rimmed in red. He must have actually thrown up. "I'm Ari of South Sherda. I'm still alive, so no one can be convicted of my murder." His tone tried to make a joke of it, but his voice wobbled. There was nothing funny in his shattered gaze. "I can testify that those images are fake. If I say the duchess is innocent—"

"You can't!" I leapt up. The rest of my words died in my throat as I realized anything I might say would be an admission of guilt.

Ari flinched. "Please don't make this any harder for me. Just let me speak."

"I won't!" I could tell from the duchess's sudden frown that Ari's lie was *not* according to her plan. Ari had the power to completely and utterly screw over whatever twist ending she intended. But at what cost? Ari had been chasing revenge ever since he was a small child. To deny his parents' murders would emotionally destroy him.

My head hurt. This damn heavy hat was giving me a headache. I wrenched it off, yanking out several hairpins and letting my curls fall down over my shoulders. "This has gone too far. Duchess Hedri is guilty, and I'm not her. *She* murdered Ari's family." I pointed at the smirking killer.

"But—" Ari began.

I grabbed his wrist. "I promised you the day we first met. You'll have your revenge."

"You're more important to me," Ari said, so quietly I almost didn't hear it. "I released you from your oath. Now I release you from any sense of obligation to help me fulfill my revenge."

I squeezed his hand. "I never needed to be forced to help you. And I'm not going anywhere. Worst-case scenario, we can flee to Conollia together." I glared in defiance at the stunned jury.

The duchess smiled. She'd wanted me to make this confession. That must have been the entire point of this strange game. But why? What did she gain from switching our identities back, right after confessing to deadly crimes? There was something I must be missing. It nagged at me, lurking at the back of my mind, a thought not quite finished.

Before I could quite figure out what was happening, the Living Shadow erupted from the floor and stabbed Duchess Hedri clean through her borrowed chest.

CHAPTER TWENTY-THREE

A sad whimper escaped my lips as I watched my real body hit the floor. I'd tried to resign myself to being stuck like this forever, but deep down, I still wanted my own body back. I might have hated it and hurt it at times, but it had been mine.

The Blood Duchess, in *my* body, stared up at the ceiling, her eyes glassy. A pool of blood spread around the sword impaled through her heart. *My* heart. Oh, Sun God, my body was bleeding out!

The terrifying tyrant had gone down so easily. I could barely think through my panic.

The other Twelve (well, formerly twelve) Avengers materialized out of the shadows, holding weapons. Nine total, including Ma'qas.

"She's still breathing! Finish her," Durnip cried. He advanced with a dagger. The entire courtroom wisely took this moment to evacuate. The Conclave's Gifted Knights vanished as easily as everyone else, apparently possessing no loyalty. A picture tumbled off the wall as someone knocked into it. In the stampede, I could barely see or hear what was going on.

"Kaine, Alzira, cover me!" Ysabel vaulted over the pew railing. "I've got to heal my sister's body."

Why? It didn't matter if my body died, when I'd resolved to stay in this one. Yet I could not bring myself to say those words aloud, to give up hope. And judging from the look on my sister's face, she also wasn't ready to watch my body die in front of her. She was moving as fast as she could with an awkward pregnant waddle.

Alzira made a jerking motion with her hand, and Durnip's dagger flew out of his grip. Then she chased after my sister.

Kaine cast a glowing net, dragging down the Living Shadow and two other Avengers. Two stayed down, but the shadow oozed free and nicked Kaine's leg. The thing had sprouted a million tiny tentacles from the pitch-black blob in the middle. Kaine didn't even bother to dodge the attacks because he healed instantly. He knocked the shadow away with a kick and a blast of fire. His net grew and expanded, stretching toward the others and yanking them down. Only the shadow could not be contained, slipping through the holes. From the cold look in Kaine's eyes, I knew he would use lethal force next time.

How could I help? If I leapt down there, I'd only get in the way of those two. Everything was happening so fast, I couldn't think straight. Ugh. Useless again. Letting my sister handle everything alone *again*. I felt sick. Was guilt the only thing making my stomach so nauseous? Or was it something more? I had a bad feeling, but nothing actionable. If I shouted the wrong thing, maybe I'd just make everything worse.

My sister stepped on the pool of blood. Ari started forward.

"Wait," I said, grabbing his wrist.

Ari frowned. "I might be able to talk to the other Avengers. Maybe I can deescalate this."

"Something is wrong," I said at the same time. Strange as it sounded, after pretending to be the Blood Duchess for so long, I *knew* the Blood Duchess. She was paranoid, surrounding herself with magical defenses at all times. She kept people on their toes with her mercurial murderousness and by spying on those around her. Everyone was terrified of the Blood Duchess. She was cunning and careful, yet also willing to take risks to achieve her goals. "I would swear she provoked that attack." I didn't fully piece together my thoughts until the words left my mouth. "The timing didn't seem coincidental. But why? What does she have to gain?"

I kept asking myself that same question, even as Ysabel reached the body stolen from me. What did the Blood Duchess want? She wanted power, obviously. She wanted to take over Arahasnor. She craved blood as if the murderousness was a compulsion granted by a gift. But she didn't have a gift . . . did she? She was just an ordinary person obsessed with drinking the blood of people with beauty and powerful magic. Funny how improbable that sounded when I strung the thoughts together. If she wasn't completely insane (a generous assumption), then drinking blood sure did sound like the type of inconvenience that popped up as the price of strong magic. And she was right next to Kaine and Alzira, the two strongest magically gifted people on the continent. Three, if you counted my sister, who had a very exceptional ability even if it wasn't combat-oriented.

My gaze snapped back to the scene of the battle. The pews were empty and abandoned now. Kaine and Alzira had driven the Avengers toward the door, standing protectively between them and my sister. Leaving her alone with the Blood Duchess. Ysabel crouched down, about to heal the duchess.

I had no idea what was about to happen, only instinct. I screamed, "Yzzy, stop! It's a trap!"

Ysabel froze. But I'd spoken a fraction of a second too late. The Blood Duchess sat up and slashed a dagger at my sister's wrist.

Alzira leapt forward and yanked Ysabel backward.

Duchess Hedri shook a drop of blood off the dagger into her mouth. "You fool. I've won." Her injury completely faded away. The sword through her chest vanished, too, as if it had never existed.

Wasn't it a bit soon for her to be declaring victory? Hadn't I stopped whatever had been her trap?

Alzira made a strange croaking sound, then sank to her knees. I'd never be able to forget that wounded, confused expression as she gazed up at the only person she was completely unable to hurt. Her own blade had been shoved into her gut, and my sister held the sword. For a moment, I thought it must be another illusion. Ysabel would never have stabbed her own beloved friend. Then I saw the glazed look in my sister's eyes.

Control. The duchess's gift was control. That was how she'd killed Araceli's family so long ago, how she'd risen to such a powerful position from her start as minor nobility, how she'd convinced the Conclave of her real identity and to back her move for power, and the *real* reason why she drank blood. No wonder she'd hid it. The gift would have been useful in the World Games, but it was far, far more useful as a secret, allowing her to puppeteer powerful people behind the scenes and get away with any crimes she pleased. Now I understood her plan. But I was too late.

"Ari," I screamed. "The Blood Duchess is controlling my sister. You have to stop her!"

"I hate when someone gives away the surprise ending." Duchess Hedri pouted. "Holy Maiden Ysabel, kill yourself if anyone attacks me."

Blank-eyed, Ysabel put the sword to her own throat.

Every muscle in my body stopped at once. This couldn't be happening. Not my sister. Not Ysabel, who was always so perfect and implacable and took care of both of us. The world took on an unreal and blurry quality. Why hadn't I stopped Ysabel from trying to heal my body? I'd already given up on becoming Bora again. If I'd just stopped her sooner, this never would have happened.

It was all my fault.

I didn't dare take one step forward with my sister's life at stake. My fingers gripped Ari's sleeve to stop him, but he'd frozen, too. Kaine, about to lunge, stopped in midair so fast he must have used magic on himself. Agony filled his face. There was no one else left to do anything. The Avengers had already been taken down by Kaine and the room had been evacuated except for Donya, standing by the door as she helped the last elder through. Alzira was bleeding out on the floor, and I couldn't even lift a finger to help her. I was useless yet again.

"My dear shadow, toss me your real weapon," Duchess Hedri called. As she spoke, she twisted the smoky quartz ring on her finger. It flashed black. The ring must be a relic, and all along the shadow must have been a tool controlled by her.

The Living Shadow threw a sword to her. Red dots gleamed on it. I hoped that wasn't Kaine's blood.

My hopes were dashed when Duchess Hedri licked the blade. Kaine's eyes took on the same glassy sheen as Ysabel's as he fell under the duchess's control. "Ah-ha! The man with thousands of gifts is mine! The power rush feels amazing." Her eyes gleamed in the shadowy room. She threw back her head and laughed. "Kaine, you could have conquered the world, if you hadn't fallen for a woman too weak to use you properly. Now you'll turn *me* into the final Dark Lord, the one who wins and claims everything."

Most of the Avengers were already unconscious under Kaine and Alzira's assault. Those trapped in the net looked stunned by the betrayal of the Living Shadow.

Duchess Hedri smirked and petted the shadow at her side. "You lot of revenge-seeking fools never realized why you were so ineffectual. Maybe you shouldn't have trusted my own servant to aid in your plans to kill me. The shadow was never a person. It was always me talking to you through it, enjoying your pathetic attempts at revenge."

Over the Duchess's triumphant laughter, I barely made out a scraping on the floor. My eyes snapped over to the sound. Donya had slipped through the room, ducking low to hide under the pews, and grabbed Alzira's body. As quietly as she could, she dragged Alzira toward the door.

The duchess hadn't ordered my sister to kill herself if anyone tried to leave, but of course that could easily change. I had to distract the duchess before she noticed in order to give Donya time to save Alzira. Although the injury didn't look fatal, Alzira needed immediate medical treatment, and if the Blood Duchess took control of Alzira too, it really would be all over for the world.

"I still have your body! I'll kill myself if you don't surrender!" I shouted.

This was definitely a bluff. I didn't seriously expect it to work. Still, I was surprised when the duchess laughed in my face. (*With* my face, too. That was so annoying.) Duchess Hedri looked unconcerned. "If you don't kill that worthless body, then I'll murder it myself. I forced you to reveal your true identity because I'm planning to stay in this body forever."

That didn't sound good. Only my extensive experience careening from crisis to crisis was keeping me from panicking. Groping for ways to keep her talking, I said, "And you don't care if anyone finds out about your crimes because you're going full dark lord."

She shrugged. "With Kaine's power, I'll crush the Conclave beneath my high heels."

"Very ambitious, I admire that. But aren't you sad about not getting your body back?"

"You can keep that old sack of bones. I want this younger, hotter body." Duchess Hedri placed a hand on her chest.

I gasped. "Do you really think I'm hotter? That's crazy. I thought you were more beautiful than me from the moment I laid eyes on you." To be honest, this was largely me babbling and doing a desperate imitation of flattery to distract Duchess Hedri, as Donya had nearly made it to the door. It was true, though. I'd never been much of a liar. "Do I have poor self-esteem? Do we *both* have poor self-esteem? Is this about how Falael used to insult your body? Because the man is an ass. He got into my head so badly that he made me start throwing up my food. Don't listen to him! You're gorgeous!"

"How nice of you to say, but I'm still going to kill you and everyone you love. Wait, are you trying to distract me?"

"I'm sorry, I couldn't pass up on the opportunity. I did mean every word I said about your beauty. Never believe otherwise."

"Are you brain damaged?" The duchess managed to pack more scorn into her voice than I'd heard in my entire life, and I'd been subject to plenty of scorn. "No matter. Kaine, kill everyone in this room."

"Hey! I thought we were having a moment!" I yelped.

Ari made a noise in the back of his throat and stepped in front of me. I already knew it was hopeless. Not only could we not defeat Kaine, I'd be forced to surrender if the duchess threatened my poor sister again. At least Donya had made it out the door with Alzira. I'd done a tiny amount of good.

Kaine's neck twisted at an unnatural angle to look at the duchess. Tremors ran up and down his body. "You haven't beat me," he sputtered.

The room fell into confused silence.

The Duchess frowned. "I drank your blood. I know I did. I'd heard about your legendary simplemindedness, but surely you can't overwrite reality by being too dumb to accept it. Your power belongs to me." She looked down at the sticky blade. "Was it not enough blood? Come over here and let me drink more, or I'll kill your wife."

Ysabel stood still and unnaturally empty-faced, the sword still at her throat. I uttered a strangled choke, trying to calculate if I could jump and stop her, knowing I'd never been an athlete in either body. The distance was too far.

In a strange, crackling voice, Kaine said, "Even if you control this body, the magic can only be taken by someone who overcomes my will. That is the inviolable rule of *plunder*. I—we—I can't accept a weakling who relies on other people to fight as a master!" His head jerked back and forth with unnatural speed as he spoke, as if warring with himself.

What the hell was going on? I had the odd sensation that it wasn't Kaine talking. Kaine would never be able to look away from his wife while she had a blade aimed at her throat. This must be about the secret price of Kaine's gift. He'd once let it slip that someone who overcame his will could steal his powers. On the flip side, since the duchess hadn't fulfilled the price, she couldn't use his magic. But was this good or bad? I was only alive as long as Kaine did not follow the duchess's order. But my sister would die if he disobeyed.

Ysabel started to move the sword, and I screamed.

Duchess Hedri shouted over me, "Stop, Ysabel! Not yet! If I die—if I'm seriously hurt—then kill yourself. Kaine, I don't know how you're doing this, but get on your knees before me or your woman dies. You, useless Holy Maiden, show him a little blood."

Ysabel pushed the sword into her throat, just enough to draw a line of blood. She did not make a sound of pain. It was sickening.

Kaine doubled over, clutching his head. "No, stop!" he howled. "The will is not as strong. Don't you dare submit. *We* refuse! All of our prices must be paid!" One of his knees bent, then his own hand shot down to brace his leg. The bone cracked, but healed itself straight just as fast. A dozen different colors of energy crackled down his body. The conflict was literally ripping him to pieces.

Ari grabbed my arm. "While she's distracted, run."

"No." I jerked my arm away. "Not without my sister."

Even *I* didn't know what I was doing. My knees shook. I'd sweated through my fancy dress. I was completely, utterly, irrevocably out of my league. I didn't have the ability to take on people as powerful as the Blood Duchess or Dark Lord Kaine. I'd always been relying on my big sister to protect me and tell me what to do, and now she'd been turned into a puppet.

For my whole life, I'd become accustomed to giving in, running away, and losing what mattered to me. I'd stood by, a silly helpless child, on the day the slavers took away Ysabel. When the guards came for our refugee camp, I waited for someone else to save me, and let my sister again sell herself for everyone else's sake. When Falael stole my money, I'd never even considered revenge—I'd accepted it as what I'd deserved for being a fool. Every time my mother insulted me, I made myself a bit smaller and forced myself to throw up as if punishing myself. I'd never even asked what Calum was doing the day he'd left for the city, and I hadn't known when he'd died. In the final battle against the former Head Cardinal Jiang, I hadn't found out what was going on until later. No one had expected me to join the fight. An out-of-shape farm girl with no useful magic or combat training would have been no use, but oh, how I'd wished to be someone helpful. If I'd been something other than a burden to be protected, Calum might have let me help him. But I'd been afraid to offer because I'd probably just screw it up.

When the Blood Duchess had come to execute Donya, and Donya had told me to run away, I'd left her like a coward. When my sister showed up in the city, I let her take over because it was a relief to have someone telling me what to do. Ever since I'd been dropped in this strange body, I'd let other people give me orders. Even now, a big part of me wanted to run away again. But I could not give up on my sister. I couldn't lose another sibling, not like I'd lost Calum. Here was my line in the sand. Here was where I'd make my final stand and fight to my death—or better yet, to the death of anyone who got in my way.

The look in my eyes made Ari let me go. "Do you have a ring that could paralyze Ysabel and stop her from using the knife?" I asked.

Ari shook his head. "I would have used it already. Ma'qas's poison could do it—but Bora, we don't have much time."

I knew exactly what Ari meant. Half of Kaine's hair was coated in ice, the other half on fire. The energy had spread out from Kaine, sending cracks down the floor and up the walls. Shards of wood fell from the roof. This building was about to go down. The Blood Duchess ducked behind the chief judge's throne. She had not yet ordered Ysabel to die. Hostages were a one-shot deal. She had to know that if she killed Ysabel, then nothing would stop Kaine from killing the duchess. We could use that. I could not believe how coldly I was thinking.

Duchess Hedri screamed, "Shadow, stop Kaine! Kaine, you madman, what do you think will happen if I put a blade into your wife's pregnant belly? If you don't care about the woman, then do you at least care for your legacy?"

Absolutely no one was paying attention to us. Ma'qas had fought free of the net and was dragging it along the floor, taking her unconscious companions with her. My sister had been right about villainous monologues being a useful distraction. The Blood Duchess didn't seem to care about anything except screaming at Kaine.

I ran over, Ari fast behind me. "Ma'qas, I need a poison to freeze Ysabel."

Ma'qas winced. "I screwed up. I shouldn't have trusted our resident shadow. But I don't owe you enough to die for you. This place is coming down, and it takes me time to create poisons. I'm out of here."

I grabbed Ma'qas by the throat and dragged us so close, our noses touched. "The Blood Duchess doesn't have her hands around your neck right now, Ma'qas. *I* do. Create a paralyzation potion or I will kill you."

Ma'qas's eyes went wide. "I thought the villainess bit was an act."

"If you don't believe her, you know *I'm* capable of murder," Ari said.

"I believe you!" she squeaked as I tightened my grip. "I need an object! Fast!"

I yanked off my necklace and shoved it into her chest hard enough to bruise. She closed her eyes, concentrating.

Behind us, the shadow flew at Kaine in a blast that ripped up the floor.

"Done! The poison is in the largest diamond," Ma'qas cried, then fled.

Ari took the necklace by the clasp. "I'll save Ysabel. You get out of here." There was a grim set to his mouth, like a hero making a sacrifice. I knew full well he did not expect to make it out of the building before it collapsed. Before I could stop him, he twisted one of his rings, becoming invisible. His footsteps trailed away from me.

More pieces of ceiling came down. I would not run away and leave my loved ones to die. Not this time. Instead, I charged straight at Kaine.

The usual Dark Lord Kaine would have heard me coming a mile off. His reflexes or a few hundred abilities could have protected him. Whatever was going on with him, he did not have enough control to use his powers or his body properly. He didn't even resist as I grabbed a wooden beam off the floor and smacked him over the head. Holy shit, that worked?

Kaine dropped without a sound. The Living Shadow sailed over his head, embedding in the wall. The energy coursing through the room ceased.

Ysabel went slack. A certain invisible someone yanked the sword from her hand, then dragged her away. I tried to pick up Kaine and leave, too, but he was heavier than a heifer. Oh dear. I couldn't leave him, but I didn't think it was a good idea to stand here. A falling chandelier struck right next to me with a sound that shattered the air. I yelped like a child and dodged the glass shards.

"What?" The duchess gaped, too fixed on Kaine to even notice her hostage getting away. She repeated, "What?" Her gaze locked on me. "You know, of all the people I hate in the world, I think it might be you the most. The stupid little farm girl who always ruins everything. Constantly making a fool of me. I'm going to kill you."

"I'm s—" Nope, no apologies. I bared my teeth. "You hurt my sister. That's *my* line."

From the doorway, a young girl's voice called out, "What's going on? Why is everyone running away from here? Ari?" It was Queen Antonia.

NO!

Unfortunately, that was the precise moment when the roof came down.

CHAPTER TWENTY-FOUR

I activated the shield on my ring, as Ari had taught me. Kaine was close enough for me to shield him from the blast. But what about Ari and Ysabel? Had they gotten out of the building in time? Desperately, I prayed that Antonia hadn't gotten hit by the rubble. She hadn't stepped inside the room yet, but she'd been dangerously close.

The impact flung me up in the air, then I bounced off the ceiling. My gift still worked even when I was under the magic shield. Huh, I learned something new.

We careened through the air, hitting the ground and then flying again. Kaine slammed into me a few times, but my power protected me. As for him . . . hopefully he was tough. He'd married my sister, so he must be. Shards from the crumbling building and dust rained against the surface of the shield. I couldn't see or hear anything beyond it. When it stopped, I lowered the shield and staggered out. Knee-deep wreckage surrounded me. "Ari! Ysabel! Antonia!" I screamed. All my efforts would have been for nothing if they'd died. The massive pileup around the doorway prevented me from seeing Antonia, but since she'd been outside the building, she was the most likely to be okay. It did bother me that she hadn't replied to me yet.

"Over here!" Ari screamed.

I ran toward him. He grabbed my shoulders and examined me. "Are you injured?"

"No, forget me," I said impatiently. "Ysabel?"

"I bandaged her with a scrap of my shirt." He pointed at the ground. I dropped to my knees in front of my sister. When I touched her forehead, it felt feverish. Ari had tied her hands together with another bit of shirt.

I was confused for a moment, then I realized. "She'll obey the Blood Duchess's orders if she wakes up."

Grimly, Ari said, "Worse. She was ordered to kill herself if the Blood Duchess gets hurt, and that's happened. I'm afraid of what she'll do when the paralyzation wears off."

Regular Bora wanted to panic, but I was still Villainess Bora. "Do you remember how the Blood Duchess ordered Ysabel to do it"—I could not say the words out loud—"if she died? Then she changed it to seriously hurt? The Blood Duchess's gift must not work after she's dead."

"Of course." Ari snapped his fingers. "Magic rarely lasts after the user dies. If Hedri finally took her rightful place in hell, then we'd be safe."

At that exact moment, the rubble groaned. A tendril of shadow poked out. Then it flopped over, limp.

"Or she used the Living Shadow to shield herself." Ari groaned. "I'm going to kill the Blood Duchess and end all of this. Please protect Antonia and Ysabel." He started forward, holding his sword. Light danced from one of his rings and ran down his hand.

The Living Shadow erupted with a howl. Ari met a tendril with a sword.

In the distance, I could hear bells. If the guard was coming, they weren't close enough. Should I help Ari fight? I'd just defeated Dark Lord Kaine! I could do anything, dammit! Okay, realistically I'd be useless, but I could provide moral support.

On second thought, Antonia needed to be my top priority. I absolutely hated to leave my sister lying on the ground, but I couldn't abandon a missing little girl, either. It felt like my heart was being torn in two. Grunting, I lifted Ysabel onto my back. Damn, she was heavier than she looked.

I stumbled over the fallen chunks of tile, calling, "Antonia?"

A soft groan responded to me.

That didn't sound good. I picked up my pace, slipping and scraping my knee. I didn't dare look back at the fight behind me. I had to trust Ari, as he'd trusted me to look after our girl.

Antonia lay sprawled on the ground with dirt splattered across her face and turning her hair grayish. Her lips half parted, she moaned. Blood dripped onto her right ear from a cut. A block had fallen on top of her arm.

With a scream, I ran forward. In my panic, I nearly forgot about Ysabel on my back. I remembered just in time to lower her carefully and gently to the ground. I had no time to pick a good place, so I propped her up against the closest rock. Then I turned to free Antonia.

One of my fingernails broke on the cement block. Howling incoherently, I ripped the stone off Antonia and flung it away. Adrenaline had given me mad strength. Then I collapsed to my knees, because something had given out in my back.

I reached for Antonia, then stopped when I noticed her horrible injury. Her arm was bent funny. Kneeling down, I ripped off half my sleeve and fastened it around her bleeding the best I could.

Antonia's eyes snapped open. Sweat dripped down her forehead. "I think my arm is broken." She sounded weirdly . . . happy about it? "I'm in a lot of pain."

"I'm sorry." I applied pressure to the cut on her forehead. "Sweetie, do you think you can run away? I hate to ask it of you, but you need to get out of here. Ari and I are fighting the Blood Duchess."

"I know. I came to help."

"That's noble of you, but—"

She interrupted, "I can swap your bodies back. I always could have, from the moment you first asked me to." Each word sounded strained. Her gaze lowered, her cheeks pinking.

A roaring sound filled my ears. She always could have? And she'd left me like this, even when it looked like I might get executed? Selfish, just as expected from a royal. Cold, ugly anger reared up inside me. Villainess Bora wanted to grab her and—

No. This wasn't like threatening Ma'qas. Antonia was only a little girl. I wasn't going to mistreat a scared, abused kid. She had good reasons for keeping me in the duchess's body. I took a deep breath, and my anger faded away. Villainess Bora left, leaving only tired and scared Bora. "I understand. You didn't want the real duchess back. It's okay."

Antonia gnawed on her lip, digging into an existing cut. "I didn't . . . but that's not all." Her words came out laborious and strained. "I lied . . . about not knowing . . . my price. It's . . . pain."

Suddenly it seemed obvious to me. The Blood Duchess had been whipping Antonia when she'd first accidentally swapped us. All powerful gifts had nasty prices. I remembered Antonia pinching herself when I'd asked her to swap me back. She'd been trying. Antonia's gift required more than mild pain—she needed to be in agony in order to use it.

Tremors shaking her body, Antonia whispered, "I was afraid . . . if you knew . . . you might hit me . . . to get your body back. I'm sorry . . . for lying."

"Oh *no*." Tears filled my eyes. "I would never. If the alternative is hurting you, then I'll stay like this forever. I'd resigned myself already, so it's fine."

"You don't understand," Antonia said. Her chest heaved. With great effort, she spoke clearly and articulately. "I can swap you back right now. Should I?"

My world shifted on its axis. This was it. The only time that Antonia would be in great enough pain to use her gift, because I had no intention of ever letting such suffering happen to her again. My one big chance. It was now or never. What did I want to do?

That was the wrong question. What would be the most useful thing to do? The lives of my loved ones were at stake. If we swapped, the Blood Duchess's gift would follow her no matter what body she was in. I needed to kill her if I wanted my sister to survive. If we traded bodies right now, then at least I'd know where to find her. But swapping now would put the Blood Duchess right next to Antonia and Ysabel, which didn't seem like a good idea.

I took off my ring. "Antonia, this ring has a protective bubble. If you activate it, then it will keep you and my sister safe. I need you to stay with her and protect her for me. Don't lower the bubble for any reason. That way, when I swap back with the duchess, she won't be able to hurt you."

Although she took the ring, Antonia pointed out, "Then the mean duchess will be outside and free to attack my Ari."

All right, I hadn't thought this plan entirely through.

I turned around, realizing the sounds of battle had gone oddly silent. Ari stood panting, his sword impaled in a fallen mass of darkness. He'd killed the shadow. A line of blood ran down his leg, but not enough to bring him to his knees. It seemed to be over. But where was the Blood Duchess?

The faint sound of a board shifting gave her away. Duchess Hedri pushed aside the wreckage to partly get free, squirming her upper half out of the hole left by her shadow. Ari's back was turned, not seeing her. She inched a finger toward him. No, she was aiming for the trail of blood. Her finger dipped, then moved for her mouth. She was about to control Ari, too.

In a mad panic, I screamed, "Antonia, swap us now!"

Antonia stared at me with wide, confused eyes, wasting valuable seconds. But she trusted me in the end. She triggered the shield in the ring.

Light blinded me. Then my world changed.

I lay on the ground. My neck throbbed. Dust stung my eyes. A heavy weight dug bruises into my back. I tried to move my one free arm. I saw a familiar brown hand with calluses from farm work. I'd returned to my own body.

A shame this had happened right when my body was trapped.

I gave up moving. It wasn't happening. Instead, I called, "Help!"

Ari turned around, the expression on his face entirely unfriendly. He raised his sword.

Crap, I definitely did not think this through. "Wait!" I screamed. "Please, it's me, Bora! Antonia swapped us back! She can tell you . . ." Oh, no, based on my personal experience, the shield blocked sound, and I'd ordered Antonia not to lower it. How was I going to prove myself? "Just give me a second to think of something to say that only I would know." That sounded lame. Ari would probably be smart to kill me.

Yet Ari hesitated, his gaze angry. He did not quite seem able to bring the sword down.

Duchess Hedri ran forward, looking far less injured than me, her lovely blonde hair wild about her face. She cried, "My love, she's lying!

How could we possibly swap back? Kill her, quickly, before she pulls out more tricks."

Why, that shameless . . . I groped for the right words to convince Ari. Something no one else would know. My mind was blanking. Of all the moments for my tongue to freeze up.

The duchess clasped her hands together. "Please, love. Remember how you saved me from the poisoned bracelet and even fought your own comrade to protect me."

Ari's gaze cleared. "We never told anyone else about that, after Ma'qas became our ally." He turned toward me, raising his sword.

"Wait!" I yelped. "I'm Bora! I don't know how she found out!" I thought fast. "Ma'qas must have told her, when she spilled everything to the Living Shadow." That was probably how the duchess knew about our romantic relationship, too.

Duchess Hedri cried, "Your favorite fruit is oranges! You get easily carriage-sick! You can't sleep during thunderstorms!"

Dammit, I didn't know all those facts. The Blood Duchess had lived with Ari longer than me. What if she knew him better?

"You promised to run away with me if the trial went wrong," I said.

At the same time, the duchess said, "You promised to stay with me forever."

Sadly, she'd gotten it right. That had been a predictably romantic guess. "Please—" I started to say.

"Please," Duchess Hedri said at the same time, clasping her hands together and looking innocent and adorable.

Ari hesitated. He looked between us. He bit his lip and twirled a lock of his hair.

I had no choice but my last resort—embarrassingly sexual details. "Ari, remember when—" I stopped. I looked at his hand playing with his—no, *her*—hair. Yes, biting the lip, too. I recognized that gesture. I'd seen it several times before. "You're not Ari right now. You're Araceli."

Araceli startled. "You know?"

I smiled. "I'm starting to get the hang of telling the difference. I'm right, aren't I? If not, I'm sorry."

"Huh?" escaped from the duchess's lips.

Araceli whirled around. A green blade shot from her ring. It slashed open the duchess's throat. Our enemy fell in a spray of blood. I jerked my eyes away, because I didn't want to see. But I still heard the sound when the body hit the ground.

"Oh dear, I wasn't even completely sure about my guess . . ." What if I'd gotten the difference between Ari and Araceli wrong this time?

Araceli met my gaze. "I knew beyond any doubt." The emotion burning in those eyes took my breath away. "Do you think the duchess ever apologized? Only you would pick a moment like that to say sorry."

"Hey!" I cried, feeling mocked.

Araceli dropped to her knees before me and took my hand. "I love you."

A creak came from the rubble trapping my legs. Araceli leapt to her feet. "And I'm going to get this off you right now." She readied a ring, blasting the wall off. Then she dragged me to my feet.

"Thank you," I gasped, choking on the dust.

Araceli brushed dirt off my face. "You're even more beautiful than I imagined." She tucked a curl behind my ear. "You wear this body better than the duchess, too. She lacks your cuteness." She tweaked my nose.

I blushed. "Oh, I, uh, you're even more—that is to say—it's not as though you've had a body swap, but if you had, then I'm certain you'd be devastatingly attractive—sorry, that sounds stupid. I love you, too."

Araceli pulled me into a crushing hug. "You're still the same, no matter the body," she murmured.

As much as my heart fluttered, a groggy moan from behind me reminded me of the others. That had probably been Kaine. Antonia and Ysabel were still stuck in a bubble. And I really hoped Donya had gotten medical aid for Alzira. "We'd better go help everyone else."

"One more thing first." Araceli kissed me.

The tentative touch made me tremble all the way down to my toes. The aches and pains all over my body faded away as I became lost in this moment. Araceli deepened the kiss, and our tongues got involved. I knew I ought to break it off so that we could handle many important matters, but I could not think straight. Her lips were so soft and hot, I melted. My breathing roughened, becoming ragged and desperate. Our bodies pressed so close I could feel the frantic pulse of her heart, matching the speed of my own, until I did not know where one ended and the other began.

In the end, Araceli drew back first with a cocky grin. "Done."

EPILOGUE

I wiped a tear from my eye as Araceli swore the oath to become regent for Queen Antonia. I knew this wouldn't be an appropriate occasion for clapping (Donya had drilled that into me during my etiquette lessons). But I wanted to. My heart was about to burst from joy and pride.

Next to me, Ysabel reached over Kaine's lap and squeezed my hand. Since she couldn't heal herself, a bandage peeked out from under her lacy collar. Fortunately, the cut hadn't been deep. The royal doctor had reported her fetus to be unharmed. Even so, Kaine and Alzira had been more clingy than usual. The two of them sat on either side of Ysabel, sandwiching her away from even me, her own sister. Ysabel had healed Antonia, Alzira, and Kaine, fortunately. I'd even gotten to witness my eternally proud sister apologize to Alzira. That had been a rare sight indeed. However, Alzira had insisted it was her own fault for failing to protect her charge, and somehow it had turned into a screaming match with both of them shouting that the other one didn't need to apologize until Kaine intervened and shoved them into a hug. Those three were an endless source of entertainment.

The surviving Avengers sat in the back. I'd felt a bit weird about inviting them, but they were the closest things to friends that Araceli had in the entire world. Also, my sister had fined them of all their money as a punishment and soaked Durnip's bandages with hot peppers, so at this point, I thought they'd suffered enough. Ma'qas at least was smiling sincerely.

Donya sat behind Ysabel with a small perfume bottle full of ice-cold water and a scowl. After Ysabel found out about me bringing a prostitute to the last coronation, she'd joked about topping me with something even more scandalous. It had definitely been a joke. As a sister, I could tell from her tone. Donya had taken it deadly seriously and vowed to spray anyone who disrupted the ceremony with water. I would swear she was watching me, too, even though I was happily partnered now.

After the oath concluded, Queen Antonia leapt up from her seat and jumped on Araceli.

Araceli caught her and spun her around. "Whoa, there."

"You're staying with me forever now?" Antonia asked hopefully.

Araceli's smile was gentle. "Yes. Forever and ever."

Since Araceli had revealed her identity as the rightful heir to South Sherda, she'd taken over the deceased Blood Duchess's role as the queen's guardian and the royal regent. Sherda had accepted this because they were denying all responsibility for anything the duchess had done. They seemed to be pretending not to see our kingdom. Since the Blood Duchess had proven to be a criminal hiding her unregistered gift, we'd turned into heroes for killing her. Just like that, our past crimes had been swept under the rug by a grateful Conclave of Kings—grateful no one was questioning their association with an attempted dark lord, mostly.

Araceli had privately confided in me that she suspected she'd have a more difficult time taking back her former duchy. At least Arahasnor was secure and under our control. We could build up our influence enough to fight for Araceli's original family lands, too. We had Conollia and Kaine's backing.

In the meantime, we were plenty busy straightening out Arahasnor. Everyone knew about the body swap now. Since I'd claimed to have amnesia at the trial, this had been used as a polite fiction to allow me to escape the consequences for impersonating a duchess. I suspected that almost everyone I'd personally come into contact with knew better. Whenever I met someone whom I'd encountered during my acting, I squirmed with embarrassment. I kept expecting someone to be angry at me. Instead, most people seemed intimidated, as if facing a mad dog. That might be even worse. I'd desperately brainwashed myself during my masquerade by telling myself that no one would ever know *I* had done those things. Now I'd been left helplessly exposed. I felt off-balance. Sometimes I found myself painfully shy and nervous, as if to compensate. Sometimes I felt tempted to slip into a villainous persona rather than be myself. Araceli assured me that I could still throw my weight around, and she'd back me up. But I'd rather develop my own style of leadership. I wanted to be confident without being mean. It was a work in progress.

Looking over Antonia's head, Araceli's eyes caught mine. She looked absolutely stunning in her green dress with layers of lace flowing from the skirt. She gestured me over. I stood up and joined the group hug. Honestly, it was a welcome excuse to avoid the tension dripping off my sister's pair of paranoid bodyguards.

I myself wore a pink sleeveless dress with flowers winding down the skirt. I'd swept my hair up into a bun with a silk lily on the pin, attempting to finally set a new fashion trend and get rid of everyone's love for heavy hats. They gave me a headache.

Antonia carefully examined my face. She'd seemed a little uncertain about me after my body first swapped back. She looked at my features as if she wanted to memorize me, then smiled. She grabbed my arm. "It's you, Bora. I know it."

I smiled. "I'm back in my body, thanks to you."

"She still has that same silly, blank look," Antonia whispered to Araceli.

"Hey!"

Araceli laughed. "I know. It's cute." Okay, that made me feel better.

Antonia shook her head. "How did you ever have trouble telling her apart from the Blood Duchess?"

"I figured it out almost immediately!" Araceli protested.

I shook my head. "I'm never, ever acting the part of the Blood Duchess again. It's a relief, honestly."

"Mmm, I wonder about that." Araceli winked. "Maybe we'll need a villainess again someday."

From the pews, a nobleman in a gray doublet muttered, "Just look at him, parading around in a dress. This is our lord regent? Disgraceful."

Araceli flinched slightly.

I marched over. "Excuse me, I heard what you just said. Perhaps my sister's last sensitivity training wasn't sufficient for you?"

He leapt to his feet. "Fine, I'll say it again! It's disgraceful that our future queen might be raised to see men in dresses as something normal."

"You look tired," I said with fake sympathy. "I heard your wife had a new baby recently. How wonderful! But you must be exhausted between changing all the diapers and still carrying out your usual duties. Have you heard about my sister's newest suggestion for improving society? It's paternity leave. I'm removing you from the Council so that you can spend more time with your new family. You'll thank me later!"

His face reddened. "What nonsense are you talking about? Babies are women's work! I don't change diapers!"

My smile deepened. "Don't expect to return to the Council until that changes. I'll be watching you. Guards!"

Half a dozen guards stepped forward. Laurent, now Captain Laurent, winked at me before he dragged the sputtering nobleman out.

I turned around. Araceli and Antonia regarded me with identical amused expressions.

"I see you still have a bit of the Blood Duchess in you," Araceli said.

"That was me being nice," I protested. "The Blood Duchess would have thrown him in the dungeon."

"The Blood Duchess would have killed anyone who crossed her. I'm glad you're better than that."

"Err . . . even as head of the Council, I didn't exactly have the authority to remove him without talking to you first . . ."

"I'll have the decree stamped by nightfall." Araceli smiled, then bent over to kiss my forehead. "I appreciate you standing up for me, love."

Sometimes I missed being tall, but I found it cute when Araceli did that.

Antonia beamed. "Someday I'm going to annihilate all my enemies, just like you two."

I hoped we weren't being as bad an influence on her as the nobleman had claimed. She was scary enough already. (I was just kidding. It was nice to see her smiling, unlike the terrified child she'd been when we'd first met.)

Leaning over to Araceli's ear, Kaine spoke softly. "I meant what I said before. It means a lot to me, to see you living openly like this. Maybe because of you, more people will feel free to do the same someday."

Even at a whisper, he didn't dare speak of himself in a public area. I felt a pang of sympathy for him. Someday.

Araceli turned around. "Thank you."

"I should be the one thanking you," Kaine said.

"You already have," I said. "Many times." It had started to get excessive, honestly. "You don't have to keep bringing it up."

"Yes, I do." Kaine cleared his throat. "Bora, I owe you a debt. You saved my life, and you saved Ysabel, who means more to me than my own life. There is no greater debt possible for me to owe. If you ever want a favor in return, name your price. You can have anything, even if you want me to destroy the world."

I frowned. "I can't accept. Even leaving aside that I don't want you to destroy anyone, Ysabel is my sister. I'm not doing *you* a favor by saving her life. If anything, I should be the one thanking you for making my beloved sister happy. You're my sister's husband; it's only natural for me to help you if I can. Frankly, bringing up debts insults me."

"I understand. I apologize for my rudeness, little sister." Kaine swept me up into a hug. "There are no debts between family."

He had spoken "little sister" with such solemness, as if bestowing a royal title on me. I tapped his arm. "Oxygen . . ."

"Sorry." He set me down. "I'm excited about having a new family member."

Ysabel came up behind her husband and took his arm. "Bora is already family." Alzira lurked behind her, glaring hard enough to scare everyone away from us.

"But now she's *family* family," Kaine said. He beamed at me. "You'll have to come visit us soon."

It gave me a strange feeling. I wasn't entirely sure what I'd gotten myself into. "Wait, visit you? Are you leaving already?" I asked, disappointed.

"I was enjoying the vacation, but Ysabel says we have important political nonsense back home."

Ysabel sighed. "We left abruptly. The court will be in disarray without me. Give me some time to set my affairs in order, and then I'll be able to take time off for a longer visit. We'll definitely come to visit after our child is born." She touched her stomach.

"I can't wait," I said, smiling at the thought of my future nibling.

Ysabel said, "We'll stay for one last dinner. I've already arranged a feast."

Come dinnertime, Ysabel was true to her word. She'd arranged for a fancy fountain of cheese and another, chocolate fountain for an elaborate fondue. We enjoyed dinner in a private dining room: just me, Araceli, Antonia, Ysabel, Kaine, Alzira, and Donya.

After the meal, Kaine pulled Araceli aside, offering political tips from an experienced ruler to a new one. Most of his advice seemed to involve beating up people. I was fairly certain that Araceli was only politely nodding along. He also showed off a few fighting moves. Araceli paid more eager attention to those.

Ysabel dragged the rest of us into a game of cards. "I learned a new game in Conollia called Last Dragon. It's a variant of Bluffer. The goal is to avoid being stuck with the dragon in the end. I'll teach you how to play; it's loads of fun."

Donya nodded. "I've played a few times with Ysabel. She always wins, but I'll beat her next time."

"Can I play?" Antonia asked.

"We'll need you," Ysabel said. "The game requires four people, and I can't play with Alzira because she always takes the dragon and loses. I don't mean by accident. She does it on purpose."

"It's my duty to ensure your victory under any circumstances, Your Holiness," Alzira said.

Ysabel sighed. "It doesn't make for a very fun card game if you deliberately lose to me. That's why I'll let you play on my team. We can share the same set of cards. Come on, stand behind me to look."

"I'm honored, Your Holiness," Alzira said.

As Ysabel dealt the cards, I noticed a flash of a card vanishing up her sleeve. I snorted and grabbed it, too fast for her to stop me. It was a dragon. "Sis, ditch the extra cards. Play fair."

"Her Holiness would never cheat!" Alzira cried. "It's part of the game for her to keep an extra dragon up her sleeve. That's why she always does it."

Ysabel winced. "Alzira, don't incriminate me."

"I'm sorry, Your Holiness."

Donya rolled her eyes. "Is this why I keep losing to you? I should have known. Roll up your sleeves, Ysabel."

Hanging her head, Ysabel rolled up her dress sleeves. Three more cards fell out.

Donya inclined her head at me. "Want to team up to beat her?"

I nodded. "Yes, absolutely."

Antonia raised her hand. "I want to be on the same side as Bora, too. She's amazing, and she knows how to win."

Ysabel pouted. "That's not fair."

Donya snorted. "Don't talk about fair when you always cheat. It's the only way we can beat you. Besides, you have Alzira on your side."

Alzira nodded. "That's right! Her Holiness and I together are unstoppable. Even though Her Holiness currently has the real dragon in her hand, we won't lose with such a small handicap."

Ysabel sighed. "I told you to stop incriminating me."

With Alzira's facial expressions completely giving her away, the three of us effortlessly beat my sister into the ground. She tried to cheat a couple times, but I was good at catching her. I had to admit it was satisfying, given how often she used to beat me at games as a child. I now realized she'd probably been cheating back then, too.

Donya and I bumped fists. "You're good. You're like a less-evil version of your sister," Donya said, though there was a fond edge in her voice as she glanced at Ysabel. "I've been avenged. Thank you."

"I couldn't have beaten the evil queen without you." I beamed.

"Was I useful?" Antonia asked hopefully.

I ruffled her hair. "You tricked my sister into taking the dragon twice. Far more experienced monarchs haven't been able to pull one over on the Holy Maiden. Be proud of yourself."

"I'll get all of you next time." Ysabel counted up the points. "The final winner is Bora. What a coincidence! I have a prize for you." She grinned and tugged my arm. "Step outside with me. I need to have a word in private."

I followed my sister. We seemed to be going toward her guest bedroom. I'd finally started to get the hang of this labyrinth of a palace. "What did you want to talk to me about? Do you have political tips for me, too?"

Ysabel shook her head. "You'll do fine without me. I saw how you handled that snooty nobleman at the coronation. You've grown up, baby sister." She slapped my back. "That's why I prepared a grown-up prize. I custom-ordered it just for you. Believe it or not, I was going to cheat to let you win, but you kicked my ass without me needing to."

"Oh? What is it?" I was becoming curious.

As she pushed open her bedroom door, she smiled mysteriously. "That's a secret—" Her eyes fell on my ankle, noticing the bandage there. "How did you hurt yourself? Who do I need to murder?"

I grinned and plopped down on a chair. "No one. I got a tattoo." I tugged down my sock and peeled back the bandage to show her. "Do you like it?"

"I love it!" Ysabel clapped her hands. "Elegant and stylish. Mom is going to faint. Please let me watch through a linked book when you show it to her."

"Crap, I don't know how I'm going to explain my new position to our parents." I'd already written to Benoni to tell him and apologize for my earlier lies. I couldn't let my own little brother find out from the news circulating around the kingdom. My parents were more difficult, because I couldn't count on them to be happy for me. Dad would inevitably show up looking for money.

Ysabel snorted. "To be honest, I don't understand why you still talk to either of them." She hesitated. "Sorry if that was too blunt. It's your choice."

"Don't be sorry. You're right. Maybe it would be funnier if everyone back home found out through the town crier. I have guards now to keep people away. If our father tries to borrow money, I don't even have to look at his face. Communications with Mom can travel through a linked book. If she comments on my appearance, I shut the book."

"That's my daringly villainous sister. I'm even more certain you'll enjoy my gift."

"Don't keep me in suspense. What is it?"

Ysabel went to the dresser, removed a black leather box fastened with a padlock, and handed me a key. "Guard this carefully. I want you to know that all of these are new. I ordered them to be made shortly after I came to the city. Some things, even sisters shouldn't share."

Now she really had me wondering. I started to put the key into the lock.

Ysabel grabbed my wrist. "No! Not here. Open them with your lover." She waggled her eyebrows.

"Ugh, you're driving me insane with curiosity."

Ysabel pushed me out the door. "Go back to your room first. No need to return to thank me when you see them. I know you'll be otherwise occupied for quite a while."

"Fine, be mysterious." I laughed and let her shove me down the hallway.

Once back in my bedroom, I locked the door *and* barricaded it with a chair. I would not tolerate any interruptions this time. Ari already waited for me, sitting on the bed. He'd changed into male sleepwear.

"Ari?" I asked, just to be sure. I had a strong feeling, though. Not only the clothing, but also his posture and aura was different.

He nodded. "Your sister whispered something about a present for us if I met you here."

I gestured at the box. "She's been very mysterious about it. You hold the box, and I'll open it." I inserted the key and pulled back the lid. WHAT?!

The box contained several dildos of different sizes, a butt plug, padded handcuffs, and a blindfold. Oh dear. I knew my own sister—so I should have seen this coming. My mind went largely blank, only sororicide remaining. "I'm going to kill her."

"Why, what is it?" Before I could stop him, Ari turned the box around and looked. "Oh. What is this stuff?" He picked up a harness with a dildo attached.

I winced. "I believe that's, uh . . . something for me to use on you. Hypothetically speaking."

"You're right. It came with instructions." Ari picked up the card. "How intriguing. Look, she included numerous sheathes and those new thinner condoms."

From the heat on my face, I knew I'd turned bright red. "She's dead. I'm going to become the oldest surviving child in our family the next time I see her. She won't resist; she knows she has her murder coming. I saw that smirk on her lips. She even told me to open it with you!" Really, I already knew that Ysabel was shameless. I felt angrier at myself for not having the foresight to open the box alone. My outrage covered up a certain level of interest. I'd never seen such fancy toys before.

Ari grinned. "Actually, I think it was quite a thoughtful present. I find this rather intriguing." He held up the harness.

"Oh? Do you want to try it?" My voice squeaked. I was embarrassed to admit how much the idea interested me too.

"Another time, absolutely." Ari smiled in a toothy way. "But tonight I'm feeling a bit more dominant."

While I was trying to think of a calm, reasonable, charming response, a moan escaped my lips.

Ari's pupils dilated. He reached up to tuck a lock of hair behind my ear. Leaning close, he whispered, "I'd like to try the handcuffs."

"That could be fun," I said. From the predatorial smirk on Ari's face, my fake casualness wasn't fooling him.

"Then allow me," he whispered, pushing me back onto the bed with one finger.

I fell backward with a gasp. Ari was on me in an instant, straddling me and kissing me. I opened my mouth without a second thought. His hands mapped my jawline and neck, as if I were a fragile and precious treasure. It felt different, being touched by someone I loved. I was so focused on him that I didn't get lost in my intrusive thoughts.

Ari kept moving downward, undoing the laces of my dress as he kissed circles on my breasts. Every single bit of skin got sucked. I was half naked and completely breathless when he said, "We were going to try the handcuffs? Where should we put them?"

Ugh, I had to use my brain at a moment like this? I looked around the room. At first glance, I didn't see a logical place to fasten cuffs. "Hmm, maybe if we loop them around the bedpost?"

"It's worth a try." Ari dove back into the box. "She got two sets for different sized wrists. How does she even know my wrist size?"

I groaned, desperate. "I don't care. Hurry up and get over here." I cast my dress to the floor. It needed to come off before the cuffs went on. My panties followed.

Ari ran a finger around the handcuffs. "They're padded and look custom-fit. Let me know right away if they chafe." He looped the cuffs around the bedpost and then fastened them on my wrists. A look of confusion crossed his face. "How do we do this?"

I understood his dilemma—I was now cuffed to the corner of the bed, rather than the center. "What if I bend over the bed? We haven't tried that position before. It might be fun."

"That does sound fun." Ari cleared his throat. "I mean, bend over for me, wench!"

I dissolved into giggles.

Ari chuckled. "My intimidating act needs work."

"No, no, you're doing great."

"At least I'm confident in my ability to do this." Ari traced a finger down my bare spine. I shivered in response.

It was an intriguing sensation, yielding to the notion that I was a mere passenger as Ari's fingers played with my body. No need to think, just feel. I moaned and jerked on the cuffs as he stroked a sweet spot.

"Are you still doing good? Are your arms okay?"

"They're great," I groaned through a dry throat. "Hurry up. I'm ready."

There was a rustle of a condom. Then Ari slid into me.

Grabbing the bedpost, I pushed back, making him gasp. I chuckled.

He leaned down and kissed my bare back. "If you still have the breath to laugh, then I need to try harder." He thrust again, rubbing me with his finger at the same time. I cried out.

"Good spot?" he whispered.

"*Yes.* Do that again. Make me lose my mind."

To my profound relief, he did it again, and again, a slow and steady rhythm. The pressure became nearly unbearable, a hot press of being filled, intoxicating like the edge of drunkenness. Each thrust sent starbursts of sensation through my core. The heat had consumed my entire body. I barely registered the moment when Ari came, because my world had turned white and crackling. I let myself fall headfirst into the sensation of pleasure. Overstimulation and exhaustion made my head spin, treading an exquisite line between pleasure and not-quite-pain.

I was still collapsed and breathless when Ari unfastened the handcuffs. He lifted me up and tucked me under the covers. Lying down next to me, he cradled my body close. One hand massaged my wrists. "Still good? Did it bruise?"

"It didn't hurt my wrists at all. It's my brain you nearly fucked out." The post-orgasm mood had loosened my tongue.

He laughed and kissed the top of my head. "Flatterer."

"Only the truth."

"You did wonderfully. I can't wait to see what we can do with the rest of the toys."

Ugh, would I have to thank my sister for that gift after all? How mortifying. I sighed and nestled deeper into Ari's shoulder.

He whispered into my hair, "I love you."

I squirmed around to face him, then kissed him. "I love you," I said into his mouth.

Ari groaned. "If you keep rubbing against me like that, you'll rouse me for a round two."

Adopting a joking tone of my own, I said, "Then I'll just lie here like this." I pulled back the blanket and struck a pose on my side with my head in my hand and my hair falling over my neck.

His groan and immediate physical reaction were gratifying. "That's cheating," he protested.

"I'm not even touching you," I said with mock innocence, jiggling my chest.

He fell on me in a flash, kissing me like he wanted to fuck his tongue down my throat. I grabbed a fistful of hair. Even with both hands, I couldn't touch everywhere I wanted at once. I freed my mouth to nip his earlobe. Then I kissed a trail down his neck, planting a hickey on that gorgeous collarbone. Each desperate noise spurred me on.

I curled my tongue around a nipple, teasing out the most fun reactions. With great reluctance, I kept kissing my way down his chest. I was in the mood to take control. At this angle, I could see his blown-out eyes and flushed cheeks. I reveled in finally being able to touch him back. It felt absolutely perfect, that moment when I took him into my mouth and his pupils dilated. His butterfly tattoo seemed to flap wings every time he moved; it was intoxicatingly sexy. I wanted to see my always polished and confident Ari lose control. Slowly, I slid my lips down and teased until he finally cried out, "Please!" Then I took him all the way.

His thrusts went wild and suddenly neither of us had control, lost in the animalistic pace, until he came so deep I barely tasted it.

Exhausted, I sagged against the side of the bed. Ari tugged me onto the bed alongside him and tucked my head on his arm. Soft adoration filled his gaze as he kissed my forehead.

"You're beautiful," he whispered.

When he said it like that, I could believe it.

Ysabel, Kaine, and Alzira stood together in the courtyard. "Last chance to say goodbye," Kaine said as he summoned shadows around his body.

I hugged my older sister. "Make certain you write frequently. When you're close to your due date, I'll come down and help you."

She hugged me back. "There's no need to make a fuss, but I'd be glad to have you visit any time."

"Of course I want to be there for the birth of my first nibling." I smiled.

Ysabel examined me. "You look rather cheerful this morning."

I bit my tongue to stop myself from flushing. "It's a very good morning. Bright and sunny. I'm sad to see you go, of course."

My sister whispered into my ear, "It's okay, you don't need to thank me. The fact that you're not walking straight tells me everything I need to know."

Then she teleported away, robbing me of my opportunity to either thank her or kill her.

I'd promised to take Antonia toy shopping as a reward for sitting through another boring coronation. Araceli had a ring that could make people not look directly at us so we could blend in with the crowd and enjoy the day under a cloud of anonymity. Our heavy coats hid our noble clothing.

People bustled down the street full of shops, walking carefully to avoid the ice patches. The snow had started to melt, running trails to the gutters. Signs hung over the glass doors. Most of the shops had a second floor above, where the owners usually lived. Younger entrepreneurs set up temporary stands along the sidewalk to hawk wares. It was good to see how many more stands had opened up. Even more so, it was good to see people smiling and carrying flags to celebrate the coronation. Winter was ending for Arahasnor in more ways than one.

At a street stand, a teenage girl held up a painted gold hairpin with a fake flower on top, shouting, "This is a replica of the pin Lady Bora wore at the royal coronation. Only available here!"

Araceli laughed. "Already? Word travels fast."

Hats would be out of fashion within the week. My gently evil style of leadership was working.

"I told you that everyone would love your hairpin," Antonia said, nudging me with the proud grin of someone who'd helped design it.

"It *does* look great on me." I smiled at my own reflection in the glass, adjusting my pin slightly. "I tipped off the local hat sellers in advance to start producing a new product."

Antonia clapped her hands. "You're a pigeon plucker."

I choked. "Where did you hear that word?"

"My tutor said that it means a very smart person."

"It means a scammer." And it seemed to have entered the upper-class vernacular since I had lied to some of the nobles that it was a compliment, but I decided to make that not my problem.

Antonia giggled. "I'll remember." Her gaze latched on to a hobby horse in the window. "I want that!"

I was already reaching for my wallet.

We loaded down the carriage with toys for Antonia, the first ones she got to pick out for herself. She refused to be separated from her new velvet stuffed rabbit.

As I sat down in the carriage, my sock hitched up to reveal the bandage. Brow furrowed, Antonia pointed. "What happened?"

"I got a new tattoo." I glanced at Araceli. "I think it should be okay to remove the bandage now?"

She smiled and nodded.

I unwrapped my ankle to reveal a small red A. The stroke through the middle of the A looped to form a heart shape, such that the letter seemed to be sitting half inside the heart. A tiny crown rested on top of the A. "I got this to remind me of the three most important As in my life: you two, and Arahasnor. This is my promise to protect all three."

"For me?" Antonia gasped. "Can I touch it?"

"Sure." I held out my leg.

"It looks cool." Antonia traced the A, entranced. "Can I get a tattoo?"

"Not until your body is done growing," Araceli said firmly. "The tattoo would end up stretched funny. Besides, you should take your time to think about what you want, what would be meaningful to you."

"Aw." Antonia pouted.

"I can show you how to temporarily paint on your skin."

"Yay!" Antonia held up her rabbit. "I want a bunny."

This would definitely scandalize the court, but who cared? They needed some scandal to keep them entertained. And they should count themselves lucky I wasn't throwing anyone into the dungeon any longer.

I'd thought long and hard about my first tattoo. It was supposed to symbolize my journey. I'd considered something related to the Blood Duchess, but although my version of the Blood Duchess had been very important to me, I didn't like the real Duchess Hedri or want her on my skin. I'd picked an idea with several layers of meaning so that even if my life's purpose changed later, it would still be connected to me. In the end, for me, what I got as a tattoo ended up being less important than having the courage to do something I'd always wanted but never thought suited me.

It was about bravery, and loving my body, and making my body into my own.

ACKNOWLEDGMENTS

So very many people helped bring this book to life, it is difficult to list them all. Podium Publishing shaped this book from its rough draft stage to the published manuscript in front of you. Thank you in particular to Cass Dolan, Stephanie Beard, Taylor Bryon, Erin McClary, Nicole Antos, and Crystal Watanabe. To my cover artist, Francell Garrote, thank you for the beautiful art that took my breath away. Thank you to my wonderful agent Stevie Finegan who always went to bat for me.

I am eternally grateful for the support of my family and friends. Thank you to my critique partners: Kelly Barina, Becky Bosshart, Carol Rickman, Keith Srutowski, Hayley Garrett, Paul Dick, and the DC Speculative Wordsmiths. Thank you to my family for encouraging and promoting my writing. Finally, thank you to my readers: based on the philosophy of subjective idealism, this book does not exist without you to observe it.

ABOUT THE AUTHOR

Katy Nyquist is an economist in Washington, DC, who writes humorous fantasy novels to take a break from the constant math jargon. She has had short fiction published in *Abyss & Apex Magazine*, *The Arcanist*, *Every Day Fiction*, *Strange Changes*, and *Magic, Mayhem, and Monsters*.